C000068565

CHRIS BERRY
TOUGH SEASON

GREAT NORTHERN

TOUGH SEASON by Chris Berry

First published in Great Britain in 2019 by Great Northern Books

Copyright © Chris Berry 2019

The right of Chris Berry to be identified as the Author of the Work has
been asserted by him in accordance with the Copyright, Designs and
Patents Act 1988.

All rights reserved. No part of this publication may be reproduced,
stored in a retrieval system, or transmitted, in any form or by any
means without the prior written permission of the publisher, nor be
otherwise circulated in any form of binding or cover other than that in
which it is published and without a similar condition being imposed on
the subsequent purchaser.

All characters in this publication are fictitious and any resemblance to
real persons, living or dead is purely coincidental.

A CIP catalogue record for this title is available from the British
Library

ISBN: 978-1-912101-09-2

Cover design by Caroline Berry

Great Northern Books
PO Box 1380, Bradford,
West Yorkshire, BD5 5FB

www.greatnorthernbooks.co.uk

Chris Berry is from the north of England and lives near Leeds. He is a writer and performer. Feature writer for the *Yorkshire Post* for 20 years, author of several autobiographies, singer-songwriter both as a solo artist and with his band. He's a keen sportsman and currently runs several distances from parkrun to half marathons. Born in Kingston upon Hull he is a staunch Yorkshireman. *Tough Season* is his first novel.

Also by Chris Berry

NON FICTION

TONY CHRISTIE The Song Interpreter

JOE LONGTHORNE The Official Autobiography

SUGAR IN THE MORNING Joe Longthorne

LES BATTERSBY & ME Bruce Jones

BOXSTER'S STORY The Truth Behind the Bull

THE J.D. IRELAND STORY

www.chrisberry.tv

TOUGH SEASON

CHAPTER 1

"Mmm … yeah…!" Susie was seconds from her moment, eyes closed as she rode rhythmically, her teeth making a soft indent to her bottom lip.

"Oh … babe…" She stretched her neck a little further back, blonde hair caressing her shoulders, breasts swaying effortlessly, nipples erect.

Greg was enjoying every move and the view as Susie moved gently and sensually above him.

"Oh … My … God!" she gasped. *"Yes darling … O baby…"*

She was almost whispering, her hands moving behind her head. Greg added a playful spank as they neared precious fulfillment together. Now they were as one, bodies entwined, their tongues and lips playing and darting around each other's eager, excited mouths.

Two minutes later, fulfilled by their passionate embrace and its desired culmination, the shapely mature blonde with ocean-blue sparkly eyes and a figure that girls in their late teens would envy, and her handsome, dark haired, delightfully toned man, were satisfied once again.

CHAPTER 2

"I don't give a shit what you think! And I don't care what the fuck it takes! There's no way I'm letting up now..."

A pause – the voice at the other end of the call interjected.

"Yes, of course I fucking well know what's happened! Do you think I've not thought this all through? We always knew there was a chance. It alters nothing.

"Well whatever you have to do, just do it ... now fuck off and stick to the plan!"

The voice handing out the tirade threw his now empty whisky glass across the room with the customary result of such action as it hit the wall.

For fuck's sake, he had invested so much time and energy into this. His planning had been meticulous. It was he who had seen this opportunity, masterminded the whole thing and was looking forward to the big payday. Whatever it took, he was going to make sure it happened. Whatever it took.

CHAPTER 3

"Bloody disgrace!"　　*"Come On Town!"*　　*"Run it straight!"*
　"Get 'em onside!"　　*"This is shite!"*

Half-time came and went. The second half fared no better. Grim voices, from the ever-faithful Hopton Town Rugby League Football Club fans on the terraces, were matched in the faces of the thirteen trudging figures on the pitch. Another disastrous game, another heavy defeat.

"That's it! Go on! ... Go on!"

Any optimism fans had of urging their team to registering late points was soon dispelled as the ball spun loose from a set of despairing Hopton hands for the umpteenth time.

"Bloody 'ell!"

"Useless ... bloody rubbish!"

The groans and moans around the ground said it all. There had been little by way of expectation before kick-off, but this just added further ignominy.

'Town' had been annihilated. The hunched shoulders of the mud and blood splattered brown-and-black hooped shirts trooped slowly off the rain-drenched mud bath of what now loosely fitted the description of a professional sports ground.

Greg was amongst them, hands on hips shaking his head in frustration. They had been impotent in the extreme, unlike his bedroom exploits the previous evening.

The next day's newspaper report told in detail what had happened in the immediate aftermath of the game. Parting with their head coach – and in Hopton's case their only coach – wasn't unexpected news for any team languishing at the foot of a league table and without a league win in months. Something had to be done:

"Hopton Town coach George Ramsbottom was sacked yesterday following a catastrophic run brought to its tumult by the parlous performance away to Axby Axemen. Town were hopelessly

outclassed by a team just two places above them and it is becoming increasingly difficult to see them remaining in the league for next term. Now into the latter part of their league programme and fast running out of games, they can thank their lucky stars fellow-strugglers Ensideleigh also lost. One bright note was the form of 17-year-old wingman Vincent Venus, the new signing from Transpennine Amateurs, who ran in a try on his debut. He must have wondered what he has let himself in for as he and his new team-mates recorded their biggest defeat for three years!"

Flying through the air, the *Hopton Messenger* landed unceremoniously on ex-Town prop forward and now club chairman Bill Garside's desk. His 18-stone frame was as imposing as ever, albeit a great deal flabbier than it had been thirty years ago when he had taken Town within a whisker of their greatest achievement – Challenge Cup glory – only to falter in the final seconds.

Bill had led the charge valiantly, losing in the final minute to the most amazing penalty kick from an incredible 75 yards and a couple of inches out, the longest ever successful penalty kick in rugby league history, beating the previous record set by Artie Atkinson in 1929 and scored by a man who became known eternally as The Boot.

Since that historic cup run, the club had spiralled downwards, stacking up ever-increasing debt. Town now held the league record for finishing bottom more times than any other club, but this season their fate would be sealed if it happened again.

In a new league structure scheduled for the following season, the club finishing bottom would be banished to the amateur divisions. Tension was palpable in the club as games had begun running out.

Greg Duggan had sent the door of the chairman's fusty, damp wood-paneled office at the rear of the grandstand very nearly off his hinges as he had burst in. It was he who had thrown *The Messenger* towards Bill. Greg wasn't one for harsh words with the club chairman. He'd known and respected him for years, but enough was enough. He kept it brief.

"This can't go on, Bill. We're in a mess."

Greg – the angular, jet-black haired, granite-jawed giant – was far beyond angry. He'd endured the club's lurch from crisis to crisis both on and off the field and although the previous day's defeat may not quite have been the last straw, it was getting close.

He'd been selected for the Great Britain youth team in his early career, but senior international opportunities hadn't come due to his desire to stay with Hopton and hold down a 'proper job'. He'd been hailed as Hopton's *'last great hero'* by Ted Brewiss, the *Messenger*'s chief sports reporter.

"Greg, we're doing something about…"

"It's a shambles!" Greg interrupted. *"You've sacked George, but it's not his fault and you know that. He's had nothing to work with. Pete's done his hamstring. Dave's suffering from that blatant head-high tackle everyone saw but the ref. Paul's just joined the fire brigade because we can't afford his wages. Mike and Bri say they can't afford to play anymore because their jobs are on the line and that's just yesterday's news, as well as conceding 80 points in one sodding game! Maybe it's time for me to go too…"*

Greg still couldn't get his head around that – 80 points! He had no desire to leave. He loved playing for Hopton. He was born and bred Hopton, but he longed for success – even one game's worth would do at the moment – but he was starting to wonder just how much longer he could carry on. There were other clubs that would be more than willing to sign him.

"I shouldn't think that'd be necessary, lad."

There was someone else in the room. Greg hadn't seen him on his enraged entry, but heard him now. Greg turned to face the epitome of the 'self-made man'. Smart suit, matching silk tie and handkerchief, gold watch, a man whose aura gave off money and success. He stood from one of the two large leather armchairs, smiling broadly across his tanned face of some fifty-odd or sixty-odd years. He offered his hand.

"I'm Bob Irvine…"

"*Our new owner,*" cut in Bill.

Irvine was still smiling, his hand outstretched. Garside had anticipated Greg's scepticism. This wasn't the first time a new owner had come along. People with finances and big ideas could rescue Hopton in the short-term, as several had previously, but turning fortunes around in the long-term required a fortune too.

Takeovers and what had turned out to be several dodgy deals had littered the past decade.

"*Greg, I'll tell you straight,*" Irvine said. "*I've bought out the other guys because I've always enjoyed the game and I'm in a position to help. The other guys wanted out, they couldn't afford to lose any more money. I'm in a better position. I've got money to pump into the club, enough to build us a team to compete at the highest level, in the fullness of time, but I know there's a lot of work to do before we think about that.*"

Bill caught Greg's eye. "*Greg. Bob owns Ringstall Glass, Borough Chemicals, Castlegate Press Group, BI-Comms and...*"

Irvine interrupted. "*I'm sure you're not in the slightest bit interested in what I own and what I do...*"

Irvine's dismissive tone seemed genuine and it played well with Greg. He didn't go much on bigheaded bastards.

"*...what you want to know is how me being involved affects you, here it is. Bill stays as chairman. I provide the funds to get us out of debt and into the Super League inside three years, but first of all we need to survive this season.*"

Were Greg's eyes giving him away? Had Irvine noticed his look as he glibly announced his highly ambitious three-year plan? What did this guy know?

"*Today you take over as coach,*" Irvine continued. "*If you want the job. Bill tells me you're up to it, you know the players, you're already qualified, you want to win and you're a bloody good player. Too good to be playing for us by all accounts, but you are and I want you to take Hopton Town to the top – eventually.*"

Greg hadn't been expecting anything like that. Suddenly he was being offered the job of coach of his hometown club, at just 26 years of age.

Bill was studying Greg. He knew he wouldn't turn it down.

Greg finally allowed himself the slightest of smiles, shrugged his shoulders, took a deep breath and gave a nod, no words.

Irvine returned the motion. He was eyeballing him now. This was business.

"I'll give you the funds to build a team. I'll make sure you're looked after. And I've got contacts. It's up to you and Bill to tell me what you want."

Irvine started towards the door. The meeting was over. His phone gave a warble, his hand ready to press it to his ear.

"Now, I've got to get away gentlemen. I'm due at a board meeting twenty miles away in half an hour. See you tomorrow."

With another nod to both Greg and Bill, Irvine strode out of the ramshackle office. Garside was the first to break the silence. He stretched out his hands and gave the widest of smiles as he announced:

"So how many new players do you want, my boy?"

There was nothing that could have prepared Greg for what was to come, nor for a future that would have little to do with playing the game he loved.

CHAPTER 4

George Ramsbottom had been Hopton Town's coach for the past two years. His departure had been the last act of an initially enthusiastic, yet increasingly exasperated and rapidly becoming destitute group of three well-meaning and locally based directors who had run the show for the last four years.

If Irvine's ambition of reaching the Super League was to be anything more than a pipedream wholesale changes were needed. And time was already running out.

The league's governing body had ordained that at the end of the season the bottom club would be replaced with a new franchise from a city further away from the traditional M62 corridor as part of the game's constant expansionist policy. Moscow, Leningrad and Chicago had all been mentioned.

It was now Wednesday, just two days following his appointment and Greg's problems were mounting. Half of the squad was unavailable for various reasons. He had no other players to call upon as Hopton's reserve and youth teams had been disbanded three years previously in cost-cutting measures.

Greg's first game in charge was to be Sunday's Challenge Cup tie at home to promotion-chasing Sherwell Shredders and it didn't even look as though he had enough players to provide a starting thirteen, let alone substitutes.

Hopton hadn't reached the second round of the cup for the past ten years and had twice been knocked out by part-timers from the lower amateur divisions during that period. At least this year's exit would shock nobody.

Greg had wasted little time in attempting to get new acquisitions to the squad but there had also been more bad news. The training session held at Hopton's Parrot Lane ground the previous evening had yielded another problem – stand-off Chris Hardwick hobbling off to hospital with a suspected broken ankle!

One thing Greg had learned from his coaching courses had been that to ensure success on the field you needed a solid team of backroom staff. His first appointment was to offer scrum-half Mike Rodley a place on the coaching staff as assistant.

But he desperately needed new blood: with no second team to call upon and a squad that at best only ran to 19 players, Greg set about bringing in whoever he could as quickly as possible. His first signing was local amateur Richard Brent. He'd played amateur grade rugby league for many years without ever being snapped up by the pros. Greg had played against him as he had made his way in the game and had always felt that Brent could cut it. Now thirty-three years old, Brent had the opportunity to ride a late dream and was fit and ready for the challenge. He wasn't a big signing by way of finance, but he was another fit player to add to the somewhat depleted ranks.

That still left Greg with four gaps in his starting line-up. Bill had told him plenty of players would be interested in signing once they knew the club was being bank-rolled, but the reality of getting hold of them quickly was a different proposition and the clock was ticking.

After two days of making calls, sending texts, posting on social media and a multitude of emails, even Bill was beginning to lose a little faith that players could be found before Sunday.

Bill's phone rang just as he and Greg had given up for the day and were heading out to drown their sorrows at one of the local hostelries.

"…yes it is … *now then, how are you? … you what? … Who else?… well, yes, certainly we're interested.*"

Bill nodded giving Greg a thumbs up. His eyes were gleaming, eyebrows dancing, his free hand clenched in a fist with try-like euphoria.

"*I tell you what. If you can get across here tomorrow morning, we'll see how you go. It's Greg's decision of course…*"

Garside wound up the conversation and pumped his fist into the air.

"*Hey, hey! We've got a team!*"

CHAPTER 5

Her black stockings, satin basque and six-inch heels had been too much for him after leaving Bill and explaining that he hadn't the time for a drink. Greg's day had taken a turn for the better earlier and was now complete. She smiled the gorgeous smile that had turned him on even before they were together.

"That was so good, darling…"

Greg's cares of the day earlier were gone for now, his hands propping him up over her glorious body as she smiled again and once was never enough for the pair of them.

"Mmm … O, don't stop … yes, yes … Oh Greg … again…"

Susie's blonde hair framed her face beautifully amongst the gold and white pillows. Greg might well have been one of the fittest blokes around, but even he was almost out of breath.

"Mmmm … yeah…" Greg was on the verge as both were intoxicated by their passion…

Stress over finding new players for his first game in charge was over and this was such a great release. They'd been texting each other all week, teasing.

Right then, Greg had no idea that his new role at Hopton was to change everything.

CHAPTER 6

Greg usually reached Parrot Lane before anyone else. It was easily done as he lived just a short distance from the dilapidated ground, home of Hopton Town since their formation nearly a century previously.

There had been just time for a quick morning kiss for his raven-haired wife Diane, and their 2-year-old son Kyle.

Yes, wife. Yes, mother. Yes, Greg was the father. Yes, married – and yes, there was Susie. You're up to speed. Well almost.

Greg had been all set with some manufactured excuse about being back late when he'd arrived home: difficulties with getting players, drink with Bill, but it hadn't been necessary. Diane had been asleep.

It wasn't that he didn't love Diane, but life was just great with Susie. Everything about it was fun and he loved being with her in ways he never felt with Diane.

Diane was a beautiful young woman, ambitious too and making headway in her career designing websites and search engine optimisation. It was the kind of work she could do from home so it fitted in nicely with looking after Kyle.

Greg couldn't fully explain anything other than he loved being with both Susie and with Diane and Kyle. He wasn't condoning his appetite for being with Susie but she transported him to a place where he felt not only fulfilled sexually, but also happy in lust, love and friendship. He knew what they had was something that was wrong on so many levels, but he knew it also felt so good. If he could somehow manage a balance between the two his world felt right for now, or at least as right as it could be for him. He wasn't looking for any kind of exoneration of he and Susie from anyone else. He just wanted his separate worlds to never collide. If they did, well that was for the future. Sure, he knew he should feel guilty too, but what the hell he felt, let's just not go there.

Susie and Greg were good from her side also. She was married too, although in her case no longer living with her husband. She was in her mid 50s, but more attractive and sensual than any other girl Greg had ever known – and he'd known a few.

That morning before setting off for the ground, Greg had been all set to tell Diane he and Bill had been hard at it all night. The thought of the unspoken line brought a smile to his face, as it would have been factually correct to a point, but he was careful over taking pleasure in something that would ridicule, even though Diane might not catch on. He knew that wasn't right, especially as Diane was pregnant again, seven months.

Greg loved being a dad and although he and Susie were great, Diane's feelings were still very important to him too. He would do all he could to make sure she, Kyle and the new baby would be okay.

Greg also knew his wife was much more astute than him. He wasn't about to get over-cocky, another smile quickly sent to the back of his mind.

It occurred to him that Diane might already know of his relationship with Susie. She was usually aware of much more than he, but his thought process was such that if she did she may have been either hoping it would play itself out or maybe she was simply ignoring it completely. If what came out in the end, if it ever did and with all the repercussions that would come with it, then he'd just have to deal with it. Consequences of his own actions after all.

He had slipped back home around midnight leaving Susie to a luxurious lie-in at the Marquis de la Maine country hotel several miles out of town. He'd known her for three years and they had been passionate lovers from the start, but there was something far more than love. They shared a bond in some way that Greg would never be able to articulate. It was like she was his confidante, not that he would use that word either. They just worked.

She lived fifty miles away in a city location. They had met first in a village pub a few miles out of Hopton when Greg had enjoyed an evening with the Hammerton twins much more than he had thought. He had been cajoled in to joining them to watch their elder brother play drums in what turned out to be a truly awful covers band where the singer/lead guitarist should have been named reverb or echo-echo-echo. The noise had been deafeningly loud.

Susie had been the reason for the evening to turn on an upswing. She had been out for the night with her friend Lorraine who lived nearby. They had smiled, chatted and exchanged numbers. Subsequently they had met for lunch, then more lunches and had grown as a couple, enjoying each other's company.

As Greg walked to the ground, thoughts of Susie, Diane, Kyle and the baby were pushed to the back of his mind as he focused on today. His mood was positive. He knew Town had little chance of overnight success, certainly not on Sunday, but he was looking forward to taking that first step on his new road. The thought of new, experienced and talented players getting involved with the club, particularly those Bill had mentioned the previous night, was encouraging.

"Morning Greg lad, give 'em some stick, eh?"

Greg hadn't been the first to arrive at the ground after all. The crumpled features of Fred's lived-in face gave way to a grin that would have sparked nightmares in those who attempt to keep ivory piano keys in good condition.

Fred was the man who put the T into Town – or rather, he made it – the tea. He had been a loyal servant to the club. He wasn't on the payroll but was always there, the sort of man who always seemed to slip under the taxman's radar. Programme selling, gate money, boot cleaning, car park attendant, tea-making – name the job, Fred had done it!

Greg decided not to tell Fred, the only name he was never known by, that the game wasn't until Sunday so the 'stick' would have to wait a while longer. Fred wouldn't have acknowledged it anyway. You had to *'give 'em some stick'* every day in his book.

Greg walked through the side entrance at the end of the stand and paced down the corridor until half way, reaching the coach's office. The door was wide open already. He stopped. Irvine was there. Cigar smoke filled the room, phone in hand. He perched on the corner of Greg's desk and broke off from his call motioning the all-clear.

"Come in, Greg. How's it going? I've made a few contacts. Did you get a call last night?"

He then held his hand up so that Greg knew the conversation was presently one way, bearing in mind the other he was currently conducting. This was Irvine's world, the way he did things. He finished and turned his attention back towards Greg.

"You're sorted for Sunday? Or do you still need me to make another call or two?"

Irvine's question brought about an inquisitive look. Greg wasn't annoyed just yet, more perplexed. Irvine smiled generously and unaffectedly.

"Look lad, you'll have to get used to me. I talk quick. I move fast. I like action. I can't slow down – it'd kill me. Did Ron catch you last night? I said you'd be here. They all want to play."

"Coming today."

"Sign 'em," said the express train of a man with a mission as he moved to leave.

"And keep enough ink in your pen for a bit later on. I think you're going to need it." He looked back again as he reached the doorway.

"Right, I'm off, got to dash. Another bloody meeting. Call or text me if you need anything."

Irvine was gone by the time it took Greg to register all that he had said. The last words were still bouncing off the echoing corridor walls as the provider left. But what had he provided?

CHAPTER 7

"Dear God!" said Bill as, half an hour later, his doorway filled with faces.

"I wasn't going to believe it until today," he said enthusiastically as the three entered.

"Now then, Bill. What's us chances? Do you reckon he'll want us?" Ron Rigson beamed at Garside.

"If you're fit then you're good enough for us, we're grateful for anything right now," said Bill with fit players suddenly almost as scarce a commodity as any player at Parrot Lane.

"But let's see the boss. He's out on the pitch."

Hands on hips, the new coach was trying hard to convince himself that he could play some of the fringe players who hadn't featured so far this season.

"Come on, Tony! Get a wriggle on … move it!"

Ron Rigson flashed past the unfortunate, harangued Tony and intercepted the ball. He came to a halt right next to Greg.

"How's it going coach?"

He wasn't breaking sweat and asked it with the kind of cheeky grin associated more with diminutive half backs than rangy centres.

In front of his eyes, Greg's problems had been resolved threefold. The players Irvine had been in touch with had all either retired or not had their contracts renewed with Super League's Castlegate Park two seasons ago. They hadn't played since, but through Irvine's business contacts he had fallen upon their burning desires to get back in the game. They needed no introduction to Greg.

Ron Rigson, the speed merchant and spokesman for the trio, had been a top-class centre. He had led 'Park' to the Super League Grand Final on three occasions; had topped the try scoring lists one season and had represented Great Britain seven times. He'd made way for the younger talent and had put a greater emphasis on his business career since, but had found it boring and now fancied making his way again at 34.

The other two were Keith Denny and Trevor Prentiss, both with bags of experience. They'd all played in the Super League although Greg recalled that Trevor had been dogged by injury. Keith Denny played in either half back position whilst Trevor was an out-and-out wingman. Greg did as Irvine had said and signed them.

That left one place in Greg's starting 13 to be filled. Could Steve Benson, normally a scrum half, step in to play at hooker? The positions were sometimes seen as interchangeable, but it depended on the player.

Benson had only played one full game all season having been hampered by injury, but he was keen. It looked like lethargic Tony Webb, the subject of Greg's earlier wrath, would be set to make his full home debut in front of what looked like being Town's biggest gate of the season. Webb's lack of pace had led him to be Hopton's nowhere man through the season so far, one of two players never selected for the starting team nor on the bench, but desperate times looked to be calling for even more desperate measures. Webb was set to make his season debut.

The higher than normal attendance was anticipated due to Sherwell always bringing a good following and they were currently a club on the up.

Time was running out for Greg's first match in charge. He was close to his starting thirteen, but who could fill the one gap he had left? Second row or prop forward Mark Merrioneth had come off the bench most of the season, but if he played it would be out of position and not ideal, but then again nothing was ideal at Hopton Town – and all was to be even further from ideal pretty soon.

CHAPTER 8

"Now then Duggo! Whatcha got for me then young fella?" The beaming smile belonged to the sizeable girth of Ted Brewiss. His years of investment in the local brew *Tannersfield Bitter* had created a substantial midriff on the *Hopton Messenger*'s sports columnist as he sat in Greg's office following the training session.

This was the man who had steadily added to Greg's reputation by devoting inch upon column inch of vivid detail on the young man's rugby league prowess since joining the club as a junior. Ted was a good 'un, a trustworthy journalist who didn't pull any punches when necessary. They'd spoken on the phone since Greg's appointment. This was the first time Ted had been down to the ground since. Greg was straight with him returning Ted's smile.

"Quite a few debuts on Sunday, surprisingly enough."

Ted raised what could only be termed a sarcastic arched eyebrow. He'd turned up as training had been coming to an end.

"The Dad's Army Squad, eh?"

Greg knew Brewiss's humour and that this would probably be his headline, but the reporter was devoted to his hometown team and knew better than most their constantly precarious financial state. Ted came to his main point, the reason for his visit as a journalist.

"Well, Duggo. So what do you think to him? … Irvine…"

Greg gave a shrug, spread his arms and hands.

"You tell me, Ted. Every time I see him he moves so quick and talks so fast that by the time Bill and I get round to asking him something, he's gone again. He's a bloody whirlwind. But he has got me three new players."

"And that's not all, lad!"

The tone was loud, confident. Greg had only heard the voice a few times, but now knew it instantly, its rasping deep timbre.

The benefactor was back. One thing Greg had learned about Irvine in this short time was that the man never came to the club without a purpose.

Ted let out a low whistle through his teeth and rested back in his chair. His copy for the next day's edition was now staring right in front of him. Irvine made the introductions.

"*Greg – Kenny; Kenny – Greg.*"

The famous gap-toothed grin, the designer-stubble, the mass of black, tousled hair – there was only one Kenny Lomax. Four Aussie Grand Final wins, eighteen Australian test caps, 'Man of Iron' winner – Kenny was simply the best.

"*As you know,*" said Irvine, "*Kenny's been out of the game since the early part of the last Aussie season with a spot of knee trouble…*"

It was time for the Antipodean legend to say his piece. He opened in customary Aussie style.

"*G'day mate, I came over to see a specialist and I'm out of contract back home. I've been putting myself through all sorts of tests in training, but I really need to get some stiffer tests before going back to Oz.*"

The double act of Irvine and Lomax switched the baton. It was Irvine's turn.

"*Bill told me we were really short of a few class players and then a business pal of mine in Australia, who just happens to be on the board at Kenny's old club, told me Kenny was available, or at least he could be for a short time.*"

Greg glanced across at Ted, who was enjoying every minute of his sporting scoop for the day. Greg wasn't the world's greatest talker, yet at times he had a way of putting across a message with the same clarity as he used through his ball-handling skills out on the pitch. This was one of those times.

Irvine hadn't seen this side of Duggan until now.

"*Right!*"

His tone was final.

"*You two! Out!*"

The new owner stared in disbelief. Ted heaved himself out of his seat, winked at Greg, and moved away towards the door.

Bob Irvine had just found out what set Greg Duggan apart from the rest. Standing up to people was his trademark both on and off the pitch regardless of their reputation or their money.

"Come on, Mr Irvine. It's time we left him to it."

Brewiss shepherded the somewhat shell-shocked, but also soon to be impressed magnate out of the office, ready to ply him with questions for a future edition.

Greg's strength of character in getting rid of Irvine created an immediate bond between himself and Lomax. Greg was keen to make sure Kenny was on board properly and that he knew what he had walked into. Greg also wasn't about to be overawed by the presence of a genuine superstar in his ranks. He wanted to get things straight from the start. He was deliberate and took his time.

"Kenny, it's great to have you here, but just what has Irvine told you about us? I guess you've looked at where we are in the league and also which league we're in?"

"Listen, mate. I know exactly what I'm letting myself in for. You're struggling and you need to win games, otherwise that's it, you're out of the league. I'm a winner, mate. I want to be back in Oz for a shot at a fifth Grand Final if I can, but to do that I need real matches and because I've been out so long I need someone who'll give me a fair go. I also need someone who is prepared to take the chance I might break down in the opening stanza. Your guy – Mr Irvine – heard I was coming over to see a specialist and suggested I stayed on for a few weeks so I jumped at it. Simple as."

Greg knew having Kenny around was great news, unbelievable news in fact. What's more, barring another catastrophe he now had a team all playing in their respective positions. Greg nodded his appreciation of Kenny's words.

"So, mate ... when do I start?"

It was the easiest question Greg was to answer for the next six weeks!

CHAPTER 9

"Yeah, it's all set up. Not a hitch…"

"Good. Now let's just see what happens. Hopefully we won't have to do anything more…"

The second voice was far more rational, calmer than it had been in their conversation a few days earlier. His man had moved quickly. He was happier now. He smiled across the fields that were stretched out away from his home in the country. Things were back on track.

****

Bob Irvine had begun fulfilling what he'd told Greg. He'd given him more players to work with, better players who had a pedigree. The team already looked light years ahead of the dispirited clan that had trooped off the field so miserably the previous Sunday. The new boys and the remaining fit players had worked on a couple of set-plays, which were developing, but were as yet nowhere near the finished article given the limited time. Greg had taken well to his coaching duties including watching recent videos showing Sherwell in action. There was a long way to go, but progress was being made.

Although he wanted to win his first game as coach, and every game he ever played in, Greg was a realist. This cup game would at least give him an opportunity to plan for the games that were of greater significance, the ones that held the key to their survival.

Greg knew he could use this game as a way of looking at the new guys and checking on those who hadn't featured much so far. If they won it would be fantastic, as well as a bloody miracle. The only player problem Greg had identified was with second-rower Andy Colquhoun who had immediately slapped in a transfer request after hearing of Richard Brent's signing. Colquhoun had been on the fringe of the first team for five years and had only been called upon when there appeared little option to do otherwise. His transfer request was met with rather more humour than he had anticipated.

WE'LL SHRED SHERWELL! *says King Kenny*

"*Aussie test star legend and Hopton Town debutant Kenny Lomax has thrown down the gauntlet to title-chasing Sherwell for tomorrow's big game at Parrot Lane. Lomax is one of five new recruits in Greg Duggan's first game in charge. The team also includes ex-Castlegate Park trio – Rigson, Prentiss and Denny – whilst local signing Richard Brent makes his debut in the second row alongside Tony Estorino for the clash that is set to attract Town's biggest gate of the season. One doubt is full back Ian Sissons who received a dead leg in training and faces a fitness test tomorrow morning.*"

Ted's pre-match report had gone on to include further background on Kenny through an interview and Greg's thoughts. All in all, it had been a positive take on life since the previous week's humiliation.

Tough news was to follow in what had already been a tough season. Ian Sissons didn't look good. Greg wasn't at all sure about him, but had little option available apart from 16-year-old Paul Davy.

Greg gave Sissons the nod. Whatever injury he may have been carrying, Greg still felt his experience was worth the risk. That left the team as: Sissons; Prentiss, Rigson, Thomas, Venus; Denny, Rodley; W. Hammerton, Lomax, J. Hammerton, Brent, Estorino, Duggan. Subs: Steve Benson, Mark Merrioneth, Tony Webb and young Paul Davy.

CHAPTER 10

"Now, Greg! Give 'em some stick, eh?" Fred was there. He was always first at the ground on match day. *"New programme looks good..."*

Fred thrust one at Greg. Until now, the matchday programme had been in danger of defying dictionary definition. Its most recent format had consisted of two sides of an A4 sheet of paper folded more like a team sheet. This was a smooth, shiny 24-page issue of 'TOWN'.

The cover had two brown Vs and one black V on a white background with the Hopton Town club logo in the bottom right corner. Inside was advertising from local businesses and one or two of Irvine's own companies, a full team listing, articles on leading players, namely Greg and Kenny, and THE TOWN STORY by Ted Brewiss offering a complete history in this and subsequent issues charting the club's 97-year existence – plus one particular piece of information which always gave Greg a warm glow. Record try scoring feat in one game –

G. Duggan 5 tries v. Ensideleigh. That had been five years ago.

Greg should perhaps have twigged by looking at the front cover but didn't until he walked into the dressing room. Hung on the pegs were new kits for the whole squad – no more the hoops of yesteryear or indeed last week, but the strip represented on the programme's cover.

"You get a sponsor's name on the front once we've started winning matches," said Irvine as he appeared seemingly out of thin air once more.

Irvine might be a quick talking go-getter, but Greg didn't want him carried away with a belief that success was around the corner. It was about time someone told him the harsh realities of Rugby League.

"Look, Mr. Irvine..."

"Bob, lad, call me Bob."

It still didn't feel right. *"Look, Mr. Irvine. I appreciate what you're doing. I really do. What you've done this week is given us a chance to start building a team, but it doesn't give us an automatic right to win games. And I'm not saying we're not going to win today. We'll give it our best shot, but…"*

He let his words tail off. He'd said his piece. He shrugged his shoulders.

Irvine listened. His black leather gloved right hand rubbing his chin. His mouth was closed, lips firm. He gave no hint of his feelings as he moved off in the direction of the directors' area.

Greg didn't know whether he had blown it before he had even started. It couldn't be often a millionaire walked in offering the kind of riches many could only dream about, but hey! kick-off was only an hour away. Game time!

The team was in high spirits. Bill came into the dressing room.

"Good crowd. Must be two and a half thousand."

Sherwell's colours of cherry red and thin gold hoops were the first to emerge from the mid-point of the grandstand. They had two ex-Parrot Laners in their side – Gary Vernon and Jeff Turner.

Greg led out his team to rather more boos than applause. The Sherwell supporters outnumbered the home side by at least 4 to 1. The new Hopton strip was received in customary rugby league fashion by the red and golds' supporters who were in good voice.

*"What the ****ing; what the ****ing; what the ****ing 'ell is that!"*

"Get back in the bag with all the other liquorice allsorts!" shouted one wag as Greg lost the toss.

Greg caught a passing glance at the new owner. Irvine was smiling and chatting with Bill.

Referee Harry Stead blew his whistle. The crowd roared. Hopton kicked to Sherwell playing from right to left as you looked from the grandstand. The ball went straight into the hands of Sherwell's wing sensation Glyn Edwards. He sidestepped two weak efforts, taking him to just over his own 25, then slipped the ball to the full-back who was the first to suffer the famous Lomax 'brick wall' tackle. The full-back looked stunned already. The crowd were even more stunned but it had little to do with Kenny's initial effort!

In the middle of the park lay the prostrate figure of Ian Sissons. The gamble had failed. There was no way he could carry on. The opening kick of the match had also been his last. Within that first minute Greg was to find out the difficulty of being both coach and player. Decisions had to be made.

Mark Merrioneth peeled off his tracksuit. At six foot four, the second-row substitute was about to become the tallest full-back in League Two. Greg gathered his team as Sissons was led from the field.

"They're gonna put Mark under pressure every time. Give him support. Get back and help."

The next half hour went well. Merrioneth had been steady, concentrating hard on catching each high ball put up by Sherwell. Town were looking good with ten minutes to go to half-time. The score was locked at nil-nil and Hopton's fans were beginning to see hope.

"...well yes, that's right Ron. And you join us here at Parrot Lane with Town pushing hard. They're ten yards into Sherwell's half. Lomax is at acting half-back. He feeds Estorino – oh, what a burst! Venus is on his shoulder ... oh, this could be a try! ... well I'm sure that could have been a try but Vincent Venus, who played for the first time last week was brutally taken out by Sherwell's Eric Mellor ... and he's off! Ten minutes ... the referee's given him ten in the bin! Well, I'm not sure that Mr. Stead has made the right decision there. In my book he should be off for the rest of the game. The Sherwell supporters don't agree as you can probably tell ... Venus looks OK ... a bit groggy as he gets to his feet but he seems to be moving better now. I know it might not be the way to play the game, but maybe if he'd stayed down longer as they do in football then Mr Stead would have red carded Mellor. Anyway, it's up to the referee.

He's the whistler, he's in charge. He knows what he's seen and he's given a penalty. Mike Rodley will take it. It's slap bang in front of the posts ... and it's there! Hopton 2 Sherwell 0. And it's not often, Ron, that you can report that!"

Whilst Terry Derbyshire eulogised on Dalesmoor Radio, the crowd looked on in disbelief. Glyn Edwards had taken the ball from Hopton's kick-off, beaten the first wave of defence, barged past a recovering but not yet fully recovered Vincent Venus and gone inside full-back Merrioneth. All in the space of 12 seconds! With the conversion going over Town went in at half time shell-shocked rather than ecstatic, down by 6 points to 2.

Physio Dave Hardy, a master of pessimism, gave Greg the news while he was leaving the pitch. Of all the club's characters Greg had always found Hardy the most difficult to get on with. His attitude didn't fit with the new Duggan regime – as he was soon to find out!

"Six weeks at the very least," but Ian Sissons' injury, despite the lad being one of Town's most loyal servants, was not exactly top of Greg's priority list at that moment. Not half way through a game that, remarkably, they were making a decent fist of with a team that hardly knew each other. Greg wasn't in any mood for pessimism right now, his adrenaline flowing freely.

"Dave, I don't give a fuck what's up with Ian right now. We've got a game to win. What I want to know is what's wrong with Vince, so just get him in there and take a look will you. And take a look at Jeff too whilst you're at it."

The anger and frustration with which Greg let rip through clenched teeth and match tension had the desired effect on Hardy who rattled off quickly to check on his latest casualties.

Hopton were still in with a chance of a remarkable cup upset – or so it looked until the last twenty minutes – but, Sherwell, back to their full complement with the return of the offending Mellor, turned on the style as Hopton's resilience wavered. One swift incisive move of slick handling and great pace was enough. The locals started drifting away. The effort had not quite been big enough. Edwards touched down for his second soon after, leaving half the Hopton side sprawling in his wake and Merrioneth understanding why he would never be a regular at full-back.

Hopton's fans would have to wait a little longer to see Greg's work and Irvine's money take effect. The hat trick of tries for the Welsh wizard was duly completed and to cap it all ex-colleague Gary Vernon added insult to injury with a drop-goal from 30 yards out. Sherwell won 17-2.

"Sure, I'm a bit disappointed, but there was enough passion from the lads to show me that we can get ourselves away from the bottom of the league. I thought Mark (Merrioneth) summed up our commitment today and the fans … well, all I can say is keep coming and we will get the results."

With a nod to Terry Derbyshire, Greg took off in the direction of the dressing room after completing the post-match interview.

"Thanks, fellas. You gave it your best shot today. We had Sherwell worried for an hour. They thought we were just going to lay down and die, but then we got tired. So I want to see all of you down here tomorrow night and every night this week. If we can compete for a full 80 minutes we will stay in the league."

Greg wasn't just going to let things happen around him, he wanted to make things happen. He saved his next words for the Aussie legend.

"And I don't want you dying on me the way you just did out there Kenny. I don't care how much Irvine's given you to play here and I don't want to know, but I won't be selecting you if I don't think you're fit, even if I only have 12 players on the field. So you'd better get to work."

Lomax gave out a grin. *"Sure boss."*

Greg didn't yet know Kenny well enough to be sure the message had got across the way he wanted, but he gave Lomax the benefit of the doubt. Richard Brent, Prentiss, Rigson and Denny all received similar lectures, but Greg saved his best for the makeshift full-back.

"You did us proud today, Mark. Great performance."

The beam growing ever wider on the face of the gentle giant said it all. Recognition. Despite his inexperience and occasional failings on the day, Merrioneth had typified what Greg held dear. Honest, hard-working, skillful players who could run all day.

"*Where is he then?*" Greg entered the players' lounge and club bar at the far end of the stand. There was no sign of Irvine.

"*No idea. Shot off a couple of minutes before the end. Not too bad a start, Greg. How are the lads?*"

"*Dave (Hardy) says Ian's out for six, but knowing Dave it'll be less. He's such a bleeding pessimist! Vince is still not quite right, but I think it's just a dead leg. Jeff's got a slight strain … We've a lot of work to do, Bill.*"

Garside had been around long enough. "*Aye, but I think we'll be all right, especially with Irvine involved. Just look at what you achieved today. We didn't win, but Jeez what an immediate improvement on last week.*"

"*That's just it, though,*" said Greg. "*I think I may have blown it before we've even got started. I can't quite put my finger on it, but there's something about Bob Irvine.*"

Bill Garside's look was one of incredulity. "*What are you trying to say, Greg?*"

"*I really don't know, Bill. I just don't know.*"

CHAPTER 11

"No chance ... played like a bunch of big girls' blouses! Didn't see them string more than two passes in a move the whole game." The voice echoed off the walls of Victoria Street Garage the next morning.

Greg carried on with his work paying greater attention to the servicing of an Alfa Romeo Giulietta that had seen far better days than the conversation. The comment didn't upset him as it was directed at the fortunes of a local football team's woes. The other two mechanics were putting the world to rights. Greg's phone burst into life. He took the call.

"Greg, we need to talk. See you at The Old Swan tonight. Nine o'clock."

Greg was left with no opportunity to answer before Irvine had gone, just as quickly as he always seemed to when he was in front of him. Maybe Greg had blown it already! Maybe Irvine was already opting out, but if he was going to do that he didn't need to tell him face to face. The rest of the day became a blur. His day job at the garage was important to him, but rugby league was his life – along with Diane, Kyle, soon the new baby ... and Susie!

The Old Swan was one of Hopton's more salubrious hostelries on the edge of town with hills and fields beckoning beyond. Greg was there first only to find the meeting didn't just involve himself and Irvine. Bill was there too.

Irvine arrived and bought a fresh round of drinks. They sat at a table away to one corner. He then spared little time on pleasantries.

"Gentlemen, I thought we'd better get a few things straight. First, I want us to do well and second I don't want to rock the boat, but I bloody well will if that's what's needed to get things sorted here. I know things don't happen overnight, Greg. But we need a belief instilled into everybody connected with this club that we really can win every game

we play no matter who it is we're playing. From now on, I want everything that we do to be aimed at one thing. We're going to be winners. And before you start saying it, I already know you're going to need more support, even more money and even better players."

Greg couldn't just sit and say nothing.

"All right, Bob," he said. "I know you've bags of experience and you know how to make business work, and I'm not saying you're wrong about treating Town just the same. But your money won't buy a winning team instantly, it just doesn't happen that way."

Irvine was back as quick as a flash. "Look, I'll keep out of the playing side altogether. Just to let you know, I don't just want to win – I need to! And I know it doesn't happen overnight. First, it's about belief, then winning comes. We need both bloody soon."

It was the nearest yet that Irvine had got to a threat. The meeting was soon over following various instructions from Irvine to Bill and one major instruction for Greg, that Hopton must not finish bottom of the league come hell or high water.

Town had finished bottom in five of the last seven seasons, so the omens were not good. This time though it was critical. Bottom would mean nearly a century of tradition piled on the scrapheap, consigned to a history with no future and that would also mean an abrupt end to Irvine's money. Forget everything else.

Greg's phone warbled: a text had arrived. Susie was there.

"Bill. Bob. I'm going to have to get off…"

The pair were moving towards the door, Bill earnestly getting across matters that he wanted rubber stamping with Irvine while he had him. Irvine just wanted to get away.

Twenty minutes later, Susie and Greg were back in a room at the Marquis de la Maine. Their relationship wasn't all about sex, but they always looked forward to when it was! And this was another of those nights.

Susie was wearing white stockings this time. She knew how much he liked what she wore. Another night of arousal and mutual satisfaction saw Greg head homeward around midnight while Susie once again enjoyed the luxury of their shared room.

CHAPTER 12

Town's next game was against mid-table Woodenhow Bay and presented the team with their best possible chance of a result in weeks as Bay's season was as good as over. They had been Town's only scalp of the season – a dour, hard fought 8 - 4 win in the early weeks when neither side had managed a single try! If Hopton won, it would be their first on foreign soil for over two years!

It was now Tuesday. The game was Sunday. Full-back Ian Sissons was definitely out for six weeks following the aggravation of his groin injury; Trevor Prentiss, who had debuted on the wing, was back on the sidelines as he had been on numerous occasions in his earlier career – this time it was a thigh strain; prop forward twin Jeff Hammerton was carrying a knock that required treatment; and Vincent Venus wasn't 100%. All Greg had was young Paul Davy for the wing spot, but full-back and prop were also still to cover.

The influx of new recruits the previous week had been bound to put someone's nose out of joint, effectively telling those who hadn't been selected previously they were surplus to requirements, and in Hopton's case it had been second rower Andy Colquhoun. He felt insulted that 30+ year old rookie Richard Brent had walked in where he felt he deserved the nod.

Colquhoun had hardly been a match-winner in his four and a half years with Town, but given Greg's increasing injury list he was coming back into his mind. The thought didn't last. Colquhoun signed for 'The Bay' on Wednesday! He would play against Town on Sunday. Recruitment was still the order of the day.

"No, they can't get into the side. It might be worth giving them a go. They're just kicking their heels at the moment. Why not give them a month's trial? You know them Greg, it's up to you, what do you think?"

Bill Garside was at the other end of the line on the trail of new players while Greg was at the garage. Greg finished early at Victoria Street and took to the hills!

Vaille versus Kimmelsea was the biggest game of the season in Cumbria, one that yielded patriotic, parochial fever in the top-class amateur rugby league ranks.

Situated just five miles apart, this was the archetypal local derby, as well as being on this occasion the Cumbria Floodlit Cup Final at Super League side Quissant's ground.

Kimmelsea were the young pretenders to Vaille's throne in the North West. Their success in finding young talent and developing players had been instrumental in supplying the cream of their crop to what was now a very strong Quissant side.

The match was as good an advertisement for the sport as Greg had seen for months. Fittingly, it was sealed in the final seconds by a towering drop goal from 35 yards out by Vaille's John Biggar – a loose forward of questionable speed yet unquestionable thought. Kimmelsea's young pretenders would have to wait until next season before they were to land the silverware.

Shopping wasn't Greg's favourite pastime no matter what the subject matter. He had studiously avoided getting involved on that side of home life. Diane had taken on that role – as indeed she had with everything else that needed doing other than playing rugby league! Greg had never had to buy anything more exciting than a copy of the *Messenger*, but that night Greg began his own purchases for the club.

The team for the match against Woodenhow Bay had sorted itself: Webb (lethargy man); Davy (debut), Rigson, Thomas, Venus (still not 100%); Denny & Rodley; Willie Hammerton, Lomax, Harper (back in at prop), Merrioneth, Estorino & Greg himself.

Benson and Brent were on the bench – just two substitutes this time! It would have been easy to bring in players that he didn't know just to bolster the squad, and they needed them, but Greg just hadn't had the time or the right approaches from others since Sunday. The guys he had fit, or even part-fit, had trained hard, but they would all need to give an almighty effort with just two players to interchange from the bench.

This was also the game that, dependent upon other results, could see Town go rock bottom. If they lost and fellow perennial strugglers Ensideleigh won their game, it would see them return to the foot of the table.

The faithful five hundred, well perhaps not even that many since Bay was a fair drive for the supporters, were feeling better about their team after the cup game and having seen Town beat The Bay earlier there was a chance of a victory. An away win? They could but hope.

Bob Irvine had been true to his word so far. He had provided Greg with what he needed and the benefactor was at Woodenhow Bay's quaint little stadium at least half an hour before the Hopton team bus arrived. It was a newly liveried and more luxurious coach than Town had ever travelled in previously.

Irvine appeared relaxed, chatting with Woodenhow's chairman who kept harping back to their good old days. He showed Irvine the framed photographs of their championship-winning side of two decades ago. Not once did he refer to the side's present mix of has-beens, never-beens and never-would-be's! Irvine had his mind on other thoughts. He lived for the day!

"Right, boys. I don't give a knack when it comes to the result today, 'cause I know we're gonna win. But I want us to win well! Now remember what we said last night. 'Crazy's' gonna wanna get even with some of ya – so watch ya temper out there and don't lose ya heeds otherwise it could cost us! Right, let's go!"

Duggan listened with the rest of the team to his most expensive signing so far.

The man was kitted out in a tracksuit with a brand new Hopton Town emblazoned zip-up jacket and the letters PT. The words were coming from Greg's midweek signing. His visit to Cumbria had brought about the acquisition of Phil Trippett as assistant head coach, handling first-team matters whilst Greg was on the field and in the dressing room.

Greg had tempted Phil from Kimmelsea with the lure of money and coaching in the professional game. He and Greg were old friends. Greg had switched Mike Rodley's off-field role to that of resurrecting the 'A' team – a reserve side.

Rodley was to be next to Trippett on the bench when not playing and alongside would be Greg's other signing who had never played a game of rugby in his life!

Dr Veejay Ranjitshah had replaced a disillusioned Dave Hardy who had walked after last week's cup defeat vowing never to return.

Veejay, a quiet man in his forties, was a professor at the local college. He wasn't a doctor of medicine but a dab hand with a sponge and had answered the call courtesy of Ted's latest offering in the *Messenger* on Monday in an appeal for off-field talent.

"Let's just make them wait a bit longer ... and let's have that ball coming out wide! Vincy's got pace to burn down that left flank, so use him, get it out there!"

Trippett was making it clear that his role was to be more than just some willing assistant. He'd worked with the players for three sessions.

The Bay weren't exactly the division's form team, but they'd had better form than the Parrot Laners. As they took to the field in their bright green shirts with a red V, Town's following at Thornwater, Bay's ground, went berserk!

It was the announcement of one of the members of Woodenhow Bay's team that had sent Town's faithful mental! It was Bay's new signing – Andy 'Killer' Colquhoun! The announcement of this newly acquired nickname brought jeers of derision and no little laughter from those who had witnessed some of his earlier exploits in a Town shirt. Killer! WTF! As they say in text land.

A killer he wasn't – unless he had undergone some major transformation during the past few days! He'd been known as 'Crazy' at Town, but not because of any positive moments in the club's colours, more because it was the only song he knew and always sung it wherever he went. The announcer had provided an unintended lift for both Hopton's team and supporters. If 'Killer' was all they had to fear, then their future would be a little more secure inside eighty minutes.

"Give 'em some stick, lads!" came the familiar wail from the terraces. Fred was there with the customary few busloads of travelling fans, plus those who had come under their own steam, knotted together under the shed that thinly disguised itself as a grandstand on the opposite side to the main stand.

Thornwater hadn't exactly been their happiest hunting ground. Hopton had only won there once in the past thirty years and, inside ten minutes, history looked set to keep that stat unchanged. A cheeky break by one of the Bay half-backs wrong-footed the Town defence; their wing turned inexperienced Paul Davy inside out to go over for the game's first score. Tony Webb made sure of a little damage limitation by forcing him out to the corner, his lethargy seemingly replaced with energy. Bay missed the conversion.

Irvine made no comment as Garside shook his head and took a deep breath. This could be another long game. On field, young Davy looked as though he'd had enough already, his head was down. As the team stood waiting for the conversion attempt Ron Rigson caught his elbow and motioned to the main stand where he'd seen in warm-up that Davy's dad was watching.

"And he's fluffed it. Well it was a long way out. Now let's see what Town can do. They haven't had the ball in their hands yet. I must admit, Gerry, I was surprised to see young Davy on the field today and after that opening gaffe I'll be surprised to see him for much longer if his head goes! Hopton just can't afford to carry any passengers in their predicament."

"No, Ron. You're absolutely right. They're in one hell of a state at the moment and that try won't have helped one iota. Having said that, you have to be fair to the lad and say that it wasn't all his fault."

"Yes, Gerry. I'd agree with that, but as you said, it won't have helped him."

BBC Radio Westcoast appeared to be doing their level best

to sign Hopton's death certificate, typically as partisan as most local stations. Bay was their team.

A penalty to Woodenhow was soon calmly slotted over and, to make matters worse, Mike Rodley gave away another and Town finished the half 8 - 0 down. It was a scrappy game with neither side performing well.

"*And the latest scores are…*" The public address system, which had been Hopston's ally prior to the game, was about to turn against them. If the scores remained the same right now Ensideleigh would leapfrog Town and they would be well and truly staring into the abyss.

Greg trooped off field last with the tannoy's words ringing in his ears and the dressing room, when he arrived, had that air of despondency which pervades teams when every match is a struggle.

No-one spoke for seconds. Greg was about to say something when he was stopped in his tracks. A ball flew past his ear and would have thundered into the white-tiled wall. At least it would have done if Kenny Lomax hadn't been in the way! The ball zeroed in on the back of his shoulder causing him to turn round once he'd regained his balance sufficiently. Trippett didn't give Lomax chance to respond.

"*That, my little rays of sunshine, is a rugby football! I brought it in here because I reckon I could make more use of it in 1 second as you have done with it for the past forty minutes!*

"*You see, what you are meant to do with this is pass it between yourselves, move forward and sometimes, kick it. You don't give it away when you've had enough! You don't drop it unnecessarily. This is your prized possession. If you do lose it then you try very hard to win it back. You tackle the ones in different colour shirts to your own.*

"*Lomax! You showed more aggression just a few seconds ago when I hit you with the ball than I've seen out on the pitch. Sure you've had a bad injury, but my God man I thought you Aussies were supposed to be bloody tough – let's see you play this half! Dave (Harper) you're off – Richard (Brent) will take your place. Mike (Rodley) you're off too, and Steve (Benson) you're on. This lot are*

*ready for a stuffing lads. Let's give 'em one this half. They are crap
– beat them!"*

The silence that followed lasted only long enough for
everyone to take in all that Phil had said. Greg followed up.

*"Right, lads. Let's show 'em like Phil says. I've had enough of
playing second fiddle to shit teams like this lot. We can beat this lot
easily if we get our act together. Let's make people like 'Killer' look
pretty stupid."*

Greg hadn't seen Phil in action in a dressing room situation,
but he had now and was certainly pleased with his purchase. He
slapped him on the back as he made his way back out to the
match. Now all they had to do was perform!

One look at the face of Hopton's Aussie hooker as he lined
up for his second stanza would have been enough for most to
run for cover. The Lomax blood was positively steaming! He'd
played at least 3, shit, maybe 4 or 5, classes above this level for
virtually all of his career and he had certainly not lost the will
to win!

When you're down, you're really down, so it goes. The rub
of the green can go against you and if you don't have that
mental toughness to come through you are finished.
Woodenhow had all the possession for the first fifteen minutes
of the second half, but it was to prove Hopton's most consistent
tackling stint for years. 'The Bay' weren't making headway. And
then Hopton's moment came. The ball was slipped out to
'Killer'. Trying to make the big impression against his team-
mates of just a few days previous, he came onto the ball like an
express train. Lomax proved to be his buffers! The ball spun free,
Venus kicked on, kicked again and dived over the line. Fred
went wild! The bench went wild! The team went wild! The fans
were in ecstasy.

The referee rose to his feet. No try.

*"Well, I just don't believe that, Gerry! Would you credit it?
Hopton's first real attack of the game and the referee, Mr Spooner,
can't keep his feet. The touch judge has flagged for a knock-on.
Desperately unlucky."*

"*Absolutely, Ron. They've never looked like scoring until then. That really is cruel luck, but great for The Bay, of course.*"

Whilst Radio Westcoast continued their affectionate but somewhat biased commentary, Steve Benson took charge out on the park.

"*Mark, Tony – on the burst! Let's see you fly past this sack o' shite. If we can break 'em once, then we can do it again and again and again.*"

Kenny Lomax had a smile as wide as Christmas Day! He was back. In one tackle he had convinced himself that his injury wasn't about to reoccur. He felt strong, he felt fit and he was about to wreak some serious havoc!

Greg was delivering other instructions. He knew this was their time. The word passed through the front row whose gleam in their eyes gave a foretaste of what was to come. There's not too much more that a front-row likes to do than batter an opposing team into submission, but on this occasion their attack was single-minded. One individual was about to be the target of a hit squad!

'Killer' was about to be hunted down! Every time he touched or looked like touching the ball at least three men descended on him and all strictly legal, or just about! Within five minutes of this intensity he was losing himself down the line at the play-the-ball.

Irvine, watching from the stand, held what some might term a slightly pessimistic view of business, but others would see as realistic! '*It gets worse before it gets better*' was a mantra he was used to and now with what he was watching unfold he could see something developing. There was light at the end of the tunnel.

Town's tackling was no longer purely hard, it was now bordering on GBH! Perhaps they had gone too far? The referee thought so. He had reclaimed his faculties from the fall and had no hesitation when the opportunity arose to award The Bay a penalty right in front of the sticks. Woodenhow popped it over: 10-0. The moral victory though, when the ball had disappeared into the street behind the goal, had been Hopton's.

'Killer' was helped off the field to the kind of rapture he could have done without from the Town fans.

The Hopton pack was now on top and Colquhoun's replacement received similar attention with the first ball he received. Lomax ripped the ball from his grasp and put in a superb short ball to Keith Denny who raced away from three desperate lunging tackles. He shifted course to drag the full back out wide and caught sight of Alan Thomas on his shoulder just at the right moment. Denny unleashed the pass that sent the flying centre in at the corner for his fourth touchdown of the season. Hopton were jubilant and this time the referee was still vertical!

Although the kick was missed the impetus was now evident to all. Bay had made some headway into the Town half and put up a speculative kick. It went straight to Vincent Venus who collected beautifully, nimbly keeping himself from going into touch. He started well, burst into full throttle and went for the line. His pace totally disarmed the opposing defence as he tore past some pedestrian tackling. His shirt was caught just 20 yards out, but he ripped away from the challenge and hurtled at the under-siege full-back.

Only one other player could live with Venus at that pace and just at the right moment he was there again! Alan Thomas collected and went over! A brace inside two minutes – what planet had Hopton fans landed on? They were certainly in a different world. Greg tagged on the goal. 10-10.

8 minutes to go!

Irvine made no comment. Bill leapt in the air pumping his fists. Trippett chewed.

Hopton were soon camped on the Bay's line again. Five tackles had been completed. The referee raised his arm signalling the last tackle to come before the hand over. Town had been pushed out to the wing. Lomax motioned for the ball to be played back into the middle with Greg positioning himself for the one-pointer drop-goal attempt. The ball never came. Brent played the ball to Lomax at acting-half. Lomax dummied, shimmied and crashed over in the corner beneath a mound of protesting Bay defenders. The resultant grin when he finally surfaced was unmatched by anyone else in the ground.

"Now, that's how to score, mateys!"

Kenny was now in full flow and the confidence was suddenly surging through the whole team. Stand Off Keith Denny completed the celebrations by going over for his first try for the club in the final minute.

"You kicked like a moron!"

The greeting for the captain was met with a beaming smile from Greg and a similar one from the revitalized Aussie. At the final hooter, the Town fans had gone crazy. The whole team went over to applaud the loyal following. Irvine allowed himself a smile. It was as though they'd won the cup, not just two points to stave off extinction!

If only Irvine, Garside, Greg and Kenny had known the passions they had ignited elsewhere! This may well have been the start of their revival, but also so much more!

THE KENNY & DENNY SHOW

"Town burst into life with their best second-half display seen for many years and left Woodenhow sunk in their own bay! Playing with confidence in their own ability is something the brave Town followers have not seen a great deal of in recent times, however this was one to savour! Breathtaking runs by the new recruits and rejuvenated performances left the crowd breathless yesterday as Town put their terrible away record to the sword…"

The superlatives didn't stop. Ted had been waiting for a game like this. All the players received rave reviews, not just the headliners Kenny Lomax and Keith Denny. Ted never wasted the opportunity of turning disaster to euphoria and he'd had precious little chance to work on the latter recently.

Irvine wasted even less time! If the noble benefactor had gone a little cool prior to the second game under his money, then the win was about to supercharge him too!

CHAPTER 13

"Just keep calm. No need to panic. This could be temporary – you know, better initial performance under new management, happens everywhere. It may soon dissipate. They've just got to finish last, that's all."

"Fuck that! We need to do something soon before they get on a roll. I've seen it all before – one match won and suddenly there's a good feeling. We need to keep them feeling sorry for themselves, kick 'em back down!"

"All right … set the ball rolling and get back to me with anything you need!"

The first voice was conciliatory, the second the man who had been calling the shots in the earlier calls. The real drama was set to begin.

It was Tuesday evening when Parrot Lane next burst into life, two days after the first win of Greg's fledgling coaching career, which had been duly celebrated in energetic style by he and Susie, wearing nothing this time but a smile when Greg entered the room with a bottle of champagne.

It was now the next phase of Hopton's regeneration and Mike Rodley had taken to his A-team responsibilities with real enthusiasm. In ultra-quick time, thanks to Dalesmoor Radio, *Hopton Messenger* and social media, Rodley had managed to get together a trials night for prospective players. Trippett and Greg were there too, but it wasn't to be the success Rodley had hoped.

The weekend's victory may have set the players and fans aglow, but it had done little to inspire others to come along to the first trials night in a decade. Only six hopefuls turned up. A couple showed promise, but there was little they could do with the low turnout. It was all over far sooner than they had imagined and the coaching trio decided it would be better to discuss the night's finer points at a local hostelry.

"…I thought young Wainwright looked pretty sharp, and if that

lad who said he played prop was a bit fitter then I could see him being useful."

Mike was keen to bring out the positives. Greg wanted success just as much as Irvine, but he also knew that one of the long-term keys was to rebuild the club with both an A team and a youth side. Greg followed up Rodley's comments.

"*Well, we've made a start and we'll try again with other nights. We will make this work. It'll just take time.*"

CHAPTER 14

"What the 'ell's going on 'ere, Fred?"

Fred didn't know what was going on: indeed, it was amazing that he knew anything as he had been almost permanently paralytic since Sunday's celebrations!

The reason for Greg's question had been the sight of men in white overalls, not just one or two, but around half a dozen, working feverishly around the grandstand. Something Irvine had sorted no doubt. Greg would probably come back out of his office to a stand displaying two brown and one black V.

Greg walked to his office only to find that, once more, it was already inhabited. He mused that one day he might just walk in and find it empty.

This time there was no Bob Irvine, Bill Garside or Ted Brewiss. Instead, there were three guys who looked like they were from *The Sopranos*. They filled out Greg's office so much he could hardly get in, their initial silence and suited appearance would have unnerved many others, but not Greg. It didn't take Sherlock Holmes to deduce that these guys were here for a reason and Greg hardly thought it was to be pleasant. VAT men? Tax collectors? Had they come with a winding up order?

Greg chose humour as his opening gambit.

"Sorry lads, the trials were last night, where were you? We could have done with you two big lads."

The smallest of the trio, more Danny Devito to the Klitschko brothers, looked the leader. Greg couldn't help but feel he was in some low-budget, corny British movie until this point as the smaller guy, about 5 foot 4, sensing he hadn't garnered Greg's fullest attention, shut the door calmly and then turned to face Greg. No smile.

"Mr Duggan. Just listen. Congratulations on your win last Sunday, but we're here to tell you that whatever happens Hopton must finish bottom of the league, otherwise a number of people will

be seriously pissed off. Win again this weekend or any game from now until the end of the season and you'll find out how much of a bastard life can be – here, at home, or wherever you lay your head. That's all. Lose, finish bottom, no problems. We'll see ourselves out."

Greg prided himself on never being shocked and what he really wanted to do was hit these guys where it hurt and send them on their way, but threats on his family, threats against the club? And what did they mean about wherever he lay his head? He felt instantly they were talking about Susie. They knew. They had to with a comment like that as it was so barbed. Shit! Shit! Shit! But he had to act as though none of this was affecting him, keep cool. Who the fuck were they? It still felt more like he was in some really bad movie. Danny Devito turned back towards Greg to deliver his final salvo.

"And don't make us prove a point. It won't do you any favours."

His smile turned sinister before being swiftly wiped from his face as the door opened smartly, smashing against the back of his head and propelling him into orbit over the desk. The door opener had clearly been in a hurry.

"Sorry, guys … Are you all right, mate?"

Greg would have found the scene hilarious if he hadn't still been trying to come to terms with what the smaller guy had just relayed. And in truth he still found it a little that way even so. He repressed a smile as Mr Devito recovered from the door-opening salvo of second row Tony Estorino. He and his aides left with no further comment.

"What's wi' them?"

Greg answered his question with one of his own.

"What did you come in for, Tony?"

"Fred said he'd seen some strange blokes coming into your office, so I said I'd take a look."

Before Greg had time to congratulate Tony on a job well done, it was nearly time for the second-rower to take a dive in similar fashion to the other guy.

"Greg! Outside, son! You've gotta see this…"

The final words were left trailing in the wake of a wailing Fred who made his way immediately back outside. When Greg and Tony reached him, Fred told Greg what the smaller guy of Greg's three visitors had said as they had left.

"They said you'd know what it meant, Greg."

Fred looked at Greg expectantly. Greg didn't understand what Fred was talking about at first. Then he turned to where Fred pointed to the back of the stand.

The boiler-suited lads who had been working so industriously on Greg's arrival at the ground had disappeared. Greg had assumed they had been just another part of Irvine's on-going work to smarten up the club.

"What the 'ell does DON'T FORGET mean? Don't Forget what, Greg?"

The words were painted big and bold right across the wall just behind the Perspex covered dugout.

"No idea … let's get rid of it…"

So what was it? What was this really all about that required a team of what seemed like at least half a dozen in overalls and three idiots in suits?

While Tony and fellow second-rower Mark Merrioneth tackled the whitewashing of the rogue sign, Greg went back through what the shorter guy had said. The suits and overalls visitation was all about making sure Town finished bottom, but why?

What possible explanation was there? What about the threats? Someone knew about him and Susie too. Shit, they didn't even mention her. Maybe he was reading too much in to the wherever you lay your head comment? But what about things happening to his family? Diane and Kyle? Greg shook his head as if the various questions and pieces needed freshening up.

When he focused again it was on why? Why finish bottom? The club would be out of the league, but it would carry on in the part-time amateur ranks rather than the present part-time semi-professional league and aim to get back. It wasn't all over.

Bob Irvine rang next in ebullient mood. This time on his car phone.

"Greg, lad. I've some absolutely brilliant news! Hold on a sec, I'm just going under a br…"

Greg was thankful for the lost signal as it gave him time to digest what Irvine was saying before the next tirade.

"You hear me? … It's clear now I think, Greg? … They're a bloody nuisance at times these phones, but I couldn't do without them … Greg, I've just got wind of some guys from New Zealand, play for one of the big teams in Auckland. Are we interested?"

How could he not be?

"Yeah, I'm always interested, Mr Irvine, but…"

Another bridge interrupted the conversation again.

"Mr Irvine … Bob…"

It was all Greg could muster. Irvine came clear again.

"Look, Greg … bloody 'ell, another damn bridge … that performance on Sunday was just great and just what we all needed to show we're heading in the right direction. I felt as though we had really achieved something! And that's why I want to keep up the momentum. Getting new players in, better than we've already got, will at least mean we've something to build on next season. I really can get this club back on its feet you know, with you and Bill, and I'll give you everything I can to get us promotion next year."

Bob Irvine was in no mood for any lessons this time around. He was high on success.

"These lads from Auckland. Friend of mine tells me they might both be in the running for the Kiwi tour next year. They fancy a bit of experience over here and I've already told 'em to get the next flight out. That's all. No commitment from our side. Just look at 'em and see what you think. Yeah?"

Greg had by now sat down whilst Irvine's sales pitch went on. He'd just thought Irvine had drawn breath when he stunned him with another salvo.

"And there's this Ethiopian. He's absolutely lightning, although whether he can hold a ball at the same time is another matter. That'd be your job anyway."

Greg only knew one Ethiopian – Olympic 100 metres Gold Medalist, Raynard Baki.

Suspense wasn't Irvine's strong suit.

"Raynard Baki – ever heard of him? Never played the game so far as I know, but dear God his pace will be amazing and another crowd puller. You've got to think of these things."

Greg was struggling to keep up now. What next? Mike Tyson for hooker? Roger Federer at centre and Tiger Woods at loose forward? Just because someone was fast – OK, very fast – didn't mean they could play a completely different sport.

"Anyhow, he's coming to see you tomorrow. Greg? … Are you still there?"

Irvine wasn't to be stopped.

"And I understand Ringstall are having an end-of-season clear-out."

He spoke as if it were the Post-Christmas sales.

"If there's anyone you fancy get in quick. I got a tip-off from a friend of mine … Anything for me, Greg?"

Greg decided against telling Irvine about the threats and the sign. The time didn't seem right, Greg was still trying to sort things out in his head and bringing that up on a crackly, wavering signal was never going to be easy anyway. Irvine's mind had already transferred itself to another strand.

"Listen. If you see anyone you want just sign them. We can do this Greg!"

And with that the benefactor was away again! But was it the benefactor who was the problem here? Greg's first thought about this, the daubing, the visitors, was Irvine. New owner and a businessman with connections, but probably also enemies.

Irvine was completely wrapped up in absolutely not finishing bottom, and yet next minute Greg was receiving threats from people who stated Town must finish there. Maybe Irvine, while being apparently the most enthusiastic owner Greg had ever seen, and bringing good news to the club, had also inadvertently brought something far worse!

CHAPTER 15

"Baki! ... BAKI!!!???"

The voice was as much astounded to the point of humour as it was to amazement.

"The sprinter? The guy who...?"

"Should be arriving any time today."

"But has he ever seen a rugby ball?"

"...it's Irvine ... more a publicity stunt than anything else."

Diane was still impressed such a celebrity could be turning out for her husband's team when he'd told her at breakfast the next day. He was putting on a front even though his head was spinning.

This was the first time Greg had ever looked at both Diane and Kyle and had wondered what he'd feel like if anything ever happened to them. He thought about Susie too. What if something really did happen to them and all because Town won? It was stupid.

He couldn't think like this. He'd rung Phil Trippett to let him know about Baki so that he didn't hear it from anyone else. Greg knew it was a wacky idea, but he could see Irvine's point. It would provide good publicity. Trippett had more practical news on the playing front.

"Well, I can't give us guys who'll help in the headlines, but I can raise us two more forwards. They're both in their teens, but they've been playing for a local club around here. I first saw 'em when Kimmelsea played 'em in a friendly. I mentioned that we were trying to get the 'A' team back together. I've rung Mike and he's well pleased."

Town's next game was at home to league leaders Rugg Town. They'd totally outclassed Hopton earlier in the season and had gone from strength to strength since. If Greg fielded the same side as three weeks ago he knew it would have been no contest, but the previous week's win had set expectations higher.

Greg knew it would be a difficult match. Their win last week had come against a side with nothing to play for, not the division's top team on the hunt for promotion. He knew expectations could be managed this week. A good hard-fought game would be enough – and although Irvine would want a win as Greg wanted also, things had now changed. What would happen to Diane, Kyle, Susie or the club if they were to confound the critics, turn the trick for a second weekend and win again? He didn't want to think about losing, but he had no choice.

Baki hadn't arrived and no message had been received to say that he had been delayed; the New Zealanders had sent a Facebook message to say that they were definitely interested, but weren't sure they could get over in time for the last games of the season; and Ringstall's impending clearout had been nothing more than offloading one or two players who were ready for being put out to grass, but not on a rugby league paddock!

On a brighter note, by Saturday, the day before the Rugg Town fixture, Mike Rodley had almost put together a 13 to play friendlies on the run-in to the end of the season. Their first game was scheduled the following Wednesday against Castlegate Park 'A' thanks to Ron Rigson's contacts with his former club.

Greg's mind was still constantly going back to the suits and overalls and what it might mean. Bill wasn't around to ask his thoughts as he was visiting an aunt down south. Greg could have called him but decided to sit on it.

Susie also sat on it, but that was an altogether different matter. It helped take Greg's mind off the visit of the trio in his office as both Susie and Greg varied location and positions from the Marquis de la Maine to the Juniper Court Hotel 15 miles further into the countryside.

Susie must have noticed something because, at one point after they had climaxed together and were laid in each other's arms watching television, she mentioned Greg had appeared tense beforehand. She didn't take it further. Greg had cast the comment aside as he had with Tony and Fred when they asked what *Don't Forget* meant. He didn't want to worry Susie or Diane, even though, by not telling either of them anything, was he leaving them more open to danger?

CHAPTER 16

"Are you all right, Greg?"

Diane usually knew when something was troubling her husband as he was now, but he couldn't let her in. He didn't want her worrying while carrying the baby and he couldn't very well relay his other concerns. Typically for him, he went into a kind of shell. He'd generally always been quiet at home anyway and had never been a man of many words, but he knew a certain type of quiet would convey he may be worried about something. He certainly wasn't his normal self as he woke the next day, that much he knew Diane would figure.

He'd arrived home in the early hours. Diane wouldn't have thought anything about that. She knew he always worked long and hard whether at the garage or at the club and it was a busy time at Town, but he knew this kind of restlessness would unsettle her. He'd taken it that she had felt an aura of tension in his body, in much the same way as Susie had the previous night.

Dark-haired and exceptionally pretty, Diane was far more than the good-looking girl-next-door type. She was alluringly attractive with a fabulous body although clearly now larger than usual due to their impending arrival. She and Greg had been together from schooldays from the same school year. In another few months, their family would be four. No scans to see the baby's sex, though, they'd agreed. Diane preferred the natural approach and they would be happy with whatever the baby was going to be, so long as it was healthy.

Greg just couldn't tell Diane what had happened. He didn't want her feeling stressed, yet knew a totally different stress would come if she found out about Susie and now it seemed someone was using this as a threat. But as yet, it was nothing. Nothing, so he could handle it.

They were unlikely to win against Rugg. Play well. Defeat.

No problem. Irvine wouldn't be happy, but he could get by with that. What if they won other games? Greg had now been told things would happen if they did. Still. Not to worry at present. Work it out. There was plenty of time so long as Sunday was a return to defeat.

Maybe they were nutters? Cranks? He knew they weren't. They may have been like something from a crappy TV show, but the shorter guy had meant what he'd said. Greg was sure of it.

"I'm OK. Just thinking about the game today. Plenty on."

She let it go and smiled, putting her hand on his shoulder as she helped Kyle with his cereal.

"You've said it will take time to get it right … you'll do it."

The threats continued to prey on Greg's mind as he gave his attention to completing the starting line-up for the afternoon's game. The team that finished the match against Woodenhow Bay had been his starting point. Steve Benson was definitely due a run at scrum-half. He was in. Tony Webb wasn't the right class for this game. Paul Davy needed more time and would be the first beneficiary of reserve grade rugby. Pete Smith was still a long-term casualty, but both Ian Sissons and Trevor Prentiss were back in the frame. Jeff Hammerton was still troubled, but could perhaps give Greg 40 minutes. The pack that finished against Bay would be unchanged, handing Richard Brent his full debut and at half-back the pairing of Denny and Benson had worked. Rigson, Thomas and Venus all looked sharp and although young Vincent was carrying a slight knock his presence and speed were invaluable. Trevor Prentiss was to come back on the right wing, leaving him with just the full-back position to fill. Sissons, Davy or Webb? He'd gone back upstairs to grab his bag ready to make an early start for the ground, to get prepared before everyone else got there. There was a knock at the door. Diane answered it.

"Greg! There's a man down here for you…"

Greg's first thought was fear. Jeez, why was he thinking this way? They hadn't even played a game since the meeting, so there was nothing to worry about yet anyway, was there? Maybe this was one of the three guys back to remind him. Diane's voice hadn't sounded troubled and it probably would have if those three had been stood outside. She'd only mentioned one man anyway. He scooted downstairs.

"Hello, Mr Duggan!"

The hand that was held out before him to shake belonged to a man who looked at least three times Greg's age, but still looked fit on it. Greg felt he'd seen him somewhere before, but couldn't place him.

"Sorry to disturb you, Mr Duggan, but I've a lad you ought to see. I'm Joe English, by the way, you might have come across me before, but it doesn't matter if you haven't. Talent scout. I wouldn't bother you at this time normally just before a game, but I know you're on the lookout because I've been reading about what you're up to and had a word with Ted last night. I know you haven't much time, but there's a lad who's playing this morning and not far from here that I think would do you a job."

Greg really just wanted to get to the ground and didn't want anything else getting in the way, but the man was charmingly persistent. He also came up with a winning line that convinced Greg he should take the chance.

"I suppose I could get him to come down to your next trials night, but I think he's good enough for your senior side already and if you think so you could always play him as a trialist today! I reckon he's a shoe-in to most teams in your division. He plays full back."

It was as if Joe English had just read his mind. The man's eyes radiated enthusiasm and he was one of a dying breed. A talent scout. There'd been hundreds thirty years since, but the age of agents, social media and the Internet had seen their number dwindle to almost nothing. He was small, wiry, weather-beaten, but with enough character about him to charm anyone he talked with. The ice-blue eyes and expectant look were the added features that usually sealed the deal. Here was a man who acted on impulse and Greg was taken with that. He had to go with this man.

Greg's morning was kicked into life along the way as they drove out into the hills. Joe's rugby league knowledge was encyclopaedic. He could relate players, teams and the way they all played from decades ago. He'd played at scrum-half for several teams before knee ligaments saw an early end to his career. He'd been a journeyman player, different club each season, but had picked up a couple of medals along the way and had represented Yorkshire in the War of the Roses matches that were the equivalent of Australia's legendary State of Origin games. Joe was incessant. Facts, information, stats – he seemed to have a handle on everything.

Joe's car was totally unlike its owner. It was big, long and ideal for where they were heading. Mitsubishi L200 4x4 twin cab pickup. Joe was a farmer, or at least had been. His sons had taken over years back, but he enjoyed the power and status of a large vehicle. Their progress had been somewhat encumbered by sheep, tractors and latterly a herd of cows. They'd been driving for about 25 minutes and Greg was just beginning to wonder how long this was all going to take when Joe veered to the right, sending them half a mile down a lane already jammed with abandoned cars, vans and trucks. The pitch that met Greg's eyes was a cross between a bog and a recently ploughed field. How the hell could anyone play on a pitch like this? Joe was already out of the car by the time Greg had got his bearings. He read Greg's mind again.

"Not much to look at, is it? But we're not here for the ground. This lad's only eighteen and took up the game six months ago, but I really reckon he could go all the way!"

Energy and enthusiasm bristled from him, but although Greg had listened with great interest and had found Joe entertaining, he was still wondering just why he had come at least fifteen miles out of his way on the morning of an important match to see a player he didn't know, having been driven by a guy he had never previously met. That well-known sports phrase 'it's a funny old game' came to his mind. They had arrived with literally seconds to go before the start.

"There he is!" Joe pointed a finger at the blond haired, bearded, six foot two hunk who looked as if he had just been carved out of stone! Greg saw enough in the first twenty minutes to realise that the old man was worth having on the team alone. He could obviously spot a good player and he had the contacts, as Greg found out, to find even more.

No question about his tackling. Turbo charged in his running game. Handling and passing specialist. Greg signed him up at half-time! Bradley Warrener was a Hopton Town player from the second-half onwards, scoring one try, making another and generally decimating an increasingly fraught and distraught defence. Dartfield Dragons had lost a great asset. Joe was Greg's second signing of the morning!

An hour later and just after midday Greg was back at Parrot Lane. Brad (Bradley) couldn't play after all. Greg had checked and it was too late to register him. Since he'd also signed he couldn't play as a trialist either, but the trip had been worthwhile and invigorating. It had given Greg perspective. Suddenly he'd felt renewed. These bastards weren't going to mess with his head. Fuck 'em. He'd set everything up to win the game come hell or high water. That still left the full-back dilemma to be sorted. With the game only two hours away, young Paul Davy had won his vote. Young or not, he had the definite edge over Tony Webb. Ian wouldn't be risked.

Rugg Town had not lost in their last six outings and were on their way up. The fans who had deserted them over the lean years were pouring back on to the terraces. The royal blue shirts adorned with broad and thin white Vs and royal blue shorts now ran out to rapturous applause home and away. One thing was certain. This was not set to be Hopton's easiest game. As well as being top of the league, Rugg were also renowned as one of the toughest outfits in the league, a reputation that had been founded on years of facing adversity. Sometimes their only face-saving merits for their fans had been that their side hadn't gone down without a fight, and boy could they fight – for real! Some of the fans still recalled those times with fond memories. They may not have had much to cheer on the trophy front over the years, but they had at least found solace in baying for the blood of the opposition.

Their image had been hard to change and they had retained it through a pack whose fierce determination was a match for any in the league. It was as though Foreman, Frazier, Tyson, Marciano and Hagler had all fused together in one sheer fighting force – and for good measure, this season they had augmented the line-up with their own Muhammad Ali – Jeff Toovey – a loose forward par excellence – but like the rest, as hostile as a rabid dog!

The keen, mean Rugg Town fighting machine had been made even more powerful by a speedy and hard hitting back division and the whole show was orchestrated by tireless ex-Great Britain scrum-half impresario Dave Rowntree.

The morning's activity had been a useful diversion. As well as providing the new signings, it had served to give Greg some balance, but as he ran out to what was now a dreadful day at Parrot Lane with the rain pouring in torrents, the threats preyed on his mind.

Greg knew the side he had begun to assemble were starting to believe in themselves. They were not going to be walked over again as they had been in George's last game in charge.

"…*And with just a minute or so before kick-off here this afternoon a rejuvenated Hopton Town will be looking to carry on the good work they completed last week when claiming just their second league win of the season against Woodenhow Bay, Greg Duggan has made two tactical changes to the side that finished the game. Tony Webb's place at full-back is taken by young 16-year-old Paul Davy who played on the wing last week, and Trevor Prentiss, one of the trio of ex-Castlegate Park backs now in Hopton's squad comes back on the right after being missing last week through injury. That means Steve Benson starts only his second full game of the season and Richard Brent starts a game at prop for the first time since he turned professional a few weeks ago. With me in the commentary gantry today is regular full-back Ian Sissons who's still not quite ready to return. Ian – thanks for coming – is this the right game to be putting young Davy in at full-back?"*

"Well, Terry, thanks for inviting me ... I don't think Greg had that much choice. With the injury situation the way it is we're a bit stretched. He could have put Tony Webb back there again, but I think he wants to give the lad a go."

"Well that's Greg's job isn't it and a pretty good one he's doing by all accounts, especially bearing in mind last week's victory. So, what about today? After all, Steve Benson had a good game when he came on last week. How's he going to fare in a full-blooded eighty minutes...?"

Terry Derbyshire was in full flow for Dalesmoor Radio. Ian Sissons, one of the more articulate rugby league players around, was a regular interviewee and pundit when injured.

"It's Hopton to kick off. Left to right from our position here. I have to say that it is really a most unpleasant afternoon. We've had driving rain for the past hour. Thankfully, it looks as though it's now subsiding, but the conditions are certainly not good."

There was one man missing from Hopton's new backroom staff – Veejay. He'd been away for the week on business and had planned to be back in time for the game, but the poor weather had held him up. He'd sent a text to Trippett who was now doubling up as physio, although Bill Garside had tracksuited himself ready to help out if needed.

Both sides struggled with the weather. The ball slipping from increasingly wet hands like a bar of soap. Young Paul Davy was acquitting himself well this time. More game time was certainly benefiting. The backs were seeing little of the ball as the game stayed in the middle of the park with both packs working hard against the elements. Heavy tackles and what had quickly become a quagmire of a pitch had turned the game, only fifteen minutes old, into a scene more reminiscent of films depicting life in First World War trenches. Then, suddenly, out of nowhere came a match-changing incident!

Richard Brent – all brawn and raw power – made for a day such as this when finesse came way down the list of priorities, slipped the ball deftly to an on-rushing Tony Estorino. He was no more than 10 yards out and with the line at his mercy when he spilt the ball straight to Rugg Town centre Ian Boswell!

The Hopton defence was caught flat-footed. Boswell soared past a despairing Lomax and sprawling Benson with only young Paul Davy left! A hopeless task!

Not so! Davy took him out! The smother tackle could not have been more properly executed!

Ian Sissons was in raptures in the gantry. Terry Derbyshire was in ecstasy! Referee John Simpson awarded the try!!!

Derbyshire changed from ecstasy to utter disbelief. Sissons from rapture to eruption. Paul Davy – from delight to self-destruction!

Nearly all of the other twenty-five players on the park joined in a mass of flying fists and lunging limbs which had turned the game – in one move – from mundanity to insanity! When Terry Derbyshire regained some composure, breath and an element of reason, he handed the question directly to Ian Sissons.

"Well, Ian, what do you make of that?"

In an extremely pained and higher pitched voice that was crackling with frustration, Sissons tried to make sense of what had just taken place.

"Well, Terry – Paul's made a great stop, absolutely fabulous. And I just can't see why the referee has awarded it in a million years. Boswell clearly never grounded the ball. How could he? Paul was all over him. Neither the referee nor his touch judge were anywhere near what was going on, so how they could see that beats me! I think the crowd have convinced him, like he's reacted to the Rugg Town crowd behind the line ... oh, but look what's happening now! No, no, no, no, no..."

"Paul Davy has got his marching orders. It's a red card. Because, as a result of the referee's actions, I'm afraid he rather lost it. And he's off! ... and here we go again ... it's started again. Another fight has broken out. Well, Mr Simpson has got to do something to cool this situation. Unfortunately, there's little doubt that Davy had to go. He's taken a pop or two at Boswell and he's then given such a

verbal to the referee. You don't have to be a lip reader. We could pretty much hear it from here! The decision obviously incensed him, but oh dear oh dear. And there are two Rugg Town players needing treatment…"

"To be fair, Terry, there's a lot of peacemaking going on out there. Greg and Keith Denny look as though they've brought it back under control a bit."

Kenny Lomax and Rugg's Jeff Toovey walked too, but just for ten minutes in the bin as the referee tried to restore law and order. Davy and Lomax were booed from the pitch by the Rugg fans and the conversion kick for two points added to Hopton's sense of injustice at conceding the try. Rugg coasted towards half-time with their six-point advantage untroubled. Trippett Time was about to begin!

"I don't want any of you to say one word. Not one! Not even a whisper! Don't sit around moping. Just keep it buttoned … Right, now think about what we're going to achieve in this second half. Think about it. Do you want to win? Do you really? I mean really! Really want to win? Because you can. This shower are top of the league, can you believe that? And they are just one try ahead of us thanks to a lucky break. Now go out and earn one yourselves. Believe! Now get out there and play for this club!"

Ten minutes into the second half and indiscipline on the back of a feeling of injustice saw Town concede four successive penalties! Rugg had been able to attack without hardly touching the ball. They were now camped ever nearer Hopton's line and making headway. Four tackles down, Greg saw his chance.

Rugg made the move to sling the ball back for the drop goal. The conditions were still poor and they clearly thought a seven-point margin would more or less kill off Hopton's hopes. Greg was on his way. Beaming in on the prospective kicker. Rugg players and fans immediately called for offside. The Hopton fans drew breath, ready to shout down the referee once again.

Not many referees, regardless of what the decision should be, are bold enough to give four straight decisions to one side, let alone five! The Hopton following thanked their own gods that the law of averages fell in their favour as Greg got his man and in one move blocked him, held him and dumped him to the ground.

One more tackle to go. Rugg kicked through. The ball went straight to Vincent Venus, doubling as full-back in the absence of Davy. Vincent sidestepped past two oncoming players, lost his footing and fell awkwardly with two players bearing down on him. Just before he hit the ground he released the ball backwards. It popped up from nowhere and was gathered at pace by Alan Thomas! Thomas burnt through, this time catching the Rugg defence flatfooted as they had all stopped a little early thinking Venus was about to be tackled. Thomas took a diagonal run crossfield from the left, straightening up at the halfway line, and Ron Rigson took over from a sweetly completed reverse pass leaving only the Rugg fullback in the way. Crunch time for Ron! He'd have beaten this guy in his sleep four or five years ago – this was his first real opportunity to register a score since!

Indecision can be one hell of a price and Rigson found himself engulfed before his momentary hesitation could be remedied. Hopton kept up the pressure though and for a total of sixteen tackles they hammered away at the Rugg line.

The tackle count was forgotten for several minutes when one of their props sent a bone-cracking right uppercut that inflicted serious damage on Steve Benson's looks.

Phil Trippett was no physio, but he knew it wasn't going to be pretty! One look at Steve's eyes, let alone his nose, which by now resembled a crushed and splattered strawberry, told Trippett it was the end of Benson's afternoon!

The Rugg forward, who had typically received high-fives from his teammates and cheers from the fans, was given ten minutes in the bin. Ten minutes! Once again the referee was unsighted – rather like Benson was for real right now. The Hopton fans had had enough – and they let the whistler know in no uncertain terms.

No words were needed by Trippett. Mike Rodley was stripped

and ready for action. Greg slotted over the penalty. 6 - 2. Ten minutes to go and they still had a chance. Greg tried to blot out the memory of the three unwelcome visitors during the week and their painted warning. He was playing a game. He wanted to win. He couldn't throw it could he, if he had to?

Trevor Prentiss didn't look right. Willie Hammerton appeared to be carrying a knock, but they were in no worse shape than Rugg appeared to be.

It was Lomax Time! Hopton had forced their way back just short of Rugg's quarter. The bearded Aussie turned, his back to the Rugg line, dummied, came off his left foot, turned again and scampered as if his very life depended on it. He ducked under three dangerous challenges and threw himself at the line.

"What an absolutely brilliant breathtaking try," exclaimed Terry Derbyshire after the briefest of breathtaking pauses. *"And Hopton will hit the front with only minutes to go if they get the conversion."*

Ian Sissons was back to high emotion. *"And it's no less than we deserve, Terry. We've been playing against fourteen players out there today. Mr Simpson really hasn't helped us one iota. But the lads have battled hard all afternoon. Now they've just got to hang on and they've got us a great win."*

"Indeed it will be if they do. But I'm afraid it won't be with Kenny Lomax on the field. He's coming off. And unbelievably it's another nose job I think."

"Yeah. That's right, Terry. I think he got a knock from one of the Rugg Town players as he's dived over. He looks OK, just a bit groggy. Anyway, he's done the hard work, now all we've got to do is hold on."

"And that gives Dave Harper a few minutes in the final seconds of this game. Duggan's slotted over the conversion. That's Hopton in the lead for the first time."

He hadn't bottled it after all. Greg had debated the matter with himself as he was lining up the kick. Shit – he just had to go for it. Winning was what mattered, not what three twits without a brain cell between them had to say, but as the ball disappeared from view behind the Rugg Town uprights there was still that nagging doubt in his mind. What would happen? Would anything happen? One thing was certain. Greg was going to find out one way or another.

What a great day though. Here he was, on the verge of one of Hopton's best moments in years. Back to back wins and he had been contemplating a losing scenario! This wasn't him. He shook his head in order to clear his mind as he made his way back for the restart.

"*...And would you believe it! They've knocked it on from the kick-off. Hopton's head and feed at the scrum ... the ball's come clear. It's Thomas who receives from Denny, then Rigson and now it's Harper! My word, he was just in the scrum seconds ago! He's in the clear. He's gone past one ... two ... three ... there's no-one near him! Just the full-back to beat, he chips through ... and collects ... surely he can't ... he can ... he caaaaaannn! He's done it! Well, if we thought Kenny Lomax's try was remarkable, then that was truly amazing! A dazzling try from Harper!*"

Whilst Terry Derbyshire was fast running out of superlatives once more, Greg calmly booted over his second conversion inside three minutes. Ian Sissons was no less effusive.

"*Well, Dave's only been on the pitch for a matter of minutes and you couldn't ask for a better try than that!*"

This was the league leaders not some mid-table side with nothing to play for. Hopton were competing and indeed beating a team which was allegedly on its way out of their division the positive way! Rugg were now eight points adrift, with almost as many seconds to go. It might just as well have been eighty-eight. There was no way back. The faithful few hundred on the terraces were delirious. Bob Irvine, conspicuous by his adopted lower profile for this game, sprang to life, clutching and dancing with Bill Garside at the final whistle. Greg saw them as he left the field. They were in sheer ecstasy, but Greg, try though he did, could not feel the same joy the rest were reaching. What had he done? Perhaps it hadn't been much of a threat after all. Just that. Just a threat never meant to be carried out.

Try as he did though it wouldn't go away. Something was going to happen, and now, with the win, Greg was powerless to do anything about it.

Paul Davy was over the moon and, whilst Benson and Lomax nursed their respective and as yet to be diagnosed but almost definitely broken noses, Trippett began making notes for next week's game.

Two games won in succession! Hardly a club record, but the price of success had been hard. With Veejay missing, Phil tended to the wounded. Benson and Lomax were sent off to the local infirmary for X-rays; Trevor Prentiss, Rigson and Willie Hammerton were all carrying knocks; add to those the sending off for young Davy and half the victorious team was out for next week's game! But it wasn't all bad news! Some of it was terribly worse!

CHAPTER 17

Veejay had returned in reasonable time from his trip and he'd set off in good time for the game. He'd taken his usual country lane to link up with the motorway as he lived around 20 miles away nearer Ringstall than Hopton when a car had come directly at him forcing him off the road and causing his new Audi R8 to strike up a close relationship with an oak tree.

Veejay had been terribly shaken and hadn't been able to describe anything about the car that had caused the accident except it was black. By the time he'd explained everything to the police, arranged alternative travel plans, car recovery and had his body, mind and soul back together the game had been over.

Just some mindless idiot going too fast.

Diane never came to the matches anymore. She had when she and Greg had first dated, but had soon lost interest. Sundays during the rugby season were now trips to the park and the swings with Kyle. Today had been most definitely an afternoon to be inside. She and Kyle had been to see her mum and dad and had waited until the rain had stopped before heading back.

Diane was crossing the road near the park. Kyle was now asleep in his buggy having accumulated his fair share of sweets and having achieved the rare distinction of being sick on grandad's head when he had lifted him up on to his shoulders just minutes after lunch. It had all happened so quickly.

There was a car approaching as she crossed, but it was a straight road and she could see it was a long way off. What she hadn't banked on was the occupant of the oncoming vehicle would treat pedestrians as the equivalent of the far end of a ten-pin bowling alley!

She heard the surge in power from the now fast-approaching car and put Kyle into full throttle. At the vital moment, as she reached the kerb, she lost her footing and flew towards the footpath!

The car swept by within inches of Diane's flaying ankle. Kyle, meantime, had been propelled, somewhat miraculously by his mother as she fell, in such a way that his buggy had landed wheels first and was presently rolling gently down the path, oblivious not only to the lifesaving effort made on his behalf, but also to the fact he was now heading for the next danger – a junction.

Diane was powerless to do anything more than watch and screech. It took on epic proportions as Diane saw her son disappearing agonisingly from view. There was nothing she could do. She tried, but she couldn't move.

"Kyle! … Kyle!!! … somebody, please!"

Kyle had reached the junction and was still rolling as a waggon approached from the right. As his buggy's wheels hit the road, so the waggon driver's feet effectively hit the tarmac. The driver was out in a flash, darting in front to head off the stray buggy.

Amazingly, after all that had just happened, Kyle was still hard fast asleep! The driver turned in her direction smiling in triumph. Diane's face greeted him with a mixture of emotion that should have encompassed anger, frustration and agony, but most prominent of all was the outpouring of sheer joy and relief that her son was safe!

Right now, she couldn't think about anything other than what had happened as she lay in a hospital bed having been given a lift by her truck driver rescuer to A&E at the infirmary.

Kyle had woken, but only for food. She'd rung her mum and dad and Greg while in the truck. Her parents were on their way. Her foot hurt like hell and the fast-developing balloon that was once an ankle was thankfully the worst of what she had suffered as a result of the rather abrupt end to her afternoon. The only thing that really mattered was that Kyle was safe, but what in God's name was the driver of that black car thinking? Bloody joy riders.

There are some who don't see things until they are staring

them right in the face and there are others who can calculate immediately what is going on and add two and two to make four rather than five. Diane fitted in the latter camp. The sound of the engine roaring into full power as her foot touched the road would stay with her. The driver had meant to harm her, shake her or even kill. Greg had been bottling something up. Was there a connection? She didn't believe in coincidences. She'd find out.

Greg had seen the inside of more hospitals than most. It went with the territory as a rugby league player, but this time it was different. Apart from when Kyle had been born, this was the only time he had ever needed to come for a reason other than his own. He had received the call from Diane within minutes of getting out of the shower at Parrot Lane.

Until the call he'd been starting to bask in the sweet success of the afternoon when his world had suddenly came crashing down.

Now, in an instant, he had been made aware of the consequence of today's win. There was no doubt in his mind the reason Diane was in hospital was down to the threats. No doubt in his mind at all. What the fuck was going on here?

The infirmary was a new-build some three miles across town. Anger and sheer panic had by now taken over. He had to see Diane and Kyle. The baby! God, the baby! Greg prepared himself for the worst. Or so he thought. If only he had believed these guys and what they were capable of and thrown the game if he'd been able to.

By now he could have been playing catch with Kyle, with his little rugby ball, whilst Diane looked on smiling as she always did. Greg had kept the radio on from getting into the car. Local radio with the sports news. It came as no help, announcing Hopton's result as by far their best game of the season. But what had the result done to Diane? What had he done to his wife's life by winning?

Parking as near to the hospital as he could, car parking always being at a premium at the one place where you need to be parked quickly, Greg sprinted to the reception area and bounded up the six flights of stairs which led to Diane's ward.

Through the doors to the ward Greg met silence. Serenity, with nurses gliding from room to room down the corridor. Safe. Was Diane? It couldn't be that bad, what he was about to see or hear, could it? But why keep her in? Observation? Diane had rung him so it couldn't have been too bad surely? She didn't sound overly traumatised.

"Mr Duggan?" The smiling face of the nurse that greeted Greg was one which had been perfected over many years of training, giving away no air of impending doom nor offering too much comfort that all was well when in fact it certainly wasn't.

"My wife and my son ... I got a call ... how are ...?" Finishing sentences was suddenly a major problem, almost as though he didn't want to ask the questions for fear of the inevitable.

"I'll call doctor and tell him you're here." Reassuring though words from the doctor might be, all Greg wanted to do right now was to see Diane and Kyle. He had already resigned himself to the fact that the news was bound to be bad in some way, but calling the doctor confirmed it.

Within seconds of Greg's arrival, the doctor appeared. He was early 40s.

He forced a smile as he introduced himself to Greg, at which point any last remnants of hope faded from Greg's mind.

"Mr Duggan." Greg wasn't in the mood for introductions and pleasantries.

"What is it? What's the matter with my wife and my son? Diane rang, she didn't sound too bad on the phone, but with you here..."

Greg's words trailed off. The doctor motioned for Greg to sit down.

"Mrs Duggan and Kyle are here," he paused very slightly. *"Kyle is absolutely fine and is asleep at the moment in a bed near to his mother's room, but I'm afraid the force with which Mrs Duggan fell..."*

The doctor finished the bad news that Diane had lost their baby. He had gone for it, straight out, slight pause, but otherwise straight there. He'd looked into Greg's eyes and seen the man simply wanted to know exactly what had happened. No messing.

The words hit home with all the impact of a dagger to Greg's heart. What the fuck had he done? But, dear God, he hadn't expected something like this.

"It will be tough for her ... she's doing as well as she can under the circumstances ... Mr Duggan?" The doctor was trying to ascertain what level of shock Greg was under. Silence was Greg's only reply. The doctor decided to carry on.

"From what Mrs Duggan tells us, someone drove straight at her as she was crossing a road. Mrs Duggan, Diane, managed to save your son, but in her attempts to get out of the way of the car she broke her ankle as she tried to reach for safety herself. It was how she landed that caused the abdominal trauma that brought about the miscarriage. I really am awfully sorry. I've given her a sedative and she's drowsy at the moment, but she desperately wants to see you, of course..."

"Does she ... I mean, does she know she's lost ... the baby?"

"I think she probably had a fair idea after hitting the ground the way she did, but initially she was just so glad to see that Kyle was safe."

They turned into a separate room. Kyle was asleep on the bed opposite Diane. As the Doctor and Greg entered, she opened her eyes slightly. The sedative had kicked in. She was drawn and pale, tears were in her eyes, rivulets running down her face. Greg went to her side and held his wife in his arms.

CHAPTER 18

"Yeah. I shouldn't think he'll be able to concentrate on anything right now."

The voice delivering the line wasn't venomous, more matter of fact and that the job had been done. The other was cautious but determined.

"Remember, he's not everything. They won. We can't do with them winning again. Whatever you think you can get away with to keep up the pressure just do it, because if they win again, then it could be game over for all of us."

Right now, Greg had one thing on his mind. Revenge. Those bastards! Fire raged inside as he made the journey home. Diane had woken long enough for him to stroke her hand, look into her eyes and tell her how much he loved her. She had said she was sorry for losing the baby.

Greg held off his tears with a struggle while Diane's flowed. He wanted to cry so much, but just couldn't. The anger was too much. All he truly wanted to do was to go out and get them. To do to them just exactly what he had in mind, to chop their fucking balls off! Yes, he loved being with Susie, but he also loved Diane, and knew she needed him. He wanted to be there for her.

Kyle had slept right through Greg's visit, seemingly undisturbed by anything that had taken place. Greg had only left them both when he was sure that Diane was back asleep and her parents had arrived. Greg had told them he needed to get some of Diane's things. He'd be back soon.

Now he was out of there all he had on his mind was to hit back and quickly – but how? Call the police? But what would they be able to do? What did he have for them? Report a dangerous driver?

So far, all he'd had up until earlier this afternoon had been threats from the three who had visited him, nothing substantial. All he had to go on were three faces. The black car that Diane had mentioned gave him nothing additional. He could inform the police at least. Give descriptions of those who came to the ground.

Irvine? Surely this must have something to do with him? Irvine was the only person he could think of outside of the people he knew. Crazy though. Blood crazy! Why would it be him? He was investing, encouraging. It didn't make sense.

Why go after Diane? Their baby, formed and just two months away from birth, now dead before it had chance to even see daylight. Tears weren't far away, but his anger forced them to dryness. These guys had to be found and strung up. Either that or just kick the living shit out of them.

Greg drew up in front of the house and sat for a short time, engine still running, brain still running, both turning over and over again as he tried to make sense of all of this. Here he was, just a rugby league player, but no longer! Now he was a rugby player who had to lose matches and he was a rugby league player with a vendetta. His head was clearing – these guys needed dealing with whoever they were – and fast!

At last, he turned off the engine and made his way to the door. As he stepped inside, his phone rang. Surely not the hospital again with even worse news? Not this time. Withheld number.

"Now you know what it's like to lose something. Just make sure your team goes back to doing the same!"

The voice wasn't one Greg had heard previously, but he knew what it meant. He was back outside the door looking into the night for any clues as to where the voice was coming from. Whoever was calling had known when to ring and was probably watching him. Greg's eyes darted as he talked, moving back out into the road.

"Listen, you fucking heartless murdering fucking bastard. I'm gonna find you and when I do you're gonna wish you'd never started this…"

The phone had already clicked soon after the 'heartless bastard' vitriol had been delivered. He hadn't heard the rest of Greg's verbal attack. Greg saw the line had gone dead. Within seconds it was ringing again.

"And don't get any stupid ideas about getting anybody else

involved, cause we're watching you real close. The police would be a very bad idea."

Greg didn't say a word. He was thinking. In the instant between the two calls, he'd had a clear-thinking moment and had set his phone to record the voice. This situation needed his skill, not his brawn. Bullish, aggressive behaviour was out just for now – it was time for tactics.

Why had the call come just as he set foot back in the house? A second call so soon after the first also meant that surely the voice had to be somewhere close or there was some kind of camera trained on him, although the latter of those seemed absurd. This was boring old Hopton not some downtown San Francisco. Greg was outside checking cars in the street as fast as possible. The voice started again.

"If you go anywhere near the police or contact them in any way then you can look forward to visiting your wife in hospital again. There's only one way you can get out of this. Lose. Don't win. It's easy. Good night, Greg."

Bastards! Why did they need Hopton to lose? The caller had gone. Greg looked all around in the street. He walked calmly, slowly. No sign, no sound, no movement. This new voice, authoritative and assured, was something far more professional than the visit he'd had from the three stooges.

Greg took stock of his situation as he went back inside their 3-bedroomed detached home on a small new-build estate they had moved to earlier in the year. Diane was in hospital, wrecked physically and emotionally. Kyle there too, albeit unscathed, but that afternoon he and Diane had lost a child, a perfectly formed baby girl who they had decided if the baby was a girl, would have been called Kirsty. Greg wasn't one for tears, but this was different. There was nothing else he could do. He wept now with tears of both despair for Diane and Kirsty frustration.

Surely this kind of thing only ever happened in books or films, not here in bloody Hopton! But here it all was, happening directly to Greg.

CHAPTER 19

There was nothing he could do immediately. He had no idea whose voice he had just heard, although he'd recorded it. He would have been able to give descriptions of the three who had visited him, but that was it, nothing more.

He'd been warned off going to the police, threats were not just being made but also being carried out and he now had every reason to believe that, given the latest call, more would take place if he didn't fall into line.

Diane and Kyle were in hospital and they were his priority right now. He had to see them. He started the car complete with changes of clothing. Diane and Kyle, while neither were in danger, were both staying in hospital under observation.

Greg had to talk with someone, rattle through what had happened, bounce ideas around – but who? Diane always knew when there was something not quite right, and he was pretty certain she would have answers, a plan, but hell, not now! She needed him where he now was, alongside her bed in hospital. He couldn't burden her. But what good was he doing here? This mess needed sorting and quickly, if it could be. Greg needed someone to talk with. Bill? Ted? Even Irvine? Susie came to mind too, but no, but then what if these guys turned their attention on her next? Wherever he laid his hat?

The one person who stood to lose anything here so far as Greg could see was Bob Irvine. He'd invested in the club. He was the new factor, the one factor that was different, that might have caused this. But why? Irvine had only been here a matter of weeks. Was this some personal vendetta, some businessman's war, some fight that had clearly got way out of hand?

Surely Irvine was the guy to tell Greg just what the hell was going on? Irvine, it had to be, didn't it?

Diane opened her eyes and smiled. The kind of smile reserved for those moments when every part of you is hurting, but you're still alive and you see a familiar face you wanted to see when you opened them.

Greg felt guilty about the threats and what had happened, as though this was all his fault. He also knew it was stupid. He'd not been responsible for driving a car at his wife and the consequences of that, but he still felt guilty and he knew he was no bloody use in the hospital. All he felt was frustration. What could he do for Diane at present apart from giving her his hand, kissing her on the cheek, and, well, just being there at the hospital. It might have been enough for some, but it wasn't Greg's way particularly, given what had happened. There was only one thing that kept resurfacing in his mind – revenge!

Going to the police was ruled out, not just because of the threats, but also because Greg honestly didn't feel there was anything they could do. He knew they, the police, were the right option, but what about anything else that might happen if he went to them? The threats were real.

When Greg left the hospital for the ground there was still no plan taking shape. He knew involving the police was the right way. It had to be sorted! He'd rung Bill who was still at the ground in the bar with a number of others. The celebrations had lasted a good few hours and it was now around 10pm. Bill was his best bet.

"Yeah, he's leaving the hospital now … No, he's not talked with anybody. I think he's just scared shitless at the moment … Yeah, I'm watching him night and day, just to make sure this doesn't go all pear-shaped … I'll catch you later…"

Driving in to Parrot Lane had always been a pleasure to Greg, sweeping through the main gates and wandering around the ground. It was hardly a theatre of dreams in the grandest of manners, but it held an affectionate place in Greg's heart. Not so now! This was serious heavy millstone time.

Greg felt a pulse in his pocket. His cell phone was on vibrate. He took it out as he got out of his BMW X5.

"Hello, Greg. How's your wife? … and your physio?"

The text was meant to deliver another blow and it had. He

hadn't heard about Veejay – but was soon made fully aware of his predicament from everyone he came into contact with at the ground who all proffered sympathy over Diane and the loss of the baby.

Greg had taken it all in and had been relieved to hear that, despite everything, Veejay was okay and would be back the following day. That was his outward reaction. Inside, Greg had, in fact, been utterly distraught by the revelation. No-one else knew they had to be linked.

Another incident! But this time it had been before the match had started while Diane's had been just after the result. They'd been watching her, but these bastards didn't really care what the result was going to be.

Bill caught Greg's mood, although in truth it wasn't easy for Greg to hide his anger and frustration. Bill knew all the young man's ways and had seen and dealt with them throughout Greg's career. Greg had explained about Diane and Kyle earlier when he was on the way to the hospital the first time and Bill had questioned whether Greg should have even bothered coming to the ground right now.

There were only a handful of players and supporters left in the club lounge, but that was still too many for Greg. He motioned for them to go to Bill's office.

Once inside, Bill opened with the question.

"What is it, Greg? … What are you thinking?"

Greg leant back against the wall, tight-lipped and with his hands locked behind his head, eyes closed. He opened them and stared for a few seconds, then closed them again shaking his head.

"I dunno, Bill. I just don't know … If I told you all that's happened in the past week or so, you'd never believe me. It's like something out of a fucking nightmare."

Bill certainly did want to know. But he could wait.

"Look, Greg, why don't you get off and get back to Diane and Kyle. You're more use to them than you are here at the moment…"

Bill didn't have to wait long.

"No, you don't understand. Bugger me, I'm not at all sure that I do, but you've got to listen to me. Don't tell anyone else what I'm gonna tell you. Do you understand? ... Otherwise ... look I need to tell you, and by telling you, well you could be right in the shit too..."

Bill was dumbstruck. Greg paused. He had walked over to Bill. He sat on the edge of the desk staring at the floor, then bit his bottom lip and closed his eyes. He'd known Bill for donkey's years, trusted him completely. He had to tell him.

"Diane and Kyle's accident ... well, it wasn't ... an accident ... they were driven at by the same stupid bastard who tried to get Veejay. And before you say it, yes, I'm dead sure. I've been receiving threats from a group of thugs and now it's gone real."

Greg watched for a reaction from Bill. He didn't know what he had expected Bill to do or say, but hadn't expected the blank expression he now saw.

"These guys, they're getting worse. Every time we look like winning or doing well, I get more threats and yesterday, well..."

Bill resurfaced from his trance-like status. He was muttering rather than being at any meaningful volume.

"I bloody well knew this would happen."

Greg was pacing up and down the office, shaking his head and running his hands through his hair in exasperation. He stopped, mouth open in jaw drop fashion. His cell phone vibrated again. This time he left it. Bill bloody well knew what?

"What do you mean by that, Bill?"

Bill rallied and countered quickly.

"There's more to it, Greg. There's more to it. If I'd have known..."

Greg couldn't believe what he was hearing. He certainly hadn't expected to hear Bill had kept something back about what may have been going on, but this was also progress. Maybe this was something to cling to, some information he could use to exact his revenge on what had happened to Diane and now Veejay. But this was also Bill, who should have put him straight on what was happening. Greg was slow, methodical and simmeringly brutal all in one go.

"You know all about it, don't you? You know what's going on ... Fucking hell, Bill. You've let me suffer a living nightmare. Diane's in hospital, we've lost our baby and Kyle could've been killed! Now I find out about Veejay. What the fuck is going on?"

Bill steadied himself. He sat down, having got up to try and calm Greg initially. He was at a loss, too.

"I don't know, I really don't ... I don't know any more than you ... it's just..."

Bill was starting to regain his composure.

"Greg, I don't know about anything for sure. All I can tell you is that they warned me too. Three guys. Said something about making sure we finished bottom of the league. Told me not to talk with police or Bob (Irvine)."

Greg was mellowing. All Bill had done was the same as him and kept it all in. Sensing that things between them were getting back to normal, Bill carried on.

"Honestly, Greg. If I'd have known for one split second what was going to happen, I'd have been down to your house, picked up Diane and Kyle and taken them somewhere safe, but I just didn't know how heavy it was all going to get and I still can't believe it's happening now."

Greg put his hand firmly on Bill's shoulder by way of acceptance. Neither knew more than the other.

CHAPTER 20

"So…" said Susie, as they laid on the opulent bed in Greer's Retreat, a fabulous 5-star rated hotel named after a General in some 17th century battle. Allegedly, this is where he'd retreated, shielded by forestry and woodland.

It wasn't that Greg didn't care about home and family, especially now, he cared more than ever, but there was little point being home. He couldn't not see Susie and it wasn't because he was fueled with lust either.

He'd visited Diane earlier in the day. She'd smiled, but behind the smile he knew she was hurting like hell. Losing Kirsty, well, you would, wouldn't you? She was doing ok, the nurse said, but was being kept in for observation. Nothing untoward, they'd said, but they'd rather just keep her in for the time being. Diane's parents were looking after Kyle. Greg's parents had emigrated to New Zealand several years ago. He'd visited Kyle at their place after leaving Diane. He'd played with him and seen him fall off to sleep before heading off to Susie.

Greg needed someone else to talk to, someone close, someone he could trust who wasn't involved in family or the club. That was the reason this time. He and Susie had met many a time without the need for their urges taking over. He also felt a responsibility to her as well as Diane and Kyle. If anything happened to any of the three of them. Anything further than what had already happened. He had to tell her too, in case. They'd spoken rather than texting. Greg was by now aware someone might be reading texts. Hell, they might be listening to conversations too, but he'd had to get a message to her to meet up. Bill had mentioned about the phone being hacked in some way. His too. He'd already thought. Greg had bought a Pay-as-you-go, just in case.

Susie had had a manic day on the road in her role as area rep for a leading perfume company and Greer's Retreat was a special treat on her expenses. Having Greg there was even better, but she knew this was serious. Their relationship went far deeper than sleeping together for both of them. She now knew all that had happened. What she didn't say, and she was always careful with what she said, never giving much away about herself, was how she was feeling. She left it with Greg's thoughts.

"What are you thinking? … You're going after whoever did this, I know, but is that going to make things better? … or far worse?"

Greg had been through it all, over and over. Susie's hand propped her head as she lay by his side, she was asking the questions slowly and with affection. Greg had his hands behind his head, his eyes alternately either closed to establish some form of contemplation or staring at the ceiling. He sighed the largest of sighs and closed his eyes again. He was at least more relaxed here, albeit still fully clothed on the bed. There had been no action between them tonight.

"I have no idea … I've just got to do something … I've got to find out who did this … and that means finding out why … why we mustn't win … why we need to finish bottom … it's all bloody stupid."

Susie tried to help.

"Have you thought any more about your idea … you know, this Bob Irvine character? … Big boys in business usually have people they've trampled over on the way to the top … not that it happens at all in the cosmetics or perfume industry…"

She gave a smile and raised her eyebrows at her own irony, it happened all the time.

"…Small rugby league club … no offence about the small, but maybe an easy target if someone wants to get at him? … Just be careful … Maybe it would just be better to go along with what they want? I know you don't want to and I know it's wrong, like who loses games on purpose? But maybe that way everyone stays safe?"

"Nobody's safe," were the first words that came into his mind and he was sure Susie read what he was thinking.

He'd intended to make this about letting Susie know what was happening, but not to worry her even more than he was already stressed about everyone. Veejay too. There was no logic to it being anything to do with Bob Irvine? What other reason? Greg couldn't think of any other.

He might not have come out with the words, but she would have seen from his shrug of shoulders it was what he meant. She picked up her glass of wine from alongside the bed, put on the television with the remote. Susie was settled for the night.

"Are you staying?"

For once he did. There was nowhere else to go.

CHAPTER 21

Mike Rodley's re-launch of the Hopton 'A' team had consumed much of his time in the past weeks. Ron Rigson had pulled a few strings with his mates at Castlegate Park who had agreed to the friendly against their Youth team. Rodley wasn't expecting too much from his thrown-together side, but he was excited by the prospect of building a new Hopton Town future.

Sissons, Hardwick and Jeff Hammerton were all experienced first team regulars coming back from injury, giving Rodley confidence that at least his team was going to be no pushover. The next trio were totally untried – scrum-half Stu Wainwright, prop Stan Reevers and hooker Tony Tynan – all having attended the previous week's trial.

New signing Bradley Warrener was looking to make a big impression and the Auckland boys, centre Jon Entish and second-row Warwick Player, had miraculously materialised just hours before the game, as he had been starting to wonder whether he had a full 13.

Brian Goram, who had disappeared after the massive defeat in George Ramsbottom's last game in charge, had jumped at the chance of a game when Rodley had made the call. He hadn't wanted to give up the game altogether. It had been more the pressure of keeping his job which had dictated at the time.

Rodley's cousin, Andy Ainscough, had turned out once before for Hopton earlier in the season when they had been so short through injury that Andy had made the transition from terraces to playing staff. He'd enjoyed his first taste, hadn't looked out of place and for friendlies he'd be okay while Rodley found the real guys he needed.

Rodley could have started the game himself, but he wanted a decent look at his new charges. He had held out hopes that Raynard Baki, the sprinter, would surface as Irvine had planned – but to no avail.

He decided to use some of the other guys who had come along to the trial on the bench. Phil Trippett showed his versatility by rolling back the years to turn out in a full match for the first time in a decade; and Paul Davy took the opportunity of getting a game in on the wing before his expected ban.

The game was never going to prove anything other than being an indication of the club's recent progress. Castlegate hadn't seen it as any more than a run-out for the young lads and they had finished easy winners. But it hadn't all been plain sailing as Town were within six points of them until the final quarter. A combination of Kiwi jetlag, coming back from injuries and general fitness levels had taken their toll on what had been a gritty display. At 36-12 Rodley felt the score line flattered the hosts, but he was far from disappointed.

"Wainwright and Warrener – they were the guys who shone for me tonight. Wainwright's got great skill – how he sent their lad the wrong way was pure genius ... and Warrener, well, you've got to say the lad's just awesome!"

The ex-first choice scrum-half was bubbling over with enthusiasm. Trippett and Greg were happy too. They'd made a start – and at least, thought Greg, this was one game he'd been able to watch without worrying about the connotations the result brought about.

"We've a lot of work to do on making sure these lads can get to the right standard. Joe and Warry the New Zealand lads obviously haven't played for a while and they'll need to work hard for the next few weeks – but they should be ready if we need them. We've definitely got something we can make a start with."

Phil Trippett was next to eulogise about the Joe English signing. Joe had been there to watch Brad Warrener too.

"I've got to say Greg, Mike's absolutely right about Brad. He looks the part and could really do some damage out there. Him and Stu (Wainwright) they're both worth at least a place on the bench with us."

Greg was finding it difficult to concentrate right now. He

wanted to be a part of all this. It was his future, the club's future. Mike and Phil were both excited, but his mind was elsewhere. So far he'd come up with absolutely nothing. Neither had Bill.

Greg wouldn't have gone to the game at all if he could have seen a way out of it, but he felt that he just had to keep everything appear as normal as it could be at the moment. The rest of the club knew about Diane, they had also heard about Veejay, who had turned up to physio at Castlegate, but they knew nothing other than they had been a couple of unfortunate accidents. Greg came out of his trance.

"Yeah, great performance, Mike. They did you proud, but just one thing. That loose forward could do to lose a few stones, let alone pounds!"

The six-foot frame of the recent coaching signing, who had debuted for the 'A' team at forty years of age, took the comment in good part. Sat in the snug of Castlegate Park's closest hostelry, The Coach and Crown, the rest of the conversation between Trippett and Rodley made for a useful diversion for Greg.

CHAPTER 22

Two wins in two games was form stuff from Hopton. Town had now created a two-point cushion between themselves and basement side Ensideleigh, but with two of the last five matches of the season pairing both together it really was going to be bum-squeaking time. The final five games were all in a tightly packed three-week period.

The first of the run-in would see the return of promotion-chasing Sherwell, who had accounted for their Cup demise just weeks earlier when Greg's first raft of new players were just settling in.

If Greg hadn't now been so concerned about what would happen if Town won, then he would have been excited to see just how far they had come in such a short time. Sure, they were still the underdogs against Sherwell and that would fall in Greg's favour if Town lost. They had to lose this week. Either that, or beforehand, he and Bill had to come up with something that sorted out this mess. They still hadn't a clue – and since Sunday's antics there had been nothing, not a word from the callers who had been on his case. He knew they hadn't gone away, they were waiting for the next game. Why? Why? Why? There had to be some explanation.

Having played a number of away games earlier in the season, four of their last five games would be at Parrot Lane, and Ensideleigh were next at home after Sherwell.

It was now Thursday. Diane was still in hospital, but due out hopefully tomorrow. He'd visited her twice a day every day, while juggling his job at the garage and his role as coach at Town. Diane had been consoled as best she could, but the proliferation of flowers, cards and chocolates was never going to do it. It was going to be a while before everything was back in order in her life and the pain of losing Kirsty kept sweeping over her like a tidal wave, but at least Kyle had come through unscathed. Although no instant consolation for the loss of her unborn child, she had nonetheless been given the all-clear regarding future family. It was scant consolation at present.

But Diane was a determined, driven woman who had more about her than she felt most gave her credit. She wasn't about to wallow in grief. She had Kyle to think about. She knew the scars of losing Kirsty would take time to heal, but she had more about herself. As soon as she was able, she would throw herself back into her work. Their hopes of expanding the family could wait. And she had another thing on her mind. Why? Why? Why did that car go for her? There had to be a reason.

Greg hadn't mentioned anything. He'd been playing the attentive husband, but she wasn't a fool. She knew in her heart that Greg had something burning inside him that he wanted to be able to tell her, but just couldn't find a way. She knew he thought he was protecting her, but she wasn't emotional now and she was focused. She wanted to know. She wanted to take him on about what had happened when she was fit and ready. She'd dealt with him previously over other things and she would get it from him soon, just not today.

Diane's parents, Tom and Trudi, were both retired and offered to look after her and Kyle whilst she recovered fully. It made sense, they said, since Greg was at work, either at the garage or at the club. Diane had found it difficult to say no and Greg was relieved that she hadn't. She would be safer with them than with him.

For now, the spotlight was back on the next game. No more messages delivered by B-movie gangsters, just a festering feeling no matter what he did, or was about to do, there was someone watching.

It was Ted Brewiss who next noticed something was different about Greg. Ted called the club daily, as every good local reporter would. He also had a tendency to drop by unannounced and on this Friday, two days before the Sherwell match, that's exactly what he did. He wasn't about to stand on ceremony. He was firm, but in no way unfriendly.

"Are you going to tell me what is going on or am I going to have to go through some stupid rigmarole … and we're not talking sport here … you know what I'm talking about … I've been digging…"

Blunt and to the point, Ted had entered the office where Greg had been getting down to the brass tacks of management and was in the process of putting pen to paper over what needed doing for the weekend's game.

Ted towered over Greg's desk with searing eyes. Greg felt their pressure. He reasoned that Ted couldn't possibly know what had been going on, unless Bill had confided in him, but Greg and Bill had said they'd tell no-one and Greg had told Susie, so maybe Bill needed to talk to someone else too. He let it ride.

Greg's lack of immediate verbal response confirmed one thing in Ted's head. He had been right to attack. There really was something wrong. He smelt it. He hadn't dug very far, but enough to know that Greg wouldn't have kept so tight-lipped under normal circumstances. He'd talked with him enough in the past to know that.

He knew how to smoke out the story and it was time for his 'Uncle' Ted Brewiss approach as the nice guy he was. His eyes never wavered from Greg's as he relaxed a little from his tension-based opener and sat in the armchair opposite the now slightly less red-faced Duggan. 'All friendly like', as he had a habit of telling local audiences when he was acting in a guest speaker role, relating how he uncovered his next headline.

The two sat in silence for what seemed to Greg to last an age, but in reality was just seconds.

"Ted…"

Greg hadn't wanted to open up to anyone else and he didn't know what to say for fear of what might happen, but then he knew Ted of all people was more likely to be able to keep information under lock and key, at least until he published. Ted was already on his wavelength.

"Whatever it is, you can't tell me can you? You've been nobbled."

Ted was psyching him out. He'd done this many times before. Starting with the negative tended for some strange reason to put interviewees at ease. Once he'd set them up that way, as though they didn't have to tell him everything they invariably did, but not always straight away. There was a story here, but maybe it would have to come out later. He could wait, but tried again, just for the road.

Greg shrugged, tight-lipped. It was the shrug of an extremely frustrated man with something to spill. Ted had seen it all before. He came forward to the edge of his armchair.

"Let me just put it to you this way, Greg. I've seen you play and I know how you react to situations. I know something is wrong here. It's bloody stupid, of course, because after your last two games you should be on a real high, but you're not. It's pretty obvious why you're not over the moon, but there's something more than all this. I get it. Diane loses the baby; Kyle nearly gets killed, your physio has a close escape the same day ... and just before that you get something daubed on the grandstand ... Fred told me that ... It doesn't take Einstein to realise that something's going on here, so?"

Again the pause, Ted was working his man. He could see the turmoil going on behind Greg's eyes.

"OK, Greg. OK."

Clearly there really was something more, but Ted was the local sports reporter who cared about those in clubs who gave their heart and soul and unless for some reason he had come to find his trust misplaced he had a natural concern for those he associated with regularly. He was their friend, even though sometimes he had to write that their performance was also crap. Truth had to be told.

However, regardless of any other consideration, if there was a major story somewhere that he could uncover, like any self-respecting journalist he would try his level best to get it.

Ted had seen a great deal of shenanigans in the world of sport and Greg's current demeanour bore the hallmarks of something rather more serious than others Ted had come across in years. Attempted hit and runs were certainly not in the everyday sports news manual.

"If you can't tell me at the moment, then fine. But just give me a

call when you want to. I know there's something going on here. I can taste it, smell it. And you can't tell me for some reason ... but you just might need me sometime. I'll leave it like that for now..."

Ted's mind was already clear as to his next port of call. He may not be pursuing it with Greg, but outside he would begin digging in earnest. He'd had confirmed what he thought. Greg was scared shitless. He made as if to leave.

Greg had really wanted to open up. Ted was probably one of the best people he could have confided in. He knew so many people and could probably find out answers better than most. But the last thing Greg wanted was to start including others. It was better just between himself and Bill. Yet Ted seemed to know so much already, but maybe that was journalistic bravado. He gave way marginally as Ted left.

"Ted ... I will ring you ... and thanks!"

Training that night brought good news. Town's season definitely appeared to be on an upswing. Greg knew the enormity of the task against Sherwell and despite winning the previous two matches the fans surely wouldn't expect a third in succession against a strong, confident team they'd lost to just a few weeks prior. But maybe they would. And winning breeds winning. Success breeds success. It was hard to get away from these mantras, even though Greg knew that for the sake of his family, and God knows who else at the club, it might just be better if Town lost for this week at least. Buy himself a bit more time to work out what was happening.

He'd found out nothing about last Sunday's mayhem makers. Bill hadn't either. They'd talked during the week. They'd texted. Nothing. Greg reasoned if Town lost this one they would still be okay as Ensideleigh were two points behind them. If Ensideleigh won their match this weekend and Town lost they'd be back dead level and with two of the four matches then left pitching them together those results would be vital. He and Bill had to find out who these guys were before those games.

Just as he had no magic wand to create a winning team, he also held no wand to turn a fast-improving side into a losing team and even if Greg wanted to throw a game it wasn't all down to him – and he'd started assembling a team that was now made up of natural winners.

Training went well and morale was good, even though Davy, Prentiss, Benson and Lomax were all sidelined. Davy, following his sending off against Rugg, had been handed a four-match ban.

"No way," said Bill, in reaction to the young lad's first ever offence. The rest were all out with injuries. *"Can't believe that. Poor lad, that's the rest of the season pretty much."*

With Willie Hammerton also missing for the first time with a dead leg picked up during the Rugg victory, that meant at least five changes to the starting line-up from the previous game for Greg's fourth match in charge.

Kenny Lomax would be sorely missed. He'd given Greg real hope that he was getting back to his Aussie legend status with his last performance. Stu Wainwright was to be handed his debut at scrum-half in place of what the X-ray had found to be a broken-jawed Benson; Richard Brent, who had filled-in for Jeff Hammerton in the previous game now provided the same function for brother Willie on Jeff's return; Dave Harper was back at hooker after his try-scoring reappearance as substitute for Lomax the previous week; and Brian Goram was rehabilitated fully after his run-out with the 'A' team to be back on the right wing. The bench was looking stronger too, with Bradley Warrener all set to burst on to the Town stage for the first time and, the forgotten man of Parrot Lane, Chris Hardwick, back on the scene. Chris hadn't played since Greg had taken over, sidelined with a hamstring injury for the previous six weeks, until getting a run-out with Mike Rodley's new A team. The others on the bench would be the Kiwi duo of Jon Entish and Warwick Player and Tony Webb. Of the fit players, that meant just Mike Rodley missed out. It was a disappointing end to Rodley's week after having put so much effort in to the A team. He'd hoped to at least be on the bench, but was completely made up with Stu Wainwright's debut at scrum-half and had also championed Chris Hardwick's return.

The announcement, that Friday evening, that Wainwright had received the nod after one trial game and one 'A' friendly was enough to tell Rodley his first team career was perhaps coming to a close.

The young, proud new possessor of Town's number seven shirt's size and physique was bound to force commentators and spectators alike to utter the oft-used and ever affectionate rugby league phrase 'pocket battleship', seemingly reserved for every well-built diminutive scrum-half. The five-foot-six dynamo's face told its own story when he heard of his selection. From stacking shelves in the local supermarket to playing in front of thousands, okay not many thousands in Hopton Town's case, but still enough for him right now, all in just three weeks!

"*Amazing!*" was the nineteen-year-old's brief summary of his selection. The grin that followed and whoops of delight were just what Greg needed to raise his own spirits, even if a disastrous debut for the lad might also work in his and the club's favour on Sunday. But Greg, while happy for the lad, had gradually become more consumed with concern for someone who he hadn't talked with and the only other person who knew everything.

Since he and Bill had spoken earlier in the week, there had been nothing. Under normal circumstances prior to Greg's appointment as coach, they hadn't been together that regularly. They had generally picked up after training and discussed vital matters after a game on the Sunday, but they had spent a great deal of time together immediately following Irvine's initial commitment to the club and since their heart-to-heart earlier in the week they'd been texting at least twice a day, even if there was nothing to report, but then nothing at all today Friday. It was only one day.

The remainder of Friday and all-day Saturday passed without meaningful event and also no contact from Bill. Greg tried him several times with calls and texts in between visits to the hospital.

Diane and Kyle were going to come back home on Saturday but, given Greg's club involvement, Trudi had suggested that it might be better if they continued staying over with them at their place until after Sunday's match.

Anything that shielded his family appealed to Greg. If they were with others there was less opportunity these maniacs would get to them. But now he had other worries. Where was Bill?

They had started planning, but so far their talk had been just that. What if Bill had gone out on a limb and found something? And then something had happened to him?

Greg kept coming back to why the hell hadn't he just gone straight to the police and asked for protection for his family? Why hadn't he done it so far and why wasn't he doing it now? But he'd been warned off, as he kept coming back to, threatened with more of whatever they could make him suffer if he had.

One call, that's all it would take and he could hand this whole thing over to people who would know what they were doing. But he couldn't.

It was Sunday morning. Greg held his head in his hands once again, this time in his office. He'd been first there, apart from Fred. Reclining gradually in the chair at his desk, he let his hands slip from his forehead to his cheeks and then placed them at the back of his neck, cradling his chin with the heels of his hands. He was desperately trying yet again to process messages he had received. He went through it all from front to back and back to front.

Irvine! It had to be something to do with Irvine. Everything that was going on had started to happen once Irvine had become involved. But was that right? Maybe it had started before Greg took over, but he'd been targeted now because he'd taken over as coach? Had George (Ramsbottom) suffered too? Greg shook his head. Bill hadn't said he'd had any contact until around the same time as Greg.

But why carry out an assault on Greg if this was all to do with Irvine?

He returned to the George Ramsbottom thought. Had he and the consortium been pressurised before Irvine took over? George had been a decent coach, but had lost heart in recent times. Greg had seen his enthusiasm disappear.

Casting aside the contacting the police option, Greg felt he had just two alternatives today. Try to sort it out and risk others being hurt while continuing to play to win, or playing to lose and hopefully losing without having to throw the game.

Could he pull it off if he wanted to anyway? The club was now suddenly more geared to success than at any other time in the past two decades, all in the space of four matches! And that too was down to Irvine! That had to be the connection surely.

"Morning, boss!" The tone was unmistakably friendly and from one guy who was determined to be on a high for the whole day! Debut boy Stu Wainwright was all set, in eager anticipation and readiness for the most important match of his life.

His greeting was as quick as that. Popping his head in and with one bound down the corridor and off to the dressing room to prepare – six hours early – before Greg had time to respond.

"Now then, Greg lad! Don't get up."

There he was again. The man Greg so wanted to question.

"I hope Diane got the flowers. I was really sorry to hear about what had happened. Really sorry. Your son okay?"

Did he really care? It certainly seemed so. Greg wanted to believe there was something about Irvine's tone, but he saw nothing in front of him other than Irvine the businessman and Town owner. He wanted to confront him, but what with? He had nothing. Maybe just a question, surely that would be reasonable? But what would he ask and what kind of reaction would he get? Are you involved in something that caused my unborn child to die?

He stayed calm. Better to stick to talk about the game. He was keen to convince Irvine that winning was not a guarantee because they'd won the previous two.

"Look, Mr Irvine, Bob, don't get your hopes up too much for today … with all of the changes I've had to make, it won't be the same as the past two weeks."

Irvine held up his gloved hands.

"Woah! Steady up, Greg. You don't have to tell me. After the last few games, I also know you've got what it takes, and I know you

and Phil will get the best you can out of the boys. Just make sure you keep us in the division, that's all. Then I guarantee I'll bring you everything you need to get us a promotion place next year."

Greg was pleasantly surprised. Perhaps Irvine was getting the idea.

"We'll be giving it all we've got."

And as the words were leaving his mouth Greg knew that one of the thirteen who were taking to the pitch was somewhat compromised in that regard.

"Give 'em some stick, lads!" seemed to ring out even louder from Fred into Greg's ears as he took to the field six hours later.

How the hell could he 'give 'em some stick' with all that was going on? He spotted Irvine in the directors' seats, addressing what seemed to be a decent sized group of similarly adorned businessmen. Well-heeled types. For a split second, Greg thought he recognized one of the guys Irvine was with. The face.

"...and it's Dave Harper at the play-the-ball, to Wainwright, oh, he's dummied Pearson and he's gone past one, two, three Sherwell players! He's made fifteen, twenty, twenty-five yards. Sensational! And there's Alan Thomas. He's just got to get it to him. Yes. Yeahhhhhssss! He's in at the corner. It's Vincent Venus! Electrifying pace from the new lad Stu Wainwright made that – what a superb try. And I've got to say that we might go a long time before another one is scored like that. Real top drawer stuff! ... Mike, there's your boy already making a fantastic impact on his debut..."

Terry Derbyshire was already in eulogistic mode. It was Mike Rodley's turn alongside him in the commentary position halfway up the main stand.

"That's right, Terry. Stu only turned out for our newly started 'A' team just this week, now he's scoring against one of the side's toughest defensive units. We'll have to see how he goes for the remainder of the game, but that try and how he worked it just confirms what we all think ... this lad could have a big future!"

Greg had to admire the artistry, even though this had already put him under pressure. Of all the times when Hopton had been behind in games, they had to start taking the lead now! He'd have wished for this four weeks ago when they were getting mercilessly drubbed and a strong part of him still couldn't help enjoying it now. But it was not exactly what he could do with if worse was to follow. Town were looking good again.

Greg was hurled his kicking tee for the conversion attempt. This was his first ever moment in the sport he loved when he was actively thinking of doing something that would not help the team. It was the one thing he could handle himself, down to him, and it had to be done. He had to miss with this.

Right now he had his own opportunity to make sure their lead was not an extra two points. It was hard to line up to miss when you practise to score and yet miss well enough for it to look as though it was unlucky.

Greg straightened the ball slightly off-centre from where he would normally strike. This had to look as though it was just a slight miscalculation, enough to skew wide of the posts, enough for commiserating applause from the loyal faithful.

He had been the club's kicker for the past five seasons and the fans knew his style. There would be analysis and reanalysis if he missed as to how, but not why. Greg readjusted the ball slightly as he crouched looking at the posts. He raised himself and took the six paces back he always took, then two paces sideways to the left, bringing his right foot across to meet his left each time. He splayed his feet apart enough so that he was relaxed and in position for his run-up to the ball. Greg blew hard, settled himself. Hands on hips. He took one last look at the target. He was kicking from near the touchline and, though the odds were always more against kickers from out wide, the Parrot Lane crowd had seen him kick more than he had missed. He started towards the ball. Perfect run, sweet contact. The ball immediately looked good. It sailed high, it sailed close … it sailed so close that it hit the upright – and it went through! 6-0! Six points to the good inside the first few minutes!

Greg very nearly let slip his innermost feelings as his head dipped slightly when the ball went between the posts, but then quickly changed it into a shaking of the head and with an ironic smile made his way back for the restart.

Two minutes later, it was 8-0 and Greg had done the damage again. This time with a penalty right in front of the sticks! He couldn't feign some kind of miss from there. 10 minutes later Town extended the lead even further!

Stu Wainwright was overjoyed! A drop-kick from the new recruit! Everything the youngster did was coming off just fine. The crowd had a new hero and Greg couldn't quite believe what was happening. Nine points ahead was too much! Too big a gap! Nine points was also the biggest lead Hopton had held all season!

And they held it! They pressed. Inching closer and closer to the Sherwell line, benefiting from two outrageous decisions from the referee, which had the visitors penned in their danger zone for the best part of twenty consecutive tackles. The Town fans roared their appreciation!

Sherwell's defence held firm, as it had done for most of the season. Town spun the ball out wide. Alan Thomas came up fast, on the burst again, the ball was laid off just a smidgen too slow. And that was all it took for the league's high flyers. Glyn Edwards intercepted before it could reach Vincent Venus and the Welsh flyer re-opened his account against Town with a 75-yard run, marshalled by a fleet of foot Ian Sissons, who, although he couldn't catch him, made sure that the kick was difficult enough for the ensuing miss. 9-4.

The Parrot Lane faithful had seen false dawns before. This might just end up going down as one more, but they were hoping for better. There was disappointment too for Greg's new mix of young, raw talent and energy and experienced old hands.

Greg's outer disappointment was an inner relief. Five points in front meant that Sherwell only had to score one converted try to secure the points and in so doing extend Greg's and his family's immediate health for another week – and probably that of people from the club too. Thank God the mistake had not come about as a result of him! The half-time hooter sounded.

"The stronger side will always score at the death in each half if you give them just a sniff. You lot only gave them one loose chance in the

whole of that half and you got punished. But you've got the fuckers worried. You're making them think they're not that good. Now, go out and show them just how good you really can be this half!"

Sherwell might well be worried, but not half as worried as Greg was becoming if the match went Town's way.

9-4. Town 5 points ahead. He couldn't afford to leave it until the end to make a mistake otherwise it might be too late if Hopton were to score and get ahead. It would look too obvious near the finish – the blunder or whatever it was to be. He couldn't also aim to throw the game at that stage as there was no guarantee he'd get the chance. Something had to be done earlier. He knew this was against everything he believed in and wanted from the game, but it had to be done for now.

Greg needn't have concerned himself. Sherwell came out a completely different side in the second half. Their team talk at half time had settled the table toppers, who'd taken over from Rugg Town courtesy of Hopton's defeat of them the previous weekend. Sherwell tore into Town's resolute but as yet not quite cohesive defence sending them awry with a bewildering set of planned moves obviously well-rehearsed during the rest of the season.

Sherwell ran through their playbook and picked up two quick tries within ten minutes of the restart, finishing with another just before the hooter. Ironically, it was Sherwell's kicker who had a nightmare day missing all four conversions that kept the score respectable at 9-16. Town had fought gamely enough to maintain the respect and admiration of their home support. All was well in Greg's mind. For now.

The Hopton revival had been quelled at least for one game and any gaffs that had taken place had not come from Greg's making, indeed he had emerged with great credit and once Sherwell had hit the front he had felt able to contribute far more positively to the game.

He wasn't religious, but said the briefest of prayers, shutting his eyes momentarily as he came back off the pitch. He looked into the stand as he made his way towards the tunnel. No Bill.

Many Town fans were still applauding in appreciation of a gallant fight and the players returned the compliment even though they had lost. It was heartfelt from both sides. The fans were enjoying having a team that now competed and the players were delighted they were pleasing them, even if today's performance hadn't been sufficient to send them home ecstatic.

Little did anyone know that some wouldn't be going home for a while yet.

CHAPTER 23

Greg and many of the other players were still making their way off the pitch as it happened.

Three explosions. All in the main stand and all echoing like gunshot all around the ground propelling a mass of debris into the air including seats, metal, plastic, timber and lumps of concrete. One explosion sent a hole through an area of tiered seating; another damaged one of the stanchions that held up the canopy of the main stand that had been erected in the 1920s. For a split second everyone froze.

Seconds later it was pandemonium. Panic-stricken voices rang out into the early evening air and it seemed as though everyone was either screaming or shouting while also trying to get the hell out of the stand as soon as they could.

In moments, an awful, grinding, creaking sound began as the damaged stanchion weakened. The impact sent everyone further into meltdown.

If one stanchion went it could trigger a collapse of the whole stand. While those in the crowd may not have understood the science, good old-fashioned common sense comes into play remarkably quickly. Get out!

Often regarded as local heroes for their clubs, the players who had been leaving the field of play threw themselves into helping spectators get clear of the catastrophe in any way they could. The scene had fast developed into a melee of bodies trying their best to escape and the pitch was their best hope.

Another stomach-churning crack rasped out from the damaged stanchion, but it remained in place as hundreds of sets of eyes willed it to stay up.

The disaster was all over in about a minute and a half. Wailing and weeping lasted longer, mixed with shouting and screams as families and friends were reunited. Bumps, cuts and bruises, perhaps the odd broken bone, but thankfully first impressions were that there didn't appear to have been a fatality.

There were no further explosions and the fires caused by them were small and were fast being quelled by the more quick thinking who knew where extinguishers were placed around the stand.

By one massive piece of good fortune the explosions had all taken place in one area of the stand that had been free of spectators at the time they went off.

The whole stand was soon cleared and everyone including officials and spectators alike gathered on the pitch.

The regular matchday St John's Ambulance team was doing the best it could under the circumstances and had suddenly found more work inside 60 seconds than they had ever been called upon in all their years at the ground.

As ambulance, fire engine and police sirens began wailing in the near distance and the first of them, the early indications were confirmed that, somewhat amazingly, everyone had come through. Battle scarred, yes, and blood clearly flowing among the less fortunate as a result of debris catching a few heads and limbs but otherwise not as bad as it had sounded or looked just minutes earlier.

The explosions hadn't been as bad as they could have been, but had still been forceful. Those with active imaginations may have thought this a terrorist attack, but ISIS in Hopton? It was swiftly disregarded, although it wouldn't be by the authorities. Hopton and Sherwell fans alike were just pleased to be alive.

Greg knew. He knew instantly. These weren't bombs from some terrorist organisation. They were controlled explosions. They were designed with one intent. As a warning, but hell what a warning! There was no other explanation. But now they had gone too far. At least this way something would have to be investigated. At least he hadn't needed to call the police. They'd be here soon.

The emergency services took over the playing surface. Paramedics, firefighters and police officers appeared from everywhere.

It was soon evaluated there were trauma victims, but no lost limbs, no blindings, no fatalities. Many were suffering from shock, others being held by loved ones and friends but most were texting, emailing, sending photographs of the scene on Snapchat, Facetime, Facebook, Twitter and Instagram.

One fan who had been at the game with his brother for his birthday had been filming him on his i-Phone when the explosions had occurred. He had loaded it on to YouTube and it had already scored over 50,000 hits in five minutes.

For Greg, it was the continuation of the nightmare. He looked up to the stand from where he was crouched in the centre of the pitch.

The stanchions designed were at 15-metre intervals along a 45-metre stretch making four in all. The one in danger of giving way completely was at the left end when viewed from the pitch. It didn't look well.

Diane, Kyle, their still-born baby Kirsty, Veejay and now this! And where the hell was Bill?

Now! ... Now! ... He had to say something. Christ, there really was no way that he could not say anything to the police.

People from outside the ground had come running to offer help and had then joined the throng in the pastime of taking even more images for social media.

It could have been far worse had it not happened when it had after the final hooter, when some had already left including Bob Irvine.

Dalesmoor Radio's Terry Derbyshire made national coverage for the first time as Johnny on the Spot!

What was going on here? Bollocks, this just had to be sorted, no matter what. A paramedic had reached him and despite Greg's half-hearted initial protest had gone to work on the cut to his head that he'd received when rescuing one of the fans. Greg had stumbled and had caught his forehead against the sharp Perspex corner of the teams' dugout.

"Bloody 'ell, Greg! I've seen some finishes to a game in my time, but this tops the bloody lot! Are you all right lad?"

Ted Brewiss's tone was as affable as ever and seemingly unaffected by what had just taken place. This was Greg's perfect opportunity, Ted coming to him just at the time when his resistance was at its lowest ebb. Now was the time! Spill it! Tell Ted everything. Get it all published in the paper. Forget the rest. Forget what else might happen. Forget telling the police first. Blow the whole thing out of the water. But he needed time after this to gather his thoughts properly as that might put Diane, Kyle, Susie, Bill, Veejay, everyone in danger. Where was Bill? And what did he have that he could share with the police or with Ted? And he'd been warned off telling anyone anything anyway. Ted looked into Greg's eyes and could feel Greg was close to telling him something. He saw worry and pain inside.

"Greg? What's up, son? Listen, there's nobody seriously hurt. You've done everything you can…"

It was the last Greg was to hear of Ted, or anyone, for the next few minutes. He collapsed. He knew he was OK immediately, but he also knew there was no way he could communicate that to the rest of the assembled throng. It was as though his life had gone into slow motion. Frame by agonising frame he could feel himself moving eyelids, fingers, toes, but that was all.

"…it must be some kind of delayed reaction…"; "…give him some room…"; "…Mr Duggan. Mr Duggan? … Can you hear me? … I don't think he's done anything serious, but we ought to get him off to the hospital just to check him over…"

CHAPTER 24

When Greg recovered consciousness, he was laid on a bed, although not exactly the type of bed he might have anticipated as his last memory had been a mention of hospital.

"Hello, Greg." The tone was relaxed but authoritative from the man sat on a chair by the side of the bed. Greg's wrists and ankles were tied to the bed. His dignity preserved with just his compression shorts otherwise naked. For Christ's sake! What the fuck was this all about!

The tone was between fatherly and condescending. Instantly Greg knew where he had seen him before, but to the other side of the bed was someone new. It was his breath he smelt first – of whisky, cigars, the mix of alcohol and smoke. His teeth. Greg looked back at Danny Devito from the three that had visited him at Town. He moved away with his back to Greg. Whisky and Cigars to the other side took over.

"Greg. Your team is causing us some serious concern." He was matter-of-fact, reasonable.

He moved around the end of Greg's bed, his hand stroking his close-cropped beard. *"We need to make sure you get the message once and for all."* Another little walk so that he was now at the opposite side of the bed to which he started. Time to get closer to Greg again.

How long had Greg been there? Minutes? Days? Hours? What had happened whilst he had been knocked out? How far from Hopton was he? How could he get out? It amazed Greg just how many thoughts could be processed in a nano-second – and that included that this guy was a prize twat.

"If I'd had all that has happened to you happen to me in the past few weeks, I'd at least have tried to make life a bit easier on myself."

Under normal circumstances, the mix of drink and smoke wouldn't have bothered Greg, but here he felt nauseous. Wherever here was.

"You see..." said the little guy who'd had his two larger cronies with him when he'd visited Greg weeks earlier. *"We really don't want to hurt you or anyone, Greg..."*

Hurt. What the hell were they about to do next? Greg stayed calm. This was ridiculous. Almost naked, tied to a bed. Presumably, hopefully he felt this was because they didn't reckon much to their chances if he was free, but what if they planned something more?

Whisky and Cigars scratched behind his ear, then rubbed his right hand slowly back and forth on his chin.

"... you, Greg, are making this whole exercise a fairly long drawn out and unnecessary affair. We just want to see the job over and done with. You're causing them grief."

Greg rolled his eyes. Town hadn't even won that latest game and yet he was causing them grief!

"You've got my employers feeling jumpy. They're feeling in danger of some very real sense of loss."

Loss! For Christ's sake! Who was this guy? He should try the fucking loss of his wife's stillborn child. Greg shook his head. Whisky and Cigars leaned closer. God his breath was foul.

"It's really very simple. All we want you to do is to ensure your team finishes bottom. I don't care how you do it. Just do it! That's why I'm here, to make sure the message gets through! What happened at the ground. What happened to your wife, your child and your..." He stopped for a second. He decided to miss the word stillborn completely. He raised his hands slightly, taking a deeper breath. The air filled with the smell of cigar and booze once again. *"Just think about what happened to your doctor, the one who hit the tree."*

Greg desperately wanted to get up from the bed, tear out their throats and chop off their balls, but he also needed the whole job sorting out so that no-one else got hurt. Why was it vital that Hopton finished bottom? Where was the gain in that? Irvine wouldn't gain. Who else? Who else might gain?

It was time to find out more. He needed to know, to understand. Calmness first.

"Finishing bottom," he started, waiting to be shouted down

immediately. *"Why?"*

Greg tried the question again, differently, speaking softly in order to try for a positive reply, thinking the softer he approached his would-be jailers the more receptive they might be.

"We're only a poxy little club, you know, no threat to anyone."

Whisky and Cigars drew breath deeply.

"Gre-e-e-g," his tone conciliatory. The kind a father puts out when he feels his son should know better. Greg's hopes of any kind of reasonable reply disappeared as he saw him smile.

"So, why am I ... Where are we? And what the fuck is all this about? And what did you do to me?"

Greg gestured as best he could about his present situation.

"Look, Greg. All you've to do is finish bottom. We need to see you losing your games and not even looking as though you might win them. We can't handle that kind of stress, you see. You're now bottom because the other side beneath you won today, so that's where we want you to stay. We just gave you a shot of Ketamine that's all, to get you here. Your kit's on the floor."

Today! He hadn't been knocked out too long. It was still today, Sunday, and surely that meant he couldn't be too far from Hopton.

"...just make sure you don't go above them again and you'll be ok."

That was all very well, but with two of the remaining four games against Ensideleigh, their fellow strugglers, it wouldn't be easy. The first of those two encounters was due to take place in just three days on Wednesday at Parrot Lane, but would the game even be on, given what had happened that afternoon?

Greg had to find out more about these guys, who they were working for, but when Whisky and Cigars moved from his chair, fastened his coat and put on his gloves he sensed some kind of relief. Or was he leaving for the others to carry on? What had they planned for him? He gave Greg a final word.

"Finish bottom, Greg. Believe me, it will be right for you. You can make sure it happens. There is a lot hanging on this job. It's what

everything comes down to in the end. Business…"

Whisky and Cigars had made it to the door. He paused. Another final word.

"Frank's boys will let you go in a short while, Greg. You'll be taken within a couple of streets of your home…"

Frank, so that was the little guy's name. Finally he had some kind of information, not much but more than he'd had previously. Whisky and Cigars' tone changed to that of a father chastising his son for the umpteenth time. The final, final word.

"…but just don't for fucking Christ's sake win any more matches … then you'll have nothing to worry about … but, if you win then … just don't, Greg … at all…"

He made his way from the door and back to halfway between door and bed for possibly this time the final words. This guy had obviously been trained in the school of fucking melodramatic art.

"For every game you lose – no action!" His arms were making a crossing movement by way of confirmation. *"If you win…"* His arms raised, he paused before shaking his head slightly.

Whisky & Cigars left, this time not even looking back. No pause. He was gone.

Frank moved across to where Greg was trussed up as his two colleagues who had been with him on the visit to Greg weeks earlier replaced Whisky and Cigars. It was his turn to deliver a few lines. Greg just wanted to twat him. The guy was too much – and he could do to stand in a Growbag for a year or two.

"My lads enjoy their job, Greg. They don't give a shit about what they do to others, just so long as they get paid. And we get paid real well. Win a game and you'll find out just how well they conduct themselves."

Greg remained calm. There was absolutely no sense in becoming embroiled with Frank apart from making a mental note to volley him straight in the bollocks first chance he got. Greg was better employed in finding out whatever else he could about who was really pulling the strings. Sure, this guy had the better of him at the moment, but there would be other days as there always were.

It was the last thought Greg would have for a while as the Klitschko tag team delivered a swift blow to Greg's head, followed by another to the stomach and another dose of Ketamine was administered. Greg knew very little about it at all.

CHAPTER 25

Stop messing around with water! Greg flinched as if to avoid it, jumped from his prostrate position, but it continued, dripping away at him, he was soaked. He flinched again and then, startled, opened his eyes. He was coming around.

He was laid on the front lawn outside his house in darkness except for a streetlamp around four houses away. The drips were the remnants of an earlier heavy downpour. He didn't know how he'd got here, but his best bet, quickly assimilated, was to get back inside and get sorted out, his head throbbed. His ribs hurt.

Slowly the vision of what had taken place came back, rather like pieces of a jigsaw floating into the picture.

After all this time, whatever time it was, Greg was still in his kit from the game. His memory hadn't yet recalled the near nakedness. Muddy, wet, with damp stenches of sweat and congealed blood from his mouth, he wasn't about to earn any points for presentation. It was evening, although Greg had no idea whether it was midnight or three in the morning. He had no keys, but he tried the door in the vain hope it would open automatically.

Who the hell was in control of his life right now? It certainly wasn't him anymore. No matter what he did or where he went someone always seemed to be there before him. In a fleeting moment of paranoia, he considered others knew what move he was making next. As Greg turned the handle and pushed the door, remarkably, it opened. Had he left it unlocked? Had they been in? Had Diane come home? He slumped on to the floor in the hallway. Aah, home! Warm, dry, that'll do.

CHAPTER 26

"Greg! … for Christ's sake … what the fuck's happened?"

Greg couldn't speak. He was in no fit state for pleasant, or indeed any conversation, thanks to Frank the Wank's – his new name for him – parting gift of a lip-splitting, chin-jarring knuckle duster induced delivery after the Klitschkos' heavier efforts; and having focused momentarily he had been taken aback having not seen his brother for the past two years!

Colin was just an inch taller than Greg's 6 foot 3 and a little heavier. Jet black hair and looks which had always won him at least as many admirers as Greg – and had landed him in serious matrimonial problems in the past. He'd had the bruises to prove it too, from numerous irate husbands. Colin had spent the past three years in Scotland, working for an agricultural research organisation. All about shit and sex was how he described it.

Slowly, in what seemed like an age to Greg, but to Colin no more than a rather elongated pregnant pause, a smile surfaced. Colin moved to hug his humongous mess of a brother. Not enough to betray too much affection, but enough to show natural brotherly concern.

"What's going on here, Greg?"

It was almost delivered in a whisper as they first clasped arms, then followed with a brief embrace.

"And why are you still in these?" as Colin pointed to Greg's kit with a casual flick of the hand. As they broke from the brief show of affection, Colin caught his first real sight of Greg's recently rearranged facial design.

"Have you seen how bad it is?" Colin pointed his brother to the mirror. Greg's left eye was catching up fast with the state of his mouth.

He didn't really want to talk with anyone right now. All he wanted was bed, rest, time, sleep and a great deal of nothingness. He just wanted to be allowed to drift off and get away from all that was happening for a few hours – distraught wife, endangered son, stillborn child, club physio run off road, ruined ground, threats to his players, abduction – there had to be some way out of this, but all Greg wanted for the moment was peace. Shut down of the lot, body, soul and mind.

But here was his brother. Wanting to know what was going on and at last he had an ally, someone who he could perhaps share the load with since Bill hadn't surfaced.

For one brief moment, Greg considered the possibility that Colin might be involved in some way. Why would he be back just now? How had he got in? No. That really was paranoia. No chance. The doubts quickly subsided. Greg slumped back against the wall of the hallway from which he and Colin had not yet progressed.

"How did you get in, Col?"

It had been the first thing on Greg's mind since he had touched the door and found easier entry than he had anticipated. It was still bothering him even now. It wasn't the concern that Colin had got in, but just how he had managed it. Had Frank's guys broken in and then Col had just managed to stroll in as a result? Was it all another warning? What was missing?

"It was easy, mate! All you have to do is know the right people."

It was said with such a twinkle in his eye that all fears Greg had were immediately dispelled.

"Diane sends her love," said Colin. *"There was no-one here when I arrived, so I rang her, found out about you know what, so sorry about that Greg, really, heartbreaking..."* He left an appropriate moment before continuing.

"She gave me a key. She'd decided to come back tonight, but said since she'd not heard from you she was staying with her parents tonight and looking at you right now that's probably just as well ... I said I'd surprise you, but man you've beaten me on that one ... So are you going to tell me who did this to you and what the hell is going on?"

Greg was still reeling. He moved from the wall to the stairs where he slumped again, on to the third step, running his hands through his mop of matted, bloodied hair. Colin leant against the banister, on the hallway side of the stairs, looking over at his brother.

"You'd never believe what's going on, Col. I can't believe it myself. It's like something out of a gangster movie – and not even a good one at that!"

Colin had got into his fair share of scrapes in the past, and some of those had been exceptionally hairy, but all of his affairs had been just that. Affairs, break-ups, love triangles. This was different gravy.

"…if I don't sort it all out soon … well fuck knows what is going to happen…"

It was as near as Greg had come to tears. At last he was offloading some of the baggage, what was going on inside. Sure, he needed sleep – and to get out of this stinking blood and mud smeared kit, but the adrenaline was back flowing again.

Greg proceeded to give Colin chapter and verse over what had occurred in the past weeks, whilst finally ridding himself of the playing kit and getting his body back into something like a fit state. Col's reactions to it all were only surpassed when Greg's massively bruised torso was revealed as he finally took off his shirt.

CHAPTER 27

Parrot Lane had become a hive of activity long into the night. Lights beamed everywhere as assessments began on the damage, what had caused it and what needed to be done to make the ground safe.

Miraculously, the worst physical injuries sustained by the crowd had been restricted to one or two broken limbs and around 40 non-serious lacerations. Over 70 spectators had made the journey to Hopton General in order to be checked out, with only half a dozen having to be kept in. Within two hours of the disaster, the ground resembled more of a building site than a playing arena.

Bill Garside returned to the ground just as the last ambulance had left. There was never a doubt in his mind about how the devastation he now witnessed had come about. He breathed deeper and heavier, puffing out his cheeks at the sight.

Perhaps, thanks to his efforts in the past days, he would be able to do something in order to redress the balance.

CHAPTER 28

George Ramsbottom had left home after being sacked. That was the first fact Bill had found out when he had started looking for clues as to how he and Greg could put an end to the threats, intimidation and violence.

Bill had been so upset with himself over not talking with Greg about the threats he'd received that he'd decided to fly solo and dig where he could.

George had lived just outside Hopton in a comfortable enough existence, but nothing out of the ordinary. Bill had tried contacting him on his phone, had sent several texts and emails to him, but to no avail. George had studiously avoided any type of social media.

Action was the order of the day. Bill had driven to George's place. Perhaps George wouldn't be able to give Bill any clues, but it was worth it, as the police say, if only to eliminate him from his inquiries.

Bill had known George for several years, but not well. George had played for Hopton too, but a decade later than Bill, he had always been a handy player able to fill in either in the second row or at centre or stand-off.

The area Bill lived seemed reasonably affluent. George had a respectable job with a local printing firm. It was as Bill strolled up to the front door that he noticed something interesting. The garden didn't look particularly well tended and from his limited knowledge of George's private life he was aware of his love of gardening and plants. It wasn't until he received no reply that the idea fertilised in his brain. George not only wasn't there, he hadn't, obviously, been there for some time judging by what he could see as being a reasonable volume of mailshot detritus lying liberally on the floor inside his porch door.

"Been gone a few weeks now if you're after George," the call came from an attractive lady in her early thirties as Bill was

backing away from the front door to look up for any sign of life upstairs.

"*Is Mrs Ramsbottom still here then?*"

It was the first thing he could think of in reply. He wasn't certain that he would ever make an undercover cop. The lady had been happy offering her initial comment to him as a stranger, but somehow answering an actual question brought about a slightly more defensive tone.

"*Why would you want to know?*"

Her tone had changed from being helpful to a touch more inquisitive. He didn't want to appear anxious, but he now desperately wanted to know where George had gone. Knowing George was no longer there had set little alarm bells ringing in his head. Could be a plausible reason, of course, but he hadn't heard of any reason why George would leave.

He'd been with the printers for donkey's years and Bill hadn't read or heard of any redundancies. He would surely have heard from someone in the club if George had lost his full-time job as well as the coaching position. Maybe he was just away on holiday, taking a break?

Bill moved closer to the woman. There was a small fence, dividing the two driveways leading up to the conventional 1930s style semis.

"*I just thought I'd pop by and see George,*" Bill felt he didn't sound very convincing at first go, so he added further information. "*I'm an old friend ... played for Town, both of us ... just wanted to see how he was.*"

The woman was fast losing interest and decided there was no harm in talking.

"*Well, all I know is that they were here. Then they weren't. Seemed to happen all of a sudden. One minute we, Mrs Ramsbottom, Janice, were talking about how we were going to repair this,*" she pointed to some rickety parts of the fence between her and Bill. "*Then they'd upped and gone. Bit of a surprise all round. We got on well. If you look through the windows you'll see they've taken everything. I think the house must be going up for sale sometime soon, but who knows? Not me."*

"Did they tell you where they were going?"

Bill tried to ask it as calmly and as naturally as he could. He felt he was on to something. There was no way George would have made any swift decision to go just like that. He might not have known him that well, but it seemed out of character and odd that he would do it now.

It was too much of a coincidence surely? Sacked as coach. Leave home or move home. Or was he just clinging on to whatever spurious bit of detail he could.

George had only left Hopton after all. It wasn't like he was on a football manager's wage! He might have been so severely pissed off with being sacked that he'd just snapped and thought sod it let's get out of this town. It still didn't wash with Bill, that's not how George behaved.

The woman simply shook her head.

"Not a word. Like I said, one minute they were here, both of them. Next they were gone. I work during the day most days you see, and one night when I came home I noticed there were no lights on at all. That's unusual for them. Then I noticed it again the following day. They're not ones for going out and not leaving some form of lighting on. Not seen 'em since. Then I had a look through their windows just the other day and there was nothing there."

The woman shrugged again as if to signal that this was the end of any information she had.

Bill replayed all she had said as he got back in his Mondeo. It didn't add up. He now really wanted to find George and ask him about whether he'd received the same threats as Greg. It was a wild goose chase. He kept telling himself. But maybe it wasn't.

George's sacking had been amicable enough. No bad blood, so far as Bill was concerned. Everyone had realised he'd had to do the job with no money for signings, no incentives. He'd done the best he could on meagre resources.

Two seasons ago he'd given Town their best league placing of the decade, fourth from bottom. It wasn't much and even then he'd had to sell a couple of that side in readiness for balancing the books over the close season. George had accepted the board's decision.

Perhaps George leaving home, presumably with Janice, was purely innocent. Maybe it was down to the job? Had he got a new one? He could check that. Maybe a holiday? None of it seemed to stack up in Bill's mind.

It happened as he turned the ignition. The tap at the window. Bill rolled it.

"They've got a caravan – one of those big static things, up in the Lakes. Janice usually goes up there quite a bit in summer. Coniston Water. Nice place she says, well it's all nice up there isn't it?"

"You wouldn't know whether Janice mentioned the name of the site would you?"

The woman performed her now customary shrug. Bill thought how much more attractive the shrug made her look every time she had done it.

"Can't tell you, but Janice said it was near a big watersports centre. Always talking about the fellas' bodies and how they looked great in their kit ... and through it, if you know what I mean. Lots of Australians there, by all accounts."

With a giggle and what Bill saw as a delightful little wriggle, as she was clearly enjoying disseminating this information, the woman made off back to her house next door.

Bill was left to conjecture upon what he might have discovered if he had been a little more forward earlier. He made a mental note to have more confidence in any further questioning he took on – and not to miss out on a spot of flirting if the opportunity arose again.

"Thanks, Mrs..." he called, with the final word hopeful of a reply from the intended recipient.

"Tunney!" came the reply. *"Jennifer Tunney ... and it's Miss."*

Less than an hour later, he was within sight of a misty, rainy, Coniston Water. A hundred and one thoughts raced in and out of his mind on the way. Had George just had enough and wanted to simply get away? He'd been coach for long enough, he'd worked hard all his life. None of this was earth shattering news.

Maybe he had won the lottery? Unlikely, of course. Maybe he and Janice had just taken off, maybe they weren't going to be there at all. Maybe the whole thing was a total waste of time.

Yet why would they leave home without saying anything? Why, if all of this was so innocent, why wouldn't they tell their next door neighbour? It was like they had done a moonlit flit. There had to be something! There had to be a reason. It wasn't just coincidence that, within weeks of leaving the club, the club he had loved and played for, that he had also left the town too? Was it?

Bill had put in a call to where George had worked when he'd left George's now ex-home. He'd left a message. His call was returned right now just as he was driving alongside Coniston Water.

"Handed his notice in and left the same day, about three or four weeks ago. I can check the exact date for you. Completely out of the blue, no warning. Good, solid company man. Wish him all the best, of course."

Bill had spoken with George's boss. This was no coincidence. This had something to do with the club, but was he just manufacturing things here?

Bill turned his attention to the task in hand finding George. How to play it now that he was close? What to say? George might not be there anyway, but what if he saw him straight away? Bill spent the first half an hour journeying round the lake, checking out all of the signs, the caravan sites.

It had seemed the obvious thing to do at the time. Just set off and worry about the finer details when he knew he was actually there. What he hadn't appreciated enough was the sheer length of Coniston Water stretching, as it does for five miles and littered with caravan and camping sites – and watersport centres every hundred yards.

Not only was it misty, it was also dark. There was no chance of making headway tonight. Better to start afresh in the morning. Bill pulled into a hotel car park and checked-in.

Not long after, a black car pulled alongside.

The next day was a typical British response to the day previously. This time, no mist, no murkiness, no rain. Instead, a pleasantly sharp start with pure blue skies and a strong sunshine. Bill hit the road early after enquiring with the woman on reception about the caravan sites that also boasted watersport centres alongside. Two had their own watersport facilities, but a further four were possibles since the facilities were close by. All had Aussies!

He had only travelled as much as a couple of hundred yards when the first of the two main sites came into view. And a fabulous sight it was. Mountains reaching high on two sides of the lake, giving the impression that they were in some way guarding the water, framing the landscape, with a forest to the other side of the lake and the sunlight glinting all the time, cascading for miles across the water.

Preparing himself for a day of asking the same questions, but no doubt getting the same negative reply, Bill was astounded when he struck oil at his first attempt! He'd acted as nonchalant as possible and had hoped he wouldn't receive the reply most gave that they couldn't give out information.

Yes, the lady in the Coniston Glades reception had said, the Ramsbottoms were on site, and yes, so far as she knew they were in their caravan. She pointed out where it was on the site plan that adorned the rather plush office. These were long static affairs – second homes to their owners or as Bill conjectured possibly George and Janice's first home now. He left his car at reception and set off by foot.

Exchanging a few nods and good mornings, Bill made his way on to Donald Campbell Avenue, which gave a panoramic view of Coniston Water.

"They say the boat just exploded right there!"

The voice came from the steps of the fifth static along. It had been a while since Bill had seen Janice, and whilst he had been told which caravan, he hadn't quite expected to hear a voice immediately. On first impression, Janice was pleased to see him.

Bill made his way over to her. She was coming toward him, but with little of a relationship in previous years, there was no embrace or peck on the cheek.

"Janice," Bill was aware of treading carefully. "How are you? Are you and George ok?"

"I'm fine!" came a voice from somewhere inside the aptly-named Country Hideaway 40-foot lodge. Surely these weren't really regarded as caravans? "Just getting dressed, Bill. Be with you in a minute!"

Bill had no reasoning for his next thoughts, but he felt as though they had been expecting him to call. He and George had no real past form of ever being best buddies or drinking partners. Bill sensed something. A kind of over friendliness. There was definitely something not right.

As he waited for George to appear, Janice set to work, providing cups of tea and biscuits.

"I hear the lads are turning it around!"

George called from somewhere further down the caravan or lodge.

"Yeah. Really getting it together!" Bill responded. "This bloke Irvine's got the bit between his teeth at the moment and Greg's made a good start…"

Bill was acutely aware that what he'd just said might rankle, hearing the young man who'd taken his place was doing a better job. He hadn't intended it so. Wished he could take it back.

Janice passed the cuppa. She smiled. It seemed she had no more words. She looked as though she wanted to say something, but could Bill detect that she was too frightened for some reason he couldn't fathom?

Bill wasn't certain, but he felt that he had learned more in those few seconds in the almost silent company of Janice than he would learn from George. She was on edge and had disappeared into the back of the van as George took her place, all smiles.

He appeared, drying his brown hair vigorously with a towel

and wearing jogging trousers and sweatshirt. He was still a fit man and by no means ready for any scrapheap in his mid-50s. He was friendly, but also on his guard.

"I wondered when we'd get a visit from somebody. I must admit I'd not expected it to be you."

He took a sip from his mug. Bill smiled back in return. There was a hint, from George, that they felt he was interfering with them. Disturbing their peace. It wasn't going to be an easy conversation. He tried to be diplomatic.

"Nice place George ... Have you moved here permanently? I can see why you would."

"We've had this place donkey's years. Love it out here, away from it all. No-one harassing you, nobody trying to get you doing things you don't want to. It's beautiful."

George smiled again at Bill, but Bill hadn't spent the best part of the last two days for this.

"This place is fabulous, Bill. We always said we were going to retire here when the time came, and that's exactly what we've done. It's days like today that make me realise we've made the right decision."

Sod it! It was time for a little less beating around the bush and a little more getting straight to the heart, as far as Bill was concerned. It was a defining moment in the conversation. Bill took the lead. He was measured. It was time to find out and get beyond this front.

"Tell me. Why are you here? I mean the real reason. Don't get me wrong, I can see why you'd want to be, but there's a lot of things that just don't stack up. You leave home without a bye or leave; you jack in the job where you've been happy for years. I can understand you not ringing anyone at the club, bearing in mind what happened, but tell me, why now? Why this moment?"

In an instant, George changed from genial gent to viper-like venom. Bill felt as though he'd struck oil or gold, but either way it was the end of the tea and biscuits and the pleasant morning in the country.

"What the fuck's it to do with you what I do?" said George.

Janice reappeared from the depths of the caravan. *"I never saw you come running, looking to help me."* George was in full sail now. *"Get out! Piss off right back to Hopton."*

"George!"

Janice's actions once again spoke louder than her words. She was frightened by something. Was it George himself? What was the matter? Her tone had been final to her husband.

"Tell him."

Janice told George firmly, but with a hint of surrender, shoulders dropping. It was the first real time Bill's mind strayed to whether whatever they might tell him might put George and Janice in any danger too. No wonder they hadn't ventured anything earlier, if that was the case. And he hadn't even told them why he was there.

As Bill said his goodbyes to a chastened George and tearful Janice, the fear heightened in his mind. He knew there had been something. He had needed to know what it was. Now he knew his chest had tightened, his breath seemed shorter. As he left the couple, he couldn't stop himself from looking all around for any sign of being watched.

When he reached the car park, Bill was greeted again by the lady on reception that had directed him earlier. She was in her early thirties, slim but not thin, attractively attired in smart blue jeans with brown ankle boots, white T-shirt under a short leather jacket.

"You found them then?" She smiled. *"They keep themselves to themselves do Janice and George, you'd never know they were here. Been here years."*

Bill smiled back, as best he could under shocked circumstances. His head was not just beginning to swim, it was looking up for a lifebelt.

"Hey, are you all right?" The lady's expression changed from good-natured to incredibly concerned. Bill passed out.

He'd never blacked out before. Five minutes later, he was coming round. He'd been knocked pretty much unconscious many a time whilst playing for Hopton, but never what he'd just suffered. They'd hauled him in to the site office. Josie, the leather jacketed girl, and a couple of local lads who had been working on the plumbing in the toilet block ready for the main holiday season to get started.

"*Where'd you pick this one up from then, Josie love! Not one of your regular types!*" had been the banter Bill had picked up on when he came round.

"*Are you okay? You just went – like that,*" said Josie, clicking her fingers. "*One minute you were about to say something, next you were in a heap at my feet.*"

"*Jus' 'ow Josie likes 'em, innit, Jose?*" said one of the now guffawing country boys.

"*Dave and Dan,*" said Josie, by way of introduction. "*They carried you in here.*"

Bill nodded by way of appreciation. "*Thanks.*"

"*S'alright, mate. See you later, Jose!*"

The double Ds left to continue fixing their flues and flows. Bill closed his eyes. He had to take in what had just happened. Finding out what George had told him, then next minute knocked out by something. He looked at Josie as she poured him a coffee.

"*I'm sorry for all the bother.*"

"*It's not a problem.*" A sympathetic smile as she offered him the now steaming mug. "*You didn't half scare me out there. As you were coming towards me, I thought you looked ill. I hadn't expected you to fall for me so quickly.*"

She gave a wry grin. It suited Bill's ego.

"*At your age, you need to be careful, you know.*" That comment soon put his mind quickly back on track.

"*How long was I 'out' for?*"

"*Oh, only about five minutes or so. Don't worry, you've not missed anything. The world hasn't changed.*"

If only she knew just how much Bill's world had changed in the past few weeks and now in the past hour. Her concern still ran deep as Bill thanked her for the drink and help and began making his way back to the car.

"Are you sure you should be driving. I mean, don't you think you would be better seeing a doctor? I can ring for one, if you like?"

Bill opened the door to the Mondeo. Shaking his head slightly, he gave another suppressed smile to his Florence Nightingale.

"I'll be fine…"

All he really wanted to do right now was leave and get back to Hopton. He tried to make sense of why he had lost it momentarily.

"Look, it's your life, love, but if I were you I'd go careful. No sense taking risks with your health – and I should know! My ex-husband. He never took no notice of the signals. Third heart attack saw him off … still, I suppose you know best."

Bill hit the road.

There was much to take in. Yet at the same time there was so much missing. Finding George Ramsbottom was only the beginning. No wonder George had left in the manner he had. Little wonder he had flown.

"They've got it in for the club! They'll do anything!" was the ringing endorsement George had given after Janice had calmed her husband.

CHAPTER 29

"...yes, I knew what we were getting into at the start, but this ... this is all too much ... it's way beyond what I expected."

The voice on the other end of the line was laying down the law. The anxious voice had reached serious stress level. He was feeling the pressure.

"...no, no, no ... I know we can't pull out now, but ... yes, I know. All I'm saying is we don't need to go as far as that..."

Greg's body was not in great shape right now, but at least he'd had some respite from yesterday's game, the abduction and the treatment that had been rendered to him.

His phone, both phones, were still at the ground from yesterday, so it was the landline that rang ... and rang ... with a warble of phones all around the house. He and Diane had invested in five phones on the basis that at least one would be close by, but it never was. Three seemed permanently out of charge, while the other two always ended up in the same room furthest away when they rang.

The ansafone clicked into gear. Greg's immediate thought was it would be a sales call. Either that or it would be Diane or her mum or dad checking up on him, making sure he was all right. He hadn't had contact with anyone except Col since the match, the collapse of the stand, his passing out, the abduction or the threats. Col had called Diane to let her know that Greg was okay so that was unlikely. Or was it another message from Whisky and Cigars? It had been his voice previously. He now put a face to an admittedly convoluted name.

"...Greg ... it's Bill. I'm at the ground ... When you get this message give me a call."

Greg lunged for the phone. He may not have felt like any activity seconds ago, but it was amazing how quickly everything kicked in.

"Greg?" Bill had heard the click of the receiver being picked

up at Greg's end. All Greg could hear was noise at the other. He managed a low 'yeah' as Bill went on raising his voice in competition.

"*This place is a nightmare. It's crawling with suits and men in hard hats all waving about at each other and no doubt building up to something they'll laughingly call an invoice at the end of the day. Anyway…,*" sensing the need to get on and to his main point his voice changed to serious.

"*When are you coming in? We need to…*" – there was a hesitation – "*…discuss team selection.*"

Greg would never have put himself down as the sharpest tool in the box on uptake, but given the past 24 hours he'd endured he felt similarly that Bill's final words were not the main event.

"*Soon as I can.*" And with that he turned his aching body back over in bed for another half hour before venturing first to the hospital and down to the garage. He could catch up on Bill's news later, but first he had family to see.

Diane was slowly getting better, taking solace in the company of her mum, but still feeling pretty low overall. Kyle was fine. He could still play and, since that was all his 2-year-old life centred around, he was okay. Diane wasn't ready to pursue Greg as yet and could see he was in pain too.

Greg also made visits to the half dozen fans who had stayed over having suffered the most damaging injuries at the ground. It was the least he could do and it helped put smiles on their faces before moving on.

Greg knew that none of this had been his fault. Yet at the same time he felt some responsibility. What if he had just gone along with these idiots right from the start? He wasn't a yes-man. He wasn't a loser. But what had his pride let him and others in for?

Someone grasped Greg's arm!

People of all shapes and size, overalled and suited, still crawled right around the ground. Greg had called into the ground in between jobs at the garage and visiting the hospital and Diane and Kyle.

Colin had called at the ground while Greg had been at the hospital and had picked up Greg's bag and clothing left since yesterday's match. The brothers had met up earlier so that Greg was back live again phone wise.

Susie had only called a mere 18 times and had sent at least a dozen texts. Diane had called and sent slightly less on both counts. Susie had caught the national news on television and had picked up on everything on her tablet. Diane had been watching a TV series on catch-up on her laptop when it had pinged on Facebook. She knew Greg was ok as Col had got to her beforehand, but she knew nothing of the abduction. All she knew was he was going through something and he was attempting to shield her from it. Susie's last message had hit hard.

Training was due that evening, in preparation for what should have been the biggest night of Hopton's season so far with the bottom two clubs playing each other and a league place at stake. Level on points now, Hopton and Ensideleigh were scheduled to play each other twice in their last four matches.

Greg turned as he felt the grasp.

"Greg, lad. I'm pleased I've caught you."

Bob Irvine obviously had some kind of instant materialisation kit from the Starship Enterprise. There was no instant response from Greg. He waited to hear what was to come next and whether Irvine would give him any new information.

Greg's real purpose for being here was to catch up with Bill. Fred had informed him he'd missed Bill by about 20 minutes.

Greg and Irvine were stood in the Hopton Town car park, which was presently full of white vans and assorted other workmen's vehicles. Irvine had appeared just as Greg had made his way out of the stadium having found Bill had left. He now noticed Irvine's car, parked up alongside a maintenance van of sorts.

Irvine seemed totally unfazed by what had happened.

"Greg, I just wanted to say. Nobody could have done more than you on Sunday on the pitch and off it and no matter what has

occurred here, it's at times like this we all stick together."

Greg was in no mood right now for anything other than getting to work on 'team selection' with Bill.

"Sure, Bob. See you later."

And he was off. Not Irvine this time, but Greg himself. Or maybe he wasn't. As he turned Irvine spoke again.

"It's like this Greg…"

Now it was Greg's turn to take Irvine by surprise.

"It's like fucking what, Mr Irvine! It's like," Greg shrugged his shoulders and put out his arms in semi-Buddha type pose, mockingly. *"It's like let's get on with winning the fucking game. Is that it? Is that what you were about to say. Cause if it is, then let me tell you something for nothing. My wife, my kid, my still-born kid, Veejay, the fucking stand. Do I need to go on! If you were about to give me some sort of lecture you can fucking well think again."*

Greg was amazed that he had lost it with Irvine, but wasn't about to apologise. He hadn't accused Irvine of anything. Irvine stood tight-lipped. He looked intently at Greg. Eyes cold set firmly on him. There was no friendly warmth. Perhaps here was the real Bob Irvine, ruthless businessman, coming out in the open with the hard exterior that had earned him his fortune.

His voice, when it did come, wasn't menacing, but neither was it the noble facade he had cultivated since buying the club. He was now the calculated, cool professional. Sure. Certain. Confident.

"You're wrong Greg … very wrong … no lecture, no recrimination. One piece of advice, though … strength in adversity. Tough season, but we'll get there."

One last hard stare deep into Greg's eyes, a slight nod and he was away. Greg stared in his wake before shaking his head in trying to make sense of it all.

CHAPTER 30

"Full of crap!" was Colin's instant reaction to Greg's retelling of his car park confrontation with Irvine in The Ship, their 'local' from when they were kids. *"The guy's full of bullshit by the sound of things!"*

Greg's stifled laugh at his brother's summing up loosened his tension over what had happened. Colin hadn't been idle. Being an analyst, albeit in a totally different environment, he had a voracious appetite for facts and figures.

"Let me tell you a few things, Greg ... oh, sorry Bill ... thanks, cheers mate! I'm just telling Greg what I was telling you earlier..."

Bill had come back with the drinks and was enjoying their camaraderie.

"It's like this. Town's finances have never been much to write home about. Always struggling to keep the club afloat. Succession of backers all coming in trying to get a winning team, aiming to put any money made back into strengthening the club, right?" Greg nodded.

"Nobody's ever made any money out of Hopton and they're never bloody well likely to either..."

Greg shifted in his chair, his index finger stroking along both his top and bottom lips, he was now engrossed in his brother's findings. Colin was now moving up a gear.

"Let me put it this way. If you have a business that isn't doing well what do you do?" Colin left a momentary pause to see any reaction from his brother.

"You either work very hard to turn it around or you look to get rid of it. Sell it on if you can. Put it on the market. Sell it. Try to find someone who will cover what you're losing."

Colin was starting to lose Greg at this point. How could his brother arrive on the scene and within hours provide a different spin, the kind of thoughts that Greg would never have managed in a million years. But what was he getting at?

Colin had anticipated his brother's next question.

"So, what's occurring here?"

Colin's words, Greg's thoughts. There was still no answer coming through even given for Colin's analysis.

It was Colin's turn to shift where he was sat, on the seats which ran around in a U shape in a snug type setting. He moved forward, leaning in such a manner that Greg and Bill felt obliged to crane forward towards him too. Greg couldn't help blurting out his incomprehension before his brother could go on.

"But Irvine's only just bought the sodding club. He's not looking to get out, is he?"

Colin took a sip from his pint before adding further information.

"Have you ever wondered why the last lot buggered off? They saw him coming or they encouraged him. Took what they could get out of him. The club was floundering again. The guys who'd had all the grand ideas about Town being great again had had their dreams shattered like all the other dreamers. They'd put money in out of their own pockets, their own businesses, and they hadn't seen anything back. That's what happens in most clubs unless you've millions you can afford to pour down the drain on a regular basis. Decided to cut their losses."

"But Irvine wants us to be successful no matter what."

Colin tried hard not to look at his brother as though he was naïve.

It was Bill's turn to contribute.

"All I know is when I went to see George he was convinced there was some plan for us to finish bottom regardless of who owns the club. He says he never had the support he needed and that he was being leaned on too, maybe not as bad as us and particularly you Greg. Reckons he's better off in the Lake District now. He's bitter. Reckons maybe that's why Irvine is here, a kind of double-bluff, act as though he wants the club to do well while all the time pulling strings making sure it doesn't."

Greg thought back to his 'session' with Whisky & Cigars. Everything had been weighted against Town, no personal attack on Irvine at all.

"They didn't mention Irvine once whilst they held me."

Colin was quick to reply.

"These guys weren't likely to tell you anything, were they? They're obviously working for someone, maybe Irvine. The facts we know are one lot of guys shipped out – one guy came in – and one ex-coach is pissed off – while the other is being threatened, abused, abducted and his family and club are being attacked. Someone somewhere has a plan – and that plan is for Town to finish bottom at all costs."

While Greg didn't like Irvine, he'd seen enough to feel his words and actions had been sincere. He couldn't be that much of an actor could he, but who knew how he'd got on in business. Greg's slump back into his bench seat was indicative of his exhaustion from the past days and all he'd gone through in the past weeks.

"We're gonna sort this out, Greg. Check what's happened. Irvine's taken over at the club. The club starts winning. Within days of winning, things start going wrong which shouldn't. It's all got far heavier. There's more to all of this and I'm fucked if I know what it is at the moment, but there will be a way to sort it."

It was Colin's turn to rest back now. *"Tomorrow,"* he said with finality, *"we start digging properly."* It had been a vibrant team selection meeting! Greg hadn't learned anything really new, but work had begun with his other team of Col and Bill.

CHAPTER 31

Four games left and with the fear of threats turned to reality if Town won any of them. Nothing settled well with the player-coach as he relaxed in the bath, remarkably the bruising and swelling was going down in double-quick time. His ribs hurt and he'd need strapping and any other help he could afford for Wednesday's game, but he fully intended to play.

Without ceremony, Colin entered the bathroom, lifted the lid to the lavatory for something that had evidently been 'brewing' since their return from the pub.

All the same, it was as good a place as any for a conversation. Colin opened the proceedings.

"*I don't think any of this is about the club*", no instant reaction from Greg, who seemed more intent on taking-in the relaxation therapy offered by the tub.

"*It's maybe about Irvine. There's got to be something in what Bill said tonight about Ramsbottom … but then … what gets me and then casts doubt on it being all about Irvine is the club … Why you, why Diane? Why the stand, the supporters? There's more to all of this … someone's desperate and the problem is the more desperate he, she or they get, the more they threaten…*"

Greg couldn't find anything of any use to say. In the end, he felt he had to join in with what were obviously Col's valiant attempts to make sense out of the drama.

"*Pass us the towel, Col,*" and whilst Col duly did, Greg exited the bath, war scars and all.

"*You're gonna be in a right state by the time you retire, if this is what you're like now…*"

"*That might not be too long coming,*" was Greg's heartfelt, earnest reply.

As Greg continued drying, Col replaced his brother in the bath. The waters must have favoured his disposition because, in a 'Eureka' moment, the penny dropped in his mind.

"*What if that's it?*"

It was announced in such a way that Greg had to tune in for the next thrilling installment.

"*What if you not playing is what all of this is really about. I mean, not you personally not playing, but the club. Hopton. What happens then? You know, if you finish bottom?*"

"*Play in a lower league, I guess. Town'll always carry on in some way. It won't be the end. See you in the morning, Col, and thanks for being here.*"

Detectives from Hopton & District Constabulary arrived at Parrot Lane on Tuesday morning. The local police had been regular visitors to the 'incident' since late Sunday afternoon, along with the bomb squad and fire brigade. Everyone at the club was to be interviewed. Fans too. From both Hopton and Sherwell.

The cause of the debacle was abundantly clear. Three incendiary devices, all small-scale, but still enough, as it had proved, to cause severe damage. The professionals had fast ruled out a terrorist attack.

Bill was fielding much of the inquisition.

"*It's all bloody paperwork and filling in forms,*" had been his comment when he'd caught up with Greg during the morning, having broken for a coffee halfway through his session with them in one of the three Portakabins Irvine had loaned from one of his other companies.

The Hopton & District Police had handled some pretty impressive investigations in recent times for a relatively small unit. They had uncovered a drug-dealing cartel and had been the main force responsible for bringing the leader of a paedophile ring to the public's attention in the past two years, but explosives were new territory.

They had drafted in extra help from the larger County Division, but as yet hadn't come up with anything. They were looking for links. Previous incendiary device cases. Sources for buying? Any CCTV footage anywhere? Town had cameras. They were taking a look.

Bill was sure he'd end up filling in more forms, having more meetings, talk for ages, they'd take up far too much of his time, and end up finding out precisely nothing.

There had been talk of Hopton's next match, originally scheduled for Wednesday evening being put back, but only by 24 hours. The Rugby Football League were intransigent as the season had to finish within the next twelve days from then. It was going to be tough for Hopton. Two evening games, two Sunday games and a ram-shackled ground to prepare quickly.

Tomorrow's game had been postponed from earlier in the season, as was next Wednesday's game. Ensideleigh were now level on points going into their last three games to Hopton's four.

Axby, who Town had lost to big-style and had proved to be George Ramsbottom's last game in charge, were next up on Sunday. It was another rearranged fixture the following Wednesday against promotion contenders Brazen Bees before Ensideleigh away to finish the season.

Greg knew his charges could lose against Axby and The Bees and not incur the wrath of being labelled as throwing games. Both sides were going well, but the games against Ensideleigh? He knew that in the short time he'd had and the players he now had at his disposal his team was far better now than a bottom of the league club.

He'd encouraged Diane to stay at Tom and Trudi's with Kyle and was visiting them in between abduction and explosions. He had to keep some kind of perspective through humour. It's all he had. Diane was improving. It was still only nine days since the incident with the black car, but he knew only too well how strong she was, stronger in many ways than himself. She'd been working on new business and had won a new contract already. Her dad had vacated his office lair for her.

There had been nothing from Susie. Her last text had said there wouldn't be and not to make contact either. He'd been true to her word. He missed her, but it was probably for the best. They'd had long periods when she'd been away previously. It was nothing new. One less person to worry about. One less person to get hurt.

Irvine hadn't been around, probably busy elsewhere with all his meetings.

Tuesday evening training was taken by Trippett. Greg and he discussed selection afterwards. Whilst so much had happened immediately after the gutsy display against Sherwell, the two took themselves back to what had happened on the park.

The next four games were all going to be – as all rugby league and football clubs had a habit of saying at this time of the season – their own cup finals.

Hopton's spectator facilities were now no more than terracing, opposite the ground from the presently forbidden and soon to be condemned territory of a mangled grandstand. The three Portakabins acquired by Irvine took up the behind the posts area of the Parrot Lane end, with the car park adjacent. Bill speculated if they'd been applying to get into the league right now, as opposed to being a long-standing participant, they would have been laughed well and truly out of court. There were plans to bring in a portable grandstand on hire at the other end of the ground. Irvine had fixed it. It would arrive in the morning.

Trevor Prentiss, Kenny Lomax and Pete Smith were all definitely ruled out with injuries and Paul Davy was banned; but Willie Hammerton was ready to return to the pack, and his experience just edged out Richard Brent to the bench. It was generally accepted that Stu Wainwright had done well enough to carry on his impressive work at scrum-half and although young Vincent Venus had been carrying a knock for a few weeks, this was the match where they could really do with his pace, even if it was just for quick bursts in the eighty minutes.

The end-of-training meeting was held in the middle cabin of the three Portakabins which, strangely enough, Greg was getting used to more so than the previous office now abandoned in the main stand. These were at least modern facilities, with modern furniture. They didn't look as though ghosts of ninety years were haunting the corridors.

Greg, Phil Trippett, Mike Rodley and Steve Benson were all involved. Rodley's 'A' team exploits could wait now until the close season, but he was now part of the new coaching triumvirate with Greg and Phil. Benson's broken jaw meant he was unlikely to figure in the playing line-up as it now stood and Trippett had wanted him to remain fully involved with the club. He and Rodley were good mates too and had already talked about running the new 'A' team together next season.

Although none of them liked or wanted to say, the match against Ensideleigh was coming too soon. None of them had fully recovered. Steve's brother and nephew had suffered. Indeed Carl, the nephew, had been one of the half-dozen or so that the infirmary had kept more than a watchful eye over until finally clearing him to go home that morning. He'd taken the impact of an adult or two unintentionally using him as a steppingstone after he had stumbled as the crowd surged to get out of the melee.

Tactics were discussed, but there was no time for trying anything new. There was an underlying confidence. Phil Trippett took the lead.

"If we play the way we have for the past three games there's no way we should lose this game. If this team had been together at the start of the season, there's no way we would be where we are now fighting for our lives, but that's the way it is. We've just got to make sure that the experienced guys look after the younger heads if the going gets tough. We don't want a repeat of what happened with young Davy."

It was as they were wrapping up for the night the door to the cabin was opened and a beautiful face popped through, quickly followed by a body all four could not help but admire. The word admire could easily have been put more bluntly as ogle.

"Greg Duggan?" she enquired. *"I'm sorry, have I interrupted something important?"*

She wore a brown leather cowboy-style jacket with jeans and knee length boots. Pink T-shirt and golden flowing hair to her collar. This, to the assembled throng, was class. The young woman proved a hugely popular distraction. Phil made the introduction.

"Well, here's the man you want, love. Although why you would want to ask for him in front of me I just don't know."

"I'm sorry," said Greg. "Greg Duggan ... and you are...?"

"Oh yes, me too, sorry ... Patsy. Patsy Previn. And before you ask, no, no relation..."

Patsy had chosen the wrong guy in assuming that Greg would know anyone by the name of Previn. Phil filled him in.

"Famous conductor, orchestras, Greg. Andre Previn? Talk rugby league to him Patsy, don't blind him with arts and culture."

"I actually didn't expect to find anyone here," she said, "I was looking for Colin ... your brother..."

Colin had never mentioned her, but then again Greg had not asked much about his brother's life since he'd arrived on Sunday, but 'fuck me,' he thought. She was gorgeous!

The rest of the guys said their goodbyes as they all ventured out into the car park.

"This was the only place I could think of from what Colin had told me. Silly boy forgot to text me your address and I've not been able to get hold of him for the past few hours," explained the blonde bombshell, as she started the ignition of her Jaguar XE.

Nice touch that, thought Greg. Colin had obviously found someone with wealth as well as gorgeous looks.

"I thought I had no chance of finding a house address at this time of night, so I just came here, more in hope than anything else."

Greg pointed the way as they came out of the car park and the Jag purred out into the road.

The night that followed was arguably Greg's most relaxed of a long week.

OK, so the Town victories he'd racked up recently had been great – but having both Col and Patsy around had proved entertaining.

Patsy had regaled him with constant streams of stories over his brother's ineptitude in the romance department, but from where Greg was sitting it hadn't done his brother any harm.

Greg still wasn't quite sure why Col and Patsy had turned up out of the blue, but he was happy they were there. They'd ordered in a Chinese from the local takeaway and with wine and beer added to the mix it had been enough to put Greg's troubles and concerns away for the evening.

CHAPTER 32

Mornings were usually a bright time in the Duggan household with Kyle a constant source of amusement for Greg and Diane. This was the first morning in a while when Greg could justifiably claim to be close to that feeling once again. It was a feeling that was soon to get even better.

The door to the front room where Colin and Patsy had slept was slightly ajar as Greg came down the stairs heading for the kitchen. The sight that greeted Greg as he turned in the hallway, towards the kitchen, brought a smile to his face.

Patsy's perfect posterior as she bent to look into the fridge was instantly up there in Greg's favourite moments of the past few weeks.

"Oh, hi Greg! I was just checking out what you had in."

Fortunately, Colin had taken on the duties yesterday. He appeared from just behind Greg at that moment.

"Don't ask him, he's not exactly up to speed with much at present are you, broth?"

Having Colin and Patsy there was a great relief in many respects and a welcome breath of fresh air, but Greg was aware of concern for their welfare too. Everyone he came into connection with seemed at risk. At least Colin and Patsy, since last night, were both aware of what Greg was going through. And there was some degree of telepathy on Col's side.

"Greg, don't worry about Patsy and me. We've already started work on how we can help and I spoke a lot with Bill yesterday. You just concentrate on the games and we'll do our level best to do the rest. If we need you, we'll let you know."

Patsy leant over the kitchen table to reach for the juice that Colin had dispatched from the fridge. Greg couldn't resist a slightly lingering look. Patsy caught the moment and gave a little smile.

Greg gave himself a kick up the backside. What was he

thinking? Diane was away. He hadn't seen Susie in a while, that's what had hit hard. It wasn't uncommon if she wasn't in the area and she'd told him she wouldn't be around for a while. He was being threatened. She'd rightly cooled things off. It had helped in some ways, but not in others.

Friends', colleagues', relatives' lives were in tatters, and yet all he could think of right there and then was his brother's girlfriend! Come on, get a grip. Or rather don't get a grip. Hey! He put some humour back into his personal chastisement.

The momentary affair with Patsy now seemingly over, Greg returned his full consciousness to his brother, who was about to hit hard on Greg's behalf in trying to find some kind of lead on the guys who were causing the club's and Greg's mayhem. Patsy carried on busying herself with breakfast, whilst the two brothers looked out of the window on to the somewhat untended garden, alternately taking sips from steaming mugs of tea.

"I thought I'd drop by and see Di and Kyle," said Colin. "I've not seen 'em properly since I got back, and Di won't think much of me missing my favourite godson while I'm here. Patsy and I'll go after we've seen Bill."

Patsy moved again, this time bending slightly as she reached for a dish in the kitchen unit. No, no, get real again!

"You know what's really behind all this, don't you, Greg?"

Colin wasn't searching Greg's current 'caught in the headlights' look, thank God, as he once more returned from the land of leering. Although a full explanation would take time, he had reached one easy conclusion.

"Behind all of this, no matter which way you look, no matter how you turn, there's only ever going to be one motive. Greed. Someone wants to get rich."

"But you said it yourself, Col. No-one gets rich from Rugby League. There's not enough money in it…"

"Yeah, yeah, I know. But think back. When did all this heavy stuff get started?"

Another pause. Greg knew nothing.

"Irvine. I'm not saying it's all about him or that he's even at fault.

That makes no sense from what you and Bill say, but it's all started since he came. George Ramsbottom didn't have it the way you did, not the heavy stuff. He did have some pressure though, so Bill says. But no…"

Colin took another chunk out of his third slice of toast.

"We reckon something's happened since Irvine got involved, we're not certain what or why apart from you've started winning games. That's what Patsy, me and Bill are trying to find out … And it will be about money somewhere along the way, I guarantee it…"

Patsy was smiling at Greg as she made her verbal entry into the proceedings.

"My hero!" she exclaimed as she clasped her hands and fluttered her eyelashes at Colin. He wasn't impressed. He was trying hard here with a fairly clueless brother who knew how to play rugby league and mend cars, but that's as far as it went. But he also knew Greg had been through enough recent trauma and was doing well to just keep going.

"Has Irvine ever said anything to you, you know, given you any impression he's aware of anything?"

"I just don't know, Col. He's full of words that don't mean much. Just wants us to win. Strength through adversity, he said the other day. Sounded like he wanted to be Winston Churchill."

"That'll be a 'no' then…" Colin's slightly comical put down of his brother was the spark to ignite Greg's tortured flame. Colin's expression had been one of eyebrows raised, wide-eyed amazement that his brother could have worked out so little. Greg wasn't having any of it.

"…I just don't fucking know! What do you think this is, Col? Just another trivia quiz where all the answers are there and it's just a matter of being a little bit clever to sort it all out … This is no fucking Cluedo with the vicar and the rope in the fucking sitting room!"

Colin was already backing off now, hands half raised towards his brother, realising that despite all his efforts he had just committed the same cardinal sin he used to manage with great alacrity in their school years. He knew he'd set off the time bomb and that for the next few moments it was purely a matter of hanging in there.

"*Shit, Col, there's people getting run down, babies not being born when they are supposed to be, cars being driven off roads, people scrambling for their lives! You think I haven't been thinking about it, what's been going on! I'll tell you, all I've been able to think about for days now has been who's going to be next ... and now you're here, it could be you! ... or Patsy!*"

Greg looked back across at Patsy who for a moment hadn't known where to look. She hadn't seen the total and utter devastation in Greg's voice and face until now. She'd seen him with the coaching staff after a training session, enjoyed the evening with him and Col – and yes, she had been enjoying flirting a little this morning.

Colin knew he had pushed Greg too far. Given him little credit. And it was true, he couldn't possibly understand the enormity of what his brother had faced and was facing. Then again, he was there and he was trying to help.

"*OK, OK.*"

He left the slightest of pauses. Then, sensing Greg's rage diminishing and Patsy's now puffed out cheeks, blowing calmly, he moved slightly away from his brother and straddled one of the kitchen chairs facing Greg over its back. He clasped his hands in prayer-like style with the index fingers pointing upwards, resting just underneath his nose, and his thumbs on the underside of his chin.

Patsy enjoyed being provocative, and knew she was. But Greg's violent verbal reaction to Col had brought her back to her senses. Quit the flirting girl, right now.

"*Look...*"

Colin held his pose as he was saying this, not even looking up at Greg. He had been stung by Greg's criticism of him. Of course, he didn't see this as a game! But it wasn't going to help anyone's case if they bickered.

"*So far what we know...*"

He closed his eyes to give more credence to what he was about to say.

"…Di's been attacked…"

Another momentary pause to acknowledge what was coming next.

"…she's lost the baby … Kyle was nearly killed … your physio's been run off the road…"

Yet another pause. Colin lifted his head slightly and shifted his hands, so that now the middle fingers were touching the chin with his hands still adopting prayer-like posture. He continued with his eyes shut. He didn't want to see Greg's face at present. Didn't want to know whether Greg was taking it in or not.

"…you've been threatened … we find out that George Ramsbottom was threatened before you, albeit in a smaller way with none of this seemingly bigger time stuff … you get visits from three idiots … the stadium gets daubed … the stadium gets wrecked, people could have been killed … then, after all that, they abduct you, do that to you."

Col stopped. That was it – as far as he had made out. That was pretty much the size of it as far as Greg was concerned too, but what good had reiterating it done? Telling him what he already knew was fine, but it hadn't provided any answers. Colin had stopped deliberately.

"…and all this is supposed to be about Hopton finishing bottom? What a load of bollocks!"

Colin ran his hand across from chin to cheek and back as he now raised both his tempo and voice. God he could do with a shave!

"…it's money, Greg. And that's all…"

He thrust both hands out firmly, his fingers like talons to express his point.

"…and the only guy it leads to at present is the one guy who's got involved as owner since you took over as coach."

Colin opened his eyes and looked straight at his brother.

"It's got to be something to do with Irvine, Greg, it just has to be…"

And then added an air of finality to the breakfast

proceedings.

"…and that's what Bill and Patsy and I are going to find out."

Greg had never in his life felt so insecure. He knew he'd been letting off steam against his brother. He was an easy target.

Here was his brother trying his level best to sort his mess out for him. He needed to show gratitude. He moved to put his hand firmly on his brother's shoulder. Patsy drank it all in.

"Cheers, Col … really."

Greg moved to leave the room heading for the hallway.

"I've got to get down to the ground. See ya later, eh?"

Col nodded, more by way of slight satisfaction that he had negotiated a successful path through the last five minutes than anything else. He looked a fleeting while at his brother.

"Yeah, have a good one…!"

Greg couldn't resist a final look across at Patsy who was currently loading the dishwasher. It just so happened she was once again showing her bum off in great fashion. Stop it, Greg told himself.

"And you too, Patsy. Thanks for being here."

Patsy looked up and smiled.

CHAPTER 33

Hopton is nestled in the heart of what is often referred to as the Pennine area of Northern England. Hills and valleys that surround the town provide picturesque landscapes for film and TV programme makers and day trippers.

The town became a thriving industrial centre in the 1800s, thanks to sheep farming and its waterway system, which provided cheap transportation of wool produce that had been turned into clothing and carpets through the large woolen mill era.

The days of making money out of what grows naturally off sheeps' backs had long since passed and since WWII Hopton's employment opportunities had come increasingly via smaller, light industrial operations and the town's world-renowned Tannersfield Bitter.

The town's name, so it goes, is a quite simple derivation – Hops Town. Way beyond the time when fleeces were the major source of income, the town's tradition had been founded on brewing. Plentiful supplies of its own hops, thanks to Hopton's amazing micro climate in the 17th century, had brought about the hops growing fields, normally grown much further south in England. Water was sourced from the River Twidal that ran through Hopton with malting barley grown in substantial quantity on the non-hill land providing the other main ingredient. It had become a self-contained brew like no other. Sadly, the hops fields had gone through a change in climate – and people thought climate change was a new thing!

Today, just one brewery survives along with a handful of micros, a hefty reduction from the heady days of the early part of the 1900s when the textile world doubled the town's population to 25,000. At that time, somewhere between fifteen to twenty were going strong, but in the past decades the changing role of drinking habits, public houses and brewers had brought about a series of failures, buy-outs, mergers and the survival of the fittest had taken hold.

Tannersfield Bitter holds its own against the other northern greats and is mentioned in real ale circles in the same breath as Theakston Old Peculier.

Caill's Ales, who brew six main beers with Tannersfield its flagship, keeps the town's reputation flying high as one of the trio of major beer producing centres in the area that also includes Masham and Tadcaster.

The breweries, plus some of the larger woollen mill barons, had pretty much run the town for the past 200 years.

Tannersfield's good name continues thanks in the main to its distinctive taste, but also a clever appreciation of tradition and marketing. All barrels and casks still leave the brewery by barge on the River Twidal as they did when waterways were trafficked in the same way as today's motorways – which stands them in good stead with the council who are trying hard to increase visitor numbers – despite the fact they are then loaded on to articulated trucks just a quarter of a mile upstream. They have succeeded in capturing the imagination of drinkers worldwide.

Tanners Barge had opened as a floating pub next to the drop-off point for the casks and barrels five years ago.

To the outside world, all was well with Caill's Ales, its marketing and its future, but inside there was trouble brewing.

Greg called at Victoria Street Garage after leaving Col and Patsy to their endeavours. He was to see Diane and Kyle before reaching Parrot Lane later. Garage owner Alan Baines had agreed on flexi-time, ad-hoc hours since Greg had taken on the coaching role and work was a little slow at present, but he wanted to show willing.

Alan was in his mid-40s. He had owned the garage for about eight years and Greg had been on the brink of going into partnership with him just lately, but then the coaching job had come along. Alan knew Greg wasn't going to take up a partnership while his rugby league career still held firm, but he hadn't shut the door on the idea. They had worked well together since Greg had joined him from school as an apprentice.

Alan was under a car as Greg arrived. He heard him muttering under his breath as Greg sidled up to the car he was working on. Alan slid out on his trolley.

"Ah Greg ... Good timing, mate ... pass me that wrench ... give me a sec..."

A couple of hammer blows later, having slid back under, he was out again brushing his hands down on his overalls.

"Fancy a brew? Stick the kettle on whilst I..."

"No, no thanks Al, I've got loads to do down at the ground. Bloody coppers want to see me today – investigating what went on ... just thought I'd drop by ... check on how things are here..."

Alan let out a low whistle between his teeth as he breathed out hard. Greg didn't know whether Alan's whistle was down to his mention of police or that he was just getting his breath back in some way. Alan's hand was on the kettle filling it up at the washbasin just over to the corner of where he had been working.

"We're okay ... but funny you should come in just now ... had a feller come in asking about you just half an hour ago."

Alan was turned with his back to Greg, which was just as well because at that moment Greg's early morning good-natured demeanour disappeared in an instant. Alan turned after having switched on the kettle.

Greg tried to appear casual.

"Oh yeah?"

"Didn't say much ... sorry he'd missed you ... no message."
Alan wasn't particularly bothered about the information he was giving to Greg. In fact, he was busying himself with cleaning a mug whilst the kettle was on the go.

"Are you sure you don't want one?"

It was about the only thing Greg was sure about at that moment.

"You didn't recognise him, then? Not a customer?"

Alan shook his head. He turned back to where the kettle was

now steaming nicely, picking it up almost immediately the button had clicked for boiling point.

"*Shit, fuu…*" Alan put down the kettle quickly and put his hand under his armpit. "*We're going to have to do something about this thing. That's the second time this week I've nearly scorched my hand off as I've picked it up … What was it you were saying? Oh yeah, no, it was nobody I know … Anyhow, said he'd catch up with you sometime.*"

Greg decided against any further questions and left Alan with his hand under a cold water tap.

Typically, Fred was there to greet Greg as he arrived at the ground.

"*Crawling with 'em! Can't move for 'em, they're like bloody ants marchin' all over the place.*"

It was a little more perplexed than Fred's usual banter, probably because he felt uneasy, given his perpetual swerving of declaring income and therefore never paying income tax. He knew it might finally catch up one day. Little did he know he was still way below the minimum wage anyway, but Fred also set Greg immediately on his guard.

He'd known it was coming up to his turn to be questioned. He also knew there would be questions he couldn't answer and that if he did they would look deeper into the other happenings. He had to remember the threats. So it was time for Plan A for today.

He'd asked the whole squad, minus anyone with work commitments elsewhere, to be available for a final training session – more about light running and keeping the boys together for the day than anything else – from 10.30 that morning.

At least this way he could see they were okay. Training was also a delay tactic from talking with the police. He was already kitted up for a run.

"*Fred, do us a favour would you?*"

Greg's head slightly cocked towards Fred as he spoke under his breath.

"Tell the lads we're going for a run and get them out here."

Five minutes later, the party of around 18 disappeared into the distance with Greg and Phil Trippett.

Threats, explosions, Diane, Kyle, Kirsty, Veejay, Bill, Irvine, Susie, Col, Patsy, Whisky and Cigars, the Klitschkos, black car, money, greed. All these came and went in Greg's mind as he ran – in bed with Susie, Patsy's pert bum. He felt guilty fantasising over Patsy. Guilty about Colin. Guilty about Diane. He loved them all, but now he found he also wanted Patsy. He laughed at himself for how ridiculous he was as he ran. Such a twat, he told himself.

Greg's thoughts moved from his private world to concentrating on checking out the rest of the lads. Young Paul Davy was running hard and keen to be back from his ban. Stu Wainwright was into the banter. The cheeky scrum-half had quickly slotted in as the guy the rest of them could never shut up. Brad Warrener looked in-shape and had struck up a friendship with Mark Merrioneth and Tony Estorino. Keith Denny, Ron Rigson and Kenny Lomax – the three with the most experience – lagged a little, but they knew how to pace themselves. Alan Thomas and Vincent Venus had their own agenda. They'd brought a ball with them and were practising offloads on the run along with Ian Sissons and the New Zealanders Jon Entish and Warwick Player. Right at the back were the Hammerton twins, Dave Harper, Phil Trippett and lethargic Tony Webb. Others were either at work or were injured.

It was a route they regularly took, taking them past the intoxicating airs of Caill's Ales; then alongside the river, before climbing back uphill toward the recently-completed by-pass which would bring them back on course to Parrot Lane. Roughly five miles – not the usual for everyone the day of a match, but if the players were following their own fitness levels properly, not unusual in their daily schedule. Greg wanted his team fit no matter what was going on – and for the moment, at least, within his eyesight!

As he looked over his shoulder to check on the stragglers, he thought he caught the glimpse of a black car. It was about 50 yards behind the Hammertons, the backmarkers. Even Tony Webb wasn't as slow as them.

Whilst neither Diane nor Veejay had been able to describe the car that had run them both off the road well enough to name the make or model, Greg, especially given his job as a mechanic, knew from the merest glimpse.

It was a jet black metallic Nissan Qashqai Tekna. All pretty average stuff. There could have been one hundred of them in Hopton alone, but there was a chance it could be the same car.

They were only a third of a mile from the ground and the least Greg wanted to do was to get the licence number down. He'd dropped back to the Hammertons on the pretence of joining them. He took note of the number. Now he had to remember it. He didn't have his phone, but his legs started pumping faster to get back sooner and record it somewhere. The faster guys saw his finishing burst and responded. Suddenly, what was a reasonably enjoyable canter had brought about a sprint and Alan Thomas and Vincent Venus weren't going to miss out.

It wasn't what Greg had planned, but to see his charges reacting to what he hadn't even intended as a momentum shift was a positive by-product. Vincent Venus, despite carrying a knock, came home first with Alan Thomas next. The Hammerton boys predictably trailed in last.

Greg smiled back whilst trying to regain his breath. He'd come in a creditable fifth, but wasn't counting. He ran straight to his car, dived for his phone and punched the numbers into its memory. He then sent a text to Alan at the garage asking him whether he could find out anything about the number. It was nothing more than that, but at least he felt as though he was contributing to the efforts from Bill, Patsy and Col.

CHAPTER 34

It was as he completed his text that the first question of many came from behind him. So much for his earlier avoidance tactic.

"Mr Duggan, I'm DI Will Gill of Hopton CID. Can I have a word?"

It was clearly more of an instruction than a request.

"In the office?" he motioned towards Greg's Portakabin.

As much as Greg had tried to keep away from this moment in the past few days, he had known its inevitability. He'd just read a text from Diane as DI Gill was announcing himself. She and Kyle had seen Colin and Patsy earlier, wasn't she nice? Indeed, thought Greg.

Greg's tongue licked his bottom lip while resting against his front teeth as he tried to gather his thoughts and relax from the sprint. No matter how much this interview had been coming, he still wasn't prepared for it, but he also wasn't prepared for what was about to happen next.

As he entered the makeshift office, his phone warbled. Greg held open the door for the detective to go through while he fished the phone from his running top pocket. He'd have to shower later it seemed.

His first thought was Alan must have turned over the information he wanted pretty sharp, but it wasn't the garage. It was a text from a withheld number:

"Don't do it, Duggan! Not a word, remember!"

Whoever sent it had either seen Greg meet the DI or had relayed their information to the person now sending it. One way or another, he was being watched.

Greg entered the office to find the DI taking what appeared to be more than a passing interest in the paperwork on his desk. If he was looking for something, Greg wished him all the best as his desk did a fair impression of a horizontal rubbish basket!

"Mr Duggan, Greg?"

He asked in such a way as to be informal. 'Copper's way,' was Greg's immediate thought. Gently does it and then hope to open him up as a friend. Greg wasn't that naïve, although he was, however, on edge, even though he had nothing to hide.

DI Will Gill was around early to mid-30s, good head of blond wavy hair and dressed in jeans and t-shirt.

"As you know, we're looking into the events that took place on Sunday after the game, as you and the rest of the players from both teams were leaving the field."

Gill left his introduction there, hanging for a second, before moving on, checking for any gesture, eye movement, body shape or change in Greg. Greg was still.

"Do you have any idea why the explosions took place?"

Gill's first question and Greg was outwardly trying to appear calm and in control. Inside, his voice of reason was telling him to spill all, but his other voice of self-preservation and family preservation and that of everyone else was at the same time uttering a commanding 'no'. He tried to make his gesture look acceptable as he shook his head and followed up with:

"…I just know, it was really bad … we all tried to help as best we could … hope we can put it behind us for tonight's game…"

"Yeah, sure … Look, Greg, I've been made well aware of how much you've given to the club and that you're now more involved than ever with your coaching role…"

DI Gill was attempting to make his progress as stealthily as he could, gauging Greg's reaction to every word. Greg was trying his best to remain calm.

Seeing the Qashqai just before the meeting had been the shot in the arm Greg needed. It might not lead to anything, but it seemed suspicious given what had happened to Diane and Veejay.

"…So what's going on?"

DI Gill paused again. He wanted to see what this sudden question, fired in quickly, might evoke. A flinch? A firming up of Duggan's lips? Tension in his fists? A turn away, shutting of the eyes? Any of that might help. Gill traded in reactions. Be the friend, but not over friendly. Soften the interviewee slightly to show you're not without feeling and emotion, then question sharply, rather like a southpaw's jab in boxing. Stand back and assess the results.

Greg knew he couldn't answer him directly, but he wasn't trying to give an impression of being evasive either. He remained tight lipped, shrugged ever so slightly before responding.

"Not a clue…"

Gill knew Greg was involved in some way. Instinct and the ability to read people were among his most noted assets. Greg Duggan might well be able to read a game of Rugby League, but criminal activity was his turf. Greg thought he was handling the situation pretty well. Gill was inclined to let him think that way too.

Gill usually found if the suspect was talkative he could find out what he wanted much faster, but Greg didn't fit that category. He needed to find the key that would unlock Greg's lips. Gill wasn't about to go anywhere just yet.

"And you played your part … rescuing fans … not just a hero on the park, but in the grandstand too…"

Gill had felt a little flattery might not go amiss. Greg took the compliment with his usual shrug and felt it was only fair to respond. It was exactly the way in which Gill had intended.

"…I know you're after something more … I just haven't anything I can tell you…"

Gill resisted the temptation to jump in on the back of Greg's latest comment. His last few words were what Gill had been searching for – Greg hadn't anything he *could* tell him, which meant in Gill's parlance that there was something he should tell him that for some reason he couldn't. He let it rest for now. Move on.

Greg's eyes were fixed on Gill's. He felt if he moved his eyes away Gill would take this as some form of weakness. While Greg may have said he didn't know how he could help, the DI was prepared to wait and listen. Greg felt he had to show Gill he was trying.

"*...I've only been coach for a month. I mean, just look at this desk, it's like a bomb's hit it!*"

In retrospect, given the recent activity at the ground, perhaps not the best of phrases, but Greg was starting to open up slightly. Gill found him a curious package. Everything pointed to him being the hometown boy doing his best for the club and although Gill's instincts were that Greg was clean there were too many other strands causing him concern. Gill knew for all kinds of reasons he had to play this just right. Normally someone like Greg would have been an open book in answering questions. People without anything to hide stay in the open. And Gill wanted something, anything on Greg.

Gill saw Greg seemed too much on guard. He knew there was something not right about this whole case and already had information he wouldn't give to Greg.

But Gill wasn't about to make this session too heavy. There was a long way to go here and he needed to establish some form of rapport, build a kind of friendship whereby Greg accepted him. In truth, he was getting pissed off with his job. He'd other irons in the fire. And he had a date night coming up.

"*OK, Greg. Let's call it quits for now. We're at the early stages of our inquiries. If you remember anything or think of anything that might help, just let me know, yeah?*"

Greg couldn't help but utter a sigh of huge relief inside. It was as Gill had reached the door that he turned with another comment.

"*I've still to get around everybody and get things straight in my brain. You see, this – the stand – isn't the only thing we're looking into.*"

Keep calm! Greg tried harder than ever to maintain the straight face he had thought had worked well so far, but had been caught off guard and had closed his eyes momentarily the way you do when you don't want the other person to see the windows of your soul, but that also gives you away. He was the bloody victim here, so why should he have to feel guilty and be on the defensive? Greg knew why. Those bastards.

Gill came back to shake Greg by the hand, gave a firm nod by way of goodbye and made for the door again. This time, as he put his hand to the handle, he turned to deliver another well-rehearsed investigative line. The question that comes after you think you're done.

"*Oh ... I meant to ask ... How's your wife? ... and your son? ... and Dr Ranjitshah?*"

Gill wanted to show Greg he knew about other stuff, that was all. Gill thought he saw something this time, a tiny flicker. Greg tried to remain cool.

"*They're getting better, thanks.*"

With a faint smile the DI was gone.

CHAPTER 35

"So let me get this straight … you got involved because you're a local lad, no other reason?"

Colin was being careful. This was his third call and the first of the three members of the previous consortium he'd managed to talk to, Hopton-born-and-bred 50-year-old Des White who had built a modest fortune in the wholesale meat trade. He'd supported Hopton Town all his life, his father too.

When a long-time friend of his had approached him to go in with two others to rescue the club and take it forward he'd agreed, but far from taking it forward it had taken even more of his hard-earned cash than he'd anticipated for nil return.

"…Yes, yes, I can see why you would … thanks … err, before you go, is there any chance you could tell me how much you were offered for your stake? … no, no, that's fine … I'm seriously not a reporter, no story… just gathering information … can't tell you why at this stage … if you think of anything more or want to give my number to your friend who was in the consortium, either ring me or get him to ring, if you could … just trying to help the club … thanks … maybe see you at a game…"

Bill had stopped leafing through the club's recent past board notes and archived material and was listening intently to Colin's end of the conversation. Bill knew Des and the other consortium members, of course, but he and Colin had decided it would be better for Colin to ring around them. Fresh face.

No-one knew of Colin – or indeed Jeff Butters, the pseudonym he had added to his repertoire for this performance. Best not using Duggan, they'd both felt.

They'd discussed strategy earlier and were now located some twenty miles out of Hopton at Bill's sister Grace's bungalow in the rural village of Smedley Stricker. She'd left for a holiday and family visit in Vanuatu, one of the world's most remote island archipelago countries, where her son was running a hotel by the beach. Bill had arranged to do a spot of house-sitting for her.

Smedley Stricker sat peacefully in the bottom of a green and pleasant vale on a quiet backroad about two miles from the nearest highway. Village amenities extended to a quaint old church with graveyard, a stream known as The Stricker and a telephone call box that had changed its use to being where locals took their locally produced jams, chutneys, eggs, tomatoes and potatoes to be purchased through an honesty box.

Once Colin had been put firmly abreast of what Bill knew, and what he had gleaned having visited George Ramsbottom, he had still been sure Irvine was the key. But how could they find out more?

Phones and laptops fully charged and with chargers at the ready, they had set their stall to find out more about the previous consortium. Maybe this way they would start getting to the reason why Greg and the club were being targeted and why finishing bottom was so important that incendiary devices and abduction had added to maniac drivers. Unfortunately, the village wasn't blessed with the best Internet connection. Superfast broadband hadn't arrived at Smedley Stricker, that was for sure, but mobile phones seemed to be working fine.

Bill relayed that George Ramsbottom, while not being one of the board, had probably seen and heard and been more aware of what had been going on at the club than him during his coaching reign.

"George may have had an inside track with the consortium as one of them, Malky Mitchinson was, I think, one of George's best mates at school. I'm not sure what that might mean, but maybe they talked."

The consortium, George had proffered to Bill after he'd calmed down from his rage at the lodge, had always been wholeheartedly behind the club. They hadn't expected to see a return on their investment. They were level-headed local guys who wanted only the best for the club. Putting something back.

They'd all found it a bit of a struggle. Baling out the club from its debts had swallowed up any extra cash they had generated for the purpose of buying new players and investing further – and the on-going weekly costs of running the club constantly outstripped its income. It had been bleeding them all dry. Their initial spark had turned to disillusion and this had spread throughout the club. George had done his level best to keep his players upbeat, but never had any money to invest as planned.

Then the club's latest fairy godmother had arrived in the form of Bob Irvine and George had been dumped unhesitatingly, unceremoniously. The open wound Bill had witnessed of George in the Lake District clearly hurt like hell. They'd got away because it was better for his health was Janice's take.

Bill thought back to the Irvine deal. Bob Irvine had provided the club and consortium with the lifelines they needed. Colin's, or Jeff's, phone burst into life.

"Mr Butters? … Malky Mitchinson…"

Colin asked Mitchinson the same scripted questions he'd tried with Des White and with similar results until he incorporated the knowledge Bill had just shared over the Mitchinson-Ramsbottom school friendship axis. It appeared this might not have been as close or at least as friendly an acquaintance as Bill had suggested. Ramsbottom's name served to light the blue touch paper in Mitchinson's world.

"Yeah, I knew him at school, we've known each other years … Wasn't brilliant as a player or coach, but he tried hard… anyway, it's over now … We managed to come out of it with our pride intact, lost money, masses of it, all of us … thank God for Mr Irvine, so far as I'm concerned … I've got back to what I do well and I have to now to build up again … don't wish the club any harm though … I'll be at the game tonight, and back where I'm staying … on the terraces … hope it all works out, terrible thing on Sunday…"

Bill heard everything as Colin had put the call on loudspeaker. He'd shaken his head as he'd heard Malky's words.

"These guys were only doing what they could. It just didn't work out for them."

"But why did Irvine suddenly appear, from nowhere, and buy the

club quickly? I know it happens. Opportunities and all that, but so quickly? What about due diligence procedures, they take time. He's a businessman and I don't get all that crap about him 'always having wanted to get involved with the sport.' He takes over companies as a business interest. How much is the club worth? Do we know? ... Assets? The ground..."

"Nope, can't be that. He can't develop it because as far as I know he doesn't own the ground, or if he does there's still some kind of restrictive covenant on it that relates to sport being played, although I've never seen the deeds relating to it ... goes back years..."

It was new information and Colin was processing it.

"Bill, whether there's a restrictive covenant or not doesn't really matter to someone like Irvine. He'll have his solicitors on it. They'll find a way. It's money. This is all about money, but if Irvine already has the club then why is all the rest happening? He'd just leave it to the legal eagles. Still doesn't make sense."

The doorbell rang. Bill set off for the hallway from the kitchen where they had ensconced themselves since arrival. Postman.

"Morning! Registered delivery. Sign here."

Bill dutifully did so without first looking at the name or address. It would be something for Grace. *"Have a nice day."*

Bill looked at the padded envelope he'd just been handed and was about to pop it on the table in the hallway, which contained the rest of the post he'd put there earlier, accumulated since Grace had been away.

But then a quick doubletake on the addressee. It was one of those moments when your eyes see something that your brain computes immediately as odd, that you hadn't intended to notice, but then you have to look at again. It was his name! And this address! But why? How? And this was a package! Incendiary device! Alarm bells! Bill stared down at it.

CHAPTER 36

Greg's phone sprung to life as Gill left. Texts from Alan at the garage, giving him the information he'd come up with about the car, and one from Patsy.

"Greg, I'm in Ringstall to find out more about Irvine, can't get through to Col. Get him to ring me, please."

Greg couldn't catch Col either. He sent a text to Col too. The car Greg had clocked was a no-no, or at least it seemed that way. Alan's text came back that it was clean so far as anyone knew, owned by a local guy bought two years ago. It was as much as he had.

Bill was mesmerised. He couldn't take it in. Colin appeared. He'd stepped out into the back garden for a second while having a brew as Bill had answered the door. He clocked Bill's expression. His face was white.

"Bill! …" Colin had looked down to what Bill was holding and saw the name and address. The package. Bill's fingers were quivering. Colin took the package.

"Your name. This address. No way, Bill. No way."

Then, after a pause for both to assure themselves they were on the same wavelength.

"I know nothing about letter bombs, I've never seen one before, I don't know this is one, but your name, this address, us just turning up here, a package, doing what we're doing, guys who don't seem to stop at much and who have previous with devices…"

Colin raised his eyebrows, eyes wide. Bill was in shock, his legs crumbling beneath his heavy frame.

"We can't just leave it, we've got to dispose of it … and we've got to do it now, let's go…"

What if this was the ultimate over reaction? Even if it was, then they were better safe! Instinct. Just holding it in his hands was enough. OK, there was no ticking, nothing to tell him for absolute certain, but from all that Greg had told him Colin wasn't going to underestimate the lengths these guys would go to.

How had they been able to find them so easily. They'd been careful and they'd been sure they hadn't been followed, but trackers? They'd come in Bill's car. Perhaps they'd managed to fit a device. Don't underestimate. Concentrate. First things first, what about disposing of this?

"Is there a spade around here?" Colin had no way of knowing whether burying it in the garden would be dangerous or not if it was some kind of letter bomb. It may just contain a note, but padded envelope, something hard inside? To them, now? He wasn't going to take any chances. They could always contact the professionals later to check it out.

"We'll put it sufficiently under the ground so that no-one can get to it. Hopefully it will only react if someone opens it and this is one way to be sure that no-one will … maybe…"

Twenty minutes later, Grace had a newly dug plot in her garden. As they finished, Bill stepped back in the house and took a look at his phone that was warbling merrily. One text. Withheld number.

"Fuck off meddling in what will only harm you … If you can still read this."

Colin was on his way around the corner of the bungalow from the garden to Bill's car. He caught sight of a head quickly bobbing down from the other side of the hedge at the roadside. There was no time like the present. No soft steps from Colin. He hit full speed by his sixth stride and leaped over a gate to confront his now panic-stricken prey.

Colin stopped in his tracks, just two yards from the decrepit figure. It now appeared amazing this old man had been able to look over the hedge at all, such was his bent-double height. Colin spotted a little step ladder.

"We've a Neighbourhood Watch scheme round here you know…" The man had summoned up enough courage to at least give it a go croaky style. *"…If you touch me, someone will see you. You won't get away with it…"*

"Look, mate, I think there's some misunderstanding going on here…"

"…So what are you doing at Grace's place? She's supposed to be away for months and as far as I knew the place was meant to be empty."

Before Colin could answer further, Bill was at his side. The man changed his demeanour in an instant.

"Bill, how good to see you! Now tell me in God's name, my man, just what is going on here?"

Alec and Bill apparently went back a long way as Bill was a regular visitor to the village. Alec had seen movement at Grace's and, with a natural inquisitiveness and having founded the local Watch, had decided to take a further look. He hadn't seen anything prior to that. No postman either, although he had felt it odd that a postman had been seen at all as that was not his regular time.

They chose not to mention the suspect package to Alec. If they had learnt one thing from today's venture, it had been that no matter who became involved, nobody was safe from these guys. Col suddenly then thought if neither of them were safe then neither was Patsy.

CHAPTER 37

"She's here … yeah, sure … yeah, OK." Bill and Colin weren't the only ones being followed. Patsy had her attendees too.

Patsy had revelled in her day posing as Jenna Howells, Associate of Clark, Fitch & Daykin, a research company looking at behavioural science in business and on each call trying to learn a little more about the Irvine empire in the process. It had been fun, but as a successful mission it had proved fruitless so far.

Posing as someone else and putting on the act had been the high spots. Patsy reached the offices of Castlegate Press Group at 2.30 in the afternoon. Her exploits had allowed her to capture the atmosphere of Irvine's empire and it appeared the House of Irvine looked in good shape.

"Never see him. We just get on with it," had been a quote from one of the management team at Ringstall Glass, located on the outskirts of town. *"Who? Never heard of him,"* had been another from the logistics manager of Haul UK, Irvine's transportation company based in new buildings on a massive industrial estate. *"Lovely guy, actually quite dishy in a 50-something kind of way, see him here once a month, always takes an interest in everything,"* was the receptionist at Borough Chemicals' view. These had been a smattering of what Patsy, or Jenna, had found out. It appeared Irvine was how he appeared, owner of many companies, but not involved, other than ownership and board meetings.

Castlegate Press & Social Media Group offices were located in sparkling new premises too. An exceptionally beautiful woman, somewhere in her 30s/40s with a body that looked as though it had been poured into her stunning white dress, came towards Patsy. The woman's smile lacked warmth.

"Ms Howells? I'm afraid Mr Kraft sends his apologies, but he's been delayed and won't be back today … perhaps we could arrange another appointment, sometime next week?"

Patsy tried her level best to hide her disappointment. This had been the first meeting she hadn't been able to complete. She wasn't used to being turned down, but didn't want to slip from character.

"That's OK. It really was only a few questions I wanted to ask, no real stinkers…"

Patsy thought the last words might just make her sound light and a little like some new kid on the block, rather than someone who was attempting to dig around. *"But no worries. I can come back next week. I'll ring you tomorrow once I've checked my diary…"*

Grahame Kraft's personal assistant smiled her awkward smile once more and was on her way. Patsy picked up her bag and had reached the outer door.

"Hi! You were looking for Grahame?"

Jeff Markham wasn't the kind of man to pass on an opportunity of chatting up a gorgeous woman and also hadn't got to where he had without checking out interesting leads.

He had taken the initial call from Jenna Howells that morning, due to Kraft being unavailable at the time. There was something in Markham's head that didn't sit right about this girl's approach. Couldn't put his finger on it. She wanted to see the editor on the same day as ringing for an appointment? Not exactly earth shatteringly odd, he reflected, but normally the kind of request that anticipates a meeting being arranged for perhaps a week ahead. He'd been inquisitive. There was something about her voice, the way she spoke, that to him wasn't someone doing routine research. He was a journalist, after all.

He'd Google-searched her before putting Ms Howells through to the editor's secretary, by which time he had already ascertained there was no record of a Jenna Howells on Facebook, apart from a black girl in Illinois and an Irish clog dancer in Limerick. He'd also searched for Clark, Fitch & Daykin. The company didn't exist at Companies House, nor in any marketing and PR directory – and there was nothing online in any way. He was intrigued and had loitered around the newspaper's reception area at the time she was due, to find out what she was up to.

Patsy decided to play along. Maybe she would find something more.

"*Jeff Markham, Deputy Editor, Castlegate Mail.*"

With a warm smile, much warmer than Kraft's PA minutes earlier, Markham's handshake was also welcoming.

"*Jenna Howells.*"

"*What brings you here, Jenna? I know you wanted to see Grahame…*"

Patsy settled into character once more. This had been her domain for the day. Telling people how she was working on behalf of a market research company in behavioural science, and that she had been asked to carry out exploratory information on businesses in northern towns and cities. How they differed from the south and whether the North/South Divide was myth or reality.

"*Listen…*" It was a habit with Markham. He started several conversations with an instruction. It wasn't dictatorial, more a way of reassuring himself that he had the full attention of his intended target. "*This sounds good. I can spare half an hour? I was just popping over the road for a beer and a sandwich since we're clear of today's deadlines. Would you like to join me?*"

The Scribe was the Castlegate Press Group's regular haunt. It remained stoically loyal to its roots, although it had upped its image from spit-and-sawdust to Pimms-and-polish.

Hived away in one of the many little 'snugs' that gave the pub its intimate feel, Markham opened up the proceedings.

"*So, is there?*" He took a sip from his pint. Jenna looked inquisitive, not quite sure of his question. Where was he leading?

"*…a North/South Divide? … there probably was, of course, years back. But these days, with a more mobile population, I'd guess it's not quite so clear cut…*"

Jenna nodded appreciatively. "*That's pretty much it … but there's more to it … obviously…*"

They were sparring, but they were also both eager to continue for different reasons. Patsy wanted something tangible, something from her day. Information she could take back to the boys to prove this had not been a complete waste of time.

Markham was encouraged that she showed no inclination to hurry off. This girl wasn't giving him the come on, not that he'd expected that. He was around 5ft 10, medium height, mid 40s, kept himself in good shape. Not at all unattractive, but this was business for her and for him. The girl showed no discernible sign of wanting to know more about him personally. So, who was she and what was she after – and why the spurious names?

"Why did you want to talk with GPK? Sorry, Grahame. He's known by his initials mostly. Middle name's allegedly Pythagoras, as he's always got an angle. What's yours?" he ventured. Patsy was on her guard, she frowned and smiled back. *"How do you mean?"*

"Simple question. Your angle? Why did it have to be Grahame you spoke to? You were going to leave otherwise…"

"Always go for the main man, or woman. That's the way we do things. Head honcho. Looks better on our data files that we've spoken to the right people…" Patsy was thinking quickly. *"I don't believe in making up stories."* She was toying with him, goading him slightly. Markham enjoyed her spunky approach. He could do sarcasm. And he still didn't buy it, why she was there.

"Come now, Ms Howells. That sounds very much as though you don't believe everything you read!"

Patsy's smile and pursed lips maintained his interest in her both intellectually, inquisitively and sexually. Patsy felt it too, that the flirt in her may be helping.

"So how does it go at your newspaper company? Does the 'Divide' exist there?" She took another sip from her wine, watching for his reaction. It wasn't long in coming. Markham fired back quickly.

"Right up into the boardroom…" Patsy felt her eyes lighting up. She resisted the temptation to raise her eyebrows.

Patsy cleared her throat lightly and took another taste. Markham shot his next bullet.

"*Right through to the owner. He's a northerner through and through who believes totally in the southern softie routine, or at least acts as though he does...*" He was fishing, throwing out the bait to see what he could catch. He had no idea what would cause the bite, but he had the time and she was very pleasing on the eye in her pillar box red shift dress. Patsy had purchased it from Kaleidoscope for her role earlier in the day.

"*Oh yes?...*" Patsy wanted him to go on further, but equally didn't want to make it obvious this had been her quest. She took another sip.

"*Come on, Ms Howells ... Jenna...*" It was time to test her. "*What are you really here for?*" Patsy cocked her head slightly. Markham waited for her next move. It came after a short pause.

"*What do you mean, Mr Markham? ... Jeff...*" She was watching his eyes. They were staring straight back at her. Following her, searing through her defences. She bit lightly on her lower lip, gave a little smile, raised her eyebrows, but not confidently enough. Inside, there was panic, but she told herself to remain calm.

Markham had her number. He watched for the restraint she was now showing, the calming of her muscles. It was his turn to smile, an easy confident smile.

"*Look, Jenna, all I know is that you're not here for the reason you say you are ... And you're also not who you say you are...*" Another direct glare into her eyes and smile to reassure himself. She gave him no indication he was wrong. "*And that interests me.*"

Jenna shifted in her chair once again. This was all going wrong. She either had to make an excuse to leave or try him out. Oh well, in for a penny in for a pound! But don't tell him everything. She took a deep breath. Then held her hands up as though she'd been sussed.

"*Okay. You're right, of course. I can see why you do what you do, Jeff...*" She wanted to see how he responded to flattery. Evidently quite well!

"*Someone, I can't tell you who, because they want it done*

discretely, has commissioned me to look into the Irvine empire. I've been asked to give them the low-down on what his businesses are like and what kind of involvement he has on a day-to-day basis. That's why I've tried to talk with the people who perhaps deal with him regularly and that's why I felt Kraft, Pythagoras, would be the one at your end."

Markham's nods of approval were mentally ticking boxes in his mind where he'd had queries earlier. He still knew this might not quite be the whole truth, but it was perhaps the nearest he was going to get for now. He leaned back, pleased he had worked her so easily. He'd had enough now. This was no threat to him. Kraft wasn't being manipulative. He'd been checking her out just in case Kraft had been up to something behind his back.

"Underestimate him at your peril, that's my advice … he's totally devoted to his business interests, at the expense of everything else … he's had three wives … after the first two almost cleaned him out he made the third Mrs Irvine sign a pre-nup. She still got a good settlement, but nothing like the other two…"

"But his business interests? What kind of influence does he have?"

"…is he a control freak? Of course he is … they all are…"

And that was that so far as Markham was concerned.

"Listen, I'm sorry, but I really do have to be off…"

He didn't have to be anywhere. He'd had just enough. It was the abrupt end that caught Patsy on the hop. Just when she had finally managed to find out some sketchy data on her subject, not particularly world-endingly wondrous, by any means, but encouraging. She was losing the chance of finding out more. Markham was getting up to leave. Act fast.

"Jeff, has Irvine got enemies? Would you know…?" Her haste in trying to hold on to Markham longer brought about the question which she had hoped to cloak a little better, but desperate times required immediate measures.

Markham was back interested. Perhaps there was a story here after all, but he wasn't about to appear over eager. He took a business card from his wallet, handing it to Patsy.

"We've all got enemies, Jenna. Some of us just know how to deal

with them better than others…"

Shit, this was getting better. She didn't know what she was going to find out, but Markham had given her hope, albeit without anything solid, that her day had not been in vain. She wanted more, but did he have any more to give? He looked at his phone to check the time, putting on his best apologetic expression once he'd looked.

"Seriously, I really do have to be off…"

He saw in her eyes that she was disappointed and decided not to abandon her completely.

"Look, I've a couple of appointments to keep, calls to make, maybe later…"

He hadn't at any appointments. He was sparring again. Seeing what would come next. Patsy so wanted more information on Irvine, but was playing her own game. Firstly, she too didn't want to appear as though she wanted more. Secondly, she didn't want this good-looking 40-something to get any wrong ideas, about extra curricula activity, if indeed he was about to propose a further meeting.

"No thanks, you've been really helpful. Thanks for this…"

She flicked at the card, stood, shook his hand. And he was gone. That was that. So, what had she found out? Markham had basically told her Irvine had enemies. She had found out that information at breakfast.

What Patsy didn't realise was that without the intervention of Jeff Markham, she wouldn't have been able to talk to anyone from the Castlegate Group. Jeff had been unavailable when editor Kraft had sent word to get rid of the girl as soon as possible. Specific instructions for no conversation with anyone, Kraft had said, but Markham hadn't been around.

Kraft had been horrified to learn from his secretary, who had caught a glimpse of Markham introducing himself to Ms Howells, that the one person he had not located and the one person he trusted least, was the one who should come into contact with her at just the wrong moment.

He was mortified that it was Markham. While Kraft

mistrusted him, he also respected the man. Markham was a brilliant attritionist, well used to recognising deficiencies and weaknesses in others' arguments. The real investigative reporter. Something would happen if Markham sniffed a story, it always did.

Kraft wasn't going to sit back and just let things happen. He had immediately reported back to the real men in charge – from whom the original message he had given out to all of his team except Markham had come.

Those 'real men' were nothing to do with the newspaper, but they were in Castlegate. They had entered The Scribe by the other door as Markham and Patsy had set foot in the bar. They'd heard every word, the two of them just another pair of drinkers as far as anyone else was concerned. They split as Markham and Patsy split. Pythagoras played all the angles.

CHAPTER 38

Bill and Colin arrived back at Parrot Lane just as Phil Trippett and Greg were making their final preparations for this first of the two head-to-head meetings with Ensideleigh.

The games would more than likely decide the future of both clubs. Win them both and either would pretty much be guaranteed safety – lose them both and it would be game over. Win this game and Greg faced other problems, lose it and his family and teammates should be safe for the next few days.

There was to be extra police presence even though the crowd was not expected to be much over 1000. The portable stand had arrived and had been cleared for usage after having being erected in the afternoon.

While Bill and Colin took their places on the terraces that faced the battered and now defunct grandstand, which was ready to be totally dismantled, as it had been diagnosed *'a death trap which should have been pulled down years before,'* Greg gave his final words to the players in one of two Portakabins that were now being used as team dressing rooms at the car park end of the ground.

Mid-week games usually meant a lower turnout than if the match had been played on a weekend, but this fixture had come about as a consequence of the weather earlier in the season.

Ensideleigh were in no better a position than Hopton, fan-wise. Their travelling support normally consisted of one or two coach-loads and a variety of minibuses, works vans and shared cars. They'd been in this kind of end-of-season, bottom of the table panic with Hopton before but, since this was the first year in which a team was about to be automatically removed from the league as a result of the Rugby League's plans, this was different. Both teams were fighting for their lives, both sets of die-hard supporters giving what they could by way of vocal support.

Ensideleigh's support for the fixture had rallied as their fans hoped that here was a golden opportunity to pick up points. If they couldn't pick up points against Hopton, they were down, the feeling was mutual. And they were in buoyant mood after having won their previous game.

Packed in together, the crowd, now almost wholly on one side of the ground and at one end, were in good spirits, despite their clubs' league positions. The Hopton supporters, many still in shock from Sunday, had still come whether fit or injured to give of their best.

Irvine had done all he could in the circumstances, supplying extra Portakabins and arranging for a makeshift canopy over the terracing, so that the supporters of both sides had some form of cover where they now stood. The portable stand had a canopy too.

Bob Irvine's money had paid for all the 'extras' around the ground, including a rather plush set of four kabins at the car park end, hastily put in place and adorned with furniture which wouldn't have been out of place in a top London hotel. The four had been linked and he was busy providing pre-match hospitality to the Ensideleigh officials and notable Hopton dignitaries, including the Lord Mayor and local business leaders, including Caill's Ales' owner.

"Bryan! Good to see you. It's a bit different, but we're getting it together…" Irvine had been in bullish mood since he'd arrived at the ground an hour and a half earlier. The place was buzzing and he'd liked what he'd seen.

He had been ready for Bryan Caill. They'd had business dealings with each other years ago. Caill, around 5 foot 9, slim and with straight brown hair, smiled as they clinked glasses and responded, not exactly in kindly fashion.

"Are you sure you did the right thing coming here?"

Caill continued looking Irvine straight in the eye, before continuing with a question that was almost under his breath, but was seared with venom.

"What the fuck are you playing at, Irvine?"

Caill knew from past experience Bob Irvine was not one for being involved anywhere if there wasn't some tangible, and that meant profitable, end result. Irvine returned Caill's stare and smiled in keeping with his role as host. He reciprocated Caill's under-the-breath style.

"And why are you here, Bryan? Why suddenly so eager to come tonight? Have you laid odds on something or other? Hear your gambling is going as well as ever. From what I was told, you haven't set foot in this ground for at least the last five years…"

Their opening advances were falling a long way short of genial. Caill returned Irvine's riposte immediately.

"And the rest."

When Irvine had come across him previously, he hadn't been impressed and here he tired of him instantly.

"OK, so I'm here for the first time in a while … problem with that?"

Irvine didn't care either way, he moved on to circulate with the other guests.

The teams were taking to the field as Bill and Colin entered Bob Irvine's hospitality kabin. They'd gone first to the terracing, but realising the coldness of the night had decided to join Irvine and his guests. The pair were both still in shock from how their day in the sticks had ended. Colin was now beginning to understand first hand a little of what Greg had been going through.

He now felt he was just as much in danger as his brother and was becoming increasingly worried about Patsy as he hadn't heard from her in the past three hours since receiving her message from Greg. He was even more committed to digging further. Inside the kabin, Colin was more interested in 'people watching' around Irvine than the game itself. Colin had not yet been introduced, but immediately Irvine saw Bill he became effusive. He had a reason as became immediately apparent.

"Bill. Good to see you. Bryan's just been telling me how long it is since he's been here…"

Bloody long time was Bill's instant reaction. He gave a slight nod toward Caill as he spoke.

"Bryan."

It was affirmation of the fact Caill was breathing, nothing more. Bill had never liked him. So far as Bill was concerned, the man had never wanted to be involved with Hopton, never shown the slightest liking for the club, unlike his late-father, grandfather and great-grandfather, who had all been great supporters.

Clive Caill, Bryan's father, had always seen there was something to be gained from supporting the town's rugby league team and had enjoyed being part of the club. His son had never been of the same opinion. Bryan Caill had inherited the company, but had never put in the hours that his father had to ensure its future, nor had he his father's nous. Caill looked away with disinterest after acknowledging Bill in search of another glass of champagne.

Colin had sat over to one side in such a way as to catch most of Irvine's movements and mannerisms. Bill chose now to introduce Colin to Irvine while settling into his seat that looked out on the ground from behind the posts.

"Bob, this is Colin Duggan, Greg's brother … Just down from Scotland."

Irvine was happier than he had been with Caill. No past history to worry about here. He offered a friendly warm handshake that pleasantly surprised Colin.

"Welcome along, Colin. Do you play?"

Colin would have warmed to him more had he not been fed so much that had been negative about Irvine beforehand. Now he saw him in the flesh, he went back over the comments Greg and Bill had fed him and could see everything they had mentioned did not necessarily add up to Irvine being the bad guy here.

Maybe Irvine was the bad guy, but it struck Colin that it could just as easily not be him.

"No … not my game … you've got the right brother out there, Mr Irvine…"

"*Bob, lad, call me Bob…*" Irvine went back to the rest of his assembled throng, spreading his engaging mix of smiles, charm and pleasantries.

Even given for a slightly larger away support than they would normally muster, Ensideleigh weren't exactly bringing over-crowding to Hopton. On a cool Spring evening, there were still no more than three or four hundred of their fans.

An eerie feeling swept over many as they looked out at what was once a proud, if dated, grandstand. It now resembled something more akin to an Addams Family grotesque, ruinous appearance. For some who had been at the match just days ago, it was a little too much to bear.

This was Greg's moment to take the heat off – and he knew it. Town could lose this game and they could still beat Ensideleigh at their ground in the last game of the season, so long as the results fell well, and they could stay up. This way he could buy a little time for Colin, Patsy and Bill. Maybe they could find out what the hell was going on and together they could all then do something about it. He didn't believe it necessarily, but he had to hold on to something.

At least with this game coming on so soon after the horrendous events of Sunday, then no-one would think anything of Hopton's defeat. In fact, many were already anticipating it. Even Ted Brewiss had uttered a negative thought for once, instead of talking up the game in that evening's *Messenger*. Perhaps he'd gone soft, but the weekend's happenings had to be taken into account.

"*Don't expect miracles,*" he had put. "*Duggan's side, the staff and the spectators, have gone through an awful experience and, whilst the enormity of the game will not be forgotten amongst the players or fans, there can be little doubt the drama will have taken its toll. They have been playing better since their new owner Bob Irvine came in and under Duggan's charge the combination of fresh new talent such as Wainwright, Venus and Warrener, with old war horses like Lomax, Rigson and Denny, gives reason for higher spirits than the club has been used to in recent times, but this is a tough ask this evening."*

Brewiss's instincts hadn't been wrong. Hopton were thankfully still in touch at half-time, but while every other team in the league may have capitalised massively on Town's malaise and trauma from playing in the shadow of what they and their fans had all experienced just four days previously, these were nervous times for both teams and Ensideleigh were feeling the pressure too. Just two penalty goals split the teams as chances had been spurned time and again.

Patsy arrived as the teams trooped off for half-time. She'd seen plenty of football matches at some of the biggest grounds around, but had never experienced a rugby league match and never one in a setting such as this.

Parrot Lane, with its now even humbler surroundings, was a new and presently far from edifying experience for the girl currently using two names. Patsy made her way to Colin and Bill as the players were leaving the field at the end of the first half.

The makeshift dressing rooms were so cramped the players looked more likely to become injured inside rather than out on the paddock. The feeling was totally flat. Everyone going through the motions. The game had come way too soon after Sunday's nightmare.

Phil Trippett sensed his rallying call was about to fall on largely deaf ears. But he gave it his best shot. As he manufactured his pearls of wisdom, he looked into the whites of the eyes of the squad. The players weren't there at all. It was as though post traumatic stress had taken hold. Impending doom covered him for a matter of two seconds. The Trippett brain needed to step up a gear. He tried. They'd been in good spirits on the training run earlier, but this was different.

"Don't let all we've worked for in these past couple of weeks go just like this, guys. Those fans out there didn't come along tonight to see you just walk through a game. They want passion, commitment..."

As he said it, he knew it wasn't working, knew that no

matter what he said would have no effect. He went for damage limitation instead.

"Come on, boys. Do it for your own pride and the fans'."

The energy and enthusiasm that had charged the dressing room in recent times was gone. They just wanted this game out of the way. Greg didn't help, couldn't help. This had been his opportunity to let things slide. He'd told himself that he needed to get behind Phil, to back up what he was trying to get across, but whatever positive thought came to him was beaten back by a thought of self-preservation, not just for himself, but the team, his family, everyone. He was also still battered, bruised and partially broken from what had happened to him after the game, something only Bill, Col and Patsy knew. He'd made sure he'd changed alone before the others had arrived in the dressing room.

The players who had started dragging the club out of its terminal decline and had been motivated since Greg took over, hauled themselves slowly from the Portakabin dressing room. Greg replaced his gumshield. He avoided eye contact with Trippett as he went.

Phil Trippett was no fool and didn't suffer those who took him for being one at all gladly. Every other time, Greg had glanced back to him with a smile or a wink as the rest had left the changing room. Not this time. Perhaps Greg was suffering more from the after-effects of last Sunday than Trippett had realised, but he reckoned there was something more. He let it pass.

CHAPTER 39

Jeff Markham's temporary dose of infatuation and curiosity was about to change the course of his life.

Jenna Howells had begged further questioning. She had as good as begged him to stay. Jenna Howells. Not her name. Markham had enjoyed her company and she was after something. He already knew she was not who she said she was. He wanted to find out more.

Tracking her would be easy, so long as he kept his distance. She wouldn't know, like many before her, that here was a master stalker, for editorial reasons, of course. Jeff had found out more by trailing and watching than most had ever done by listening.

Her car had been another factor. He'd seen her on arrival and watched now as she collected her Jaguar from the newspaper's car park, whilst he sat at the wheel of his Audi 80. He'd taken a quicker route through the building and had been in his car by the time she had walked round.

The Jag didn't match the image of someone who was supposedly collecting fairly average information, but he could let that ride for a moment. Maybe she had a wealthy father, husband or boyfriend in the background, some sort of marriage break-up settlement? Maybe her job was real? No. That wasn't right.

He'd pumped her car registration details into one of his reliable sources within seconds. He'd had his answer two minutes later. Registered owner Patsy Previn. He'd then pumped her name into social media accounts, had found her on various, had seen her with her boyfriend – Colin Duggan – who had an account, but didn't use it regularly. From there the trail followed to Hopton, to the club Irvine had just bought. Within five minutes, he'd read the newspaper reports and accessed YouTube and Vimeo footage of everything that had been happening.

This was a story worth following. Jenna Howells' appearance

was nothing to do with some arty farty research. He'd known it. Five minutes later, he'd accessed and come up with a story that might just make his career. Book deal. Mini-series. Let's have it.

Patsy had rolled clear of the offices and had been soon out on to the motorway. Markham had followed, some distance back. Ten miles on and he was still following. His phone rang. Text message. He was wanted back at the paper – now! No bloody way!

Unbeknown to him, there was a third vehicle in their mini-convoy loitering just a quarter of a mile back.

Patsy drove on oblivious to the two cars in her wake. Her thoughts now on how she had had a far from enlightening day, with the ogling Jeff Markham being her only real insight into Irvine.

Markham ignored the message.

Bill and Colin had been careful over their talk in Irvine's hospitality kabin whilst Irvine was regaling his guests – and when Patsy joined them the three busied themselves with food and drink.

"*They're not exactly hitting it off are they,*" she whispered to Colin as she watched Irvine and Caill having what appeared to be a heated exchange, albeit without the volume to make it the centre of attention.

"*Look at them. I know Irvine from what we've seen in the* Messenger *and on telly, but who's this other one. The one who looks like a weasel…*"

Colin couldn't help but smile and acknowledge the comparison as he looked. Bill had heard the analogy and guffawed more noticeably. Once he had calmed slightly, Colin responded.

"*Name's Caill. Runs the brewery. Caill's Ales. Hopton's become the equivalent of a one-horse town in a lot of ways now, biggest employer and Caill's the owner of the horse, or was – I'm not sure what he is at the moment…*"

"*You think it's something to do with Caill?*" Patsy's day, whilst fruitless in most respects, had left her undaunted.

"*I don't know Pats,*" he said almost under his breath. "*It's definitely money, has to be greed. But whether or not it has anything to do with your ... weasel...*" he paused again more for dramatic effect and with a wry grin, "*...not sure. But why would he turn up now ... maybe a bit suspect?*"

Patsy took up the conjecture. "*And why make an attempt at stage managing some friendship which obviously doesn't exist. He's sly.*"

Bill added what he knew.

"*They've had run-ins in the past.*" He stopped to check on how his voice was carrying, but he needn't have worried.

"*Bryan Caill's only ever got one thing on his mind ... himself.*" It was said in such a derisory manner that Patsy wondered how far the hurt went. Had Bill suffered at the hands of Caill? Bill added more.

"*Right from the start, Bob ... Irvine ... has had big ideas. He's different. Wants to build something here, wants a new stadium, better look and feel to the whole place... Not straight away, but as soon as he can...*"

"*Not exactly the acts and thoughts of someone who only wants money out of the place. Sounds like he's true to his word.*" It was easier to see 'the weasel' as the bad guy.

Markham had parked up since Patsy had arrived at the ground and was sat in the car park at Parrot Lane, waiting, assessing, watching for the next move. Hopton Town, Irvine, the newspaper, Irvine's other interests, Jenna, odd questions, along with the rest of what he had heard and knew about Irvine, plus another story, another strand. Markham knew life was complex, he'd uncovered enough in the past to know one story brought about another and his sources were leading to that other story.

It was all adding up to something much bigger than he'd originally thought. Just exactly what, was still to be confirmed, but when things happened such as he'd found out at Hopton Town – the drive-by hit and runs and last Sunday's stadium disaster, plus Irvine had just got involved, then there were too many coincidences attached with a girl who he had now tracked back to the club. Too many. He sat, continued searching social media, the internet, phone, making even more contacts.

Town's second half mirrored their first and it was rather by luck than skill that they finished with two points to Ensideleigh's fourteen. Greg's relief was almost audible. He had acted out his part too, knowing that he should, and indeed could, have raised his game and that of his team. Phil Trippett hadn't been fooled at all. He was lying in wait. He held Greg back and let the rest of the lads go in.

"What the fuck do you think you're doing, Greg!"

It wasn't quiet, not even low key. This was tirade time. Trippett's voice stretched to its limit. Before Greg even had time to consider an appropriate reply, Trippett was at him again.

"There's something giving here and I want to know what's going on right now, otherwise I quit. Alright? Got it? Right, go! You've got ten seconds to tell me I'm stupid, I've got it all wrong. Go."

Trippett was in his face, watching every mannerism, facial movement, giveaway eyes.

True, he hadn't pushed himself, hadn't given it his all. But Greg had banked on the fact that no-one really gave them a prayer, that sympathy would be all theirs, regardless of the result. It was just his luck to have employed someone who saw through him instantly. The reply to Phil wasn't forthcoming. He couldn't tell him.

Trippett reeled away – but not in the direction of the Portakabin dressing rooms, instead heading straight for the car park. *"Don't bother, Greg ... I'm gone."* He left the words trailing in his wake.

Helpless wasn't the word for Greg's feelings. Trippett was walking out on him. Just as he had got one monkey off his back by losing a game, he now had another problem. Shit, why couldn't he see the next thing before it kept hitting him smack bang in the face! Should he stop him? What could he do? All he felt he could do was to let him go for now. Maybe tomorrow he could make it right.

"Come on, Greg, mate. We'll do it you know! We're not going to give up now." Kenny Lomax had just seen Greg at his most despondent since the Aussie's arrival at Parrot Lane. All Greg could do was give a tight-lipped half-smile, via a slight nod as Lomax patted him on the shoulder.

Jeff Markham may well have had the eye for Jenna, but he sure as hell wasn't blinded by the fact. He had interviewed many a pretty lady in his time, but his passion had always been for 'the big story' rather than anything else. He wasn't about to be deterred now. Jenna wasn't the story. He would follow, watch her movements, who she talked with.

Markham's single-mindedness was legendary. He wasn't a team player and if he wanted to get a story he would often do it all himself. Kraft knew that too. He'd had Markham's questioning of Ms Howells reported to him.

From there, Kraft had washed his hands of the affair. Whatever happened to Markham, good man on the paper that he was, became of no consequence to him. What Markham hadn't realised was just how big this story really was.

When the bullet pierced his skull as he sat in the Hopton Town car park, he had the first and last indication of its scale. He slumped forward on to the steering wheel.

CHAPTER 40

Markham had been parked on the outer edge of the car park. No other vehicle within fifteen yards. Sitting duck for his assailant or assailants in the black car that had followed him through the afternoon and middle evening. As the ground emptied, no-one gave a thought to the car in darkness in the corner.

"It's like this, Greg. Everyone Bill and I have spoken to haven't wanted to talk, but when we've questioned them further and explained what has been going on, a few have opened up a little. The news is they have been paid off to keep quiet. That's not just the consortium. Everyone who's had money in the club in the past four years."

Colin looked over to Bill for him to nod approval. Bill was next up.

"George Ramsbottom didn't tell me how much he got, but it looks like he was well looked after for keeping his mouth shut. Probably got the lodge out of it, to keep Town losing."

It was time for Patsy's enthusiasm to bubble over next.

"...and then along comes Bob Irvine – a man with a whole lot of money – prepared to resurrect Hopton Town, make it great. Buys out the consortium and Bob's your uncle. Everything in the garden is rosy for the team..."

"...except that someone is extremely upset. A big fish has come into the water – Irvine – just when this someone had neutralised all of the others in his pool. He's very angry, and because he can't, or won't, attack the big fish directly, he looks for another angle..." Colin took a breath whilst Bill took over.

"...point of least resistance. Look for the weak area, keep up the pressure..." Bill was looking directly at Greg. He continued.

"And you're it, Greg. Easy target, soft option, wife and kids – scare the living shit out of them and you, put you right off your game – concentration shot to pieces. Give you and everyone associated with

*you more and more things to worry about, so that there's no way you
or your team can perform…"*

All three of Greg's aides were now maintaining their stare
at him, occasionally looking to each other for support as they
kept their voices restrained yet audible in the lounge bar of The
George & Dragon – a rural hostelry just outside Hopton where
the landlord's pub quiz night had just finished with a win for the
soon-to-be announced as next chaser on TV programme The
Chase, Lorna Salter picking up yet another bottle of red wine.

Greg covered his face with his right hand and breathed
deeply, then moved his hand to cover his mouth whilst looking
at Colin. The index finger came to rest under his bottom lip as
the hand cupped his chin.

*"But why? OK, I get it that someone's trying to scare the living
shit out of me, but what's it about? Money? Like you said?"*

*"And it is, Greg. Someone – the someone who's done all the
scaring – wants Hopton to fail…"* Colin continued looking
straight at Greg.

*"…and whoever it is, they are prepared to do whatever they have
to do…"* Colin looked over at Bill, who nodded once again as
Greg asked the question.

"You got any idea who?"

"We can't be one hundred percent," said Bill – and then leant
closer to Greg. *"Did you notice who was watching you tonight, from
in the hospitality area?"*

Greg had been too busy with the match – and then trying to
track down Phil Trippett afterwards on his phone – to notice
anyone else. He'd sent a text.

"Caill was here, Bryan Caill." It meant little to Greg. Of
course, he knew of Caill's Ales and that Caill was a name in
local circles, but he'd probably not been playing for Town the
last time Caill would have ever been seen at a match.

"We think Caill's involved somewhere, Greg," said Colin. *"It
only really clicked tonight when we saw him and Irvine together. But
everything starts falling into place when his name goes in the frame."*

Bill took up the piece.

"Like you've told us, Greg, the frighteners are on to ensure that Town finishes bottom. Now, what we've been short of is why finishing bottom is so important. Sure, we know what it means in the sense of being chucked out of the league, but we now know there's a whole lot more to it than that."

Bill looked to Colin once again. They were double-teaming this. Colin was next.

"Being chucked out of the league means that, officially, so far as the league is concerned, you're not classed as having a professional club, even if you continue to pay players in some way and carry on in a lower league. Bill has been going through all club record-keeping and found this."

"When use of the ground was granted, back in about 1913, it was stipulated by this wording emailed over…" And he read an extract from the paper copy:

"Use to be continuous ad infinitum for as long as the club (Hopton Town RLFC) carries on with a professional rugby league team in a professional league run by a professional body and to represent this town with honour and endeavour. If the club ceases to be regarded as such, being a professional rugby league team in a professional league, ownership of said land shall revert back wholly to the owner or owners. Should the owner or owners then see fit to allow the club (Hopton Town RLFC) or any other club to carry on usage of the ground a new restrictive covenant shall be applied."

"It was signed by Titus Caill."

"So if Town finish bottom, it seems the door is open for the owner of the ground to take it back in hand. Caill. Town might not be finished as a club, but with no assets, another ground to find and pay for, buildings and grandstands to be erected and with a fanbase of 500, it's not looking clever."

Colin paused for both breath and a sip of his long dormant pint.

"And that's it. Someone wants Town to fold so they can use that clause to get the ground. And, of course, the ground is worth millions for development…"

Greg was trying to take it all in – whilst at the same time

trying to come to terms with Phil Trippett's walk-out. He shook himself back on to their wavelength. Bill carried on.

"What we're saying is Bryan Caill must know of this technicality in the contract for the ground and is perhaps aiming to use it to get rid of Hopton Town completely. There's no proof."

"You see the ground's everything," said Colin. *"Without it the club has no asset, or very little. Whoever lays claim to the ground, being the rightful heir, can do what they like with it within reason. Our guy reckons the Town Council has some say in the matter, because of the way the contract was drawn up, but he can't be certain.*

"The land was given on that stipulation, and without professional sport it would pass back into the hands of those who had granted the use in the first place – leaving nothing for the club. With no money, no ground and no league status, Irvine wouldn't be around and there's very little way Hopton could carry on," said Colin. Bill nodded in silent, resigned agreement.

Greg was getting there and offered up a thought.

"Unless Irvine's in on it too in some way."

"Not from what we've seen tonight. Or at least if they're in it together they've just made a pretty decent fist of not showing it here, the way they behaved."

"So Caill gets it back then?"

"Yeah," was Bill's response.

"But we're pretty sure he's not behind what's been going on. He's not got the guts from what we're told, which begs the question." Bill picked up his glass once more.

"Who?" said Greg.

"We'll find out tomorrow," said Colin. *"Patsy and I are going to do another spot of digging – this time around the Caill empire. Get a picture of what's what and who's who. Look into the family…"*

"Because if it's true. If Caill really does have ownership if you finish bottom, then he could close down the club and do what the hell he likes with the land … make a mint…" was Bill's latest retort.

"So where does Irvine fit into all this then? I almost wish he had something to do with all this, 'cause the guy's starting to get right on

my tits."

This brought Patsy's turn.

"He seems clean, but…"

"But there's far more to it than that, isn't there, Ms Previn?"

It was a different voice. An interjection from outside of the four who were huddled together round a table in the manner in which you would have expected of Guy Fawkes' Gunpowder Plot conspirators.

DI Will Gill's voice was part learned, part thickly northern. Greg introduced him to the fold. The look on Gill's face told them something was not right before the words came.

Hopton could never have been described as the crime capital of the north – nor any place else for that matter and Gill was hardly some hotshot uptown TV homicide cop from the States. He seemed naturally mild mannered. He stood, firm-lipped for a matter of seconds. It was one of those moments where it seems an eternity.

Greg sensed some other disaster had occurred. Bill sensed it too.

Patsy felt the pressure. Gill's first words had been directed at her. This visit had something to do with today's exploits. She stiffened her back, sitting straight, prepared to take the news.

Gill had never wanted to be the stereotypical copper and wasn't. He preferred to get things done his way. The George & Dragon was as good a place as any.

"There's a dead body in the club car park," he was playing it tight, straight-laced. *"We believe you may be able to identify it."*

CHAPTER 41

"We know you were with Mr Markham this afternoon…"

Gill watched for anything. A flicker. A sign.

Patsy looked down. Avoiding eye contact with Gill or Colin, Greg and Bill, who had all come along with her and were now ensconced back in the hospitality Portakabins at Parrot Lane. Gill hadn't chosen the police station. He wanted to keep things informal. And he wanted Greg there.

Patsy hadn't been ready for this. How could she have been? Up until now, it had all been pretty much a game. Serious, but quite good fun actually. Pretending to be someone different, getting into her Jenna Howells role had been invigorating.

Only now did she realise just how real death was – and, it seemed, murder. But then she was no wallflower either. She knew that, from what Colin and Greg had talked about in the past days, even more danger could befall any of them if they were to involve the police.

"You know, don't you, that we could easily just do this down at the station." He hated the cliched way it had come about and winced inwardly at his own phraseology. Equally, he had no intention of taking them to the station.

There was plenty of action outside. Hopton Police were sealing off the club car park and once again, for the second time in a week, Hopton's ground was the scene of circus-style press activity as more local and national media descended for yet another slice of mayhem, except this time it was one of their own.

Greg wanted to say something. Patsy and Colin were only involved because of him. They were making headway in their own investigations. Keep quiet.

Colin took the lead. Desperate as he was to help his brother, this was Patsy getting a grilling and he didn't like it one bit.

"We were trying to find out more about Irvine because of what

had happened here with the explosions. Patsy went over to Castlegate to check out some of his business interests there ... check him out..."

It was enough to get things rolling again. Gill started once more.

"So, you met Mr Markham? During this afternoon?"

"Yes." She was beside herself as to how they had known that she would recognise him. How? Had they been following? She felt she had checked using the rear view and wing mirrors, to see whether anyone was following her.

"How did you know? That I would know him?" Her voice faltered. She wanted to know that her cover had not been blown, needed some form of reassurance. Gill wasn't ready to give any information.

He felt in sparkling mood. He enjoyed this moment where they saw him peeling back the layers wherever they led.

"You were talking with a journalist Ms Previn – or should I call you Jenna?"

It was meant to throw Patsy and it did. How the hell? How could he know? Patsy went for him before she analysed thoroughly.

"DI Gill. I spent time with Mr Markham in a pub across the way from the Castlegate Press Group. I was interested in finding out more about Mr Irvine. We chatted. I was at the Castlegate Mail around 2.30. Mr Markham and I must have left there about 2.35. We were in the pub, The Scribe, I think, for about half an hour. I never saw him again. That's it. As much as I know."

"What did you talk about?"

"I've just told you. Irvine."

"And?"

"And nothing. Well not much. Just told me he was your typical businessman. Useless really. We had a glass of wine, or I did, think Mr Markham had a Coke. End of."

Gill stood from where he had been sat, with Patsy directly opposite him across a small table and Patsy's co-conspirators just over to one side, on three small stools. Taking up his coat, which draped across one of the other chairs, he took his leave. He'd heard enough from Patsy and earlier in the day Bill and Greg. He had other fish to fry and people to see. He wasn't angry when he uttered his next missive, just matter of fact, but with enough of a threat and without giving away what he already knew.

"I'm going to find any way I can to get all this mess sorted out and who is responsible here. Personally, I don't think any of you knows what you're into, running about playing private investigators. I know you don't want to let me in, but believe it or not, I can't help you if you don't. I'll be saying goodnight."

He turned toward the door and on reaching for the handle and opening the door turned again, clearly this was his stock in trade.

"He had your name on a text and your number on his log of his phone in the car. He'd been searching you as Jenna Howells and some other company name you'd given. This is murder, Patsy. Who's going to be next before you, Greg and your cronies start taking some real advice and talking to the right people, instead of playing crimebusters?"

Gill raised his eyebrows as if to accentuate the futility of what the gang of four had done so far.

CHAPTER 42

"No ... no more ... call 'em all off now ... this is far too much ... well, why the hell did you let it happen ... he was a journalist, for God's sake ... don't you threaten me ... I'll..."

The other end of the conversation hung up. There had been more. Murder was a new territory, at least for one of them.

The town's library. Erected, like many such creations, in the Victorian era, it stood just off the main drag of Hopton High Street. Its dark imposing exterior led to an even darker morbid interior. It had provided learning, reading and a place of peacefulness for all, but had long since been ignored in terms of revitalization and renovation in favour of investment in a fun-pool, ice rink and multi-million pound projects designed to keep the populate in the area for the future.

Colin, Patsy and Bill were already there poring over any scrap of evidence they could find that would give them the additional information they needed about Caill and his forbears. Colin had taken on the library's microfiche-stored records; Patsy was trawling through similarly stored copies of the *Messenger*; and Bill was checking out any other source he could possibly think of – books, biographies, local histories. They'd been under way hours, having arrived full of vigour when it happened. Each was in a separate area of the expansive ground floor and all were becoming increasingly exasperated with their lack of success.

Bill had thought he could smell something. One of those moments when you sense the smell before your brain calculates danger. No alarm bells had sounded in his head. Now they were ringing out clear and long! Suddenly his head was pounding. From the nothingness of seconds prior, it felt like he was about to explode. The heat was quick, his veins bulging. In the split second between feeling the heat and taking in what was happening, the fireball struck. One second heat, next second the rolling ball of fire. There was no time to run.

Bill fell to the floor.

"He'll be fine. Just needs rest … and a little time to himself…"

It was a line delivered pleasantly enough as Bill opened his eyes. He was now on a bed, a hospital bed. He quickly deciphered he had no burns, peeling flesh or blisters. What happened? Fireball? He looked over to see Colin and Greg happy to see him and confirming he was indeed in the land of the living, in hospital, in casualty. Bill raised his eyebrows then frowned and raised his eyebrows again. It was enough to let Colin and Greg know what he was asking.

"You passed out," said Greg.

"Just passed out while you were looking at stuff and fell off your chair into a heap," said Colin.

"They thought you were dead," was Greg's next matter-of-fact contribution.

"But you weren't and you're not are you?" said the bright, bubbly voice of Patsy as she took her place alongside the two brothers, handing each of them a coffee.

"Patsy said the nurse heard you mumbling something about a fire when you came round…" said Colin.

Bill didn't want to answer for fear of making himself look foolish. Hopefully, there was no way anyone would know about his passing out incident in the Lake District as well. What the hell was wrong with him? He'd never suffered from anything like that before.

"How long have I been here?"

"About half an hour," Greg replied. *"But you've got to stop while they take a look over you … observation … better safe then sorry…"*

"Right. We'd better crack on," said Colin as he and Greg made as though to leave.

"And don't worry, Bill. You get yourself right first."

It was the most upbeat and animated Greg had been for weeks. It was only at that moment it fully registered to Bill that Greg hadn't even been at the library and that he must have dreamed up the fireball somehow while passed out. Something like that anyway. He shook his head. So how had Greg got there? Colin noticed the slightly quizzical look on Bill's face at that split second and solved his puzzle.

"We called Greg. Came straight here, got here five minutes before you opened your eyes. True love. Man to man, of course."

Bill was out of the team to track down Caill, or whoever they needed to get to in order to work out what was happening and stop it from going any further.

Whilst Colin, Greg and Patsy had put on a brave face at the hospital there was no denying their anxiety as they left.

"Do you reckon he knows?"

"Nah, no chance."

"It'll be a hell of a shock for him…" The remaining three of the quartet debated Bill's condition from what they had just been told in morose fashion as they made their way out of the hospital. His blackout had been more than just passing out, the doctor's opening thoughts had offered little in the way of hope based on previous knowledge and experience.

The Caill residence was as grand a setting as you would find in and around Hopton. Caroline House – so named after Bryan Caill's grandmother – looked fantastic as you approached from the estate gates. The house was approximately a mile away, but the closer you reached, the more dilapidated the main features became. Castellated walls surrounding the house were in a forlorn state and two-thirds of the grand country manor were crumbling. If ever there was a need for the *Restoration* TV programme, this was it. It was a shock to them all.

Rather like his house, Bryan Caill's world was crumbling. Caill's Ales was in a parlous financial state. Where once his grandfather Titus Caill had built a business running sound and true, founded on strong values and iron discipline to the task in hand that his father Clive had carried it on to greater heights, Bryan Caill had enjoyed too much prosperity, too much silver spoon, too much of everything. It wasn't enough that he had never had to work for his wealth, he had also felt everyone should automatically cow-tow to his every word. He had money.

The world had changed. Landscaped gardens had now become bedraggled and once oh-so-carefully manicured lawns were out of control as succession after succession of estate gardeners parted company with the man who had managed to destroy, single-handedly, three generations of goodwill.

Bryan Caill's life was in ruins, and the family business wasn't far behind. He'd been the only child of Clive and Corinne Caill, making him the sole benefactor once both had been laid to rest. He had married – twice, neither time with prenups – and both marriages had failed. His more latterly realisation that they had only married him to see how much they could get out of him may have been true, but his lifestyle hadn't helped. Neither saw him again, apart from in court, where both walked away with a huge slice of the family fortune. You can only have so many huge slices before the cake is gone.

Bryan Caill had been left with his ever-decreasing group of family friends, who sought to advise him wisely, despite his ignorance and arrogance, and his business associates – an assorted ensemble of sycophants who, without his ever being aware, had bled him dry over the years. That, plus a further complication of his unhappy knack of backing horses that must have all been three-legged and a roulette wheel that never fell in his favour, had brought about a continuous downward spiral that would inevitably lead to oblivion.

The first Caill knew of it was the smell. He had been poring over various last-ditch attempts to save face for weeks, sell the business outright to perhaps foreign or any money, pay off the debts – some hope! – and start a new life when the fumes hit him. Petrol! Then he saw the black saloon disappearing.

Get out quick. His office led straight out on to the lawn. He gathered up papers, books, valuables, laptop, cell phone, then made a dash for it.

He then checked his thoughts, mind racing through all possible alternatives, and threw all his papers back inside the room he had just vacated.

"For Fuck's Sake!"

Greg, Colin and Patsy were half way down the mile-long driveway to Caroline House, approaching Caill, when the black saloon hurtled past Colin's on-coming four-wheel drive Land Rover Discovery. It had sped by on the grass. Greg's exclamation amply summed up the group, but it was the combined voices of all three that followed as the house came into view that brought the day's events to a nerve-jangling hiatus.

Colin's comment was understated in the extreme, as he whispered *"Fuck me"* under his breath; Patsy restrained herself admirably with a *"Jesus Christ!"*; and Greg let out an elongated *"Shiiit."* The house was fully ablaze. Reds and yellows of the flames contrasted brilliantly with the now towards dusk setting of Thursday evening, as though this were all some sort of stately home bonfire night.

They had come to quiz Caill. Shortly before Bill's collapse, it had been Colin who had found a vital missing piece of the jigsaw in legal records. The ground would indeed revert to Caill's control if he exercised the clause in the restrictive covenant – and he would do exactly that!

He needed the money. Caill's Ales was in deep financial trouble.

Companies House records showed that Caill's Ales and its overall holding company Caill Enterprises was in meltdown, but even more local evidence had come by pure chance when they had resumed their searches after ensuring Bill was comfortable in hospital.

Patsy had been chatting with one of the senior librarians, Christina Borrow. If ever there had been a more apt name. It turned out her husband, Gordon, had worked as one of Caill's odd-job men for years.

"Gordon would never work for him again, I can tell you that," said Mrs Borrow. *"For one thing, he treated him, and all the people he employed, very badly, and secondly, he's gambled away what was left of the family fortune that he hadn't already frittered away elsewhere. Word has it he's trying to sell off anything he can to pay off his debts and even if he does sell everything he'll still be short."*

"You bastards! You evil bastards!"

Hardly the words Greg, Patsy or Colin anticipated hearing on venturing closer to the half-ablaze house. There was no-one else around. No staff – hardly surprising really given Caill's attitude they were now fully aware of – just him. And he was coming for them! Coming their way.

It was Caill at his worst, most intimidating. His voice seemed too strong for what must have been no more than his nine and a half stone frame. He was in their faces now.

"What the fuck do you think you're doing? You don't do you? You don't know what you've done…"

He gestured back in the direction of the flames. He was right, it was too late. Far too late for any rescue mission to save what was inside.

"Mr Caill, we…" But Colin's words were drowned out by the noise coming from the blaze, the sound of windows shattering all around, and the heat that was forcing them back from the house where they had come within 25 yards.

"Just go…"

Caill began making his way to the black Mercedes parked far enough away from the house on the gravel driveway. Colin, Greg and Patsy were not to be deterred. All three followed Caill, with Patsy next to attempt the questioning.

"Mr Caill. We need to know what you're doing … and why you're doing it…"

Another window shattered, splintering glass in their general direction.

"Why the hell have you got people making Greg's life a misery? Why all the bully boy tactics just to make sure the club finishes bottom?"

She saw Caill's desperate look.

"We know about your debts and why you need it to happen, but why all the rest, why not just cut a deal? If the ground's yours, why not cash it in anyway if you need the money?"

Caill looked incredulous.

"You really haven't a clue, have you?" And then Caill turned

the situation on its head by reaching for his mobile. *"Hello. Yes..."* And with an ironic grin aimed at the trio, he continued, in now slightly more fraught manner.

"...this is Bryan Caill. My house is on fire, so get your bloody skates on, if you're not here in five minutes it won't be worth bothering ... good ... oh, and by the way, I've got the culprits right here in front of me..."

At which point he was reaching for the car dashboard, opening it, and next brandished a hand gun in their general direction – and flicked shut the mobile phone.

By way of Greg's call on seeing the fire as they approached, rather than response to Caill's call, the ringing of fire engine bells and police sirens accompanied the next seconds. They were entering into the grounds. Three-minute response, pretty impressive.

Greg wasn't fazed by Caill's cowardice or what Caill had felt was his own clever play and the gun was propelled from him as Greg managed to fracture Caill's cheekbone in three places, it would be later found, with one swift hit.

There had been little time for Caill to realise what was coming. No time to even think about pulling a trigger. Indeed, it had been so long since he had put the gun into the car that he hadn't even remembered whether or not it was loaded. It was of little consequence now.

"Fuck off out of here!"

He was clutching at his cheek, but Greg wasn't finished. He stood over the prostrate, pitiful figure, picked him up by his neck using just his right hand and, eyeballing him straight and true, headbutted him smack on the nose. Blood erupted like lava from a volcano as Greg released his grip and the 'weasel' slumped to the ground in an ungainly heap.

Now it was Greg's turn for words.

"You've screwed up my wife's life, fucking well killed my unborn kid, nearly killed my lad, nearly had my physio killed, fans' lives and their families' lives close to ruin. You're the bastard Caill. And all for what? For this? You stupid bastard. Call off your guys now and get

out of my fucking life!"

Greg's words had become harder, harsher, delivered more raspingly as he had gone on. This had been the release he'd sought. Caill's reaction to their arrival had been disgusting. To then pick up the phone and try to frame them and then pull the gun! What was he on?

"Come on, Greg, let's go."

Colin was ready to shepherd his brother out of the way. It was time to regroup, get life back to normal if they could. He'd thought he'd got his brother under control earlier, talking about what they would do when they got to Caill's place, but they'd not been ready for this, none of them.

The fire, Caill's venom, Greg's response. This was getting too much. He couldn't blame his brother for reacting in the way he had. Caill was a bastard, true enough, but Greg's rearrangement of his face in one immense hit wasn't going to set everything straight, not straight away.

Caill hadn't bargained on the gung-ho approach of Duggan to his own gung-ho activity, but it had paid dividends. Cheek bones and noses were painful, but not as painful as a stretch inside that Duggan may well be looking at for arson and GBH.

However, this was a high price to pay. He didn't want to lose his house, but who knows, it might work out better than even he had anticipated.

Patsy saw the look. She softened their approach. *"Why have you done all these horrible things to Greg's family and the club, Mr Caill?"*

Caill welcomed the fire engines and police cars with all the bonhomie of a father greeting his prodigal son.

Colin noticed there was something too confident about Caill's approach to the whole matter. He was too cock-sure that this would all go his way. Caill knew he had the situation under control and Colin knew it too, but he didn't quite know how.

Caill got there before any of the emergency troops disembarked. It was clear he was not going to stand around.

"Thank you for coming so promptly, gentlemen. These are the

people you need to be talking with, caught them skulking around, just a shame I didn't find them before all of this…"

He'd shifted easily from utter ogre to good-natured, mild-mannered high life as though his persona was meant to be this way. No wonder he had survived so long. Greg wasn't having any.

"He's way off beam…"

"Like this is way off beam, eh?"

Caill pointed towards his face. *"Well, he certainly wasn't way off with this was he…"*

Greg was seething. *"He's a bloody nutter."*

"Just ask him how I got this. And how come he's here with his cronies just when this happens."

The panoramic gesture went towards the flame-grilled building that was now being doused by half a dozen water hoses and a dozen firefighters. *"I rest my case."*

Caill's assuredness was there for all to see. He knew he held all the aces. Greg held nothing. They were on his land.

Patsy had admired Greg, seeing him in full sail. She'd wondered about him. How come he hadn't blown before now? He'd looked resigned, defeated, nothing like what you would expect from someone who was involved in competitive sport. Now she'd seen him in action she liked it. Colin was solid, analytical, dependable – he was what she wanted. But she couldn't help but feel a certain tingle when Greg had launched himself at Caill while he'd held the gun.

A further car drew up into the now crowded gravelled area in front of Caroline House. The figure that appeared from it was familiar to all. He stepped out, took a look straight across at Greg, Patsy and Colin. Greg lowered his head and put his hand on his chin, his eyes looking right back at DI Will Gill.

Gill made his way toward the trio. *"One short today? Don't you lot normally hunt in fours?"*

Caill was immediately on the case. *"DI Gill. Will. Thanks for coming so soon. I think you're going to want to talk with these three…"*

Gill was ready for him. He'd seen Caill in action many times and it was always the same. *"Mr Caill."* He delivered it with the abruptness that was meant to tell Caill he should not expect him to do anything other than his job. And then he turned back to Greg.

"Mr Duggan. Enlighten me. This your work?"

He motioned to the now smouldering debris that had been a proud residence since Edwardian days. Greg shook his head slowly and recognised a little deference in Gill's speech. Gill didn't exactly seem on Caill's side here, if he was on anyone's!

"We were on our way to talk with Mr Caill. As we were coming up here another car sped past going the other way. It was only once it had gone past us that we saw the fire and called it in."

Caill was amazed. *"You can't believe that! They're clutching at straws, let me tell you."*

His voice was raised to fever pitch with the realisation that his case wasn't being accepted.

Gill was handling it in a controlled manner. *"Mr Caill's face, Mr Duggan? Your handiwork?"*

"He pulled a gun on me! Self-preservation."

Greg changed his stance to face Caill. *"You jumped up pompous twat!"*

Gill was enjoying this in his own way. *"Mr Caill? A gun? You have a licence?"*

Gill's raised eyebrows suddenly gave the whole thing a more comic feel. It was hard for Patsy and Colin to repress their inner smiles.

Taking the matter quickly to summary status, Gill took a deep breath, breathed out strongly through his nose and embarked upon his oral essay.

"Mr Caill." He stopped momentarily, for effect, biting just on the inside of his lower lip. *"Just to be clear … you appear to be accusing Mr Duggan (G), Mr Duggan (C) and Miss Previn of setting fire to your house. And…"*

He motioned Caill to keep quiet at this point in the proceedings. *"You are accusing Mr Duggan,"* he pointed to the correct one, *"…of committing GBH on yourself."*

He paused again. The others were enjoying this. *"I am sure you know these are serious allegations and, should you wish to pursue them, any evidence to the contrary could be…"*

"You're damned well warning me off, are you?" he spluttered in rage. *"What about this?"* He pointed to his facial arrangement.

Will Gill continued. This was music to the ears of Greg, Colin and Patsy. They hadn't had much to cheer recently, but this was one small act going their way.

"…any evidence to the contrary could make things appear that you hold a grudge against these people … we have their call on log as they were approaching … you admit threatening with a lethal weapon." Another slight pause, Caill was almost ready to fill it. *"So, do you wish to press charges … or not?"*

Gill was unremitting. It was cretins like Caill that were a pain in the arse. He still hadn't learned.

"Bloody well right I do, get them off my land right now and get them locked up. Do us all a favour," but Gill interjected.

"No, Mr Caill. I wasn't asking you." He looked to Greg. *"I was asking Mr Duggan here. Brandishing a lethal weapon, causing affray, threatening with a loaded weapon, intent to kill …"*

Caill was apoplectic now. *"Oh, don't be bloody stupid, man! I'd never have gone any further than that. What do you think I am? Some kind of common murderer?"*

Caill was livid. It was about time he turned the heat back on Gill.

"I'll be having a word with Commander Allison about this." The finger pointing at Will Gill was absurd. The emotions of a boy saying his dad was going to get your dad. Gill played it straight and calm.

"If you're referring to my superiors, sir, I would be glad to assist you down to the station to talk the matter over with them personally and immediately."

"Just look at that!" He threw out his hands towards his now smouldering home in exasperation. *"Can you not see what I've been going through?"*

A little late for the sympathy vote thought Patsy. *"It's no wonder I'm stressed.*" And now louder. "*My bloody house is burning down and all you can do is stand there questioning why I've lost my rag. Wouldn't you, if your house was burning down?*"

Gill knew that irony would not help, but was beside himself not to ask in as straight face as possible. "*Insured?*" He checked his phone that had recently received a text.

"*Mr Caill. Just fifteen minutes ago, a black saloon car was seen speeding away from Caroline House in the direction of Ringstall. We have the registration, the make and the model. It certainly seems to corroborate Mr Duggan's story.*"

"*I'll be making a full and formal complaint once this has all been seen to,*" said Caill.

"*That's your prerogative, sir.*" And the head-to-head was over. Caill turned back to witness the blackness that was once his home. Remarkably, the one room that was untouched by the flames was the room he'd thrown in the papers. Bloody typical.

The Duggan boys and Patsy had exchanged nods with Gill as they turned back towards their car. It was time to regroup, work out what they had learned, find out whether they were anywhere nearer getting this whole mess cleared up, so that the club, family, friends and supporters could concentrate again on staying in the league. This hadn't done that, but they were following the money.

Lose every match, go out of the league, endure no hassle, forget or rebuild the club, it was that easy. Why not just do it? Greg had tried to meet the first part. He'd been abducted. They were now on the trail of who they needed to find. The real perpetrators. Caill wasn't going to tell them, but he must know. God knows what was to happen next, now they were getting closer. Could they find a way in the next three days before Sunday's game?

And on that score, Greg still had to make his peace with Phil Trippett.

"*Mr Duggan?*" Greg and Colin turned back immediately. "*Greg.*" Gill was coming towards them now, after having first uttered the words whilst being stood. He caught up to the party of three. *"So, what was all this about? Why come to Caill's place? What is it you've worked out?"*

After Gill's defence of them just now, Greg was more prepared than ever to open up further. But no. They still shouldn't let him in. Greg remembered the threats.

"Thank you, Mr Gill, Will, for just now. Much appreciated. We will let you know when we can."

He couldn't risk any of Caill's cronies, or whoever they were, ruining anything else. Surely to God the murder of the journalist had proved that. Violence meant nothing to them clearly. He, Colin and Patsy knew they were far more dangerous than Caill would ever be.

But how and why was Caill involved? Yes, the ground was his, but he obviously didn't have the stomach for the whole fight, to see everything through.

Gill let out a low exhalation – a mixture of exasperation and ever so slight understanding.

"Look, I'm not stupid. It doesn't look to me as though any of you are instigating what's going on, and I get that you won't talk with me because you can't..." He paused once again for effect.

"...someone's putting the frighteners on you. Watching you like a hawk. Coming here to Caill's place, you must have been on to something. Was this meant to be a showdown?"

He shrugged and held out his palms. *"Believe me, guys, I probably can help you, but you've got to let me in..."* Once again the pause. Still nothing. His face tightened, mouth tight, slight shake of the head.

"Just do me one thing. Ask for me when you need me, because if I'm right you'll need some serious help soon, whether you take it or not."

He turned back to the chaos that was still behind him – then turned back with a wry grin. Rolling his eyes at the scene.

"Glad you enjoyed the show. Stupid prick of a man."

And with another shrug, this time with an almost friendly, conspiratorial air, he moved off back to his car. In the background, Caill was now flailing his arms about at anyone who was available.

CHAPTER 43

"What have we got? Where does all today's action put us?" It was Colin who was preparing the ground for the committee of three, in between sawing off hunks of bread as Patsy threw together a concoction of grilled sausage, cucumber, lettuce, tomato, peppers, houmous and raspberries! Greg grabbed the next beers from the fridge.

Patsy sucked on her fingers as she finished putting the meal together that also included chicken and couscous.

"Well, just because Caill's so wet he needs hanging out to dry doesn't necessarily mean he doesn't get others to do his dirty work, does it? But I agree with Colin..." She was looking at Greg at the time. *"Caill doesn't look as though he has the guts. He's small-time."*

Greg was already into his second beer. *"Pulling a bloody gun on me. Stupid sod."*

"He looks even more weasel-like when you two stand next to him..." Patsy was taken with the way the brothers were now working together. *"How are Diane and Kyle doing?"* Patsy was also keen to maintain the distance between her and Greg and this was her way of doing it.

Greg had gone to see them immediately they'd left Caill's place. Things weren't going that well. Kyle was okay, Diane's father had said, but Diane was taking one step forward and then two steps back. Greg felt he should have encouraged Diane to come home, but knew he couldn't give the sort of comfort and attention she would get from her mum and dad.

"You do what you have to do, Greg", is how Diane's mum had put it, without malice, but with a little hopeful feeling they would be getting back together soon.

Although Diane never liked taking anything, she had been prescribed a series of pills to alleviate stress levels and depression. She'd started on attracting new business workwise and had always counted herself strong, but she was not in a good state. Losing Kirsty weighed on her mind.

Kyle was great though. It was as though Greg had never been away and he had spent a highly enjoyable father and son couple of hours before heading back home.

"She's good. Well, she's not good, but…" Greg's manner was enough to signal the end of that conversation. It gave him no pleasure getting into a detailed observation of Diane's plight. Partly because he didn't understand it and partly, if he was being honest with himself, he had actually started to enjoy the last couple of hours.

Gill had seemed on their side today. And, of course, there was Patsy. He couldn't help himself every time he looked at her.

Patsy gave Greg the briefest of looks, swiftly followed by a glance across at Colin to check that he wasn't watching what had happened in the slightest of moments.

And Greg was now smiling directly back at her. Had Col noticed. She thought not, but it was difficult to tell. She wondered what it was that seemed to be attracting her to Greg. I mean, what was it about him? Muscles? Yep, pretty good reason. Rippling flesh? Yep. Forget it, she didn't need any more reasoning.

"I tell you what, broth … that Gill's a real trier…" A slight pause for him to lick his fingers as he prepared for his next mouthful. *"Maybe it's time to cut him a bit of slack."*

CHAPTER 44

Bob Irvine wasn't one to let things happen around him. He was a mover and shaker and determined his Hopton project would not fail. He was also monitoring the whole media circus around the *Castlegate Mail* and what had happened to Jeff Markham. There were plans.

He'd taken on the club at a dodgy time. He craved success, but knew it had to be earned and sometimes like any business that meant making difficult decisions. He'd never had qualms about them once they'd been made.

He was at Parrot Lane when Greg arrived ready to take Friday's training session before the next game against Axby on Sunday – just three games to save their season. He'd made a point of getting there early and he'd made sure Fred was at the gate to tell Greg to see him. The car park area where Jeff Markham's body had been found was still sealed off. Police tape was everywhere. They'd covered the immediate area around Markham's car with a white and blue gazebo.

"*Greg, I'll get straight to the point…*"

Here we go, thought Greg. Another quick burst of Irvine's ideas and he'd be off.

"*Sit down a sec…*"

Greg motioned he'd be fine.

"*Greg, sit down.*" The tone was sharp, but not totally aggressive. This wasn't one of those Irvine chats, this was something more. A pause.

"*Greg, you've been under a lot of pressure…*" Irvine was watching for any reaction, "*…and I know how much this club means to you…*"

Greg could feel a 'but' coming on, "*…but…*"

Sure enough there it was! "*…But I've invested a lot of money here and I want to see this thing through. I know you don't particularly like me, and I dare say you're going to like me even less* *in a minute…"*

For someone who usually got straight to the point, Greg felt he was spinning it out.

"But I'm not out to win any personality contests. I just want results … That's why I'm taking away the coaching responsibilities from you. Phil takes over today. And I'm making Kenny Lomax captain."

Irvine stopped. Greg took a deep breath, through his nose, tight lips. He ran his hands through his hair and over his face, more by way of concentration than being distraught. He moved his right hand gradually down to his chin, felt the bridge of his nose between thumb and forefinger. What did this mean? For fuck's sake, what was this all about?

"And you're no longer taking the kicks." It was a different voice. Greg hadn't realized, there was someone in the adjoining office. The door had been ajar. Phil Trippett was back.

Irvine smiled, conciliatorily, then returned to business.

"Markham's death. Caill's fire. Your wife's accident. The ground … All the rest." He held out his hands, throwing them in the air. *"You and your brother running around the town with your brother's bit of skirt dabbling dangerously in whatever it is they are doing. There's no wonder you've ended up making mistakes…"*

He'd chosen his words carefully, but Greg knew what Irvine meant and didn't like it one bit. He shot out of his chair propelling it backwards.

Irvine stood quickly. Trippett moved forward to intercept Greg.

"I'm no fucking bottler! You come here in your fucking fancy suit! You don't know what I've been going through! And I've been keeping it together! … But this!"

"Look, I'm not saying you are. What I am saying is this. You threw that game against Ensideleigh. You know it. Phil knows it…"

Trippett released Greg from his grasp.

"Bob called me, Greg. Asked me why I'd walked out on you. When I told him what I thought you'd done, I thought that was the end of it. I wasn't coming back Greg…"

Irvine took up the story from Trippett. It was time for a calming influence.

"*I visited Bill in hospital yesterday. He's in a bad way, you know, Greg?*" Greg nodded. "*All these things that have been going on. You know, I'm hardly what you'd call impervious to them. They all mean something. So I tackled Bill, asked him what was going on, put some pressure on him, I'm not proud of that. Tackling a dying man.*" He stopped again, this time for effect.

"*So far as I know what has been going on has absolutely nothing to do with me. That's just in case you're wondering. I bought this club in good faith and, like I said, I want to win. I'm damned certain you don't want to throw games, but you've got to admit if anyone ever had a reason to, then it is you. Now what you've got to decide is this – do you want to play? – and give us your best shot – or are you going to quit? I can understand if that's what you decide.*"

"*I'm no quitter.*" It was quieter than he would have liked to have answered, but it was the best he could do. It was his natural knee-jerk reaction to the question.

"*Good.*" A quick look across at Trippett. "*Right, I'm off.*" And the leather gloves were being put back on, to add to the coat that hadn't been taken off. "*And Greg. This is the right thing to do, believe me.*"

And he was gone. The bloody whirlwind had struck and moved on again. Greg couldn't say at the time, but what the hell had Irvine done, intentionally or otherwise? Was Phil now in danger? Kenny too? How much had Bill told Irvine? No-one would ever know.

CHAPTER 45

"And the crowd responds immaculately to the minute's silence in honour of the great man."

Terry Derbyshire eulogised about Bill Garside's contribution to the Parrot Lane team in the 70s on Dalesmoor Radio, just prior to the first of Hopton's three match sequence that would decide their fate.

Bill's sister, Grace, had cut short her break in Vanuatu and had made the 26-hour flight to Brisbane and then into Ringstall International when she'd heard about her brother. She'd been at his bedside as his heart finally gave up the fight on Friday afternoon. His blackouts at the caravan site and the library had been brought on by a series of heart attacks, albeit small ones, and there had been more over a period of time in the past months. His heart had weakened so much it finally gave up.

It had been a shock to everyone. Greg, Colin and Patsy had all seen him on Friday lunchtime, following Greg having been given his marching orders from the coaching, captaincy and kicking roles.

The doctor had told them his condition was serious and there was very little they could do, but the speed of it took everyone aback. The funeral was planned quickly that same day – for Monday. Grace had to be back in Vanuatu, nothing she could do about it. A funeral had never been planned so quickly. The funeral directors and crematorium were all arranged the same Friday afternoon he'd passed away. Nothing fancy. Irvine had made sure it all happened quickly.

Greg, Colin and Patsy had all helped Grace make the arrangements. Saturday had been a sad day all round organising for Monday.

There was a deep breath after Terry Derbyshire's words following the minute's silence, allowing his own sentiments to come across the airwaves.

"*Ok, so Town will line up like this: Sissons, Goram, Rigson, Thomas, Venus, Duggan, Wainwright, Willie Hammerton, Lomax – captain today for the first time – Jeff Hammerton, Brent, Estorino and Warrener. It's a new look line-up Steve. Duggan deposed and now at stand off, Warrener at loose forward. What's the feeling in the squad going into these final games?*"

Steve Benson was Terry Derbyshire's guest at Dalesmoor Radio. "*Well, Terry, the lads are up for it. We've had an interesting week with some changes as you know, but only time will tell.*"

"*Greg Duggan, Steve? No longer coach, no longer captain, no longer kicker – if what we're led to believe is true – and switching to stand-off.*"

"*Well, Terry, Greg's pretty good wherever he plays. There's plenty of other loose forwards playing in that position these days and he could form quite a partnership with young Stu Wainwright.*"

"*Indeed he could. Thanks, Steve. So here we go, the biggest match in Hopton's history. As will be the next two after this, so long as the other results go our way. Hang on to your hats, we're following Hopton all the way!*"

It was a competent Hopton performance, a great deal better than their last debacle against Axby, just before Greg had taken over as coach for what had turned out to last just five games. But their efforts were never going to be enough.

Axby had too much in reserve when it mattered. Hopton had brought back Sissons too soon – he suffered a recurrence of an old injury once again; Vincent Venus's knock he'd been carrying for the past three games finally caught up with him big style when he just couldn't turn sharply enough to get back on defence; and Kenny Lomax – still not back to full fitness – was left flat-footed at times.

Greg and Stu Wainwright linked up well without having back-up to make the big breaks and the rest of the side gave their all, but it wasn't anywhere near enough and Axby ran out comfortable winners at 24-2. They'd now not scored a try in their last 160 minutes. Not great form going into the last two games. Possibly their last two ever.

The best news of the afternoon came a few minutes after the final hooter. Ensideleigh had lost too. Just two points still separated them. Two matches to go. But a win for Ensideleigh next week, defeat for Hopton, and the season, the club and the ground would be history.

Colin and Patsy were waiting for Greg as he came out of the dressing room. God she looked great. Greg gave a slight smile, not sufficient to show he was happy with life, but enough to give his charges a little assuredness to his well-being.

CHAPTER 46

It was as they reached the top of the stairs and the lounge area of Parrot Lane Social Club near the ground, where after-match eats and drinks were taking place, that Greg saw him. He wasn't coming towards Greg, he wasn't talking to anyone else, he was simply stood amongst a group of what looked to be business-types – three men, two women.

Whisky and Cigars! What the hell was he doing here? Colin and Patsy had walked on ahead and were at the bar, so Greg was on his own. All he could do was look directly at the man. Then a swift sweep of the rest of the room to see whether there was anyone else he recognised. He wished for the appearance of Caill or one of Whisky and Cigars' henchmen – the Klitschkos or Devito – anything to confirm they were working together. He still had Caill down as public enemy number one. Whilst keeping an eye out for his movements, Greg made his way to the bar alongside Colin and Patsy.

It was Patsy who instinctively noticed something was wrong.

"Are you alright, Greg?"

"Just thought I'd seen someone…" He felt that was sufficiently throwaway not to cause any more alarm, but Patsy had re-donned her Jenna cloak.

"Who?" As she scanned the room quickly, Colin, who had been getting in the drinks, now entered the fray.

"What did you say, Pats?"

Patsy motioned her head toward Greg. *"He's seen someone."*

Greg breathed out deeply whilst taking his pint from his brother. *"It's the guy that I told you about. The one who put the frighteners on me, did this…"* pointing to his midriff and mouth.

"But why would he be here now?" Greg was worried, he might no longer be coach, but the threats were still there and so was Whisky and Cigars, but why now? It could only be as a warning. Yet there was something else, something gnawing away in Greg's

brain. Whisky and Cigars didn't look as though he were there to eyeball him, in fact Greg wasn't even sure whether he had been clocked by the guy. He caught his brother by the elbow.

Two minutes later, the three of them were outside again.

"...*so we follow him ... find out where he goes, what he does ... and that'll lead us to who he works for...*" Colin was registering the information from Greg's account of what he felt.

"*I'll do it.*" It was the re-birth of Jenna. Whilst Patsy's last exploit in undercover work had ended in such tragic fashion for Jeff Markham, it clearly hadn't put her off. Her response was eager, yet at the same time containing just the slightest traces of doubt on her face. Colin stayed calm, looking directly at her.

"*Sure?*" It was a quick nod from Patsy.

Greg was less sure. "*Maybe it had better be me. All this is too bloody dangerous. I mean look what happened in the car park...*"

He stopped himself short of saying they should involve Gill, but that was what he was thinking. He paused, they all did. Greg put his hands through his hair again, scratched his head and walked a few paces toward the railings outside the club.

It was Colin's turn now. Firm and steady. "*You'll be no good broth. What if he spots you?*" Another pause. "*And Pats, you've already had one close call. I'll tail him.*"

CHAPTER 47

Bryan Caill's world was shattered, but they still needed him and he still needed them. The deal was done. It was logistics that needed careful management and he'd been meticulous so far. Even the fire had been planned in such a way that the insurance would have to be paid out. All his plans would soon see him clear of debt and back in a strong position. As he reflected, from his hotel bedroom, there was a knock on his hotel room door.

Greg and Patsy were taking time out. Forgotten for the moment was everything that had been going on. They grabbed wine and beer and moved through from the kitchen to the sitting room back home. Colin would call when he could.

Telephone calls were being made fast and furious from all corners of the Irvine media empire. Irvine had presently ruled himself out of contact after having given strict orders through the newspaper, radio, TV, social media and Internet teams he had at his disposal to find out just what in hell's name was going on at Hopton. And find Jeff Markham's killer.

Elsewhere in a committee room further afield from Hopton, Ringstall or anywhere connected with Greg, Patsy and Colin, a throng of suited gentlemen and well-heeled ladies covened in a meeting.

"Ladies and gentlemen, you have tonight's agenda in front of you. I would like to draw your attention to points four and five specifically…"

The chairman was a tall man of over 6ft with long wavy hair in the style of a lion's mane. Chairman of an important sporting institution, the man in charge.

Two games to go. Two games! Would the club be finished if they ended up bottom? Why these happenings? The ground? Diane? His abduction? The journalist? Caill? Col and Bill's letter? Greg kept going back through it all in his mind, trying desperately to find an answer.

Irvine? That would have made it easier somehow. Yet it wasn't him, was it? Why go through all of this in some elaborate hoax? Caill? All the reasons were there. Needed the cash, no affinity to the club, utter bastard. Someone else? Greg put his hand to the bridge of his nose as he tried to go through it all once again. He'd started relaxing, but it had soon turned to this.

"You'd be better off getting to bed." She said it affectionately without any allusion to anything more, but Greg couldn't help himself from arching an eyebrow in Patsy's direction. As he arched it he felt a tinge of guilt. He knew it was wrong, where he was heading with this? He knew everyone could get hurt here, but his eyes still lingered. Jeez, his brother was out fighting the cause and here he was, doing this. Patsy returned his smile.

The *Messenger* received a call. It was for Ted Brewiss. There was only one place to get hold of Ted at that time and fortunately his mobile was switched on.

"Can I have a show of hands for all of those in favour? ... Thank you ... And now those against ... any abstentions? ... That's settled then." The vote had gone the way it had been expected, but the real meeting was just about to begin. Three of the party made their way out to an ante-room just off the main hall.

"Who is this?" Brewiss listened intently and gave just one word replies. *"When?"* ... *"Where?"* ... *"Sure."*

It was enough to appease the caller, who had interrupted Ted's flow somewhat. Amazingly, to all concerned at the *Messenger*, he had joined the local gym and had been in the process of rowing the Amazon! He'd started from Peru weeks ago and had just reached Brazil.

"What the hell do you think you're doing here?" It was Caill's voice booming out to the as yet unseen interloper.

Two of the three who had just departed their meeting rested back in their leather armchairs, whilst the third member poured malt whiskies for all – Dalwhinnie.

"Let's drink to next Sunday! I believe we may well be on the threshold of a particularly pleasing future." He was a man with a stately air of breeding and arrogance. It was not something he

held in common with the others.

The man with the lion's mane countenanced caution over his colleague's seemingly over-confident attitude.

"It's not over 'til it's over, Geoff. Let's not get carried away. There's a lot could happen yet…" The third partner, smaller and stockier nodded his agreement with the mane before adding his line. "I don't even want to contemplate it until it's signed, sealed and delivered."

In the end, neither of them had to try, even though Patsy had read all the danger signs. Greg too. They'd put on the television, made a cuppa, sat alongside each other on the sofa. A hand momentarily touched another very slightly. The other reciprocated. A touch led to holding hands, led to a look, led to a kiss, led to passion, led to everything else. They had been watching the screen, kind of, but whatever was on wasn't as big an attraction as themselves.

But God this was still all wrong! So wrong! There was no justification either could make except this was here and now. They wanted each other now. It was still wrong. But the urge was too strong, overpowering everything.

Colin was the other side of the door. He'd followed Whisky and Cigars for around 30 miles before the man had pulled into the car park of Crestway International Hotel close to Ringstall International Airport. He'd pulled up on the roadside rather than following him in and was out of his Discovery and into the hotel reception before the man had even parked up. He'd spotted a bar area and had sat in such a position he could see anyone coming in. A young woman that seemed in her 20s or perhaps early 30s had entered the reception area from a corridor that he presumed led to hotel rooms.

Whisky and Cigars had met her in the lobby. Colin's vantage point hadn't been great, but when she had turned, as he left, she held a package. Jiffy bag. Which way next? Him or her? He had chosen her. He was now the other side of a door he had hoped was next to hers. Waiting. He didn't know what for. Goose chase came to mind.

Greg's phone sprung to life warbling from wherever he'd put it on charge. If it had come twenty minutes earlier it may have been better, the way life was to turn for him. He flung himself at it from the sofa leaving his and Patsy's now naked embrace in which they had remained since satisfying their combined lust. Clothing abandoned around the room. My God that had been good!

"Ted? ... What? ... Yeah? ... Fuck ... Shit, shit, shit..." He started gathering his clothing while still clutching the phone to his ear. "Yeah, yeah, right ... we'll be there..." Greg lobbed the phone on to the armchair as he started dressing.

Patsy was back awake from her drowsiness after what she too had felt had been their fabulous copulation, or at least words that she remembered uttering to keep Greg going until she reached an amazing crescendo, not just once, but several times. Her thoughts were similar to Greg's, if he'd known. That had been amazing. She shook herself back to the present.

"What did he say? It's not Col, is it? Nothing's happened to him?"

Greg shook his head. "Ted's had some sort of tip-off. Don't know what ... Wants me there! You stay here." Patsy had other ideas.

Castlegate Press Group had gathered the troops. Crime journalists, their snouts, sources, friends from every newspaper in the country – national and local – and any BBC, ITV and Sky journalists too.

The murder of a journalist, rather like the murder of a policeman, was a galvanizing factor for colleagues and the pack assembled were baying for blood. They had followed, harassed, tailed and trailed since Markham's demise and they were not going to be denied.

When Greg and Patsy came out of the house to go to Ted, both half-dressed, holding some of their clothing, cameras began popping and flashing. Despite everything, the hacks and paparazzi, regardless of any witch-hunt, loved nothing more than a juicy bit of celebrity nookie to fill a few pages and this would do nicely!

Hopton wasn't their usual venue for this kind of thing but, given the town's recent exposure, there really was mileage in a sporting personality, however small beer, being caught with his trousers down! There were only a couple of reporters and three or four photographers, but it was enough to send a message to Greg's brain that the night was set to be horrendous.

"Where did they spring from?" Patsy looked across to Greg as they turned in the direction Ted had relayed. She saw Greg's look as she drove. Turned back to face the road. *"It's OK, you know,"* she said, much calmer. *"No-one has to know. We were in your house, but I'm staying there with your brother. It'll be ok."*

"Get me out of here! No, not in the morning, I mean get me out right now!" The girl's voice was desperate. *"I don't care what you said before."* The voice raised another few notches. *"Now!"*

He'd made it to the corridor where he'd seen her previously, saw her use the hotel room key that turned out to be Room 156 – ground floor. The hotel was quiet. Colin had stayed outside the door, but would have to move soon if a visitor arrived or someone simply walking to their room. He opted for the lobby area where he could see anyone entering the hotel and with a view down the corridor to her room.

They were still short of their intended meeting place with Ted when Greg's mobile sprang to life. Patsy was driving, Greg answered quickly.

The nightmare was just beginning. It was Diane. She was in tears, but they were not of helplessness, but of a woman wronged. Christ, he'd only been on the sofa with Patsy less than half an hour before.

"You bastard Greg … how could you?" Greg had to think quicker than he would normally.

"Diane? What do you mean? I…"

"Greg. I'm not stupid…" The tears weren't far from the surface. How had she got to know so quickly? What was this all about? He was at the same time trying to get his head around what he was about to hear or see from Ted.

Patsy had kind of heard what had been said, taken in what

was going on and was shaking her head back at Greg mouthing the words, '*Deny it*'. Greg had stepped over the line before, not just with Susie and now Patsy, but Diane had never found out, so far as he knew. But now?

"*Diane … Whatever you've heard, whatever you've been told, it's not true … look, I'm with Patsy now. We're meeting Ted … talk with her if you like … yes, we have been in the same house, our house, together overnight, on our own … but that's because Colin's been busy with other stuff.*"

Greg heard the phone go dead at the other end. He looked across at Patsy, shrugging his shoulders. "*Gone.*"

Patsy showed him the photograph of the two of them coming out of his house that was now trending on social media. It didn't paint the best of pictures. Greg shook his head in exasperation, but any making up with Diane would have to wait.

Ted flashed his headlights as Patsy's Jag cast their beam on Ted's white Cadillac CT6.

The three left their two cars and made for the lobby of the Carlton, one of Hopton's better hotels.

"*Ted … What's this is all about?*" Greg was trying to decipher the purpose of their meeting. It was now around 2am. "*Why now? Why here?*"

They were inside the hotel now. "*I don't know exactly. Tip off. No more than that.*"

Ted was different to any time Greg had ever known. This was him in his real guise. He was keen to bring Greg into his world now.

"*I've reported on Town these past twenty-five years and never seen anything like what has happened these past few weeks. I get a call to come here tonight – something to do with Town, the caller said – I just had to come…*"

All very well, but why involve Greg? "*…the caller said it might be an idea if I gave you a shout too…*"

Brewiss was a hack, just like all the rest, so far as Patsy was concerned. He may have written great copy about Greg in his time, but he was still a journo. She had her own thoughts on him already.

"Did you set us up, with the paparazzi we've faced just now? You didn't need us here at all, did you? You just got us to come out of the house for the photographers."

The girl raced out of the room, down the corridor, through the lobby and out of the hotel faster than Colin had imagined. The driver must have arrived.

She wasn't hanging around. She was on the run. Colin followed. He'd now had his first full-on view of her. Attractive, 20-30-something, curvaceous, raven-haired. Overall rating, pretty much up there in the eight and a half out of ten stakes. She moved fast. He reached the door as a yellow sports car, almost definitely a Porsche, screeched to a halt by her side.

"Not my style, love…"

Ted was dismissive. Greg and Patsy were both convinced almost immediately. Greg first. Patsy perhaps a second later. Brewiss wasn't there to catch them out and he was only there for one reason – and it wasn't anything to do with what had now occurred over an hour ago, even though if it had then Greg and Patsy had already decided the best line with Diane and with Colin would be to deny everything.

The drinks, just tea, coffee and bottled water, which had been brought by a smartly dressed young man with Carlton emblazoned on his waistcoat, had largely been left untouched, apart from Ted's! He needed the water after his Amazon experience earlier.

"Did you know, I was a member of the consortium that was bought out by Irvine? Only a small amount compared to the main guys like Malky."

Greg wasn't shocked by anything anymore. He'd find out next that his mother was an alien and his father an alligator. Everything he thought was – wasn't how it really was. But hey, what difference did it make? OK, Ted had had a small monetary interest in the club, but what the heck? Patsy was quickly on the case.

"So how were you bought off, Mr. Brewiss? Presumably Mr

Irvine paid you handsomely for your share?"

"I only had a very small interest, love. What I made didn't amount to much, but those who had a good stake did well, by all accounts, like Des White, Malky. There had been an even bigger offer on the table right at last minute that had been pretty tempting."

"Other offer?" followed Patsy.

"Caill's," said Ted.

At last they had heard his name in direct connection with the shenanigans.

"Caill offered us a fabulous deal, but it was all promises, we knew he was in trouble and the likelihood was, with him, we'd never see his money."

Greg was nonplussed. Ted saw it. "We knew about his gambling, his drinking, his other activities. Christ, the man's a jumped-up little shit. We nearly went with him, but that's when Irvine came on the scene and since then you've been doing your Town version of The Great Escape. It's been great news, because we all put in to the club, not to get anything back out of it, got our money back and now you could just do the trick and keep Town going."

"All right Ted, but why are we here? And why now?"

"Caill's here. One of us found out earlier. He's been here since the fire. The tip-off is someone's after him. No clues as to who, but plenty of reasons why. Thought you might know or at least recognise the one trailing if we see him."

"We're all on the case, Greg. Whether sports, news, crime, education journos – all of us. We want this Journo killer. I'm just one of hundreds. We will find the guy. Markham was one of ours. He was found at Town, so there's a link. Irvine owns the club. He owns the newspaper Markham worked for. Caill was at the game on Sunday. Things are happening. Now someone's after Caill. We're not thinking it was Caill who took out Markham, but this other guy may lead us to the one we're after. You might be the link."

"What I don't get," said Patsy to Greg, "is why did he try to buy the club when he already owns the land."

"You mean the lease. The covenant?" Brewiss paused. "That's not all as cut and dried as he might think."

Greg was becoming even more exasperated. *"For fuck's sake, Ted, you know quite a bit about all of this for someone who hasn't said anything whilst everything else has been going on? What's all this not cut and dried stuff about?"*

"All I know for definite is something's going to happen here tonight…"

CHAPTER 48

Brent Dugarry's wealth had come from a succession of speculative, some might say lucky, breaks. He had a system. Buy cheap, sell high. A derelict country hospital that had been abandoned some years earlier when a city-oriented council saw closure and neglect as better than investment opportunity; a slither of non-productive land which ended up being slap-bang next to a proposed motorway junction; and an abandoned mill factory where the company concerned had gone into liquidation. Within six months, every purchase had been sold on for a handsome profit.

Some said he held the Midas touch. Others put it less kindly. Whatever, Brent Dugarry was always looking for the next big one. It was now a drug. This was his occupation – buying up land and property that could be sold on quickly. It often involved delicate negotiations or something heavier, sometimes involving hefty overnight, or indeed over-week stays, at some of the leading 5-star hotel establishments, heavy drinking sessions whilst making the appropriate contacts – and somewhat irksome but leisurely rounds of golf with people he disliked. But Brent had coped with it all rather well, never once truly letting it all get him down and coping with the splendiferous mundanity it sometimes afforded.

This latest negotiation had involved more than the usual level of setting up, but he had been aware that the prize more than made up for the work involved.

Geoff Quinigan had first come into contact with Dugarry over the motorway junction land acquisition. Skilled as he had been in his timing of the purchase, Dugarry had needed the expertise and inside track of a proficient, pliable and damned fine clever solicitor who had earned the respect of all around for looking after one's own first and foremost.

Quinigan came from old money by way of succession, but the

new money was handy for his own personal recreation. This was to be his and Dugarry's biggest potential earner yet. They felt they had all bases covered. Then came the call.

Greg and Patsy stayed in wait with Ted. It was now nearer 3am.

The one man Greg never expected to show came through the revolving doors that led to the reception of the Carlton. Everything about him made Greg angrier, more resolved than ever before. Bob Irvine. Greg was still sat in the reception area, but all he could hear, all he could see, was one man, one voice. Irvine was coming straight for him, ready to stand right up to him. Face to face. Greg stood quickly.

"Bloody 'ell, Greg lad, steady on…!" The small, yet extremely sturdy table, where the drinks had been perched, had just taken a severe battering as he'd attempted to get up. It wasn't Irvine.

Patsy helped Greg back into the real world. *"Enjoy your sleep?"*

Greg let out an annoyed yet embarrassed snort, with Ted settling himself back down to what was proving to be a long night. Patsy still had her mind on the Diane situation, but couldn't help but see the funny side of Greg reacting to his dreams.

Colin's vigil was nearly done. The girl and the Porsche were gone. It was whilst he was considering this in the wake of the getaway Porsche that he had his first brief dialogue of the night.

"Something wrong, sweetheart?"

Colin turned to see a stunning blonde of around 40-50 years old, wearing a pink dress with matching pink shoes who had arrived at the hotel seconds after the younger woman had gone. She introduced herself as Janey a friend of Livvy's.

Olivia, Livvy, being the girl Colin had just missed. They were both staying at the hotel, didn't say why. He couldn't ask why for fear of catching himself out.

"And your name?"

Colin was keen to call it quits for the night, but there was something here. He hadn't bought this casual banter. Just didn't ring true, but if she was playing then why not play along, see where it led.

"*Fergus … One minute everything was fine, next … this!*" Colin had entered into the spirit of the occasion. "*But hey, you win some you lose some.*" He felt she wasn't who she said she was too. Felt he'd cut his losses and get out.

"*They're on to us! It's his brother, he was just seconds away, but we're okay…*"

The yellow Porsche driver was obviously trying to be as reassuring and calming as possible – but it wasn't working!

"*I don't give a flying fuck what you think! He's on to me … and that means they can't be far behind…*" Paula, as of now, had one hopeful saving grace. Anna aka Janey.

"*Yes, of course I've told Anna what to do and say … yes, she'll be fine … But that doesn't hide the fact that, even if they know nothing else, they now know my face…*"

It was all over in a matter of seconds. A single, piercing shot that sent all three into a state of shock.

Greg reacted first. He leapt out of the hotel armchair, ran to the corridor entrance where the sound had come from. As he hammered through the double doors he stopped momentarily in his tracks. Gun. Shit, the gun! What if…?

Patsy was just beyond the doors. She'd moved quickly too! Ted was lumbering his way forward. Greg made the mistake of turning back toward the doors, ready to tell Patsy to stay where she was. In the split second the gunman, or woman, he couldn't tell, was fleeing from a room further down the corridor and through the double doors at the far end. He charged on, passing a body in a doorway!

Greg ran to the far end of the corridor, stopping just the unopened side of the next set of doors. He pushed the right side door open gently, with his foot. This was crazy! This guy he was chasing was armed! What was he going to be able to do? He didn't know where the guy was, he didn't know the hotel, he hadn't a prayer if the gunman was ready to take a pot at him.

He heard another gunshot. It was coming, it seemed, from

midway down the next corridor, which led again to another set of double doors at the end. As he reached halfway down the corridor, having taken the last half dozen or so steps a mite more gingerly and closer to a wall, the white, ghostly face of a man that seemed in his seventies, suddenly appeared, eyes full of terror from his room.

The old man, who looked reasonably well-built, didn't say a word. Just pointed. The turning from the main corridor led to another, shorter corridor. The new corridor was similar to the other. Royal blue carpet, fresh smell as though it had been recently laid, tasteful pictures adorning the walls, however this corridor had only four rooms. An easier area to assess, but which first?

No-one had ventured out from the other rooms having heard the gunshots. Perhaps they were all too scared to come out.

The final door on the right was already open. Blasted by one of the shots. At least, thought Greg, one of the two shots he'd heard had been used for this.

He looked into the room. Typical executive style suite, no airs and graces. Two single beds, television, bathroom, window – except the window was open. Greg ran straight for the window, ready to jump through and out into the darkness. It was madness. Surely whoever it had been had got themselves far enough away by now? He decided not to jump. Patsy appeared at the doorway, followed by Ted. Greg shrugged at them both.

"*Nothing.*"

They stayed quiet for seconds in hope they would hear something, be given a clue, it proved useless. Their silence was interrupted by another voice.

"*Just what in hell's name is going on, and why are you here?*" The intonation was expounded with deep-felt malicious intent. "*I might have known you'd be involved in this … everywhere you go it's another bloody disaster! I'll have you for harassment and intimidation…*"

It was true. Everywhere he went, things seemed to be turning sour. For a split second, he thought about Bill. Sure, his passing wasn't down to him, but he felt a degree of guilt he couldn't explain.

But wait on! This was Caill talking. Not just talking, but living, breathing! When Greg had come through the first set of doors it was Caill he'd seen on the floor!

"But, the corridor … you… "

"He missed. He ran. I fell. You came. All there is to it. Don't think you're some big hero … I know you'd rather I'd taken the soddin' bullet…"

For someone whose life had just been in grave danger, he was showing no sign he had been terrified. But this was Caill. Greg mused whether he had any feelings.

It was time for the two currently silent partners, Ted and Patsy, to interject. The corridor was starting to come alive with rubberneckers from other rooms and until now absent hotel staff.

"Who was it? The guy with the gun? You seen him before?" Ted asked Caill. He was now in reporter mode.

Caill was similarly dismissive.

"Balaclava … I don't know who the hell he was. All I know is that he came into my room and pointed a gun at me … such a crap shot … too nervous … needs some serious target practice. I'll send him your way next time, Duggan"

Others looked on incredulously. How had he come past them too? Another entrance? Caill offered nothing.

"…yes … very good … good work … well it's been a pretty hairy night, but I think we've come through it unscathed … talk tomorrow…"

Two satisfied ends of the line hung up. One – a mid-twenties or thirties-something male, the other a reassured Brent Dugarry. The phone calls could now stop for the night. They were in the home straight. Working well toward their well-earned, carefully manipulated end of millions that lay in wait.

Dugarry put down the phone and turned to his much younger partner whose hair had miraculously changed from raven black to blonde since being picked up by him in the yellow Porsche.

Her long legs stretched out, wearing just a white T-shirt and brief white thong across the four-seater settee in the warm, luxurious apartment overlooking the beautiful glistening bay sixty miles from Hopton. They'd reached there in just forty-five minutes from Colin Duggan's exploits.

She was relaxed now, putting on an over-acted but easy pouting expression as she gave her come-on smile. *"Come here Brentie…"* said the woman, who had latterly re-transformed back to her original blonde.

She found it funny that she had been able to change the way she looked to such good effect when she needed. At last her hair and beauty training had come in useful.

Brentie's expression and her giggle told her his thanks were not necessarily going to be verbal!

CHAPTER 49

What Greg hadn't realized, until he woke up to the headlines and found Patsy wasn't Patsy, or she was, but also she was Jenna, and now she was Emma, soon started becoming clear.

RANDY GREG BEDS CRIME SLEUTH EMMA;

WHO'S BEEN A NAUGHTY BOY THEN?;

RUGBY STAR MAKES MORE THAN A PASS

So, Patsy who'd become Jenna was really Emma! The papers had been delivered that morning, the day of Bill's funeral. Greg didn't order a newspaper. They were all delivered very thoughtfully by someone. *Mail*, *Express*, *Mirror*, *Sun*, *Star*, even the *Times* ran it!

Colin didn't know anything as yet – so far as Greg and Patsy were concerned. His phone had needed charging by the time he'd finished trailing Whisky and Cigars and then the girl. He'd seen what he thought was a package handed over.

Neither Patsy nor Greg had come up with the right words, the right way to tell him, that the shit was going to hit their fan in the coming hours. Colin had arrived back home just after them, about 5am. He'd looked shattered, relayed the information about the woman and crashed out.

Greg and Patsy had managed to haul themselves out of their respective beds. Greg had heard the sound of post coming through the letterbox. It was too early for the postman. He'd seen them all – the newspapers – by the time Patsy surfaced.

He needed to see Diane as quickly as possible today. She'd said that she thought she would manage to attend Bill's funeral, even with her own troubles still uppermost. But now there was this.

When Patsy arrived downstairs they exchanged grimaces at the press, both aware of an impending doom that awaited them. Telling Colin, before he found out, talking with Diane, the funeral … It wasn't going to be the easiest day they'd ever had.

"We should keep to what we said." It was Patsy who offered the first solution of the day as she buttered a slice of toast. She was talking low, however, in case Colin, still asleep so far as she knew, were suddenly to spring into earshot.

"You've already told Diane it was a set-up job, and I don't think there's any evidence that we were … you know … I think if we keep a united front we'll get through it. And neither Diane or Colin will ever know from me."

"Why didn't you tell me … I mean, it wouldn't have mattered, I guess, but why didn't you tell me your real name? Does Col know it?"

Patsy stared at Greg, looked at the newspapers, took a deep breath, turned to pour a coffee then turned back to Greg.

"I've told Colin, of course … actually, Patsy IS my real name. It's Emma Able that's the pseudonym. Yeah, I write crime novels, so what?"

"No wonder you wanted to run off and play investigator! So am I your next hero or villain? God, I bet bedding me was just another real life experience you just had to have to make the next one seem even more real."

Greg had stewed this over since reading the headlines and had been getting more annoyed the longer he had gone on, but he had resisted the temptation to raise his voice too much.

Patsy gave a new harder, more vibrant edge to her voice as she leaned closer to him, piece of toast in hand.

"Come on, Greg. That's how I earn my living, yep. But this? Don't be silly. I don't do my own stunts just to check they're right for a book."

It was said with utter conviction, but she was determined he was to believe her.

"Now don't get me wrong. I know how it looks, but you're going to have to take me at my word. What happened between us had nothing to do with my work … and yes, when I went up to Castlegate I did feel that my work might have helped – and it did."

It was a kind of 'so there' attitude to finish with and Greg respected it. If there was one thing he accepted more readily than anything else, it was when people shot, like him, from the hip. He mouthed 'okay'. They were back as one.

They faced up the day remarkably well. Colin was, in truth, a doddle. Patsy had prepared him for stories like this. True, her novels did not make Patsy a well-known face in celebrity-land, but her pseudonym was certainly amongst many avid paperback readers' favourites. This, though, was the first time her name had been attributed to anything more unsavoury than her novels. Colin accepted that a picture of his fiancée and his brother leaving a house together in the middle of the night just might make good copy, as Patsy had described, especially if someone from Castlegate Press were out to discredit Greg.

Diane had proved a tougher nut to crack, especially given her instant reaction to the previous night's shenanigans.

Greg had gone over to Diane's mum and dad's place to pick her up for the funeral. Had dealt with a stony silence by her mother. He had arrived early so that he could spend time with Kyle, whilst attempting to smooth the way with Diane. She had still come with him to Bill's funeral, so that was something. Greg felt for her, in the crematorium, more than at any other time in the past weeks. He braved out the Patsy-thing and Diane mellowed a little. It was all he could ask.

The funeral was massively well attended. Many of Bill's friends, relatives and ex-team-mates were there, along with literally hundreds of mourners who had followed Town over the years.

The service was a typically tearful occasion, with readings from his sister Grace and brother Tommy who had flown in from Canada.

Greg couldn't help but look around during the service. So far as he could see there was nobody around to cause problems. As he sat, his mind drifted back over the previous night. Colin's trail had led him to a woman – who? His and Patsy's night had been pretty unbelievable, but for different reasons.

Photographers stalking them, the bizarre shooting incident with Caill. Who was after Caill? Why? If the ground was to come back to his family and under his control, why would someone want him out of the way? But then, hadn't Ted mentioned that it wasn't all as easy as that? What did that mean?

Finishing bottom was the only way Caill would get the ground. Irvine wanted Town to do well. Caill? Pulling strings? Unlikely. So who? Why did Whisky and Cigars go from the club to the girl? Too much to take in. Overload. Back to the service.

All the current squad were there – the Hammerton twins, big Tony Estorino and Mark Merrioneth, Alan Thomas, Brian Goram, Vinny Venus, Mike Rodley, Kenny Lomax, Paul Davy, Dave Harper, Tony Webb, Pete Smith, Phil Trippett, even the new lads, Richie Brent, Ron Rigson, Keith Denny, Trevor Prentiss, Brad Warrener, Joe Entish, Warwick Player and Stu Wainwright and the bought-off consortium, including Ted and George Ramsbottom – back from his exile in the Lakes. Talent scout Joe English was there too.

And then there was Irvine, for the first time with a lady in tow. Irvine being there was really no great surprise. Irvine and Bill had got on pretty well from the get-go.

It was now that Greg began racking up Irvine's good points. He'd rescued the club, wanted it to do well, had added the funds for buying players, wanted to take the club further, arranged everything he could to make sure the ground was ok since the explosions. But there was still something about him that Greg would never bring himself to like.

As Bill's coffin disappeared for the last time to the sound of music from Mantovani, Greg wouldn't have known it was Mantovani but for Diane whispering to him that her father loved this piece – 'The Way You Look Tonight'.

Greg looked around the chapel once again. Grown men, some of them his own team-mates, were blinking fast and touching corners of their eyes to hold back the tears.

Bill Garside had been every inch a great man. In many people's eyes, he had been someone to look up to. If this was to be a measure of how much Bill's life had been worth, it showed just how much he had contributed. Goodbye Bill!

Bill had always been there for him, a constant source of encouragement. 'Come on Greg, lad,' would go with Greg to his grave. It wasn't as though he felt he couldn't do things without Bill there, but there was definitely a part of him that had gone.

Colin and Patsy had stayed at the back of the chapel. They had been able to take a careful look at everyone coming in and going out. Col didn't see anyone untoward, and, apart from Patsy getting some eyebrow raising looks from people who had obviously seen that morning's papers, there was no give-away or tell-tale sign that anything was different to a normal funeral.

The mid-twenties looking chap walked past them all without sending any shivers down anyone's spine. He fitted in to the general melee of mourners making their way out of the chapel. He'd had a busy eighteen hours – playing the part of gun-toting criminal one minute, to guest mourner the next. At least this part hadn't required him to run and jump out of windows.

This was easy pickings. Just watch them, he'd been told. Just watch them and report back on what they were doing and where they were going. Irvine came toward Greg, clasped his leather gloved hand on to Greg's shoulder by way of transmitting that words were not enough – and went.

Tomorrow there would be just six days left of Town's season and possibly the last days of the club's life if results didn't go their way. Greg had threats hanging over him and problems all around. They'd lost their last three games. He wanted desperately to win and he, Colin and Patsy were still trying to uncover who was trying to make sure they didn't.

Wednesday would be their last home match, hosting promotion contenders Brazen Bees. It looked a futile task on paper. The Bees had been on an inspired run and had gone from fellow strugglers to their now elevated position in just four months. They needed the win to keep their promotion hopes alive. Provided Town won, they would be safe for another few days with the last match of the season to negotiate against Ensideleigh. It was a pre-season fixture planner's delight!

CHAPTER 50

Tuesday. The day following the funeral. The penultimate game of the season just a day away. Greg was back at the garage. Alan Baines had called. He was one man down and needed Greg for the morning. Colin and Patsy were busying themselves with anything they could find out from anyone at either hotel where the action had been on Sunday evening, asking questions of anyone either on the staff or hotel residents.

When Greg finally made the short journey to Parrot Lane, it was with fresh heart. He'd slept, for one thing. The Patsy and Greg storm had been dealt with more neatly than they both had a right, and the macho side of him couldn't help but keep telling him that he'd actually got away with it. Mustn't think like that, but there it was. He and Patsy hadn't let things go any further and had kept everything straight. Also, he conjectured, he hadn't been threatened, abducted, hit or hurt in over a week!

Even better news had followed on the playing front. Trevor Prentiss was back available after injury, Kenny Lomax had recovered from Sunday and young Vincent Venus was looking sharp having finally shaken off his dead leg. Kenny Lomax was in ebullient form when Greg arrived as Phil Trippett led training. A last short session in the early evening, held to keep the players as one unit again.

"Greg, mate! We're gonna do it this time – for Bill!" was Kenny's contribution.

Around the ground, everyone had done what they could to make the following evening's game go well. Irvine had mobilised as many forces as he could muster. New advertising hoardings were right round the ground, the mobile grandstand used on Sunday had been replaced with a larger stand as a decent crowd was anticipated. Irvine had flung every media angle and presence he could at giving Town the best support they would have for years.

LIVE OR LIVE & LET DIE was used in a James Bond style local TV and radio campaign using the Paul McCartney hit of the 70s. Hopton was urged to support TOWN in their hour of need. This was the ultimate must-win game and Ted Brewiss was heralding it like no tomorrow – not just on the back page of the Messenger but with the editor blasting it out over the front page, thanks to a four-page pullout of TOWN – Your Hometown Club Needs You! – paid for by Irvine.

Patsy and Colin visited the hotels asking about the two women and the gunman, a yellow Porsche. Greg had asked Alan Baines to check out Porsche ownership. Surely a bright yellow Porsche shouldn't be too hard to find!

Irvine – who was the lady with him at the funeral? They had no clues there and after Patsy's last brush with Irvine's empire they decided to swerve that one. By early afternoon, they'd exhausted their questioning, nothing was coming their way.

Their efforts hadn't gone unnoticed. They were being watched from a distance by Anna aka Janey, Paula and Matt, the gun-toting man from The Carlton. Anna was at The Crestway, Matt at The Carlton and Paula was putting the information she'd received in the package from Whisky and Cigars, who had been on a reconnaissance mission at the last game and afterwards at the club, to good use. The team determined to ensure Hopton Town finished bottom was just as committed as the team that was busting a gut to keep in the league.

CHAPTER 51

Wednesday morning: Parrot Lane. Irvine had been at the ground early, determined nothing was to go wrong. He wasn't happy. The ground was to be closed.

"Closed!! What the hell do you mean, closed?"

Stood in what was now his office, having taken on the role as chairman as well as owner, due to Bill's passing, were two suits. Irvine had seen the like of them many times before. Middle-aged men enjoyed, it seemed, nothing more than carrying around bits of paper to wave under noses of the hapless, creating misery.

"Mr. Irvine, we are merely the messengers…"

They had explained that, following inspections carried out by the insurance company, with regard to compensation following the incident with the grandstand, and subsequent to the report submitted last week by the health and safety officer who had visited the ground personally, it was he (the health and safety officer) who had decreed that the grandstand, what remained of it, constituted an on-going danger to the safety of those on the playing surface.

"What a load of bollocks! We only played here a few nights ago – and there was no problem then…"

The suited pair were now playing tag team with the other taking up the council's position.

"Well, that may well be, Mr Irvine, but paragraph 2, sub-section C of the health and safety regulations 1986, clearly states, 'if there is a chance, however miniscule, that one person might suffer injury as a direct result of property that has been designated as a danger, however slight, then work shall cease in the workplace until such time as that property has been made good and has been re-inspected by the necessary public bodies…'"

Irvine was used to riding roughshod over ineffectual people, but ineffectual people wearing a council hat were always tricky territory.

"There must be a way this can be resolved – and quickly. We've a game to play here tonight. Can you not do anything to help us here?"

This was as near to pleading as Irvine was likely to come. He hoped to God that they knew this and they didn't have to see the sheer venom that was lurking just on the other side of his face at that moment. The pair looked at each other and turned to face Irvine once again. They made a call. The taller of the two explaining the situation to their boss at the council. It didn't last long.

"I'm sorry, Mr Irvine. I'm afraid it is beyond our remit. Should we set a precedent by allowing you to flout the regulations, where would we stand with any other such adherence of the rules. I'm afraid you'll either have to call off the game, or play at another ground, perhaps?"

"Another ground? Tonight? … Just go, gentlemen, just go … thanks for nothing!"

Irvine was crushed. He had put so much effort into everything, particularly since Bill had passed away, to ensure that as much as possible was going right. Totally deflated did not, however, mean he could not deliver total rage the next second – and he duly did!

Slamming down both fists hard on to the desk, sending a shower of pens spilling out of their respective resting places and letting out a deafening, fearsome roar, the council officials ran for their lives.

Irvine's business interests meant he had to be elsewhere by 10am. Despite the fact the match still had to be sorted, he really did have other fires to fight elsewhere. He would just have to work out how best to sort all of this out whilst he was on the move.

CHAPTER 52

Alan Baines was still a man down and Greg was back at Victoria Street on Wednesday morning. Greg's phone burst to life. It was Gill. How had Gill got hold of Greg's mobile number? He couldn't remember ever having given it to him, but he accepted Gill was the police and they could easily find it. His number was no secret anyway.

When Gill started talking about the shooting incident from Sunday night, Greg couldn't help but smile. It put a new slant on police response times.

Gill wanted the lot. He'd been on leave for the past four days, hence no contact and had read the incident report at the hotel. There had been mention of Greg, Patsy and Ted being in the reception area. He'd also wanted the gen on Bill's funeral, the game on Sunday and where Bryan Caill figured in it all.

Greg had been warming to the copper. He genuinely seemed on Greg's side, but still Greg wouldn't let him in. Gill sensed it, even over the phone.

"Greg, I don't pretend to understand all that's going on, but what I do know is that I'm going to get to the bottom of what's happening at the club…"

As the conversation fizzled out, and Greg carried on with his work, Gill turned to the woman and gave the thumbs up. Then winked, then smiled.

She was right there beside him, difficult not to be since they had spent yesterday evening and this morning in his apartment and in bed together for most of it. He lived near the centre of Hopton and was viewed a bright, young, upwardly mobile, no-strings copper whose career was destined for great things.

"This guy's so dumb. He hasn't a clue. Even now!"

Paula just looked slightly away, then closed her eyes, laid back, smiled, started laughing. Everything was going according to plan.

"So who was she? Irvine's woman at the funeral...?"

They were going over it all again after the previous day's lack of success. Colin asking the questions over a cappuccino for him and a flat white for Patsy in the Costa in the centre of Hopton. He saw her vacant expression. He was trying anything out, looking for some hope. In truth, he was still bruised from the paparazzi story. He'd accepted Patsy's story and Greg's, but he wasn't thick. Smoke and fire and all that. It had put a strain on their relationship.

Colin looked away, he couldn't look her straight in the eye at the moment. He looked out on to the pedestrianised centre of Hopton – and there she was! He was sure of it! Except for her hair.

She looked even prettier in daylight, and a few years younger than he had originally thought. Perhaps the blonde hair did it? She was coming out of a designer store carrying a couple of bags. He motioned to Patsy.

"Come on, Pats, game time. Let's go and talk with Livvy."

As they reached the doors, Colin stopped with Patsy just behind. They backtracked half a pace. It was Gill! And he wasn't there on police business – that was patently obvious, unless the constabulary had taken up searching people's mouths with their tongues! Will Gill and Livvy! Patsy was on the case, taking as many quick photos of the two as she could on her phone.

In the short space of time it had taken them to get up from their seats and get to the door, Gill had appeared – and how! These two were far more than good friends coming out of a door to the paparazzi. So, what difference did this make? His brain was whirring into action. But it had to operate quickly. They looked as though they were on the move.

"Come on!" This time the line had come from Patsy. She started to move. Colin wasn't quite so eager. Patsy glanced back at him. *"Look, what have we got to lose? I mean it's a chance meeting, isn't it – us and them? See how it plays."*

Patsy was away, straight towards Gill and Livvy.

"*Mr Gill, good to see you again, how's it going?*" It was dealt out in bright and breezy fashion. Patsy was on top form, she wanted to see his reaction, his first movement, she looked closely for it.

First came the flash of a smile, friendly and welcoming. "*We just thought we'd come across and say hi … to you both … we're having a coffee … fancy joining us?*"

Colin was alongside her now, the four all within touching distance. "*How's it going, Mr Gill? Any nearer finding anything out?*" Colin looked across at the girl who didn't seem overly impressed with being stopped, but was doing her best to smile.

"*Oh … I'm Colin … this is Patsy…*" Colin held out his hand to shake with Paula/Livvy, hoping he would get her to give her name. Paula put on her biggest, most sycophantic smile.

"*Pleased to meet you. I'm so sorry, but I really have to run. Come on, Will, you know I've to be back … I'm so sorry we can't stop and chat, another time maybe.*"

Gill and Paula were off. There were to be no more questions, but Colin and Patsy knew they had finally made a breakthrough.

Irvine was not to be deterred. In between meetings and also within them he had sent texts, emails, instructed everyone. The Irvine machine was in motion. This game was going ahead no matter what. If they had to play the match somewhere else, instead of Parrot Lane, then fine. But he was trying every possible avenue to avoid doing so. He'd given himself a deadline of 2 o'clock. If he hadn't found a way of keeping the match at the ground by then, he would have to accept what seemed the inevitable.

Instantly they had left he had made the call to the council's Health & Safety office. He'd called their bluff by trying to get hold of their superiors, putting pressure on them. He'd made the call, as with many others, on his mobile. It was now an hour ago. No returned call.

He spoke with GPK at Castlegate Press, he spoke with his business associates in the building game. If there was a way around it then they would know. He spoke with Trippett to make him aware of what might happen, on the strict understanding no word must get out to the players or fans yet. It was now ten minutes before his self-imposed deadline.

It was less than six hours before kick-off – but where was that kick-off going to take place? If he didn't hurry he'd be in danger of not having a game at all. It was at this point that Bob Irvine began thinking, for the first time, that he hadn't needed all this hassle of a rugby league club.

He was on his way back to the ground, on the basis that it was probably better if he was there. As he rolled into the club car park, now cleared of tape from the shooting, he took a look at the scene. Dilapidated grandstand, marquees, terracing, grandstand borrowed from a county show and a series of Portakabins. This was hardly what he had imagined when he had taken over. He hadn't been naïve, he had known Town's predicament, but he had to admit he had never before been involved in an environment that could have so much bad luck piled on day after day. His phone rang and he answered as he was walking across to his office.

"Good afternoon, Mr Irvine. You contacted us about this morning's visit you received from our Mr Jacobs and Mr Jacques…?"

He listened further whilst the lady on the other end confirmed he would have to find another venue. At any other time in the season, they could have postponed the fixture and played it a week later, but since the league had deigned all games should be completed by next Sunday, now less than four days away, there was no room for manoeuvre.

For the second time that day, Anna was able to acknowledge a plan was coming together – she had taken Irvine's earlier call thanks to Irvine having used the number printed on the business card and the 'official' paperwork left by the guys she had nicknamed Reg and Ronnie, but Greg knew as the Klitschkos! They had been picked up by Frank/Danny Devito on leaving the ground.

So that was it! The game was off. Or rather, it was to be held at another venue, but where?

Fred came around the corner from where he'd been cleaning out the toilets.

"*Dirty job, but somebody has to do it, eh, Mr Irvine!*"

Fred, not known for his in-depth study of people and their mannerisms, stopped right in front of Irvine. "*Are you alright, Mr Irvine? You look as though you've just seen a ghost!*"

Again no movement or comment from Irvine. He was immersed in a combination of self-pity and wonderment as to what he should do. Fred had one answer.

"*I'll get you a brew. That's what you need, Mr Irvine, a nice strong cup o' tea, with something a little bit stronger in it as well – medicinal, you understand. I'll get you it...*"

Irvine had dealt with adversity enough times previously. This was going to be a long afternoon, but it had to be done.

Fred came back in with the steaming hot cuppas – one for him, one for Irvine.

"*Here you are, Mr Irvine, get that down your neck. You'll feel better for it ... We'll give 'em some stick tonight, eh, Mr Irvine?*"

"*What? Oh, yeah...*" Irvine's tone was downbeat, not harsh, enough to signal he wasn't interested. His mind whirring with plans.

"*Right, I'll be back to the urinals then...*" And then, as an afterthought, "*...I 'ope you told those two jumped-up so-and-sos to go forth and multiply this morning, Mr Irvine. I'm sick o' seeing 'em round here...*"

The door shutting behind him as he left. Within seconds it was back open again. This time from Irvine.

He caught up with Fred at the lavatories. "*What do you know about those ... so-and-sos? When have you seen them before?*"

Fred, now with bucket, mop and cleaning equipment in hands, turned to Irvine.

"*Well, let's put it this way, Mr Irvine. The last time I saw them they were in Greg's office. I don't know what they were here for, but it wasn't for the good of Greg's health...*"

CHAPTER 53

When Greg finally checked his phone on the way to the ground, following a longer stint than anticipated at the garage, there were three messages. The first a withheld number and what turned about to be no message, which he suspected had been Gill before he'd got hold of him earlier; second from Colin with a 'you'll never guess who we've just seen' note; and then Irvine.

Irvine's message was brief. *"Ring me, Greg. Soon as you can. Bob."*

Paula and Gill had split not long after leaving Colin and Patsy. Paula had initially been annoyed with herself over being seen, and not just seen, but recognised by Colin and seen with Will. They had been together for some time. Both hit their phones as soon as they left each other. In the short time they'd had from being intercepted by Colin and Patsy, decisions had been made.

Paula poured herself into the passenger seat of the yellow Porsche, engine already purring, on a side street just off the main drag of the high street. Colin and Patsy weren't far away, having chosen to tail her together rather than splitting themselves and also following Gill. They knew where to find him, but it was time to follow this woman. Find out where she led, but they were on foot when Colin clocked the Porsche.

Fortune was on their side. Colin's Discovery was parked in the Pay & Display just across the road. Colin and Patsy threw themselves in and came out of the small car park just as the Porsche reached the T-junction a good 250 yards ahead of them. Patsy didn't want whoever was in the Porsche with Livvy to realise they were behind, but she also didn't want to lose them. Bright yellow was easy to spot, but not from around corners.

Paula, however, was all too aware of what was going on behind her. She looked across to the young man beside her and laughed. He smiled. Patsy and Colin needn't have worried about losing them. Paula would make sure that didn't happen.

"*You ready for some fun then?*" He drove on, checking his rearview mirror.

"*Oh, I think so Matt. These guys are starting to do my head in. You set it up?*"

"*Oh yes, I think you're going to enjoy this … it will appeal to your sick mind.*"

Paula smiled across at Matt, as he took another cursory look as they drove out further into the countryside on a day that was turning gloomier due to the cloud cover, but was brightening up their day.

Matt's phone lit up. Text. "*We're ready. In position.*"

"*Right. Enough of all this. I think it's about time we had a bit of fun with these two,*" and Matt put his foot to the floor. The next five minutes were a flash-by mix of highs, lows, dips, and turns as the two cars hurtled into the Pennines.

In the Discovery there was excitement. Patsy and Colin wanted this.

"*Thank God we didn't trust Gill after all,*" offered Colin as she drove. "*Greg was right on that one by the looks.*"

"Shit!" Patsy hammered the steering wheel with the heels of both hands. They'd lost them. How the hell they didn't know, but one minute they were on the tail of the Porsche, next minute nowhere to be seen.

"*That's right. This could be our last game here. But I don't think so, we intend to be around for a long time yet.*" There was a glint in his eye as Irvine enjoyed himself, an interview with Sky Sports News broadcasting live from the ground.

"*Tonight's game was very nearly called off. And your club's run of bad luck off the field appears to be continuing?*"

He may have been duped earlier in the day, but Irvine's business antennae seemed back firmly fixed. He knew this was his time to shine. He smiled warmly, first to the interviewer and then direct to the camera.

"*No-one ever said it would be easy. It's been a tough season for all of us, but everyone connected with the club has done a fantastic job in the short space of time since I've been involved. We've picked up a few points and entertained our brilliant, long-suffering fans. And they're the important ones. Without them, we're nothing. We're hoping for a full house tonight as we continue our mission to stay in the league. I'd just say come on down and see the boys. They're giving everything."*

Irvine was in full sail and would have gladly carried on when the interviewer took a hold. He turned to the camera himself.

"And there you have it. Bob Irvine's Hopton Town are fighting for their survival tonight. I think I've just got time for a pie before kick-off."

It was all Irvine had hoped it would be. Prime time coverage on the local channels as well as the major sports channel arranged through his media operation. The broadcasts had all gone out between five o'clock to six o'clock.

The Irvine publicity machine had been rolling throughout the afternoon and now, just half an hour prior to kick-off, the plan was coming together.

"I'm here." It was the voice that had been sending warnings, transmitting messages and generally orchestrating the play over the past weeks. The man who would be Hopton Town's Terminator!

"There's too much at stake for me to stay away now."

He was speaking on his car phone three cars from the front of the queue leading into the ground.

"Christ!"

Patsy slammed hard on her brakes. She'd lost the Porsche, but now saw nothing but blinding lights. Strobe effect too. Slap bang in front of them. No way she could see to drive. Before they knew it, lights blinded them from behind too as another car slipped to their rear. They had taken a turning from the main country road and were on a rural lane and other than the lighting all around it was pitch black.

"Get out of the car! Get out of the car! Get out of the car!" It was devastatingly loud. Police loud hailer loud, with what seemed added volume from some kind of PA system. It

continued with urgency.

"*Get out of the car!*" And then more personal, but still as instructive. "*Mr Duggan, Miss Previn. Get out of your car now. You must get out of your car now!*"

They vacated, not without fear. It was certainly time fo fear. Colin felt the beads of sweat standing proudly on his forehead, Patsy's bladder was struggling to hold.

"*Get in front of the car! Move in front of the car!*" They did as instructed, while also trying hard to make out the shapes they saw as silhouettes.

"*Take your clothes off! All of them! Take your clothes off! All of them! Do it now!*"

The voice was male. Colin decided to try talking. He made a pace forward to where the voice appeared to be coming from.

"*Look, I don't know what this is about…*" His talk didn't go any further as a single gunshot rang out into the countryside. Colin and Patsy both hit the deck. There was a pause. Then the voice started again.

"*Don't speak, just strip! Now!*"

They stripped. Colin down to boxer shorts, and Patsy to bra and panties. It wasn't enough.

"*All off … everything.*" They hesitated as though about to appeal further and a second shot rang out into the cool night air, once again rebounding through the countryside.

"*Move away from the car – together – leave your clothes – now start walking… through those trees to your side of the car, Ms Previn … both of you…*"

They could make out what they took to be a clump of trees ahead of them now. No time to think about anything, although Colin had thought about diving back in to the car.

So, they were being left there? Or what? Killed? But, the clothes off routine? Some saddo getting his rocks off?

They had no time for talk, just a look to each other. As they fled towards the trees, they could hear what sounded like laddish cackling in the distance. It didn't sound as though they were following, but they couldn't be sure.

"*Just keep moving,*" was all Colin could muster. Patsy was fit and nimble, Colin a little more lumbering – not in the same shape as his brother – both suffered from their nakedness. Their feet felt as though they were being ripped apart by the undergrowth and where it was softer underfoot the mud hindered their faster-paced progress. It was night-time, cold and just starting to rain.

CHAPTER 54

"It's him!"

"Don't get excited, will you, he's not exactly Brad Pitt, is he!"

"Neither are you, but I still love you."

They laughed.

The two Town fans, husband and wife, knew the name and the face. But that's as far as it went. He was there, that's all. Nothing more to it. That's how Jardine would have wanted.

Boots thudded and hammered from the concrete that led from the Portakabin to the pitch. It seemed odd to be running out from behind the posts rather than emerging in the middle of the field. And then there was the softness, as the studs transformed from being a thunder troop to that of a muddy squelch.

The rain had fallen like a torrent and, in just five minutes, had transformed the ground into a swamp. It was going to be another mud-bath!

I don't care what happens in these next two minutes before kick-off, just make damned sure you're ready to repay this lot's faith in you and Bill's too. I want everything tonight. Commitment, desire and most of all these bloody two points, otherwise Sunday's game will be no use if Ensideleigh win and we don't. Commitment, desire and those two points. Come on, boys.

It was no time for dressing up the words. You could be as calm as you liked, but staring at your fate and not addressing it would do no good.

The words were strong, emphatic – purposely not delivered inside, but out on the field in the heaving rain. Greg and the rest had already been willing, even before the Churchillian-style approach to their battle, but Trippett had sensed they needed something more – a galvanising force. He wasn't sure he'd given it, but they needed anything they could from anywhere they could right now.

Irvine hadn't just been busy with getting the game on. GPK had worked well with his journalists from his newspapers and others. Today had been productive. He'd made sure the game went ahead at very least.

Irvine hosted his guests – the Brazen Bees hierarchy – with bonhomie and although there was still the game to win, which he couldn't personally do much about, he was satisfied with his day's work, albeit having been duped earlier. In the past now.

"You look pleased with yourself Bob…" Irvine wheeled round.

"Julian! Good to see you. It's been a while…" Jardine nodded in support as he clasped hands with the rugby league supremo. Jardine's interest stretched far beyond the sport and the pair had locked horns business-wise over the years.

"You look like the cat who got the cream."

Irvine nudged his head to the window of the Portakabin/hospitality area. *"I got the game on – and we're going to win!"* He was at his bullish best right now. He was always this way when things were on the up. Today had been trying, but like most challenging days it had also been thoroughly invigorating.

All the same, he was on his guard with Jardine, despite the bravado. After all, this was the guy who called the shots in the rugby league world. Whatever Julian said was to happen, usually took place through some ways and means!

"You here on your own, Julian? Not come to see us die, but wish us well, I hope."

Irvine was already working on why Jardine had chosen this game. True, he sometimes acted like royalty – visiting clubs in much the same way as the Royal family – but Irvine already knew there was more to this visitation. Another small piece of the jigsaw had appeared.

GPK had been given a few names they were looking into and his was on the list. Jardine sidestepped Irvine's last comment with an ineffectual smile.

"I was due to meet a couple of colleagues. Probably stuck in traffic. You've a good turnout tonight in spite of the weather."

"Can I get you a drink? Sit with me, Julian, as we try to stay in the league."

It was said with all the intention of not letting Jardine out of his sight whilst on the premises.

"Yes. Yes. Yeeeeessss! That's a fantastic try from young Vincent Venus following a great move started by Stu Wainwright…" Terry Derbyshire could hardly hear himself as the crowd roared their appreciation of Town's fourth try of the game!

"And that's put Town right in the driving seat. It's now 20 points to 8, and the Bees look well and truly stung by Town…" Terry was in rugby league's dreamland. In the space of a few weeks, he'd been able to report on what looked all set to be a third Hopton Town win. Perhaps not that startling if you were commentating on other clubs, but this just might be something special.

12 points ahead! They were heading for the win. Greg hadn't been involved in the latest try, but this was as good as he'd hoped it would be when he'd taken over as coach.

But at half-time, just three minutes ago, he'd received not one but two texts that had reaffirmed the danger to others and himself in Town winning tonight.

Greg looked over into the makeshift stands expecting to find someone, anyone – Whisky & Cigars, Paulie – someone there as a reminder to him that he mustn't win.

Ten minutes into the second half and Greg received a high ball. He tore straight at the Bees' on-rushing defence. Slam! One of their tacklers collided with him in high impact style. It was like two oncoming cars hitting each other face on. The next tackler came in from Greg's right side sending the ball flying from his grasp and right into the arms of a third Bees' player.

Greg was down, breathing deeply. He wasn't hurt, but by God he was going to stay hurt on this occasion. He stayed down. The crowd erupted against the Bees' player who had hit hard from the right, claiming a head-high illegal tackle.

The gleeful player who had received the spillage sped away and three quick passes later, and stretching the Town defence, the Bees scored underneath the sticks to register what was a certain six points to put them back in the game.

The referee had seen nothing other than a good, honest challenge and it had been.

Trippett may have been unaware of the bigger picture of what Greg had been going through, but he felt a good judge of when a player was feigning injury. And he also knew when a player of Greg's calibre made a deliberate error. Greg really wasn't that clever in hiding it. He took Greg off with the option of bringing him back later on rotation.

They made eye-to-eye contact for the briefest of glances. Greg had looked up at him to check on his reaction. It had been enough.

"Put your tracksuit back on, Greg. Hopefully we won't need you again tonight."

Breathing hard, Greg felt the need to say something. *"I should be alright to go back on, Phil."*

Trippett continued looking at the game and took a swig from his drinks bottle. The lads were trying their hardest and were having success. When he turned to Greg his voice was a whisper.

"If I put you back on, you'll lose this for us, Greg." His words were delivered as he looked back out at the game. Greg looked back at him straight-faced.

"I don't know why you're doing it, but you must be messed up in some serious shit. This isn't you. One minute you're on it, next you're throwing the game. Look me in the eye and tell me it isn't that way."

Trippett hadn't finished. Greg's pause had been sufficient.
"Phil…"

"I don't want to know. Not now. Later. We've a job to do here and thanks to your meddling we might not do it, but by God, I'm going to do my level best to do what I can from here…"

He turned back towards the game. *"Come on, Kenny! Get a hold of him!"*

The Bees, sparked into action by the earlier try, now showed renewed vigour and following massive pressure on Town's line, they ran in their fourth and kicked the conversion. The scores were dead level. Three minutes left. Trippett couldn't help but look daggers at Greg.

Greg hung his head low as he sat on the bench. He prayed for the Bees to score as he had his head bowed. He feared. Real, buttock-clenching fear over what the recriminations would be from those who had made his life hell in the past weeks. He looked up from the bench, over at Trippett. Phil was up hollering out instructions to the defence when it happened.

Trippett collapsed!

CHAPTER 55

Greg saw Trippett's demise. It was one of those falls that leave you in no doubt it is serious. He looked on dumbfounded, nonetheless. He now knew the unexpected events – apart from Bill – were likely to have something to do with what was going on. But Phil Trippett? Surely not.

Town were not intended to win this game. Within a split second of that thought he reacted to Phil's plight, raising him from where he had fallen face first, looking into his eyes. He thought he was staring at death there and then.

Others around the bench were gathering around quickly. The game continued for a matter of the next thirty seconds. A lifetime for some, certainly for Phil! It had carried on mainly on account of a surge from Town towards the Bees' line, but the final ball had gone out of play. The commotion around the coaching area caught the attention of the crowd and then the referee, Doug Davis.

He had looked over to a mass of players and officials. He had feared the worst, some kind of melee amongst the rival teams on the bench. He called a halt to play.

"*And unbelievably the match here at Parrot Lane has been stopped. Two minutes 15 seconds left on the clock, Steve, 20-20, but something's going on around the Town bench. And I have to say it doesn't look clever…*"

Terry Derbyshire was nowhere near close enough to see through the growing crowd. Trippett rallied after a few minutes with Veejay transferring his on-field skills with the sponge to an off-field experience.

"*I'm fine, really…*" It wasn't enough to convince anyone, as Phil Trippett was stretchered away from Parrot Lane. His voice weak and his face ashen.

Greg had looked down at him as he had lain there. He'd been fastened in for his own safety and protection as he was loaded on to the ambulance that had carefully made its way from the car park across the pitch to the bench, with caution from the driver not to get stuck in the quagmire that was now Parrot Lane.

As the ambulance made its way back across the pitch with Trippett on board, Greg had watched who was taking him from the scene. Hopefully, they were nothing like the guys who had abducted him a few weeks ago.

There were still two minutes 15 seconds left. The referee, having waited for the ambulance to clear was all set to restart the game.

There was no other way. Coward or common sense? Whatever cloak he used to dress it up, this was Greg's moment. He could put the nail into the Town coffin that his adversaries so desperately wanted. All it needed was one bad mistake.

Jardine smiled briefly over what had occurred.

"Come on, mate! This is what we've been working for, remember..." Kenny Lomax was up for the fight. His regained match fitness was beginning to kick in, and he was a winner.

"Phil'll be OK, let's just win him this game." Keith Denny took a break – Greg was back on!

The Bees restarted with the ball deep in their own half. Four tackles were completed without much headway until the rampaging and skillful Bees second row Trent Mason handed off, busted through and avoided a succession of Town to reach the half-way line. Just a minute and a half left. The crowd was in full voice, both sides of supporters desperate to shout their team to victory.

Nerves jangled all around the ground, and it was much the same on the pitch. Willie Hammerton faced up to the charge of another strong-running Bees forward, catching him, clasping tight around the upper thighs. The player was going down, but he was looking for the winning pass now on Town's 20-metre line. No chance of a drop goal attempt to win by a single point. He flung out a ball that, because he was now spinning around, propelled it way past his fellow forwards and in to the path of a delighted Ron Rigson.

Five years ago, Ron would have made the line from here. His pace would have done the job, but this was five years on. What he still possessed, however, was guile, gained from nearly two decades' worth of experience. He dipped his shoulder, sending the only man in his way off balance, stepped on as much gas as he could as he cut through the gap he'd created. But it was true, he no longer had the legs. He had taken his side ten yards into their opponents' territory, still with open space in front of him, but he could feel the breath of the hopeful tacklers behind and coming from over on the other wing.

He had the sense to look and out of the corner of his eye, just to his right, he made out the image of part of a shirt that matched his. Half a second later, he'd shipped the ball, straight into the path of the on-rushing Estorino. Tony had been the first to match Ron's run. He juggled the ball slightly as he brought it under control, whilst maintaining speed. The Bees' defence was on him now. There were tacklers grabbing at him holding on, bringing him down. The Hopton crowd was at fever pitch urging him on.

Greg had gone off like an express train. He was on Tony's inside, heart pounding just as quickly as his boots had been to carry him that far. If he could just get Tony to pass it he was sure he could spill it, send the ball spinning out of reach, make it look as though he'd stretched every sinew and muscle to try, but fail gallantly. He had to get the ball.

Tony was going down, ten metres from the try line. 40 seconds on the clock. Two tacklers were on him, with a third following up fast and a fourth crashing in at his legs. Tony spun in the tackle, saw the briefest of flashes of Greg as he whirled round, backed in to the tackling mob. There was no way out, he was going down.

Just before his leading arm hit the ground Tony found, from somewhere, the strength to telescope out his ball holding arm and flick the ball away from groping limbs and into the air. Greg's eyes widened. It was what he'd wanted. But he was in the wrong place!

Vincent Venus flashed into sight at just the right time, taking the ball on the burst. Just three quick strides later, and with one tremendous lunge for the line, he was over! His first hat-trick of tries, but more importantly a fabulous, league-saving-win for Town!

Terry Derbyshire was in raptures. The crowd was going insane. Irvine beamed with the satisfaction of a job that had been well done all through the afternoon and evening. And Greg forced out a smile. He hadn't to give away his inner feeling of despair over what was to happen next. One game to go. All to play for on Sunday. But what about now?

The messages he'd received at half-time played over and over.

It had all happened so fast. The team he had set about building in the last six weeks was starting to click. The game was won. Three games from their last six.

Everyone connected with the club was in rapture.

Wheels were already in motion elsewhere. Julian Jardine had congratulated Irvine as Venus had run in his match-winning try and had made his way from the ground. He hit his car phone as soon as he set off. Jardine wasn't in the mood for excuses he was hearing from the other end.

"Look, I don't give a flying fuck what happened. I'll call you with what to do in the next hour."

Two thousand Town fans went wild for their heroes, a fourfold increase on the regular gate. Stage one completed, with stage two all set for the weekend. Ensideleigh had also won. Everything was now set for the last game of the season.

Town's players applauded their home support and the beaming smiles that came from both the fans and players was further proof that the spirit to see Town survive was alive and kicking.

Irvine joined the throng on the pitch, striding across to embrace all of the players in turn. He then raised his hands to the supporters and then, with the radio mic he had brought out with him, and through the public address system he'd had installed, and with the aplomb of an orchestra conductor managing to quieten them enough, he took centre-stage.

"Ladies and gentlemen, and not forgetting all you kids too! What we have witnessed here tonight is without doubt the best finish to any sport I have ever seen!"

The applause started once again, but was muted quickly by Irvine's gesticulation.

"I bought this club because I want to see Hopton Town not only survive, but win trophies. That's going to take some time, I know, but by God after what I've seen tonight I know it can be done."

Another renaissance of applause was heading in Irvine's direction. Once again, he assuaged it.

"But…" And he paused for yet more dramatic effect. *"But none of us can see any of that without a win at Ensideleigh on Sunday! That's the key to everything. I know that these lads will be giving it more than they have ever done before, but they can't do it alone! We need YOU there too! All of you. Now I know that's a big ask, but listen up."*

Once again he paused, briefly.

"I have just chartered forty coaches to take you all, and I will charter more if necessary, to the match on Sunday. I will pay for the lot – your tickets, the coaches, yes, even the food and drink. All I want you to do is give these lads the support they deserve. Are you with us?"

The ground erupted once again. Even the defeated Brazen Bees' supporters were impressed. Irvine was pretty amazed with himself. He'd not realised how much of an adrenaline rush today had given him.

"Shit!" was the first thought that entered Greg's head. Did these people know what they were doing to his life?

CHAPTER 56

They had arranged to meet back at The George & Dragon. It was just out of town where they had met previously and well away from Parrot Lane. Greg had arrived having dodged the ongoing celebrations back at the club near the ground. He couldn't face them. Too many happy people – and he also wanted to see that Colin and Patsy were okay. It was ten thirty. Col had been left a text message on his mobile that they would be there soon. The landlord kept him company on what had been a pretty barren night in the G&D.

"Some game or other," the landlord offered in response to Greg's possible reaction to the bar's lack of presence.

The landlord gave up on any further conversation, taking the hint Greg wasn't particularly interested. And how the hell could he concentrate on anything? So Phil was OK, resting up in a hospital bed by all accounts, but look at when it had happened. They, whoever they were, had a plan to deal with Trippett, Lomax and Wainwright. Win the game, one of the texts had said, and see what happens between now and Sunday. Each of those had been mentioned. So why nobble Phil before the result? Greg shook his head as he stared into his beer.

Greg jumped! The bleep on his mobile phone telling him he'd received another message. Each one was now almost a mini heart attack! It was Col.

"Just rolling in. Sorry for delay. Got something for you though. Come out of the back and you'll be pleasantly surprised at who you see we've got with us!"

Caill? Had they snared Caill? Or this woman they'd talked about?

Greg waited anxiously at the door, not venturing out unnecessarily, until he saw a car veering round the back to the car park. There was something about the headlights. They didn't look quite right.

It was Will Gill who got out of the car and headed straight for Greg! The rest of the car shielded in darkness. Gill seemed different. This was a bad feeling! It was time to go!

Greg retreated back inside the pub. The landlord was conspicuous by his absence. No customers. This was more than just a bad feeling! Greg made for the front entrance by means of escape. Gill entered at the back.

"*No point, Greg!*" Gill's words were strong, resonant. "*You're going nowhere!*" Greg rattled the door – bolted, locked and impenetrable. Gill softened his voice.

"*Sit down, Greg. I think we need to get things straight.*" Greg looked him straight in the eye. His instinct about Gill had been right all along. Gill motioned for Greg to sit at one of the tables and remained standing as Greg, tentatively did as he was bid.

Gill gave a slight smile, acknowledging Greg's reaction to him.

"*That's right, Greg. Not your everyday, friendly, let's get this sorted out, sort of copper.*"

"*Fucking corrupt wanker copper, then!*" He had to let it out. It wasn't in his style to keep it in. Greg shook his head. He made to get up, but Gill moved slightly as though to block. Gill raised just his finger.

"*Now, I wouldn't Greg .. think about your brother ... and your lover...*" He paused to smirk. "*...Think about Jeff Markham.*" It was matter-of-fact in its delivery.

Gill was still smarting from Jardine's words, but here he was the man calling the shots. Whisky and Cigars had told him they had Colin and Patsy. Gill had put plans into operation as he'd left Paula. Whisky and Cigars, Frank and the Klitschkos had all been mobilized. They'd picked up Colin and Patsy in the woods after they'd dealt with Colin's Land Rover.

The two looked each other firmly eye to eye. Gill chewed on the flesh inside his mouth whilst pouting slightly and keeping his lips together. He was watching for Greg's next reaction. Greg ran his hands through is hair. Not in exasperation, he was beyond that, but in a clearing of his mind. Colin and Patsy. His voice was low, determined, deliberate. *"Where ... are ... they?"* Gill looked at him hard and straight.

"No more amateur sleuthing for them. No more detective work. They're out of the way..." Gill smiled. It was more a tight-lipped pursing of the lips with a slight tilt in an upwards direction. *"I can't tell you what will happen, Greg."* It was as honest an answer as he could give. He really didn't know what was to take place. *"Just make sure you lose the last bloody game, for God's sake."*

Gill's mobile phone rang.

"Yeah ... yeah ... yeah, I'm right here ... yeah, OK..." He kept eye contact with Greg.

"Right, Greg, that's it. Lose the game, you get back your brother and..." There was a momentary pause again for effect. Gill cocked his head slightly to the left with a sly grin, *"...and whoever's girlfriend she is..."* He smiled again. *"Don't follow, not a good idea..."*

Helpless on the pitch and off it. Greg had nothing. Gill disappeared out of the pub's front door. Greg made for the door and caught sight of Gill disappearing inside a car that for once he couldn't make out.

"Gone again has he?" It caught Greg momentarily off guard as the burly proprietor entered the room. *"Can't stand the guy ... Bloody coppers ... I've had more than my fair share of 'em, but 'im! Christ..."* Greg nodded his agreement. How right he'd been.

CHAPTER 57

"...and you think that'll do it for us ... it hasn't so far..."

Brent Dugarry was at best perplexed, at worst absolutely pissed off. Their attention to detail earlier in the season ensuring Town finished bottom had been ideal. They'd had control. Irvine coming in had been their worst nightmare.

"... yes ... we go with that ... and we keep adding to their problems ... pile it on ... Geoff can deal with things where he is ... I'll have a word with Julian ... One way or another we stack everything our way ... otherwise it's all been a complete waste of time ... I could be in The Bahamas now, rather than have all this..."

In front of him, draped on one settee, was the vivacious Paula. Next to the drinks cabinet, in the corner of the room, was Matt. The drinks cabinet took the form of a globe. Matt poured himself what looked like a quadruple whisky – and passed the drink he'd already poured, a Blue Hawaiian, to Paula.

She took an elegant sip, watching Dugarry pacing as he talked on the phone. She was wearing a fabulous vivid red short slip of a dress that left little to Brent's and Matt's imagination. Dugarry stared back at Paula.

"Your Mr Gill reckons Duggan will throw the game if he can, but then they just won ... and we've got his brother ... and his brother's girlfriend who he's been shagging..."

"Yeeees..." It was a long 'yes' from Matt, the kind that gets extended and hangs in the air for a while to channel a comment. *"But none of what we've done has made much difference to him so far. I'll tell you something, I still don't think he'll crack ... unless we go much further ... it's all about this last game now..."*

It was Paula's turn to cut in. *"But he has been throwing games. That's why he's not captain or coach now ... Haven't you seen the amount of times he's made mistakes recently ... not like him..."*

"It's not enough." The voice was firm, sure and calm. Dugarry knew there was too much at stake. *"This last game has to be lost*

and we need to make certain of it … we need to start hitting them now and continually … I want to make sure they don't have their best players available, the ones that take the field on Sunday are not good enough and that they lose the game by half-time … whatever we have to do to achieve that, we need to start with now…"

"You're right, Brent. It's like we talked about when we started on with this. We knew it might take a lot of doing, and that things might get rough…"

Matt had made his way from the bookcases in the corner of the room to the piano stool of the baby grand in the other corner looking out to the garden – "…but it's all going to be worth it."

"But…" Paula's frustrations very nearly got the better of her. What she wanted to say was that her interest in this whole affair was not about money.

"You must keep emotion out of this." It was said with measured concern. Dugarry had his eyes on the prize. "Look, I know Duggan's tried to throw games, and you're right, he has helped in making sure Hopton haven't quite scraped themselves off the bottom of the league. God knows, he tried so hard to keep tonight's result as a defeat from what we've heard. But that's our problem. Duggan's not a one-man team. We now need to hit on the others, players as influential as him…"

"Lomax." Matt was direct. "The Aussie. Him next. I'll take him."

CHAPTER 58

"Do it!" Irvine was responding to GPK's latest news. Journalists and a team of private investigators were tracking movements of Bryan Caill, Julian Jardine, Patsy Previn, Colin Duggan, DI Gill and the driver of a black car that had kept popping up continuously in the course of their leads.

It was now Thursday. The morning after the sensational night before when Irvine had never felt more energized as Town had emerged victorious. This morning he was intent on achieving results off-field. Caill was being tracked ever since showing up at Town. Irvine knew he hadn't come to the ground for no reason. He now wanted to know what that reason was. He knew of Caill's debts, but what he hadn't known was the scale of them. He now wanted the full picture.

Jardine similarly had turned up out of the blue and whenever something happened that way Irvine was on alert. Okay, Jardine was top dog in the sport, but Irvine smelled something. Jardine wouldn't come to Town like that. He wasn't there to press the flesh with the fans.

Patsy Previn, the girl photographed with Greg, had been the last person to talk directly face to face with Jeff Markham. Colin Duggan was her boyfriend and Greg's brother. She had been digging around Irvine's business interests. Why was that? This was the strongest lead they had to Markham's killer.

DI Gill was everywhere. Involved with the explosion interviews, Caill's fire, not Markham's killer, as that had been passed on to higher authorities, but he was on the case with everything else.

He'd not immediately made it on Irvine's list as a prime suspect, but the amount of times he had kept cropping up seemed unnatural. Irvine wasn't into the unnatural.

"We've got them," had been Grahame Pythagoras Kraft's call at 8 o'clock that morning, still working every angle. *"They're*

holed up some place in Scotland. And get this. The owner is one Geoffrey Quinigan QC." He paused for Irvine's reaction which wasn't slow.

"We now need to bring in a professional outfit on surveillance to check out the building, who's inside other than Previn and Duggan's brother. We know they were brought here by the guy with the black car because he drove and with three others, one in the passenger seat, the other two in the back with them.

"You know I want this sorted. Get your guys in. How soon can they be there?"

"Took the liberty of engaging them an hour ago, just didn't want to disturb you 'til now, should be there from Glasgow in less than an hour. Flying in. They're armed."

"We'll get this killer, Grahame – and we're going to see where all the rest of this leads. Everything has happened since I got involved with this club. I don't regret taking it on, but whoever is responsible for the bad blood will regret taking me on. Anything you need, just shout."

GPK resisted the temptation to ask for a rise at that precise moment. And also the other mention of the other angles he had been working along the way. This was a case of him definitely understanding both sides! GPK was in Irvine mode right now though.

"Sunday. I want cameras covering every blade of grass, every inch of stadium and grounds. On ground studio, wall-to-wall screens. We're not going to miss a thing. Players, action, people, reactions. So that's cameras, more operators."

Matt Caill was a dashingly good-looking young man with a fabulous slim physique. From the Hopton Caill dynasty he had rarely come into contact with his uncle – Bryan. Matt's father had died of prostate cancer when he was 15 years old and his mother had taken her own life when he was 18, never having recovered from losing her husband. Matt had put every ounce of energy into his studies to put black thoughts to the back of his mind, and it had paid off, graduating with honours in physics at Trinity College, Cambridge.

He had also emerged as a useful middle-distance runner. He'd spent hours on the track at university and had a PB of just over 31 minutes for the 10,000 metres. Running was now in his DNA and he thought nothing of an 8-mile run before breakfast every day.

He was on the road now. The weather was cold, sharp, one of those days that looks superb when you open the curtains in a morning, but not so clever once you set foot outside.

Matt had emerged, as he always did, from the front door of his apartment overlooking the River Twidal. He was soon into his rhythm and cruised his way towards Walton Park, dedicated to one of the town's greatest ever brewers, Benjamin Winston Walton.

Clad in a predominantly black tracksuit, with white socks and blue running shoes he took the route he had completed nearly every day for the past two years.

The phone was ringing somewhere. He could hear it, but couldn't locate it. He saw the time: 8:05, heaved himself out of bed and looked, as much as his sleep-infested eyes would let him, for any light from his phone anywhere around his and Diane's bedroom, lifting discarded clothing that was littered around left, right and centre. He suddenly realised it was a landline call, not his mobile.

He loped to the top of the stairs to try out his senses on locating another handset. This time he was on form, catching up with the second handset just as the caller was being offered the alternative of leaving a message.

"*Greg…*" The tone was hesitant. It was Diane's father, Tom. This was serious. If Diane was letting her dad speak to him then there must be something seriously wrong, especially ringing at this time. This was another disaster about to happen, Greg knew it. He immediately took over the conversation.

"*Tom? What's happened?*" The slight delay in reply was interpreted in Greg's mind as another massive danger signal. "*What's wrong?*" Greg was by this time looking around to where he could find clothing and shoes.

"*Nothing … well, nothing's happened to Diane, or Kyle. They're fine but…*" This was fast becoming too much of a start to Greg's day. He let the pause in Tom's voice give way to the next line.

"*But…*" There was a huge sigh at the other end of the line as Tom prepared himself.

"*She doesn't want to see you any more, Greg.*" Tom waited a split second for some response, but Greg was dumbfounded. If this had happened a week ago, when all the revelations came out about his fling with Patsy, then he could have understood. It would have been an understandable reaction. Maybe it was delayed reaction. She'd had time to think and that was it.

"*Diane says she'll talk to you. But she's not ready yet. She just wanted me to tell you … now…*" Tom was being as cautious as he could. Steadying himself.

"*Greg, look, Diane's … we've all taken as much as we can … that story about you and your brother's girlfriend was bad enough, even if it was fabricated … losing the baby … And, well, I won't go on … just don't call her … OK … we'll talk about you being able to see Kyle later … see you.*"

Tom had sounded resigned, not apologetic, but not without feeling. Greg couldn't get his head around it. Over the past week he'd seen Diane, visited her. She'd never given him any indication that she was going to shut him out. He knew that she had been distant when he had been around. He'd hoped to mend things. Obviously not, or at least not yet.

Colin or Patsy gone too. Bill dead. Susie not around. Nobody close left that he truly trusted. Greg was due at the garage again this morning. Decided to set off straight away. Rang Phil Trippett on the way. He was fine. Not a clue as to how he had collapsed. Tests all clear. He'd be back home by lunchtime after having been kept in for observation.

"*You've not seen it?*" was Alan Baines' reaction to Greg's appearance and, before he had chance to respond, put down his cuppa and passed a copy of the national newspaper, *Morning Mirror*, to a bewildered Greg.

Alan had worked with Greg long enough to know what he

was like.

"Well?"

"Well, what?" Greg was ready to go on the defence.

"You want to tell me anything?" Alan picked up his cuppa once again, taking a sip whilst watching for Greg's reaction.

"What do you think?" Greg's morning was going from bad to worse. At least he now had a better understanding of why he'd received Diane's verdict on their marriage.

"Listen, I don't know what to think ... It's your life ... I don't want to interfere..."

"Then bloody well don't!" Greg shut his eyes, lifted his head upwards, his mouth shut firm, breathed long and hard though his nose. "I mean, do you think I could honestly have done all that's printed here? If you do, then you're not the guy I thought you were."

"Now Greg..." Alan didn't get chance to finish.

"No, Alan, don't bother. I really can't be arsed to hear your reasons why you don't think I'm the man you thought I was. Thanks for nothing!"

Greg walked out. Fifteen minutes in there had been enough. The newspaper had revealed he'd had sex with five other women, allegedly, and carried the headline RANDY RUGBY GREG'S SIX OF THE BEST. No wonder Tom had made the call.

Kenny Lomax was the archetypal competitive Aussie sportsman. It didn't matter which team he played for, he always played to win and he trained hard and long. Running, pounding the streets, was part of his daily routine and in his short time with Town he reckoned he'd run every road, street, avenue and lane in and around Hopton to at least a ten-mile radius from the centre.

Today's route had taken in the dilapidated surroundings of Northern Maltsters, suppliers of brewing malt, once a proud complex employing over 200 and now sadly run down; Caill's Ales on the banks of the river; and Walton Park.

He was as fit as he had been for years and felt good as he entered the park. He'd already completed at least eight of the regulation ten miles he promised himself every day. As usual, there were other morning runners around the park, some jogging, one or two going at it hard. There were a few dog walkers and one or two who were now reading newspapers on park benches.

Greg was now in the park too. He'd gone because he had been in such a rage when he left the garage. He'd be plastered all over social media again as he had when the photographs appeared of him and Patsy. He never reacted to it on line and would leave it to die out again now. There was no sense in making matters worse.

He was bringing himself round gradually. He stroked his stubble forwards from his neck to the end of his chin. This wasn't just thinking time and it certainly wasn't time to feel sorry for himself.

Where were Colin and Patsy? How could he get back with Diane and Kyle? He'd heard from Veejay that morning. He was on the mend. He knew about Phil, also on the mend. He had forty-eight hours to try whatever he could, but not a clue how and with nobody in support.

He stared out at the park's boating lake that lay in front of him. He'd spent day upon day down here during the summer holidays when he was a kid, and already Kyle had grown to love it. He could see Kyle's happy, smiling face beaming at him as he splashed Greg with water as he rowed them on the lake. He wished he was back in those times, either as a kid himself, or with Kyle, just at the moment. Anything was better than the position he found himself in now.

From across the park, out of Greg's sight, but not earshot, came a shriek, swiftly followed by ear-splitting calls for help. As Greg ran towards the incident he told himself life wasn't going to get any easier in the next 48 hours!

Greg had made his way across the lake's footbridge, along one of the park's famous landmarks and from its apex had seen a group of people circling. He couldn't make out anything further and only when he was manoeuvring his way through the fast assembling rubberneckers did he see the carnage that had taken place.

"The stupid bastard just came out of nowhere…" The lad, perhaps late teens, was overcome.

"Hurry up!" The woman, cradling the man the lad was talking about, was frantic.

"Look at him…" Tears streamed down her pretty face, she wasn't calling for anyone in particular. Just help.

One of the throng, a middle-aged man, tried to reassure her as he stooped to her side. *"An ambulance is on its way, love, it's on its way now."*

Greg moved away, sorry for the young man down, but relieved this was one incident not connected with Town and him. How wrong he was as Paula lay clutching Matt as his life slowly slipped away. She had been stationed just inside the park, sat in her car ready to provide an easy escape route. The plan had been that they – Matt & Paula – would ensure Kenny could not play in the final game of the season. Their aim, Matt's aim, had been to inflict some kind of injury on the Aussie and for that purpose he had carried a knife, which had become an accomplice in his own personal tragedy.

Matt had seen Lomax many times on his morning runs. They had acknowledged each other as they passed. Paula and he had watched for when Lomax came into the park. It was a favourite route he ran most days. They'd hopefully strike lucky. Matt had been wired up for Paula's call if she saw him first. He'd intended to put on a black face mask, the same he'd worn when fleeing from Caill's hotel room, slash Lomax on the arm or thigh sufficient to wound but not kill – and run!

It was a motorbike that had wiped him out. A young lad taking an illegal short cut across the park, who knew every lane and pathway like the back of his hand, and had not seen Matt as the runner hurtled around a blind corner straight into his path.

Matt was hit smack on by the front wheel of the bike – a Yamaha – ripping through his groin, his body shattered and splintered by the follow through of an engine running at least 40mph. His face a mass of blood, with a hole the size of a tennis ball in the side of his skull from impact against the lad's motorcycle helmet followed by a somersault that finished head first on tarmac. He'd also been carrying the knife unsheathed in the front pocket of his running jacket, which had jagged into his stomach.

The motorcyclist, while badly shaken, had a few broken ribs to go with an almost definitely broken leg, but had miraculously escaped further injury.

Paula wailed in the distance as Greg made his way from the scene, unaware of the greater significance the event could have had if Kenny Lomax had been involved.

Kenny had chosen not to run the park that day after all.

"Just tell her I want to talk … that's all…" Greg was determined to do something. He was on his phone making for Parrot Lane. No sense in going back to the garage today. Time to set a few things right. Let Diane know he cared, that he was concerned about her. Let her know the latest story was all lies, well most of it. They'd twisted things, as the media does. *"I'll not get in the way, but just talk…"*

He was talking to an ansafone, leaving a message. He'd tried her mobile. She wasn't picking up. Try again later. No training with the lads today, probably just as well. Nip it in the bud tomorrow. Greg's phone flashed up Susie's name.

"Hi, stranger!" It was the friendliest voice he'd heard all day.

Geoff Quinigan, Brent Dugarry and Julian Jardine had rarely met together. Their association was not one of anything other than business and even now they were not all in the same room at The Laurence Hotel & Golf Club five miles south of Hopton, nor were they all in the same building. Jardine was with Dugarry in an executive suite. Quinigan on screen.

"What the hell was he thinking about, bloody stupid idea…" Quinigan's rage was not one of someone showing compassion as Jardine and Dugarry let him continue. *"It's just bloody fortunate we're not linked to all this…"*

"Yes, but…" Dugarry was about to stand up for the late Matt who had never recovered consciousness.

"But nothing!" Quinigan's temper was legendary in court. He hammered his fist down hard wherever he was.

"I'm sorry he's gone, but it was a pathetic idea and a bizarre, million-to-one accident … And it's also time we moved on to other plans to make sure of Sunday."

Jardine took the lead.

"That's why we're here…" he shrugged and held out his palms in front of him.

Jardine stopped himself from carrying on, the rest didn't need to be said. All three were back focused on the job in hand.

"Duggan's brother and his girlfriend. They're out of the way up here. We could use them more, threaten Duggan…" Although Quinigan had uttered the words, he still wasn't convinced. Jardine had the same thoughts.

"What good will it do? Threaten Duggan again? It hasn't really worked so far?"

Following the chase into the countryside, culminating in Patsy and Colin's nudity, Whisky and Cigars, along with Frank and the Klitschkos, had driven north and all six were now holed up in one of Quinigan's country retreats. He had three. This one was a 17th century castellated country manor house in the Speyside area of Scotland.

"We need a different approach, that's all. We use them in another way. Let's get Duggan out of the equation completely. And make all those other hits we talked about yesterday, so that tomorrow and Saturday we start sending Hopton Town into disarray. I want Irvine, Duggan and all the rest of this crappy little outfit running around so much they disappear up their own arseholes. Good night, gentlemen. Have a wee dram tonight. We'll be on champagne on Sunday!"

CHAPTER 59

"Baby that feels good ... yes ... Oh, yes ... keep going ... that's it ... ohh, baby, yeah ... keep going..." Susie was riding him with such beautiful rhythm, glisteningly naked. They'd shared a bath together when he'd arrived, bottle of wine in hand. Chardonnay. She preferred white and it never failed, she said. A glass and a half and she was smiling, eyes sparkling. She always said 'never again' the next day in the wake of her wine drinking, not that it was in any way excessive.

"Oh yes ... Oh ... mmmm," she could say no more. As she played with her breasts, cupping them and stroking the underside of her nipples, lost in her own world.

Sometimes Greg felt that's where Susie was truly in her own zone, like he was when on a rugby league ground going for the win. But he loved this. For the past hour, from their foreplay, that had included kissing, sucking and licking in all erogenous zones, he had been released.

They talked, afterwards. Ordered a meal in the room. She had been keeping up to date with events and they had laughed over the press stories. She never once asked about Patsy, nor Diane, but about how he was coping with it all. He'd asked about her life. It was the most relaxed, relieved and revitalised he'd felt in weeks. Nobody at home, no-one to get back for, no real future there. He stayed. The Juniper Court Hotel was lovely, not that he saw a lot of it.

"Let's talk." Diane had sent the text he was now looking at a dozen hours later.

It was now Friday 12 midday. They'd left the hotel around 11am and once again Greg had forgotten to charge his phone. Diane's was one of several calls he'd received, many coming from responses to yesterday's news – and, so far as Greg was concerned, that's now what it was.

Alan Baines had sent one, plus a voicemail. Irvine had done

both too. Apology of sorts from Alan – plus, he needed him if he could get in, asap. Irvine acknowledging he'd seen the story, but had bigger things to discuss. Could he call at the ground? And another from Gill. Irate in the extreme.

"Where the hell are you, Duggan. You're in deep shit. Ring me."

Diane, Alan, Irvine, Gill. Time for priorities. Diane first.

"Why do you do it?" He left her question hanging. He'd rung. These her first words. He had none. Not instantly. He could do without it right now. Bad call. Maybe try later. Next call. What was he in deep shit about? And he already knew he was anyway, but what was new?

"Meet me by the bandstand in Walton Park in thirty minutes. I have a proposition for you."

Odd, he thought, he had to know – and it appeared Gill was more subdued now. Text to Irvine that he'd be in about 2 o'clock, leaving hopefully enough time between appointments. It was becoming a busy diary! Text to Alan offering to work Saturday morning. And then a text to Diane. *"Bad line, sorry. Will call later."* Now, the park!

No pleasantries. Gill on his phone as Greg arrived. Hung up as he stopped in front of him. They moved away from the bandstand where two older couples were sat eating sandwiches, enjoying the day. Pleasant and sunny. They walked and talked.

"Your brother and his girlfriend? Safe release? Yesterday's story announced as a cruel hoax and all retracted … and a quarter of a million in your bank account. Sound good?"

Greg was on it quick as a flash. Revitalised and reinvigorated from his night with Susie.

"You trying to bribe me, DI Will Gill of Hopton Constabulary?" Greg hadn't meant it to sound as though someone else was listening in, he'd enjoyed for once the sound of a line he'd heard something the like of before, in a film. Gill was on to him regardless, patting him, feeling inside his hoodie for wires. Checking his phone for recording. Greg had nothing to hide. Gill restarted, having finished his check.

"Let me put it another way then. Sod the safe release. Keep

yesterday's story. Half a million."

Gill hadn't been quite prepared for what happened next.

"You really are a prize twat, aren't you?" as Greg grabbed him by the throat and launched him into the lake. Sure, he didn't want any harm to come to Col and Patsy and he couldn't be sure that what Gill was saying meant that he knew where they were; but if he and anyone he was working with, like Caill, Whisky and Cigars, Danny Devito and the Klitschkos knew anything, it was going to take more than a walk in the park to find out. He left Gill to extricate himself and walked away ready for his next appointment. At least he'd be early now.

Irvine was delighted to see Greg twenty or so minutes later. Even more so given the news he'd just had delivered.

"Greg, thanks for stopping by. I won't keep you. I know we've had our moments and God knows we've had some crazily bad stuff going on here, but I'm on the case.

"What I wanted you to know is this. I intend to show you in the next two days how I do business. I came into this club for the right reasons. It's taken me time to get all of this, but get it I have, and I promise you we will make this club great. Just do me a favour and hang in there."

Greg nodded, not through agreement, more acceptance he'd heard. That was all. He'd said Irvine's name as he'd entered, even managed a *"Bob"* by way of friendlier acknowledgement, but it was all words so far and nothing would count until Colin, Patsy and everyone was safe. The game. Well, that was another matter. He'd still throw it if he had to. But realistically, would he? It all preyed and played on his mind.

His phone pinged. As he drove. Text. *"Come over tonight, please."*

All in all, just another day at the office, or out of it, in Greg's case. Knocked back the offer of half a million, as you do; destined his brother and brother's girlfriend, note to anyone interested not his girlfriend, to possible murder; rejected the opportunity to clear his name; dumped policeman in pool, nice one, but no doubt incremental repercussions, what were these words he was saying to himself? He didn't say them normally; sidestepped his wronged wife twice in a day, ignorant bastard, me not her; lots of nice words, but no action so far as he knew from club owner; garage boss apologetic and needing him; and another satisfying night with Susie. He'd made the right decision.

CHAPTER 60

Saturday morning 7.45am. Just over 31 hours before what could be the final game in Hopton Town's history. Greg was in his kitchen, he blew deeply, long and low. He'd arrived back home around midnight. He would be with Alan by 8am. Head straight. Hopefully ready for whatever the next 31 hours held.

No Diane, No Kyle, No Col, No Patsy, No Bill, No Susie, No Ted – just himself. No jumping around today. Garage, ground, training, coach to hotel, prepare. Today's schedule.

It was back to another terrible day weather-wise after yesterday's sunshine. Rain lashed hard at the windows and the wind drove unrelentingly at the fence that swung wildly in the garden as Greg looked out from the kitchen window.

When he'd arrived home it was to a deluge of mail through his letterbox along with emails, largely from women set in two camps – one that depicted graphically what they would like to do with him in common with some of the *Morning Mirror*'s salacious stories – the other camp called into question his morality. He read a few – gave up. Didn't these people have their own lives?

He looked at the clock on the wall, pictures of Diane, him and Diane, Kyle and him – they were all around it.

He had set up training for the afternoon, followed by shower and a light meal before the squad would board one of Bob Irvine's coaches, travel to Ensideleigh, and stop over for the night in readiness for the game.

"*I can see them!*" The voice was no more than a whisper, yet was picked up by the other conspirators in such a way that the feeling of euphoria was the same as if a winning try had been scored.

"*They're OK … no … nothing wrong, they look fine … the others? I've only seen three, and they're all in with them … no, nothing … they might have guns, not sure … hold it … it's OK …*

they were just looking in my direction…"

Irvine had mobilised far more than GPK had requested for both Scotland and Ensideleigh. Members of specialist undercover investigative teams from newspapers all over the country had been drafted, as well as ex-marines, ex-SWAT, homicide investigators, plus additional trained marksmen. Irvine had more money to throw at this than any police force, and boy, was he throwing it. It was one of the marksmen speaking now from just outside one of Quinigan's Scottish residences.

"Easy … I reckon we can just walk in … straight to the room … but let's not get hasty…"

In the past two days, GPK's reporting team had relayed all of the information about Matt Caill and Paula, had been watching Kenny Lomax on his training run, seen Matt Caill's demise and had monitored Greg's every move. They'd even managed a decent recording of Gill's offer thanks to an implant they'd managed in each right shoe of every pair of trainers and shoes Greg had while he was otherwise engaged at the hotel. They'd hoped against hope he wouldn't wear what he'd worn the night before.

Irvine had now been told, once and for all, that there was nothing sinister in what Greg had been up to. He'd had checks on him over the past three or four weeks once he'd had an inkling. Far from wanting to throw games, Greg had been shouldering most of the responsibility for the club. But there had been, perhaps understandably, given all of the circumstances, times when he had also deliberately attempted to throw games. That was Irvine's assessment, and in light of the evidence being put his way, he could see why.

That's why Irvine had to get to the bottom of this – and that's why it had been he, GPK and Trippett himself, who had formulated the plan for Trippett's mystery illness. Irvine wanted to see Greg's reaction. It had been the right kind of reaction.

The doorbell rang, quickly accompanied with frenzied knocking.

This was the start. Greg had almost been geared up for it. Hours to go and he knew something was to happen. Especially after the last two meetings with Gill. Trouble was brewing. Greg smiled. Trouble brewing – just like Caill then – ha ha!

The frenzied knocking had been replaced by more forceful, hard hitting, fist slamming, but as he opened the door there was crying too.

Tear-stained mascara ran in rivulets down the outer sides of both cheeks of what was obviously normally a very attractive face. The rain didn't help. For a second, maybe two, the pair stared at each other.

Paula didn't smile. It slowly dawned on Greg where he had seen her before. Yesterday. In the park. Shit. This was the girl he'd seen with the guy. It still made no sense.

"I'm Paula," she paused. *"Paula Caill"*.

"No, not now! Go back, go back!" The whispers into the radio mic were no longer whispers. The ambush party that had been about to take out the three before releasing Colin and Patsy, was in retreat. There were recriminations all around as to how they had all missed the fourth conspirator.

Bryan Caill was totally on his uppers. Everything had gone sour. Caroline House and grounds was an asset even in the property's now burned-out state, yet even that was now slipping from his grasp. He'd hoped the brewery could be siphoned off to new owners, with him retaining a modest interest as non-executive director – in order to assuage the mounting gambling debts, but that hadn't happened. The house had been the centrepiece of the Caill family's achievements, the jewel in the crown. It was now run-down, poorly maintained, fire-damaged and uninsured!

The ground was his big hope. His debts could be cleared in one fell swoop. Debts that had been passed on to one of Geoff Quinigan's less honourable clients. That's where Caill had first come into contact with one of the trio.

Brent Dugarry was the client and Julian Jardine a regular acquaintance of the other two had been brought into the fold to provide their perfect holy trinity. Being the Chief Executive of the Rugby Football League put him in exactly the right position to manipulate.

It had been at the end of the previous season when everything had come to a head. Caill had been faced with the ever-increasing possibility he would have to relinquish the family seat. Declare himself bankrupt.

Dugarry had started to exert pressure on Caill over his reticence in paying even the interest on his debt and Caill had been searching for anything he could to find what else he had that was worth anything.

Of course, Caill knew of the family's gift to the town, the ground for the Rugby League club, putting something into the community. What he hadn't known was there was a loophole in the deeds regarding the ground. And it was this loophole that Quinigan had been able to confirm, through Dugarry, that could be the answer to all Caill's woes and manna from heaven for the rich to get richer. Prime land for residential development and worth a fortune.

That's why Caill was now travelling north to Speyside.

Quinigan, Dugarry and Jardine were not chaps who wanted to get their hands dirty. Caill had been dispatched with just one mission in mind. Exert enough pressure on Colin and Patsy that could be transmitted into absolute fear in Greg's mind so that the game would never be in question. They had other plans too, with other players, but Caill was going to have to work for this deal to get himself out of debt and remain at Caroline House. He'd be okay once Town finished bottom. That was the only premise. Jardine had come up with the edict through the Rugby League. Bottom side out, no longer regarded as a professional club. End of.

It had been a long trip. Although Caill had kept his foot on the floor most of the way, it had been a seven-hour drive. He was exhausted. Not only was he exhausted he was also nervous as hell. What if this all went wrong? He wasn't cut out for this kind of role.

He tempered his angst with the thought of the end result. All debts paid. The house, named after his mother, would be safe and he would have money to spend and some in the bank. In his heart of hearts, there would probably be only one place it would end up going. But at least it would feed his habit a while longer.

Scotland's intense rain hammered at the roof and bonnet of his car, offering an incessant racket as he drove.

Greg ushered Paula in, taking a fleeting glance outside to check for photographers, best of luck to them on a day like today. Ten minutes later, Paula sat, perched on the edge of the settee, in the Duggan living room, clutching a steaming mug of tea.

What the hell was going on here? Yesterday he'd seen her clutching a dying man, someone he didn't know, and didn't think anything of until now. Today she was in his house. There was only one connection. Caill. It was enough.

Greg stood. She took a sip. He hadn't known what to say when he'd let her in and didn't know how to start the conversation now. What he really wanted was for her to go away. If he'd learned one thing over the last six weeks, it had been that surprises like this meant only one thing. And it wasn't good news. It was Paula who chose to break the ice.

"I suppose you're wondering what I'm doing here…" Everything she and Matt had worked for had been destroyed in one moment. A split second where all their hopes and dreams were no longer. She wasn't looking at Greg.

Greg still didn't respond. It didn't seem right. She hadn't sounded as though she had finished.

"…there's something…" She paused, thinking momentarily. *"…something you should know, something that … well, something pretty…"* And Paula left the next part hanging in the air. She rolled her eyes, biting lightly on her lower lip whilst caressing the inner side of the lip with her tongue. She dropped her shoulders and hung her head low.

"Do you know what's been going on?" It was nearly the very same question Greg had been about to ask. She turned to look

directly at Greg.

Colin and Patsy were in reasonable spirits despite their captivity. Their jailers hadn't sought to do any more than watch over them. The two tall guys seemed infatuated with Patsy and had made reference to her body any chance they had.

It had been another boring day for all six of them. Colin and Patsy were sat playing cards. The Klitschkos had offered to play strip poker with Patsy.

Colin and Patsy hadn't given up on an escape. Sure, they had been up for the chase as amateur sleuths whilst nothing had happened directly to them, but this was different. Their car had been shot to pieces while they were naked in the woods. They had been abducted.

Frank and the Klitschkos were the henchmen. Whisky and Cigars their leader. Colin and Patsy knew he was more the one to be aware of than the others. It was he who held the gun. It was Whisky and Cigars who reacted to the movement of the door first, along with a whole other team the six were blithely unaware of!

"*Stand on! ... Watch! ... He's in ... yep, coming through the door right now...*"

"*Where the hell has he come from? And who is he?*"

"*Wait. Checking.*" It was the member of the reconnaissance team stationed just outside the window of the living room who was relaying the information to the director of operations just a quarter of a mile or so away in an old railway carriage in a field that now possessed all of the necessary CCTV monitoring equipment they had set up during the past two days to check all movement and speech.

"*It's Caill. Can we get decent sound off him. I want whatever we can get. Let's incriminate this bastard right up to his neck?*"

"Gill?" She had been explaining about her brother – Matt; about Brent Dugarry and her relationship with a policeman. She'd hung her head again as confirmation.

At last he had something to hold on to, something that started knitting this whole thing together. Whatever he'd been ready for, this wasn't it. He was ready to let rip with all his angst, but this was time for calmness, surefootedness.

"*Look, I'm sorry about your brother…*" He was in front of her now. On his haunches first, then deciding he was now too close. He tore his hands through his hair. This time his voice was calmer, strained but much calmer.

"*So you. Gill. Matt. Bryan Caill. You're all in on this?*" He spread his arms. "*Do you know what you've done to my life? What you did to my wife? And our baby?*"

Paula gave her story. She and Matt, twin brother and sister had been blackmailing their uncle. All part of a Caill dynasty struggle some years previously that had led to their father being ostracised from the family and denied what had been rightfully his. Bryan Caill had orchestrated the affair for his own ends.

Paula and Matt had worked hard finding their uncle's Achilles heel and had at one time or another both worked for him, without him ever knowing they were related.

It had been in the course of going through Caill's e-mails, social media accounts texts and finances, that college intern in Caill's Ales, one Matt Lilac aka Caill, had noticed and recorded not just the huge discrepancies that existed in anything where Bryan Caill had been involved, but his consistency at losing money on horses, the roulette wheel, and unhealthiest of all, paedophilia. That's when Will Gill had been drawn into the affair. He'd been on the police undercover team determined to nail Caill.

He and Paula had become 'an item' around the same time. Not that Paula had ever seen their relationship as too much more than another necessary component in her and her brother's drive to attain what they wanted, much the same way as she had bedded both Quinigan and Dugarry.

"*Will was able to put pressure on … and when your brother came along with his girlfriend … well … another target…*"

"*Colin and Patsy … where are they?*" He didn't need to ask more. She nodded. She knew. "*We'll talk on the way … this is it for me … I'm done now that Matt's gone…*"

Bryan Caill was one of life's natural born losers. This, he had been told, was his chance of wiping out debts, redressing the state of his wealth and being able to carry on. He had no intention of doing that at all.

Bryan Caill's only intention was to suck up to those who needed to be sucked up to for as long as the job needed doing and then jet off to Thailand or some Far Eastern land as soon as he could, without any thought of paying off debts or appeasing blackmailers. He'd see Hopton Town finish bottom, pocket the proceeds of the land sale himself and simply have it transferred to an offshore account. Fuck 'em!

His entrance was met with surprise from the existing six. Whisky and Cigars was the first to respond to Caill's appearance. But it wouldn't last longer than a couple of syllables.

"*I thought…*"

Caill immediately stopped him. It had been a long drive, rain persisting all along his route. His head was pounding with the concentration taken.

"*Don't think, I don't pay you to think,*" he snapped. There was no room for anything other than a hard-hitting approach. Scare the living daylights out of Colin and Patsy. Get a call in to Greg Duggan.

Caill would then have done his bit. Up to the rest to do theirs, sad fuckers.

He was now facing Colin and Patsy full on. He'd come in wearing a full-length, well-worn, brown tan Drizabone coat as though out of a cowboy western. Proving his role, he reached inside and drew out his gun.

"*Go! Go! Go! Hit him! Right now!*"

The screams into the earpiece of the number one shot on the surveillance team were immediate and definite. There was no way back.

The two marksmen had stationed themselves just beyond the set of doors that led from the room where all seven were now sat or stood. They were on the hall staircase, had no direct target. They'd have to fire once inside the room.

On instruction they made their move just as another frantic call came through their earpieces. *"Don't! No, stop! I repeat, stop!"*

It was too late now. The pair had committed. They were through the door. Caill spun round instinctively, gun still pointing, but this time in their direction. The two needed no further provocation than that. But the secondary message they had just received sent a split second of indecision into both minds. And that indecision saved Caill's life.

Caill let the gun drop to the floor. He hadn't been instructed to, but given his predicament his brain had fast transmitted to his hands that releasing the offending item would be infinitely preferable to receiving what the two most recent additions to the room seemed to have in mind.

Colin and Patsy's first reaction as the gunmen had appeared had been to hit the deck. The Klitschkos and Frank following suit. Whisky & Cigars remained rooted to the spot, unsure as to whatever was going on around him. The last message was still ringing through the marksmen's earpieces, but they had the face-to-face dilemma to deal with first. What to do with Caill?

"Down! Get down!" They hadn't awaited further instructions. They had already come too far and now they had taken control. Shouting hard and harsh at Caill he also hit the deck. One of the two marksmen made to gather the relinquished gun whilst the other shouted at Colin and Patsy's captors.

Colin and Patsy took their chance. They had hit the floor instantly and had half a second head start on the heavily armed and suited marksmen. Neither had a clue as to what was going on, other than they had now been propelled into a far more dangerous game than they had played the past few days. This was time to make a move!

As the marksmen had made their entrance Colin had instinctively dragged Patsy down. As fortune would have it, they were at the third entrance to the room. They knew it led to another room, but didn't know where else it would take them.

In the seconds it took the marksmen to frighten the lives out of Caill and his four paid-for loonies, they had slipped away, had risen to their feet, and had gone through a second door, this time shut but unlocked. Now they saw their chance, they were in the conservatory. All they needed was another unlocked door!

What the hell had the last thirty seconds all been about? In the space of that time, Caill had arrived, they had seen him point a gun in their direction and witnessed entrance of two guys who looked as though they'd come straight out of some Hollywood blockbuster movie fully expecting a blood-and-guts flesh-flying climax.

It was unlocked! They were out in the open for the first time for days and ran. The rain drilled hard against them as the legendary scotch mist hung low and dark, even though it was only mid-afternoon, about 3 o'clock – 24 hours from tomorrow's game.

Their dash had caught the rest of the surveillance troops off guard. Those manning the equipment in the shelter continued to relay information to the marksmen that by now had been deemed useless other than as babysitters, which left just two other team members free to deal with any other activity. They were both a considerable distance away to do anything about Colin and Patsy's exit.

The marksmen had been instructed to stay with Whisky and Cigars, Caill, Frank and the Klitschkos to ensure the safety of the fleeing couple. In one sense it had all worked out for the best – nobody hurt, the guys they were trying to help were freed. Not that Colin and Patsy knew the gunmen were on their side just yet. All Irvine's hired hands needed to do now was to find them.

But they were in no hurry. Their job had been to free the captors, check out what was going on, and report back to GPK's Castlegate Press operation and from there for the information to be relayed to Bob Irvine.

The two escapees were blithely unaware there was no chasing pack behind them and fully expected to hear sounds of approaching bodies as they made their way through the grounds of what had been their country enclosure for the past few days.

CHAPTER 61

Greg had the wind in his sails. For the first time in weeks, he felt up with the game. Hell, he just called it a game! He shook his head.

Paula had filled in the gaps. Caill needed money. Those he had fallen in with, Quinigan and Dugarry, whom he now owed the money, were intent on taking the jewel he hadn't realised could be available. The Hopton Town RLFC ground. The league had come up with the rule that was to be his saviour. Town had to finish bottom. At last he knew why!

Caill didn't have the money to pay them off until he could sell the ground. That's why Julian Jardine was at the game on Wednesday. Another piece falling into place. He was tied in with Dugarry and Quinigan. Greg could see it now without Paula telling him. Jardine would ensure any rugby league nuances with regard to regulations were kept to a minimum. But it had all gone awry when Bob Irvine had entered the fray.

"*No-one really knows what Irvine's up to,*" said Paula, as she carried on explaining the tale. "*I mean, why come in and invest in a club like…*"

She paused at this point as they continued their wait at the traffic lights. "*…Hopton? No offence, but if someone like that was really interested in the game, surely they'd be able to afford better, unless…?*"

Although Greg was concentrating on the lights, it seemed he had at last found someone who didn't automatically serve Irvine up as saviour and he felt good about it. They had exhausted the motorway system and were now at the hands of Scotland's country routes, including the legendary A9 as Greg recalled had been mentioned in the Bond movie *Skyfall*.

Paula had recovered her composure. It didn't go unnoticed by Greg. She had made solid inroads into repairing her tear-strewn face and windswept, tangled hair as they had travelled. All in all,

Greg, despite everything, once again found his mind drifting off into more carnal pleasures as he took her in. Good legs, it seemed, nice perky breasts, just about perfect size, he imagined.

"How is your wife? Is she any better?" It was as though Paula had read his mind. He smiled back at the question. *"She's fine."* But Paula was working Greg out quicker than he was trying to analyse her.

"What's Gill like?" Greg was partly making conversation, partly interested in why Gill was a bent copper.

"What do you mean?" Paula was steady, assured, intrigued, wary.

"I mean was he always bent?" Greg was frustrated about Gill. He'd swung one way and then the other over how he came across. But then the pub rendezvous had put him firmly in with Paula and her cronies.

Paula let the question settle. The rain continued to beat down on the roof and windscreen. Driving conditions were hardly easy. She stared out of the passenger's window and delivered a measured response.

"I think he's always been ambitious – and you can't really make a lot of yourself in Hopton can you?"

Greg raised his eyebrows in such a way that said *'all the same, still bent'*. He took a glance across at Paula who had briefly looked back across at him. More silence. Brown signs for visitor attractions were becoming more regular features. She signaled for Greg to pull off the A9 and on to the A95 heading towards Grantown-on-Spey.

"Matt was at school with him. They'd kept in touch. We told him about Bryan. Told him our plans. The money appealed," she shrugged as if that were all.

"Matt and I cut him in."

"Just up here," she pointed at the right turn a third of a mile away. *"Only another twenty minutes once we're at the Bridge of Avon."* They'd been on the road seven and a half hours including fuel stop. They'd be there around 4pm to 4.30pm. Not the best preparation for tomorrow, but hopefully the right result here and … there.

CHAPTER 62

Kenny Lomax had reached the airport less than an hour after receiving the news. His father had been rushed to hospital in Sydney. He had to go back. He'd called Greg from his mobile. No reply. Left a voicemail. He was on the 1.30pm flight today. *"All the best, mate! Thinking of you and the boys."*

Stu Wainwright had been picked up by the boys in blue at eleven o'clock Saturday morning. They needed to question him about a break-in and they had reason to believe he had been involved. He didn't have to say anything, but what he did say could be used in evidence against him. The usual line. It wasn't the first time he'd been hauled in. A few years back, he'd fallen in with a group of lads who were involved in all sorts of rackets. He'd long since distanced himself from them, but on this occasion his name had been mentioned. He told his parents to let Greg know he might be a bit late for training.

The last messages Greg had sent before he left with Paula were to Alan, to let him know he couldn't make it today after all, something had come up. He'd be in touch. And to Phil Trippett. He'd have to take training if he could, although Greg wasn't sure whether he'd be up to it, bearing in mind what had happened to him at the last match.

Phil was fine as Irvine already knew, he was back and ready for action. He would take training and look after the guys. Make sure they stayed together. *Got it, Greg,* he'd sent back.

Trippett had been there at two in the afternoon, as planned, but his squad was decimated. And he didn't yet know the news about Kenny and Stu, all he knew was they weren't there. Seven of the rest of the squad – the Hammertons, Brad Warrener, Vincent Venus, Richard Brent, Ron Rigson and Alan Thomas – were also missing.

It was an hour later, through ringing them, that Trippett found they had been sent texts, by phone, that training had been cancelled, to enjoy their day and to arrive at Parrot Lane for the coach at seven o'clock – two hours later than they had been told previously.

Training never happened. Ironically, the ground was almost better populated by those who had made a start on pulling down the grandstand. Combined with the bad weather, it made for a sorry scene. Phil Trippett had gradually located everyone except Lomax and Wainwright. They were all about to go for something to eat before setting off.

Gill rolled into the car park just as Trippett had called it quits for the afternoon, fully aware of the consternation caused. In the course of his interviews over the explosions, he'd made a point of having forms filled in by everyone, all the players, and had addresses, emails and phone numbers. It had been easy to send the note. He pressed the button to draw his window down slightly as he hollered out to Tony Estorino as he was walking by.

"No Duggan today?"

Tony shrugged and gave a slight shake of his head, but didn't say anything. He was more concerned about getting out of the rain, and Gill had merely delayed that possibility.

Gill couldn't help his self-satisfied smirk. This was just another part of ensuring everything possible was made difficult for Hopton.

Phil Trippett was just a little further behind Tony, but already in his Freelander. He passed Gill and caught his smug manner. There was something wrong. Trippett, who now had the benefit of Irvine's growing knowledge about events, dialled on his hands-free.

They had taken the high road out of Grantown-on-Spey and had avoided the Bridge of Avon. They had just passed the sign for Cardhu Distillery and were heading towards Archiestown before veering into the hills and dales of Elchies Forest.

The long, graveled, largely unkempt road with trees everywhere, gave an impression there was little to find beyond. It had been a deliberate ploy. In the late part of the nineteenth century, the house, that now loomed large and shadowy in the clearing that followed the up-hill, down-dale route they had travelled for the past quarter of an hour, had been built with one purpose in mind – to keep others out.

The retreat resdence had been the home of one of Scotland's foremost fishing fleet owners, Magnus Macallan of Lossiemouth. Flanked on three of its boundaries by forest and woodland, they reached a gated entrance with CCTV.

Paula had taken over the driving for the past mile or so since passing the villages of Cardow and Knockando and had told Greg to keep down when they got there, in the back of the car, to avoid any chance of being caught on camera. She told Greg the game plan as they made their approach.

"The guys looking after them don't know we're coming, obviously, so you'll have to leave the talking to me. Okay?"

"And then what…?" He wanted some kind of confirmation from Paula. *"…We just get them and go? How does that work?? He should have thought of all this before, why leave it this long to start planning? *"Stop the car."*

Paula looked incredulous.

"You what? We've been driving seven and a half hours and you want to stop now, probably less than a mile away? Do you honestly think I'd come all this way with you, bring you here, if it wasn't to get them back? Seriously, I've better things to do with my life. Matt or no Matt."

Her hard edge was alluring and convincing, but whether he'd just thought about it now or seven hours ago, his thoughts were still relevant, in much the same way as the final minute of a rugby league game or any game is just as vital, if not more so than the first minute.

"How many of them will there be? Will they just let Col and Patsy go on your say-so? Just want to know what I'm letting myself in for, that's all … Well, it's not all … but if I've got them, it means I can get on with playing the game tomorrow…"

First, Greg wanted to see Colin and Patsy in the flesh and release them. Paula's grief over Matt had brought her to him. The more they had driven together the more he'd started to get to know her, but now they'd come all this way he was getting tense.

In the past few hours, he'd thought about everything. Diane and Kyle, the game, all of this, Gill, Bill, Irvine, Susie, Caill, Col and Patsy, Irvine, even Ted and his involvement.

Why had Paula come to him? Why not cry on Gill's shoulder? She seemed genuine. But why risk bringing him all this way? Shooting herself and all her cronies' plans in the foot right at the end. But she seemed genuine, Matt's death, her grief. Couldn't be an act, could it? He'd come this far.

"Get out of the car if you want, Greg. Or I'll get out and walk there and you go back to play your game. I've no idea how many there will be, maybe three or four. I can't tell you for definite how it will all play out, but you're here. You've come nearly 400 miles … still … you want me to walk instead? Leave you to go back? Your decision."

At first, Colin and Patsy had purely focused on finding a route to road. Any kind of road would suffice after running through trees and undergrowth since they had made their escape. It had been Colin's idea. Keep away from any kind of road at first, thereby avoiding any of their captors from finding them quickly, unless they were fit – and none of them looked in good shape, apart from the Klitschkos, maybe.

The couple had made what they felt was good ground. Colin had no idea how far they had come, but in twenty minutes or half an hour or so? Maybe two or three miles at the rate they were going? The first road they had seen so far was about a hundred yards away. There was a car parked up in a passing place.

They were in the grounds! Magnus' Retreat was the name on the gates. Greg manoeuvred himself back into the passenger's seat as Paula drove on through the long tree-lined driveway. Whilst the past five miles had been rough and uneven, the mile-long road leading up to the house was smooth, black tarmac.

Paula turned her head slightly to Greg and back to the lane. She felt Greg needed some reassurance. She had been mildly surprised he hadn't needed it much until now.

"They won't be looking for a fight, Greg, I'm pretty sure of that. We just need to settle all of this. Matt…" She faltered. *"Since Matt's gone, it really doesn't matter any more … all of this."*

The house came into vision. They trundled over a cattle grid and there it was, set in beautiful well-manicured gardens and with a lake in front of the house with an island in its middle.

"Kinell!" was Greg's first reaction in his head. Just the sort of place you would want to retreat and never go back elsewhere. Paula drove right up to the front of the house where six stone steps around 15ft in length led to the main entrance. No greeting. They stepped out of the car. Total silence. It was an eerie silence. The rain had stopped sometime around half an hour ago and there had been the first glimmer of sun all day.

Greg didn't need to say, *"What now?"* Paula was ahead of him. She turned her head back in his direction as she reached the first step. The words came out warm, almost tender. The smile that delivered them was enough to remind Greg just how fanciable she was.

"Now we talk with them, tell them it's all over. You get your brother and his girlfriend back."

Paula's poise was assured. She had no hesitation as she climbed the steps to the house. Greg was tentative as he approached the house, furtively looking around. He didn't know what to expect, but he had come to get back Colin and Patsy and now he was here that was the job – he hoped it was going to be easy with Paula by his side. Then back for the game. Win it, start patching things up with Diane. It all sounded so easy when you put it like that, but that was Greg's way of thinking.

CHAPTER 63

"Mr Duggan…" Suddenly, Paula was out of sight. Greg had only turned to look out towards the woodland that faced the house for a split second, but it had been enough for a significant change of scenery in front of him now.

Geoffrey Quinigan QC. Not that Greg knew who he was. Quinigan was one of those whose wealth and breeding dictated his manner, overtly warm, welcoming, well-spoken and a thoroughly nice chap on the outer, but also with that supercilious aura that some found engaging. Greg didn't. He avoided the handshake offered. This was going well – not!

"Why don't you come inside…" Quinigan stepped back and to one side, shifting from the rejected handshake to a sweep of the arm leading Greg into the house.

Quinigan led Greg through the imposing solid oak double doors, *"hewn from trees on the estate. We also provide Scotch oak whisky barrels for Speyside's finest distilleries…"* said Quinigan, as Greg touched one of the doors.

And there was Paula again, this time with not quite the same presence as they had travelled up together. Not that Greg was over-bothered. He only wanted the result he had come for, but so far there was no sign of either Colin or Patsy.

If Quinigan was meant to be surprised by Greg's sudden appearance, he didn't seem so. Greg could see it now, the way Paula stood close, alongside Quinigan, but he wasn't fazed. He'd told himself this was the day they'd try something and although he'd given his own act of appearing gullible near the end of their journey, he hadn't travelled all those miles without being aware that Paula could be leading him up the garden path. Bloody big garden though. Quinigan offered a drink, even rang a bell for service. Jeez, how the other half live.

"I'm afraid we appear to have lured you here under somewhat false pretences, Mr Duggan … may I call you Greg?" Quinigan was

still aiming for genial, yet with a heavy dose of sarcasm lacing the phrase.

Greg gave the slightest of shrugs, casting aside the comment as though of little consequence.

"*Call me what the fuck you like, I don't give a stuff about your pretences. You must be raving mad if you thought I believed everything she told me...*" It was Greg spitting his own form of venom. "*The only reason I came up here was to get back my brother and his girlfriend!*"

"*Ah yes, the happy couple...*" Quinigan chuckled a short, deep, affected tone. "*Tell me, Greg? Is their ... association ... as compatible as yours with Diane?*" He made a move with his arm to indicate that Greg should follow him through to the next room. Greg followed, with Paula tagging along next to Quinigan.

If he had expected to find Colin and Patsy, he was to be disappointed.

"*Father. Greg Duggan, he's a rugby player...*" It was said with a mixture of off-handedness and a degree of disdain. The room was massive. Three triple-seater sofas formed a U shape around a six-foot-square low table designed with a chess board inlaid to its centre. The sofas were cream, soft, luxurious and presently vacant.

Quinigan's father was obviously reaching the twilight of his life and inhabited a wheelchair, his legs swathed in a red tartan check blanket. His reaction to his son's words was minimal to the point of nothing.

"*Mr Duggan...*" The other of the two already in the room when Quinigan, Greg and Paula arrived, turned to face Greg from her position at the drinks cabinet, open and ready for dispensing. She smiled. Quinigan made the second introduction.

"*My mother, Greg, an amazingly sprightly young 93...*" he said as he moved closer to give her an affectionate peck on the heavily lined cheek.

"*Can I get you a drink Mr...?*" She wasn't good with names. "*He is staying, isn't he, Geoffrey?*"

Quinigan was clinical in his approach. *"Oh, yes, I believe so, Mother. He's going to be staying with us tonight and tomorrow, aren't you, Greg?"*

"Where are they?" It was a seething demand, not over loud. Quinigan was no doubt about to dribble out some form of witticism when Greg decided it was time to act. He turned for the doors, which he'd come through seconds earlier, now blocked off by Paula. He ventured closer to Quinigan, ready to take him by the throat if he didn't tell him where Colin and Patsy were.

As he reached Quinigan, he heard a click. He turned smartly from where the noise had come and found himself looking into the barrel of a shotgun, remarkably held steady and true by Quinigan's allegedly wheelchair-bound father.

This mirage was no longer as the man, now stood, was six feet tall and no longer wore the prosthetic face mask that had been so effective just seconds previously. Out of the corner of his eye, Greg saw the older woman take years off her appearance instantly as she too divested herself of the mask she wore.

Quinigan found the whole scenario quite refreshing. Whilst none of this was anything like what he had imagined would be necessary when getting involved with Dugarry and Jardine, he had to admit this had been one of the biggest adrenaline rushes he had experienced of late.

"I am so very sorry, Greg. Once again you seem to have become part of another inexplicably false pretence. What can I say? May I introduce my son and daughter, Oliver and Emily, studying at RADA, of course. What will they come up with next?"

"You're all bloody corrupt." But there was no easy way out. He couldn't see what he could do. After all that had happened in the past weeks, he was trapped, seven hours from home. And no backup.

"Take a seat, Greg." Quinigan moved to make himself more comfortable. There was no danger of Greg making a break. *"Let me fix you a drink."*

CHAPTER 64

GPK's undercover operation had worked doubly hard since Trippett had passed on Greg's text that also included Paula Caill's name and his car registration.

The team Irvine had employed through GPK to trace Whisky and Cigars and his cronies and Colin and Patsy had come up trumps, following them to one of Quinigan's three properties that were all within a couple of miles of each other. They were now working harder than ever. All hell had been let loose with the arrival of Caill. How had he just slipped in unnoticed?

They still had Colin and Patsy's four initial abductors in their grasp, but Caill was no longer there. The Klitschkos were having some kind of fallout over Colin and Patsy going free with Frank and Whisky & Cigars trying to break it up. At first the marksmen saw it all as relatively low key, but it started kicking off between them and finally they intervened. In the time it took, Caill had slipped away, as lithe as he had on entry – more worrying still, he had managed to reacquire his gun. Caill was a good few minutes behind Colin and Patsy, but they were on foot, he had his Lexus RS. It was at least a mile and a half to the first road. They'd had at least five minutes' head start.

It was now overkill with four people where Colin and Patsy had been held now watching over the four who had been responsible for their abduction. They were there to save and release Colin and Patsy, not nursemaid. The pair came out of their unit a quarter of a mile away and swapped rosters with the marksmen sending them on their way to follow Caill and if necessary take him down, but not kill.

Geoff Quinigan was at ease with the current situation as it had unfolded. Paula had carried out the plan to perfection. Neither he nor Dugarry had wanted to become directly involved in anything unsavoury, yet they certainly wanted to do everything they could to ensure Hopton Town's chances of winning their final game were as remote as possible.

The trio had assessed where their efforts best lay. Quinigan and Dugarry's plot with Paula was strikingly good. Play on her loss of Matt, and Duggan's weakness it seemed for anything female. Gill was proving useful for providing disarray with his social media and text skills and popping up everywhere to cause problems.

Caill was their loose cannon. He was also the lynchpin, his land the reason all this was taking place. They had to be careful with him, make him feel as though he was working for his money and important to the team effort.

Paula and Geoff Quinigan had never been an item in public. They had shared a bed on many occasions. There was something about his arrogance that appealed to her. He exuded grace and charm and projected utter confidence. When Matt had died it had been Quinigan who had been the shoulder to cry on, and from there it had led to this.

Greg couldn't see a way out. The odds were stacked against him, as indeed they had been for some considerable time. Had Phil passed on the message? It was getting into late afternoon-early evening. In a matter of just over 22 hours, Hopton Town's fate would be sealed.

Greg's last six weeks had been close to wall-to-wall purgatory and now he was sat 400 miles away from home and hadn't found his brother or Patsy. Quinigan watched over him.

"*Drink, Greg?*" Greg had the drink in his hand by the time Quinigan had finished the seemingly rhetorical question. Greg stared at the glass. But he wasn't focusing on it, his focus was more intent on Quinigan. His eyes continued to train on the glass as he spoke.

"*Why?*" It was low, controlled, asking the question of Quinigan as he moved beyond Greg to pass a drink to Paula sat opposite. He meant, why was this man involved? He had everything already. This place. He would be on hundreds of thousands as a QC, plus the 'old money' he came from.

Quinigan turned back toward him, smile in place. No reply. He returned to Greg, patted him on the shoulder and at that point made his first mistake.

Greg took hold of him by the wrist and succeeded in flinging Quinigan sufficiently off balance to wrench his arm behind his back and grab him by the throat. Before Paula and Quinigan's offspring had even realised what was going on, Greg had dragged him up by the neck and was behind Quinigan using him as a human shield.

"You bloody fool, Duggan!" Quinigan's voice was no longer calm and assured. *"You're going nowhere."*

Quinigan let out an ear-splitting wail as Greg wrenched his right arm sufficiently smartly up behind his back that everyone in the room could hear the pop of his shoulder out of its socket. *"You fu…"* Quinigan couldn't even finish whatever expletive he was going to come out with as he was in so much pain. But that wasn't all. Greg also twisted Quinigan's neck so fast his veins popped up blood-red so quickly that the man went from being in control to in fear of his life in a matter of seconds.

"Try to stop me from leaving and I'll kill him…" Greg nodded as though to affirm what he had just said. *"No word of a lie. Just get out of my way! … You!"* Greg motioned to Paula. *"Keys to the car! Gate pass!"*

Greg had no idea how this was going to work out. All he knew was he now had Quinigan and whilst he kept him between himself and the rest he held the upper hand.

"You're pathetic, Duggan! What do you think's going to happen? Do you really think I'm going to let you…" Before Quinigan had finished he was once again in agony as Greg punched him hard in his side. Paula winced. Quinigan's rib cage felt crushed on his right side and his face contorted with his eyes bulging. If he had any wind in his sails previously, he had not a breath left now.

Greg had to act fast. He had no idea how many others were around – these four – Quinigan, Paula, the young kids in their late teens, who looked traumatized already. He had to get out quickly.

"*Car keys! Gate pass! Now!*" he barked at Paula. "*Don't come near me! Just bring them and follow me!*" He motioned to the door. "*And don't get all heroic otherwise I swear I will rip his head off – and then yours!*"

The odds were still stacked against him. Quinigan was his only hope. Just what the hell he hoped to do with him he didn't know. As on the rugby field, Greg was guided by his instinct.

"*You'll never get away with this,*" Quinigan was rallying. Greg had dragged him to the front door. Paula and the kids, they looked nothing more than that, the daughter in tears, following in his and Quinigan's wake. Fuck it! Paula wasn't about to hand over the keys or gate pass. She'd try something, devious cow, she was a Caill all right. Greg hadn't seen anyone come running. Hadn't heard anything else happening. And Quinigan was becoming a heavier weight to carry.

"*Open the door!*" he barked again at Paula. "*Back away, you two!*" to the kids. "*And you!*" to the servant or butler who had just appeared, bloody 'ell, servant! These people! Paula opened the door. "*Now outside. All of you! Now!*" He was chancing his arm there was nobody else around, but what other option was there?

"*This way!*" He threw in another sickening blow to Quinigan's midriff, another crunch. "*Pleeeeaase! Please don't hurt him any more … Daddy!*" The girl was in despair. But she wasn't about to cause any problem. She was simply pleading. Greg didn't give a stuff. "*And don't even think about it!*" Greg howled at the lad who was just about showing signs of trying to help his father.

"*Keys! Pass! Put them there!*" Greg chin-pointed to the park bench style seat that looked out over the lake. His car was 20 yards away. Paula did it. "*Now all four of you. If you don't want him hurt anymore and still want your father…*" he said for effect for the kids, "*…to continue breathing, then start walking. Over there.*" Greg led with his chin again.

"*The lake?*" Paula couldn't believe it. Neither could Greg! Suddenly he had a lake fetish! Gill, now this lot!

He was still gambling on nobody else being on site and at least this way he was buying himself some time on getting away. He had no gun, no knife, this was his brawn and whatever his brain could muster. *"Yeah. Now walk! All of you! When you get to the island I'll release your dad! ... Go!"* They hesitated. Quinigan saw a chance.

"You don't need to do this..." Greg wasn't sure whether it was a call to the others or words for him and he certainly wasn't going to waste time finding out.

"Hmmpph ... Aaahhh ... fu..." as Greg launched another salvo, this time straight back into his side. *"Yes you do! Go! Now! Or else he gets more ... and more..."*

Tentative at first, they all began wading into the lake. *"Keep going!"*

Quinigan was rallying again. *"I swear ... I will have ... you for this..."* They had reached halfway. It was enough for Greg. *"You reckon?"* He couldn't resist. Releasing him at last, Greg launched his conversion kicking foot, as though the ball had to make it over the sticks from the halfway line, slap bang in Quinigan's crotch and while he was doubling up shoulder-carried him toward the lake before upending him with an illegal spear tackle into the water. No time to admire. He'd bought getaway time.

Keys. Gate pass. Go.

From out of nowhere his phone sprung to life! He'd left it in the car. Texts, emails all pinged through as he sped away down the drive. He hit the voicemails. Five. *"Greg, we need to talk..."* Diane could wait. Next.

"Hi! You're a lucky winner...!" Next. *"Greg. Bob. Got your message. Tracking you. Patsy and Colin too. You're in the same area. Help on its way. Watch out for Caill, he's armed. Check your texts, we'll keep in touch with anything."*

Message four. *"Got your message, Greg, no probs, mate."* Alan. No time for looking at texts. He was nearing the gate. Slowing as he came to it, he brought the car alongside where the card was to be placed, as Paula had.

Nothing. No way around for the car. Huge heavy iron gates. He'd need a tank to force them. Time to run. He was over the gates in a flash. Whatever had been wrong with the pass or his usage of it was of no consequence now. Mile to the road they'd come in on. He could do that in seven minutes in running gear or playing strip. More like nine or ten at the moment. It would have taken Quinigan and Paula five minutes to get out of the water, find keys, get in a car and follow and his car was right in front of the gates when they did. Keep going. The light of the day was just starting to give way to dusk.

Greg felt he must be halfway back to the main road. A car turned into the lane from up ahead, headlights suddenly coming his way. Not quite dark, so he could make out the colour – silver – coming full tilt, but now slowing slightly – should he stay or change direction through the trees. Ho altered his run to the edge of the lane on the grass ready to move. At the same time, what looked like a quad bike came into view behind him. Shit, another gate maybe or small enough to get around his car. Whatever. And now another set of lights had appeared from the road end, hurtling towards.

He glanced back. Two quads were now spraying small stones in their wake as they made their way from the gate. Forty yards in front of him, the driver of the first car from the road hit the brakes and hit them hard. The quads were now in view and maybe less than two hundred and fifty yards away. Something had to give.

The braking car was squealing and screeching with all its might and its back wheels started swinging from the back to the right, spinning the car around to face back to the road. The other car now coming towards from the road was at best three hundred yards from the car now at Greg's feet. The passenger door sprung open.

"For God's sake get in!" The voice was desperate, loud, anxious, and fortunately extremely familiar – but this was no time for familiarity. *"GET IN!"*

Greg threw himself at the seat as the car was still moving. It hadn't quite finished its spin. Legs still flailing around outside. He clutched the driver's side of the passenger seat as arms from within grappled to drag him in further.

Tyres and brakes filled the air with a cacophony of sound, but it was gunshot that eclipsed everything else. Greg's new transportation was now fully air-conditioned as a shot from the quad bikes shattered the rear window as the car straightened up and Greg finally completed his seating position. *"Forget the door!"*

It had been difficult enough to get into the car without trying to shut it, but Greg's first instinct had been to try. Another shot rang out. Greg couldn't tell for definite, as he was no expert on thudding of bullets into targets, but this sounded as though it had hit something substantial. *"LEAVE IT!!!"*

Greg saw the reason why the instruction had been given as in the next second, he was doorless courtesy of a tree. Colin had been unable to avoid the contact as, in rectifying the driving position and having accounted for Greg's pick up and subsequent rectification of body, the tree proved unavoidable. They were not yet back on the track properly. *"KEEP DOWN!"* The car that had followed was raining down headlights and bullets. One guy was leaning out of the onrushing car trained on Colin. Next second he wasn't!

Colin had taken the grass route again, just as they were within no more than 25 yards from each other. The oncoming vehicle had veered too – in response to the marksman being gunned by the quad bikers. Colin wasn't sticking around to find the outcome. There was an OK Coral feel about what they were leaving behind.

Colin had floored the Lexus now. Greg looked to the back of the car. Patsy looked battered, bruised, windswept and dishevelled. But he still fancied the arse off her. He had to bloody well stop this! She bit hard on her lower lip as Greg looked between the driver's and passenger's seats. *"You okay?"* A nod.

It wouldn't go down as the most inspired line he would ever

utter, but it had to be that, given what he had just seen. In an instant, Col was alerted. Greg had seen something in Patsy's eyes. Colin looked back. Patsy shut her eyes and kept on with the biting of her lip as she told him, breathless. *"Just drive. Drive, Col. I think I…"*

Greg looked beyond Patsy. Nobody following. Patsy slumped forward, lifeless.

CHAPTER 65

Caill had inadvertently loaned the Lexus to Colin and Patsy. He had stopped just a hundred yards or so from where they had spied him. Looking for them. At first they had remained low, watching. Desperate for a pee and reckoning there was no-one around, he'd got out and walked across to the edge of a wood, out of sight.

Colin and Patsy had grabbed their chance. But they needed the keys or whatever to start it. When they were within twenty metres of the car, Caill reappeared, pulling up his trouser zip. It was Patsy who had seen him first. Colin looked back, first in Patsy's direction then over to the emerging Caill, who in the same instant saw both of them and made a run for the car. It would have been comical if it hadn't also been so serious. Caill reached the car first and was into the driver's seat by the time Colin arrived, but he was fumbling around with the ignition. It was still a key that turned in the lock. The car was ten years old. He dropped the keys to the floor. The door was shut, but he hadn't managed to lock it before Colin grabbed him by both shoulders and literally flung him out of the car.

"You bastard...!" Caill, while winded, was not yet done. He still had his gun. But his accounting practice was clearly well out as he hadn't accounted for the second of the pair and it was Patsy who took care of the gun, kicking it out of his hand and following up with a knee into his groin.

It was Colin who took the lead from thereon, leaving Caill in a somewhat similar position to their earlier predicament by making him strip down too, and they were nicer here than his men had been to them, his bright red leather thong! Erm, yes! Maybe they would have been better taking that as well. His clothes were dumped unceremoniously in the back of the car with Colin in fits of laughter as they left him bound by the roadside. "Who's a naughty boy then, Mr Caill? You should score with the locals around here tonight. The Scots are meant to be great tossers! Thanks for the car."

Colin and Patsy had sped off in true Bonnie and Clyde style, leaving a hog-tied and infuriated Caill in their wake. If they'd known his other habits, he'd have been far less fortunate.

They had passed Tomintoul taking the Braemar route when a phone had started ringing. It hadn't been theirs as they'd lost them when they'd stripped in the Hopton countryside. It was coming from Caill's phone. They had missed the call by the time they'd retrieved the phone from his trouser pocket. Two voicemails, both from Quinigan.

"Bryan, be a good chap will you and come to the house, leave those other two. Paula is bringing Duggan, should be here any minute. We could do with your firearm, just as insurance, you understand. There's a good chap. Just in case you can't remember, it's the left turn after Archiestown ... I'll text you the postcode. See you soon."

And the earlier message a day or two ago now: "Bryan, think it might be a good idea to add a little presence to the team at Laurie's Lodge. I've had it on a nudge and a wink that we have uninvited guests nearby. Carefully does it, old chap."

Tomintoul to Archiestown was only 24 miles, but this was Scotland and would take the best part of 45 minutes. Colin and Patsy had turned back around to find him – and unfortunately now with rather disastrous consequences.

CHAPTER 66

It was a horrible sound. An excrutiatingly loud, hollow, tinny, incessant noise that had most definitely achieved its purpose within seconds. The perpetrator being the radio/alarm. Trippett was now awake. He looked across the hotel bedroom. The sumptuous surroundings had helped ease the pain of the previous afternoon. The whole squad had enjoyed a good meal, coach trip and a relaxed evening. He was still short of Wainwright, Lomax and Greg and with their small squad they would be hard to replace. Odd they hadn't heard from them though.

Bob Irvine was looking after everyone, minus the missing three, and they were being treated royally in the delightful surroundings of The Hepton Mansion Hotel and Country Club, tucked neatly away from all main roads and only reached by one excellently maintained track. The Hotel was a dream destination complete with health spa, pool, gym, tennis courts, golf course – and the owner loved his classic cars that were on show all around.

They were five miles from Ensideleigh, soon to be the scene of the most momentous game in the club's history, eclipsing even their great Cup Final appearance. Every single player understood they were responsible today for the future of the club. It was now nine o'clock. Six hours from kick-off. The skies were completely blue and the sun kissed the rolling green hills that gave way to the Country Club's golf course beyond.

Some of the squad were already tucking in to a hearty Full English breakfast by the time Trippett arrived with the Hammerton twins, determined to show the rest exactly what a healthy appetite really meant.

Gill had positioned himself in the hotel lobby area and in the best traditions of police surveillance, although not exactly for that purpose, now held a copy of a newspaper in front of him.

"Morning, sergeant!"

Kenny Lomax had marched straight up to Gill by the time the policeman had realised who it was. All Gill could see of Lomax, thanks to brilliant sunlight bursting through the massive glass reception windows, was a silhouette. He couldn't see the utter torrent of rage inside that was about to unleash itself upon him. He certainly didn't expect what happened next.

Kenny turned back away from the disaster he had just inflicted on Gill. It's often said the nose is one of the most sensitive parts of the body. Gill no longer had to worry about such nonsense as his was now sharing itself around his face – and two other parts of his nether anatomy, check, make that three, which would normally feature in the sensitivity stakes were in serious danger of never being able to be used with breeding in mind.

The hotel receptionist and another member of staff were on their way to offer assistance to the young man; a call was about to be made for the manager to come quickly. Bob Irvine appeared having witnessed the affair.

"There'll be no need for that." He looked at the staff member about to make the call.

"And you can leave him to his nose and ... other accessories ... I don't think Mr Gill would like to make a complaint..." Irvine's eyebrows raised, by way of challenge to Gill how futile that would be. *"I thought not, carry on your tremendous work here, ladies. You really have a lovely hotel to be proud of..."*

Irvine picked up the newspaper Gill had been holding, *"...but I'd prefer you had neater papers than this. Look, it's already well red!"*

He gave a comical look to those watching, to emphasise his pun, as he held the blood-stained sheets of the tattered copy by his thumb and middle finger, dropping it into the waste bin by the side of the leather armchair where Gill had once been comfortable. An audience had begun to develop from where the hotel guests, seventy-five per cent Town players and staff, had been breakfasting.

Tony Estorino had a grin as wide as his face. *"Had that coming a long way back that,"* he nodded toward Kenny. *"What happened to you yesterday?"*

The gap-toothed Aussie's telling of a cruel hoax, involving a wild goose chase half way around the world and back since 1pm yesterday that had seen him land in Abu Dhabi at 8pm and hang around until the next flight at 2.35am today landing in Manchester two hours ago, had seen Tony Estorino go straight over to Gill and deliver a head butt that Gill had told the staff was all in order. He hadn't moved for a while since.

"Let's just put it all down to a little bit of bad news. But I seem to have got it out of my system now!"

Kenny gave a click of the fingers and finger-point by way of mini-salute of acknowledgement to Bob Irvine, who had found out what had happened once Phil Trippett had reported him missing. He'd been too late to stop him catching the flight as he was in the air bound for Brisbane and the Gold Coast by the time they'd known what had happened, but calls to Etihad had ensured Kenny went no further than the capital of the United Arab Emirates.

Ensideleigh was a once proud mining town just two miles from the sea, the coal seam long rendered no longer viable. In its place was new housing, not unattractive, designed for the influx of new light commercial activity that had been promised through redevelopment agency money.

A nice thought, if that had been how it really had happened. In reality, it had been likened to a carve up. Local councillors had got rich quick on backhanders to overpriced consultants and hadn't attracted anything like the businesses required to provide sufficient employment. The reality was of a town now that had lost its identity. Their rugby league club had suffered the same. It had ridden high in the peak production pit years of the 1950s and 1960s, when crowds of 10,000 had been recorded. Today's ground had a capacity of 3500 and usually struggled to manage one-tenth of it.

Bath Street Recreation Ground had been Ensideleigh RLFC's fourth ground in the last ten seasons, the club having moved back into the town by taking over a redundant school and sports field and building a modest grandstand with terracing where the grandstand stopped and all around. What could best be described as a tin shelter ran the full length of the opposite touch line. Behind both sets of posts was open terracing, running to some ten rows of steps with the obligatory crush barriers. The steps were topped at one end by 'executive' Portakabins, not unlike what Irvine had fixed for Hopton.

A distraught and extremely emotional Mrs Wainwright, Stu's mother, had been trying to get a message to Mr Duggan since yesterday afternoon, after she had found out her son Stuart had been arrested. The policeman she had talked with at the station had been very nice, but said it hadn't looked good for him. She'd left a message for Mr Duggan, but he hadn't returned her call. Stuart hadn't done anything wrong, so far as she knew – and she knew her son. Yes, he had been a bit silly as a junior, but not now – and he loved playing for Town.

She, Maureen, had finally left a message on the answerphone in the office back at Parrot Lane this morning. When Irvine had rung in to pick up messages he had immediately set GPK's boys on the case along with his own solicitor. Wainwright hadn't been released yet, but wheels were in motion.

Julian Jardine hadn't wanted it to come down to this, but knew it was he who held a couple of trump cards. All he needed to do was to make sure Hopton Town didn't win. A draw would be good enough and of course it was quite possible they would lose without his meddling. Nonetheless, there was such a fortune riding on this one result and he was not about to leave anything to chance. This was the final hurdle.

Colin was at Patsy's side in Raigmore Hospital in Inverness. It had taken them just over an hour to get there and she'd lost a reasonable quantity of blood, but they had operated on her within an hour of arrival. She had just woken and was resting. Greg had gone for a coffee. *"Go, with your brother."* She nodded briefly, still recovering from the anaesthetic, her voice soft and low. It was midday.

"Go. You know you need to … it's alright…" She closed her eyes, as if the heavy curtains of her eyelids were too much to cope with. She spoke again, still with her eyes closed.

"God knows, I've enough material now for my next novel," she smiled. Colin held out and stroked her hand softly and affectionately. "But go … he needs you … we've not come this far to miss out now, all of us, there's got to be a way to stop what's happening here … go and save your brother's club … and watch him do it…" Again she looked at him, again she clutched his hand tight. "Go."

Dalesmoor Radio had decamped to Ensideleigh for the whole afternoon, starting at midday and Terry Derbyshire had been at the ground since 9am prepping, talking, phoning, texting, updating social media.

"Well, this is it. Welcome along to you all this afternoon, when we find out whether or not professional rugby league dies here in Ensideleigh or for our own Hopton Town. And the news isn't good. Although the official team list hasn't been issued as yet, I can tell listeners that Town look as though they will be going into this, the most important game of their lives, without Aussie Kenny Lomax, regular full back Ian Sissons or that sensational new pocket battleship inspirational young scrum-half Stu Wainwright. But it's the absence of coach and captain Greg Duggan that is the most mystifying. Perhaps recent media stories have had a bearing! Let's hope for brighter news before kick off.

"But I can tell you who IS here…" Derbyshire was currently stood by the touchline in front of the grandstand with his guests.

"With me are our very own Messenger man, Ted Brewiss – who has followed Town's fortunes for four decades; Dr Veejay Ranjitshah – the club's new physio; then there's the man you and I and everyone associated with Town simply know by just one name – Fred, but better known for his catchphrase of…"

At this point, Derbyshire cued in Fred to fill in with his 'Give 'em some stick' catchphrase. Unfortunately, it hadn't worked.

Not exactly effective radio! Derbyshire was quick to react.

"Ah, well, just listen out later folks and I'm sure Fred will oblige. And our fourth guest is the man who was coach at the start of the season – George Ramsbottom! I'll come to you first, George. Foot in two camps today? Ensideleigh as well as Town? Or do you favour one over the other?"

George had played for both clubs – five years with Ensideleigh, winning promotion with them after having started his career with Town and coming back later as coach after spells as a player with Sherwell and Axby. Terry Derbyshire had asked the question cheekily and George had responded diplomatically.

"They've both such a great rugby league tradition. It's just very sad one team has to go after today's game. Saddens me deeply." Veejay was up next as Dalesmoor Radio cranked up its momentum toward the match.

Jardine's first plan had involved a brief mobile phone conversation and a text message from the hospitality area, followed by the slightest of nods across the room with a good-looking, middle-aged woman.

"Ted, if this really is the last game that Hopton Town ever play, where will the blame lie…"

Terry Derbyshire was 'filling' as they called it in the radio trade. He'd originally planned for Phil Trippett being available, but Trippett still hadn't arrived at the stadium, and neither had the team.

Fred had arrived early with the first coach and had been around just at the same time as Derbyshire had been panicking about Trippett's non arrival. Derbyshire had known Fred for years, had kept him away from the airwaves as he was aware he could be a liability – but he had a lot of time to fill and providing he didn't have to take him off air as a result of his sometimes colourful language, he'd decided to give him a go. As Ted finished his comment, Terry tried again with Fred.

"Well, it's getting closer to that time to … how do you say it, Fred…?" and once again he moved his hands in such a way for Fred to provide his contribution with the phrase every Town

supporter had heard from him for years.

Dalesmoor Radio went off air temporarily as Fred struggled to understand what Terry wanted him to say, leading to him saying very innocently, but on air, roughly something along the lines that he hadn't a clue what Terry meant!

Jardine was working his off-field game plan that would affect the on-field result. Only one objective needed to be attained. One objective and all his manoeuvring would prove worthwhile. These hours before kick-off would be vital, but he was also an 80-minutes man. Nothing was over until it was over, busy day, but with a handsome return in prospect. He'd succeed where the others had tried, but seemingly failed.

CHAPTER 67

Town had originally planned on getting to Bath Street by noon, leaving everyone plenty of time to relax and prepare, hence the reason Terry Derbyshire had been expecting Phil Trippett. They were still at their hotel at 12.30.

Following the infinitely one-sided fracas in the hotel reception, Gill had chosen to relocate to his car in the hotel car park, where he attempted to make contact with Dugarry, Quinigan and Paula. Dugarry had been on his way to the ground; Quinigan and Paula were over 150 miles away, but also mobile.

Despite Town's recent better form, Dugarry and Quinigan could still see their pot of gold within reach. Town were without their most influential players so far as they were aware, through Gill's and Qunigan's efforts, and with the pressure Jardine could and should exert, they were in a good place, but each knew it wasn't over. This had been a long haul and it was important they were there to see it through. Gill chose not to update them on Lomax's return.

They were all also aware that, as disreputable as he was, Caill was vital. it was his land they were to earn from. His debts that had put him their way. Where was he?

Ironically, it had been Quinigan's son and daughter heading out to a fancy dress party, the source of the prosthetics earlier when trying them out, who had found a man hours later the previous evening in an 'unlikely position', they had said sniggeringly, and in dubious attire – *"red thong, really?"* – whom they had freed and offered a coat they'd had in the back of their car and a lift to Inverness where they were staying with friends. Quinigan had had no idea about it being Caill when they laughed about it together on the phone with their father, as he made his way south with Paula.

Gill had tried Caill, but no reply. Only Greg, Col and Patsy knew why.

Josie Penzance was having a ball. It was she who had talked George into going along to the game. There was no Janice around. The Ramsbottoms' marriage had become more of a pact than a relationship, their front for Bill had been just how they played it with long-time friends and family. George wouldn't get in Janice's way, and Janice wouldn't stop George from seeing who he liked – and he had always liked Josie!

"George, you'll never guess who I've just seen...?" Josie and George had become extremely close friends during his playing days, particularly when he was playing away! Josie had casually slipped her arm around George, not realising he was talking with Ted Brewiss after Terry Derbyshire's interviews.

"I'm sorry, I'm Josie..." She made a slight wave with her hand as she released her hold on George before dragging him off elsewhere.

Julian Jardine was being feted in the hospitality area at Bath Street. Pressing the flesh was a Jardine trait, very approachable, something which had made him an untouchable in the rugby league hierarchy.

"Julie!" Julian turned to face the Ensideleigh chairman, Billy Brodie, a tall, broad shouldered former powerful second row forward in his day, who persisted with Julie instead of Julian. Julian was wary of Billy's iron grip, and although he knew to offer his hand, he also knew immediately following the handshake it would need several seconds to restore the blood flow.

They had known each other for many years and Jardine was always happy to see Billy, but never more so than on this occasion.

"Come to read us the last rites?" Brodie was loud, warm and hospitable.

"Alright, Billy, that'll do. Don't overplay it." Julian was speaking under his breath. He sat down at the table as Billy had beckoned. Billy got serious immediately.

"So, what's this all about then, Julian? Let's not mess about.

You're up to something and you want me to help you, so what I want to know is what's in it for me."

Julian Jardine raised his eyebrows and feeling the bridge of his nose with the thumb and middle finger of his right hand before placing his right hand to cradle his chin, gave Billy the right answer.

"Plenty." Billy's smile widened. The pair adjourned to a quieter area where they could talk the talk.

On reaching Inverness, courtesy of the kind young couple who'd untied him and given him the coat, as well as the warmth of their car for an hour, he had made for the police station, told his story, somewhat abridged and most definitely fictitious and they had contacted Brent Dugarry who had arranged for clothes, cash and tickets for a flight from Inverness airport that morning. He'd chosen Dugarry as, minus his phone and embarrassed by his failure, he could at least spin a different story.

Town's team coach had arrived at Bath Street at 1.30pm.

The Rubber Ducks, as Ensideleigh had become known amongst their faithful, courtesy of primrose yellow home shirts and the name of their ground, were well on their way to hosting the largest attendance seen at the ground, with Hopton's coaches arriving steadily since 12 noon. The players had been out on the ground warming up from 2pm.

Irvine's word had been followed to the letter with over two thousand Town fans making the trip. They were already in tremendous voice as they monopolised the tin shed side of the ground. But the Rubber Ducks were not without support either. The atmosphere was building.

"Well, it's just half an hour to go here before kick-off at Hopton Town's Judgment Day." Terry Derbyshire was back in full flow, now safely stored in his commentary area with his summariser for the day, Ian Sissons, once again out injured. *"And some good news when we saw Kenny Lomax getting off the bus, but still no sign of Stu Wainwright and team captain Greg Duggan. It's worrying times, Ian."*

Jardine hadn't finished his preparations. There was work still to be done. Billy was on side, but now he wanted a little more insurance.

"Focus, boys! Get it right, nothing silly, keep hold of the ball, completion rate and make the hard yards…"

Mike Rodley was doing all he could in the Town dressing room in place of Trippett, who'd disappeared just prior to the bus leaving the hotel. Ritualistic preparations of strapping, tape and spray was going on all around and he was kitted out too! No Wainwright, no Greg, Town had been used to disarray, but this was more than ridiculous.

Kenny was ready.

"Look, mates. We can't let what Greg and Phil have done go to waste, and Bill! If we don't do it for ourselves, or all those guys out there…" They could hear the crowd giving it everything already for them out in the stands, *"…then let's at least do it for Bill … And let's all do it … together!"*

Thankfully, not one of the Hopton squad had been anywhere near the door as Greg had made his entrance. It had been more than any shove. The door was still swinging, albeit a little more loosely than previous.

"Think I'd miss this?" Following Greg into the room was Stu Wainwright and suddenly the dressing room had gone to a feeling of euphoria. They were back.

Trippett was next in. He'd collected them both from the helipad where the helicopters had landed within five minutes of each other in a field two miles from the hotel. Flights arranged by Irvine. He stood for a second, smiling, then reverted to hard edge and steely determination.

"All that matters is this!" He held up a ball. Paused for a split second before firmly putting his clenched fist to his chest.

"And this!" He scanned the whole room, making sure he had the attention of all as he pointed to his head. *"And this,"* as he pointed to his heart.

"Play with these three and we will get the result today… Play without it and you'll condemn this club to the scrapheap … that's it … nothing more … it's all down to you now."

Irvine was in the crowd already, wary and watchful, particularly of Julian Jardine. He'd been with Trippett to make sure everything went without a hitch over Stu's release and Greg getting there.

Journalists, hand-held cameras and private investigators were strategically placed all around the ground. One coach had been designated purely for the huge surveillance team and a TV studio van now stood in Ensideleigh's car park with producers, editors, runners and screens all trained on everywhere and everyone they could.

"*Damn, fuck, shit, bastard…*" The tirade of single word abuse went on and on as an infuriated Bryan Caill took extreme measures against his steering wheel. Having flown back into Ringstall International, he was now sat in a five-mile tailback ten miles from the ground.

The roar of the crowd as both sides appeared was more than uplifting. It was tear-jerkingly amazing, fueled with immense passion. Even Kenny Lomax was impressed, and he'd played in front of Grand Finals of over 80,000 back down under.

Dugarry was ready. Jardine had tried his best to stage manage. Ensideleigh were pumped. Hopton were resolute and as one. Referee Richard Robson, having dispensed the formalities, set the match underway. Bob Irvine had hardly had time to take his seat. He'd given more than he'd ever anticipated six weeks ago.

Ensideleigh kicked to Hopton. The crowd roared as the first impact was just a second or two away. The ball hung in the air. Ensideleigh had gone for a short high kick in order they could launch into the Hopton catcher hard right from the start. And the ball did hang. Mark Merrioneth and Tony Estorino were under it and a rampaging pack of Rubber Ducks had only one thing on their mind. Merrioneth called his ball and went up to meet it, as did the first onrushing Duck. The crowd baying for action.

And they got it! Merrioneth was taken out, thudding to the floor as though shot as Ensideleigh's second rower Dave Banger lived up to his name. As if that wasn't enough, Tony Estorino, who hadn't jumped, had been clothes-lined by another of the Ensideleigh forwards the same instant. Banger's hit had been seen and was legal, the other definitely wasn't, but Robson hadn't seen it.

The ball had sprung from Merrioneth's hands and into the Ducks'. The plan had worked to perfection. Town were scrambling in defence as quickly as they could, but Ensideleigh were moving fast as Merrioneth and Estorino struggled to recover.

They forced the play wide, then cut back, stringing the Hopton defence as wide as they could before Maori stand-off Isaac Izamua sidestepped and scooted over the line near the posts. The conversion was easy. Town fans were stunned. 6-0 down and they hadn't been playing for longer than a minute and a half.

Tony Estorino was in a far worse state than Mark Merrioneth, who was just winded. Estorino was a mess. His face resembled more a pizza at present. Veejay was back in action! Once he'd applied the cold, wet sponge, Tony's face came clear and apart from the still bleeding scar on the bridge of his nose plastered quickly, he'd be okay until they had time to take a proper look at half-time.

Irvine looked across to Jardine, who gave no indication he was at the ground on anything but a watching brief.

Perversely, going six down in the opening minute had galvanised Greg's mind. As they'd come from behind the posts after the conversion he was instructing.

"Kenny! Stu! Get on my shoulder, one of you, every time I get the ball. I'm gonna open these bastards up … Vince! Get ready to run, mate, you're gonna go the length of the field!"

"Willie, Jeff – hit 'em, boys, do some serious damage. I don't want to see a single one of their guys walking off this field at the end!"

They hadn't heard this from Greg in recent weeks. It was good to see it back.

The feeling of resolution spread right across the Hopton line from one to thirteen. Caught out though they may have been by the initial play, they were now together and tackling hard. But Ensideleigh were matching them. So much at stake.

Blow for blow and play for play this was carnage. Blood flowed, bodies crunched. Stu Wainwright had earned them a half break in the tenth minute and Ron Rigson had been unlucky not to break the line. Greg had hammered his body into at least three of the opposition to devastating effect and they had reacted similarly.

"You've got to be having a laugh…"

Jardine's reaction to Brodie's text he'd delivered, even though he was sat next to him, was audible no matter how much he needed to keep it under his breath. Billy Brodie had just upped the ante. He wanted more. He had been watching Julie intently. He was now looking straight at the game as he responded to Jardine.

"No, Julian, just taking advantage of an opportunity. It's only business, don't concern yourself."

Billy stopped himself from carrying on, even though he was enjoying himself. He had taken time to analyse what Julie had been offered and had realised there might well be far more in it for himself.

"Think about it … But don't take too long! … Clock's ticking, you know."

The Hopton fans raised their voices once again, trying all they could. Venus had taken the ball on the wing and was sprinting down the touchline having already evaded two would-be tacklers. He was in the clear…

"Ohhh!" The crowd's collective wincing reaction was a tumult of combined pain for the player and themselves as Vincent Venus's hamstring gave the impression of a twanged rubber band. He still held the ball, but was pulling up, slowing, hoping someone would appear alongside him. The Ensideleigh full back, who Vince had been approaching and had been ready to step and speed away, paid no attention to his injury and clattered him into touch. Vince was off the pitch and out of the game.

*"And that's the end of Vincent Venus's afternoon, poor lad …
he's been a great addition since he joined a couple of months ago and
after his hat-trick of tries on Wednesday, he'd have been looking
forward to this … it's another uphill task for Town, Ian… "* Terry
Derbyshire was desperate to report good news.

There was no way he could carry on and as he left the field,
somewhat lamely, the Ensideleigh team high-fived all around.
There was no way any of them was about to lose out on a
glorious pay-day they had been promised five minutes before
walking on to the field of play!

Richard Robson wasn't the world's worst referee, but he had
his moments along with the rest of the fraternity. He wouldn't
fix a game. He just wouldn't. However, three minutes before the
match started he had received an anonymous text that went
along the lines of him taking an admittedly generous sum or his
teenage daughter, presently in the company of someone other
than he would have anticipated, would suffer. No calls. No
police. Just make sure.

There had been no further definition of how this would
manifest itself and a swift call to his daughter brought no
response. Hopton Town had to lose. He had no option. He'd try
her again at half time, but for now he'd hope the game went
Ensideleigh's way and his decisions may have to help. It was
only a game. His daughter was at stake. He sent her a message.

Vincent's departure was the signal for an Ensideleigh
onslaught. Fifteen minutes from half-time. Prior to kick-off, it
would have been enough for them to preserve their league
status, but now they had been given the opportunity of a one-
off earning, something a great deal more worthwhile than any
winning money they had earned before. And bonuses for points
ahead at the end. They hit the accelerator.

Robson was astute. He hadn't been a rugby league referee for
the past twenty years that he didn't know how to work a game
himself, if he needed to. Ensideleigh were camped in the
Hopton half. They were pushing hard, but their forwards weren't
penetrating the Hopton defence.

He knew that if he was to start giving decisions against Hopton, he would have to balance up at some stage. It always seemed to the fans as though referees did that anyway, so he took the option of penalising Ensideleigh first. After all, there was no significant danger to Ensideleigh where he gave the penalty.

"And they needed that! Town have been well under the cosh for the past few minutes and that forward pass decision, which I have to say looked marginal to me, could give them chance to mount their first serious attack for some time…" Terry Derbyshire was on the case, willing the lads to move forward.

Robson blew again giving a forward pass this time from Town. Derbyshire was aghast. Town were now under pressure in front of their posts. Ensideleigh smelled blood.

Town stood firm, tackle after tackle. It came to the last tackle before Ensideleigh would have to hand over possession. Their captain, Mickey King, a crafty half back, made space and kicked the ball, bouncing wickedly towards the corner.

Warwick Player, on for Venus, hadn't yet had a touch. He sprung into the air just a metre in front of the try line to collect the now descending ball as it had kicked up high from its bounce with three on-rushing attackers' eyes focused on the intended capture, and he had it! If they took him behind the try line while holding the ball it would be a drop-kick for Town from underneath their posts, if they put him out into touch it would be a scrum, but at least they wouldn't concede.

For a split-second, Robson deliberated. This was a chance to put the game further beyond Hopton. Robson decided if Player looked to be spilling the ball in any way, or even if two players went in on him and the ball came free, then he would be in a position to award a try.

The ball had gone to a corner of the field where more Hopton fans were in attendance than Ensideleigh. Their reaction to Player's collection was one of relief, turning fast to fist-clenching salute for the substitute.

Player spilled it on impact from the first onrushing tackler.

The ball spun free. All that was left now was to see what happened as the ball fell. The referee was unsighted for the next part, a melee of flailing arms, legs, bodies, heads from in the region of eight participants masked the ball from his vision. The linesman was in no better position, with his view obstructed by players of both sides. Referee Robson had been presented with what he had been hoping. He crouched, as though somehow he could see through flesh and bone of players with a combined mass of something around 1600lbs, and clearly make out that the ball had made impact with the ground whilst being controlled by the fingertip of an attacking player. Robson pointed to the ball, blew his whistle. The try was awarded!

Greg had been a part of the desperate defence. His disappointment was enormous, his rage on a par!

"What the fuck kind of decision is that, Robbo?" he spat in the referee's general direction. Robson hadn't made it to this level as a player – and had taken up refereeing, some said, so that he could take retribution on those who he felt hadn't given him the chance he had deserved.

Robson was moving back to where the conversion was to be taken. Ensideleigh saw their chance to goad. Plenty of choice words. Troy Johnson, one of the Ensideleigh pack had his hand in Greg's face as he tried to get up. Another of the pack was at him. Others were stepping up to the mark as they returned to their feet. Kenny was there alongside, shoving the Ensideleigh hoodlums away. The Hammerton boys took charge. Within seconds all hell had let loose. Fists were flying everywhere. No-one went down. This wasn't football. Robson watched. His linesman added words to tell him what he had already seen. The crowd in the corner was incensed. The sound level was increasing. Hopton were 10-nil down with a conversion attempt to come against them, and they were starting to fall apart.

Jardine rested back in his seat. So long as it continued like this there was no need for any upping of the ante to Billy Brodie. Bob Irvine ran his hand from his nose to below his chin, trying to keep calm. Plenty of time yet.

Robson and his touch-judge consulted. The Hopton fans, it was mostly them in the corner where the try had been awarded, were blazing towards the referee. Robson had made his way from the gathering of nearly all of the twenty-six players on the field all determined to state their case.

He beckoned Kenny Lomax toward him. The 'Aw, mate, you can't be serious' routine was lost on Robson. He took the yellow card from his pocket. 10 minutes sin bin. He also pointed to Ensideleigh's Troy Johnson – he too was dispatched for a 10-minute cooling off.

Then he called for Greg. Robson now held the crowd, the game and the life of Hopton Town in his grasp. There was a hush all around the ground.

As the mass of players and match officials had collided in titanic fashion, Billy Brodie had watched, not the match, but for signs from Julian Jardine. He gestured, palms outstretched, eyebrows raised inquiringly, in somewhat melodramatic fashion, to him. Jardine stayed firm. No further deal. Slightest of shakes of his head.

Bob Irvine wasn't so wrapped up in the game that he was oblivious to the fact that there could be other things going on to bring about a result he didn't want. His people were watching intently, following on from the various revelations that had been brought to the surface in the past days. He also knew just how much Robson's next decision would be crucial to the outcome and Hopton's future.

"And he's off too! Greg Duggan, player-coach and inspiration behind Town's success in recent games since he took over, is walking back to the dug-out … and the crowd here is going ballistic!"

Terry Derbyshire, who had seen more than his share of dull moments at Hopton games in the past decade, was giving it everything in his delivery. Every accentuation he could make to add to the listener's morbid pleasure in hearing more bad news was there. He sometimes wondered why listeners put themselves through this mental torture every time he broadcast.

Robson had been reaching for the red card, kept in his shirt pocket, rather than the shorts pocket where the yellow was held. For the briefest of moments, both sets of fans were once again on the brink between ecstasy and rage. The yellow was shown. Greg was unrepentant, incandescent, unbowed and most definitely out of control.

Phil Trippett appeared from nowhere on to the pitch at super speed and managed to get Greg away from Robson and off the field. Greg turned back, spitting fire at the twisted decision he had felt had been made. Trippett grabbed Greg, turned his face back toward the stand again, then bawled shamelessly right at him.

"Just what in hell's name are you trying to do! Lose this in one go? Don't you realise what's happening here? Are you so fucking thick?!! They've got you off, Greg. After all you've done to get this club on track, after all that's fucking happened to you. Come on, snap out of it!"

Trippett stopped, they were now near the dug-out. Greg's rage was dispersing fast. He bowed his head, biting the right side of his bottom lip, rubbing hands furiously through his hair and kicking drinks bottles flying all around as if this would in some way control his emotion, then raised his head, eyes closed for a second or two. A tirade of abuse from Ensideleigh fans in the main stand greeted him. Greg couldn't hear them, or if he could their voices weren't registering. Trippett had returned to the edge of the action watching play intently, sending messages out to the currently eleven-man team.

Ensideleigh's kicker was having a wow of a game. He calmly slotted over the conversion from right out on the touchline in front of a crowd that was now ready to boo any decision. They soon had another opportunity! Robson had not only taken two of the Hopton side from the field and awarded the try, he had also presented Ensideleigh with another kick at goal – penalising Greg, now off the pitch, for foul and abusive language.

Mr Robson prided himself on remembering rules on such conduct. There wasn't much else he could have given Ensideleigh inside two minutes. He'd sin-binned two of their opposition, handed them a highly dubious try and almost kicked the penalty goal himself! 14-0.

And there were still at least ten minutes to half-time! With Duggan and Lomax removed, albeit along with Ensideleigh's Troy Johnson, gaping holes were beginning to emerge in the Hopton defence.

Stu Wainwright took charge, along with older heads, such as Ron Rigson, as the rest of the half looked set to be a war of attrition in their own territory. Estorino, Merrioneth, Lomax and the Hammertons held firm doing their very best to staunch the flow, but Mickey King had been around long enough to realise that a little imagination, added to the advantage of having an extra player invariably pays dividends, and with just one little shimmy he was through, untouched for an easy touchdown under the posts.

Jardine showed no emotion, or at least he was trying his level best for it not to appear at the surface. A twenty-point lead for Ensideleigh at half-time, added to the 8-point winning margin Hopton had to attain for survival, as a win would put them level on points in the table, but they had a worse scoring difference than Ensideleigh. Hopton needed to out-score Ensideleigh by twenty-nine to stay alive.

There was plenty of the game to play, but inside, Jardine couldn't help himself feel he could taste the riches heading his way. But then he looked across at Billy Brodie who smiled directly back.

Brodie was toying with him. Greedy sod! Ever since he'd known Billy, he'd always wanted more. Jardine thought about acquiescing to his additional demands. Then he looked across at the scoreboard. He'd leave it a while – pay more if he had to.

It was the last thing Robson had expected as he returned to the officials' dressing room. What met him gave the phrase 'a warm welcome' a whole new dimension.

"*Hello, Richard…*" Robson was without his other officials. He shut the door behind him immediately. He'd had a text from his daughter. He'd read it as soon as he'd come from the pitch.

She was good. That part it appeared had been a hoax. And with the score line the way it was, he was already a happy man – but now suddenly much happier!

Her voice was sultry, seductive – and her body was, well, on display and what a display! As Robson knew only too well, a good deal could happen on any field of play in fifteen to twenty minutes!

"God, Josie, you choose your moments..." He shook his head while beaming an amazed smile at the humour of the situation. He swiftly decided against his half-time cuppa for something a great deal sweeter. Maybe he'd have to take things a little easier in the second-half!

There was no talk in the Hopton dressing room – not for what seemed like the first five minutes. They were quiet. Heads down or shaking slightly. Beaten. Stu Wainwright and Ron Rigson were first to start rallying them.

Phil Trippett had waited a while before going in. He kept Rodley back too, along with Kenny and Greg, before they all entered the dressing room. They delivered the message between them. There was no way this ship was going down without a fight and they would battle to the end. Forget what had gone before – the next 40 minutes were everything! No-one was in any doubt about the mountain to be climbed.

"Drink, Julie?" Billy Brodie was holding court in the bar once again. *"Going well, isn't it!"* He clenched his fist in mock salute toward Julian Jardine, then turned to give a quick drinks order for his other guests.

"There's no more, Billy..." Julian said it lightly, as though he had been well and truly hustled. Billy hesitated, then gave a slight shrug and an inner chuckle.

"We'll see..." He left it for a few seconds whilst he looked Jardine straight in the eye. *"Remember just how much a game can change ... but don't worry, Julian,"* reverting to his real name for the first time today, but for effect, *"...you've probably heard of in-game betting ... Gamble sensibly..."*

"Julian." Jardine spun round to come face to face with the

man whose club was now almost no longer. Irvine was all smiles. Jardine was ready to put on his smile. *"We've certainly quite a job on our hands in the second half."* Jardine was suddenly ready to offer fake sympathy.

"Mr Irvine…" Irvine cut in. *"Bob, call me Bob … a drink?"* Jardine was starting to sweat. There was an approach coming he couldn't quite work out. *"No. I'm okay, thanks…"* He shook his head at the same time.

"If you would just excuse me a second…" Jardine turned to move away, saw Brodie still nearby. *"Have you met Billy…"* saying it in such a way Brodie turned, although in conversation elsewhere, he broke off. *"Billy Brodie. Ensideleigh chairman?"*

Irvine nodded lightly toward Billy by way of acknowledgement as he turned briefly

"…your lads are doing well. It's a lot for us to come back from…" And Irvine was going to leave it at that when Geoff Quinigan arrived and a girl he now knew from sources through GPK as Paula.

Jardine made to move across to where Quinigan had reached Dugarry. Irvine smiled, his work was done here as Colin Duggan made his way into the room having been on the phone with Patsy. Irvine and Colin moved away to talk.

Referees aren't generally known for their good looks, but Richard Robson was regarded by most as a bit of a pin-up. He possessed a mane of tousled black hair that billowed behind him as he ran, his physique just as good as the fittest and fastest on the field. As a referee he was used to the abuse, but he was also used to the ladies and always looked good on and off the pitch.

Even half-time wasn't sacred to him! Josie wasn't the first who'd offered more than a biscuit. Nonetheless, this was quite a session with nearly as much action having taken place as he had witnessed in the first forty minutes of the game!

They'd enjoyed these encounters several times in the past. Josie had always been around rugby league. She'd gone with her father who supported Ensideleigh. She'd met Richard one time after a game in the club bar. They'd hit it off and shared a mutual love of enjoying life's pleasures at interesting moments. On a duvet with a few beers al fresco up in the Dales; in a hotel lift; this was a useful addition to their collection.

She'd sent a text to ask where Richard was next refereeing a couple of weeks ago and he'd sent some dates. Josie had chosen this one as she'd felt it might be good for George, two clubs he'd played for, get him back out again. She knew Billy Brodie and many of the others at Ensideleigh.

Billy had known she and Richard were close at times, exceptionally close. She, George and Billy had said 'hi' in the bar before he game, just briefly. Billy had asked whether she'd known who was refereeing. She'd looked a certain type of look. Billy said he'd let her know about an end of season evening being planned.

They'd exchanged numbers by text. He'd sent her a text just five minutes before half-time, asking her to deliver a message to Richard. She'd sent one back saying more than happy to oblige – if the linesmen could be syphoned off somewhere to another dressing room? Billy had sorted everything. He was enjoying his afternoon.

Richard hadn't imagined this would be another venue to add to their exclusive collection, but also hadn't been that concerned for it to put him off his stride, so to speak, as Josie zipped up her black leather trousers once more and her leather jacket.

Josie and George weren't an item as such, but she had known him for years when he'd played for Ensideleigh. The Lakes were just thirty miles north. She'd taken the job at the park after George and Janice had started there with a caravan. She'd had a bad time with a bloke and had needed to get away. They'd become friends who could talk about anything. When George had been going through hell with Town and had been pressurised to lose games, it had messed with his head. She'd been there for him as he'd been there for her years before.

She'd known who Bill Garside was when he'd turned up, because he'd played in her dad's time, but she hadn't had chance to talk about that when he'd arrived at the site, nor when he'd had his turn. She'd been genuinely concerned about him as she'd had an uncle suffer from passing out incidents that had also led to his passing.

George hadn't wanted to attend Bill's funeral when they'd heard about him passing away, as he hadn't felt Bill had supported him when he should have. Josie had decided to go as she felt involved. She'd met Bob Irvine outside the crematorium, all unplanned, just two individual mourners. They'd chatted briefly. They were there separately, but had walked in together.

As Robson ran out to start the second half, Josie took her place back in the stand next to George. As she did so, she acknowledged Brodie as he returned to his seat, her huge wink to him conveyed she had given Richard his message.

Richard's daughter was definitely okay and would remain so, time to start balancing the books a bit with the decisions but to go careful. Brodie just wanted a little leverage with Jardine.

The Hopton crowd, buoyed by twenty minutes' respite, were re-charged and ready to infuse as much atmosphere as they could muster for the next 40 minutes. They roared their approval as the men in chocolate and black appeared.

Duggan and Lomax were back. Twenty-nine points needed without response, for a team that hadn't scored more than twenty-four points in a whole match all season. It seemed nigh on impossible.

The deal had been done. Julian Jardine had rubber-stamped the victory. It had cost him far more than he had anticipated, but finally Billy Brodie had agreed. Julian was cool now, assured, he could relax.

"*...and we're ready to go. This is it then. The next forty minutes will tell us just what we've got in store for next season or not ... but it's got to start happening you feel, Ian, in the first ten minutes, if they're to have any chance at all!*"

Terry Derbyshire had seen comebacks before, but never from his time commentating on Hopton Town.

Robson looked across to both teams. The ball was resting high on the kicking tee, waiting for a Hopton boot to send it soaring into the air. He signaled the restart.

"*This is it, guys, dig deep…!*" Trippett hollered. The crowd roared. Some, it was true, had drifted away dejectedly after the first half, but it was still a deafening noise as the ball was launched into the air.

Paul Davy, playing for the first time since suspension, sent the ball spiralling into the Ensideleigh half. The kick was deep. Ensideleigh collected it on their try line. Hopton charged upfield as Ensideleigh moved the ball speedily.

"*Anderson's got it away to Webster – and he's made the break!!! … just what Hopton could do without, no-one'll catch him, he's got a clear run to the line, and if you thought it was an uphill struggle before, then I don't know what it is now … but hold on … there's a merry flag waver … and it's a forward pass…*"

CHAPTER 68

Hopton gained possession from the scrum just twenty metres from the try line. Lomax and Wainwright were directing operations, but five tackles later, Town had made little headway. Robson had it all under control. He pounced on anything marginal, penalizing the home side for head high tackles that were highly debatable. Two successive penalties and the pressure was mounting on Ensideleigh's defence. Robson had taken their captain to one side after giving the most recent penalty, threatening if they continued he would be sending someone to the bin. Quite an enjoyable afternoon for Robson, especially since half-time! A minute later, he'd blown again. Another penalty. He'd sent Isaac Izamua to the bin! The Maori shaking his head in disgust at the decision. Robson couldn't believe he'd done it either, but hell, he had to do something. Hopton weren't making headway.

Julian Jardine was agitated. He knew Robson's style. He let a game flow normally. He sensed problems, but surely the lead was too much! And Hopton hadn't scored yet. 35 minutes to go and they needed to score 29 points.

He'd had to make promises, but he, Quinigan and Dugarry were still looking good.

Ten yards away from the line, Stu Wainwright played the ball quickly, jinked inside one would-be tackler and released the ball for the on-rushing Greg Duggan, who crashed over near to the posts. 20-4. Greg put over the conversion. 20-6.

The Hopton support, so deflated during the first half, was revitalised. Town were back on the rails. The players were charged up and intent, bristling with energy. The fist pumping encouragement from all around, along with the roar as they lined up for the restart, fueled their tanks. Paul Davy gathered the kick from Ensideleigh and took off on a mazy run that took him past two Ensideleigh forwards before he was hauled to the ground.

"*Up the middle … Kenny … Warry…*" Greg had shifted his gumshield to deliver the instructions as he moved. Willie Hammerton charged upfield from Davy's play of the ball to Wainwright, who'd dispatched it to the twin making another eight yards. Brother Jeff Hammerton made similar yardage next. They were now in the Ensideleigh half of the field with three tackles to go. Kenny Lomax took on the defence, ducked, and was very nearly wiped out by his opposite number.

It was enough for Robson. He let the game flow this time, while noting the challenge from Troy Johnson.

Kenny may have been nearly wiped out, but he had also released the ball to Warwick Player, who made forty metres before being hauled down only ten metres shy of Ensideleigh's try line.

Stu Wainwright was there once again to take the ball. Passing it smartly by flicking it with the outside of his hand, he sent a delighted Kenny Lomax through a gap, who flicked a dream of a reverse pass through for centre Alan Thomas. Thomas took the ball across field, evading tacklers, aimed to straighten up, was enveloped by two Ensideleigh players, but stood tall and, basketball style, popped a pass out to Brian Goram, who made a spectacular dive for the line, landing the ball one-handedly by the corner flag, but over the line and in the field of play! 20-10! Greg landed a monster conversion kick from the touchline. 20-12.

Only ten minutes into the second half and Town had reduced the deficit to just eight points, but they knew they needed another seventeen in all. It wasn't enough to just win.

Robson hadn't finished yet. He'd let the game flow rather than stopping the move that led to the try, but now he took the opportunity to call over Mickey King. He'd been the tackler who'd nearly taken Lomax out earlier. He reached for his card again. Another sin-binning!

Irvine's team were now working overtime! Cameras and recorders were collating information with amazing alacrity, adding to their existing data. GPK's video journalist team were all around the ground and had been conducting interviews on the basis of a documentary being made about rugby league.

Cameras had picked up Caill as he'd arrived five minutes ago and had seen him take his place alongside Brent Dugarry. Unshaven and bedraggled, Caill had bad news heading his way from the press.

They were also trained on Quinigan and the woman they had now identified as Paula Caill. The owner of a black car matching that which had initially followed Patsy Previn, while she had been posing as Jenna Howells, and had shot Jeff Markham.

Now they had them. The whole sorry gang. They still didn't have everything in place, but pieces were starting to fit – and for the journalists, at least, they had the killer in their sights.

But the editing crew, working from the mobile TV studio in the car park, were having the best time of all. As they ran back the events from various cameras, they couldn't believe what had happened in the referee's changing room at half-time! Josie Penzance was already their new number one pin-up!

Richard Robson knew nothing about any of that – but he did know only too well he needed to appear a little more lenient towards Ensideleigh. But not just yet! He knew where Brodie would be and took a look towards the Ensideleigh bench. Brodie enjoyed being in the thick of the action and was now alongside his perplexed coach, Tom Barrett, who in addition to having played for many years had been a useful bare knuckle fighter. Tom, mild natured away from sport, was a completely different animal within it, and currently would have given anything to floor Robson. One blow, that's all! Brodie was happy with the present scoreline.

Town's fans were full throttle in the vocal department. Some of the more long-in-the-tooth fans, who had seen all manner of strange refereeing decisions occur over the years, were getting their mind-set ready for when decisions started going against them, but none were going to whimper about what had happened in the past fifteen minutes.

"And I just can't believe that!" Terry Derbyshire's commentary added a chuckle, as Mr Robson once again penalised Ensideleigh. The chuckle quickly turned to roguish laughter. *"He's got them for being offside as they've kicked off, well now I don't think I've ever seen that given whilst I've been commentating…"*

It was too much for the Ensideleigh players to bear. They ran, as one, to Mr Robson – a seething mass. The Hammerton boys found it hilarious, which only added fuel to the flames. Richard Robson's merry flag wavers ran to his assistance, with one losing his footing as he approached the furore and unwittingly took out one of the Ensideleigh team.

Other players saw it as an outrageous attack when the linesman's flailing arm hit the player's jaw. Ensideleigh's giant prop forward, Nobby Burns, towered over him, picked him up by his shirt and threatened the linesman's parentage before unceremoniously dumping him back down again.

There was only ever going to be one way in which the whole matter was to be settled. Whoops of delight went up from the mass of brown and black opposite the main stand, and the Hopton Town fans were once again given even more hope.

"And he's off! Well, I have to confess, I couldn't see exactly what happened there, but one thing is for sure. It's a straight red, and Nobby Burns will play no further part in this game."

Terry Derbyshire's voice was on the verge of cracking. A game that Dalesmoor Radio had covered in its totality, but with, in reality, minimum of belief in their side's ability to win, was now sliding ever more their way. Ensideleigh were down to 11 men at least for the next five minutes before Mickey King returned from the sin bin. Terry Derbyshire collected himself. This needed enthusiasm and expectation for sure, but it also needed a calm head.

That wasn't exactly Julian Jardine's state of mind. He could only look on as Hopton kicked for touch deep into the heart of Ensideleigh territory. Ten yards away from their line once again. Jardine turned to Dugarry. Caill. Quinigan. The cameras followed. Something had to give here.

Greg Duggan called for the ball, this time steaming on to a pass from Kenny Lomax, his momentum alone took care of three would-be tacklers before he was forced down just a yard short of the try line. Lomax was on hand immediately. He took the ball from Greg, swivelled as though to pass, dummied, swivelled once again and bundled himself low over the line. 20-16. Twenty-five minutes still to play, Hopton fans rejoicing, Ted Brewiss having to type more detail about Hopton scoring in fifteen minutes than they usually managed in a whole game, Fred leading the fans in a new Town chant, 'We're 'Opton Town … Give 'em some stick,' and Irvine trying hard to keep in check a beaming smile. Still a long way to go. 20-18. Greg had landed the conversion. Another 11 points needed.

CHAPTER 69

"What the bloody 'ell do you think you're doing?" The voice boomed down the corridor of the main stand that ran between the restaurant and boardroom, as Billy Brodie approached him. Texts had been flying between the two in the past minutes.

"Come on, Julie! You didn't seriously think you could just waltz off with millions of pounds of assets by buying me off on the cheap, did you?" Brodie was steady, firm. *"I know what you and your partners in crime are up to. Listen. You want a result today?"* His eyebrows raised at least an inch on his forehead. *"You can still have one..."*

Eleven more points. Some fans only thought three were needed, thinking that a win would be good enough. As Greg ran back for the restart, the Hopton fans gave him what had to be the biggest reception he had ever had in all his time with the club. They were on the precipice of something truly remarkable.

Bob Irvine and Colin sat together, a distance away from the huddle that had formed between the conspirators. *"Stupid, isn't it, what money makes some people do?"* It was Irvine who delivered the words. Colin Duggan was growing to like him.

"And if you can't believe this at home, let me tell you I've just pinched myself and no, I'm not dreaming. Hopton Town are within reach of the great escape! They really can see light at the end of the tunnel. And twelve-man Ensideleigh are wondering just what has hit them in this second half..." Terry Derbyshire was eulogising like never before.

Richard Robson started balancing off the penalty count. He started with little ones, those that didn't look to put Hopton under any real pressure, and within the next fifteen minutes he had awarded five decisions Ensideleigh's way. They were within twenty yards of Hopton's line for the first time in the second half.

Ensideleigh's movement was good, the ball fed from hand to

hand quickly and expertly. Tony Estorino slipped, leaving a gap for Dave Banger to go through. And he did. He was in the clear and with only Paul Davy to beat. Banger flipped out the ball, and the now returned Isaac Izamua picked up on the bounce to race over.

The Ensideleigh crowd rose as one, it was time for their own clenched fists, gritted teeth and mutual spurring on of emotion. The Hopton fans were silent. It had all been to no avail, their side wasn't about to pull this out of the fire, after all. The collective of Dugarry, Quinigan, a recently reseated Jardine, plus Paula and Caill rose as one, delighted.

"*Well, I suppose we had to expect some kind of response sooner or later…*" Derbyshire's analysis was philosophical, even if it was depressing.

The crowd behind the try-line were the first to notice. Izamua, Banger and the rest of the Ensideleigh players had begun celebrating in grand style near the corner where Izamua had gone over. Their smiles were the biggest they had been all day.

Richard Robson wiped away every Ensideleigh smile. He wiped away the try and part of their belief. The try was disallowed. Once again, the linesmen had to come to his aide as a snarling mob descended upon him. Robson, like many more referees before him, was in his element when in the thick of it all.

"*Knock-on?*" The same words and expressions were echoed throughout the Ensideleigh team, coaching staff and fans. Robson's linesman had spotted Izamua's grounding, he'd not had control of the ball as he'd gone over. It was the correct decision. Ensideleigh's supporters turned on Robson. A chorus of '*You don't know what you're doing!*' boomed around the ground. Town's fans were in shock. They'd never been this lucky before.

To their credit, and fearing more red and yellow cards, the Ensideleigh players curbed their emotions quickly. But this hadn't all played in Hopton's favour. The incident itself had taken up two minutes before Robson had realized he hadn't stopped the clock. That left just eight minutes. Town needed to score and soon.

Greg, Kenny, Stu, the Hammertons, Tony, Paul Davy, Ron Rigson and the rest of the side, didn't need to look at each other. The disallowing of the try renewed their resolve. Their next five drives all made good ground, and with only one play remaining before having to give the ball back to the opposition, they prepared to pump the ball into the sky ready to charge forward once again in the hope they could force an error.

Kenny was about to pass to Greg for him to punt for all he was worth. The Ensideleigh players stopped momentarily in expectation of the pass, but Kenny came off his other foot and stepped inside the hole left by their statues. He hadn't won all those Grand Finals for nothing.

He was through. Forty yards to go, thirty, twenty, ten, but he knew he was getting caught. Five yards to go he was grabbed, going down, he hadn't seen anyone else who had been able to react as quickly as he had done. He was still going down – four yards, three, two. There were now three tacklers all over him, but his momentum was still with him. He managed to stretch out his right arm. The ball was no more than attached to his index and middle finger tips as he made impact with the whitewash, but a try it most definitely was.

Eruptions around Bath Lane were now reaching epic proportions.

"*22-20!! Twenty-Two points to Hopton Town! And incredibly they're now in the lead for the first time in the game and only seven points from pulling off the most sensational win I will ever have seen. Come on Town!*"

Terry Derbyshire's voice was cracking big time. "*And if I don't end up with a voice by the time this finishes, I won't care. I really won't. They can send me off to the funny farm and I'll live there happily forever just telling everybody I was here at this fantastic, amazing game…*"

Greg kicked the conversion once again. 24-20 to Town. Five points to go. They were going to do it! No matter what had been chucked at him, or at the club in this tough season, they were making it work. Four minutes to go!

Brodie smiled at the text. *"You win, Billy, the answer is yes."* Brodie looked to Robson. Slightest of movements. Nothing more today. Jardine couldn't take the chance. Quinigan and Dugarry were heading for the exit.

The job had been agreed. They'd shaken hands with Caill. It was over. Cameras recorded everything. The team in the editing suite were having a field day as all the filming flashed on ten screens in the mobile studio.

Billy Brodie wasn't worried. He'd won with his texts to Julian. Now to make sure Robson didn't do anything that gave the game to Hopton.

On field, Ensideleigh were looking a dejected bunch. They had gone from twenty points up to four behind. Five more and they were out of the league. No big pay day, no future.

"This is it, Greg. It's our time, mate!" Kenny Lomax was alongside Greg once again as the ball was placed on the kicking tee for Ensideleigh to give back possession once more, but there was a hold up. It had been as much as Greg could do to simply acknowledge what Kenny had said with a nod and a grunt. He didn't know what was keeping him going now, apart from pure adrenaline.

In the past weeks, he had been held at gunpoint, been tied up, beaten up, had his life turned upside down, lost a baby, lost his wife – he'd tried Diane again on the phone this morning, it hadn't gone well, maybe he was better off on his own, seeing Susie when they could, maybe that was better than what he was doing to Diane, she deserved better, from someone better than him. All fleeting thoughts while trying to keep focused. He was totally knackered, out on his feet, but still found the energy from somewhere.

The hold-up had come for an injury, but not to a player!

Richard Robson was flat on his back in the middle of the field. Josie saw the funny side. Maybe a little too much exercise for you, Richie, her first thought, before then showing natural concern. It was Brodie's worst nightmare. Robson was coming off.

But with only four minutes on the clock, maybe it was already all over. Nonetheless, a try and a conversion would do it and that only needed seconds. Brodie was worried for the first time that afternoon as linesman Alex Pipson took over.

Phil Trippett had just one rolling substitution left to make. He'd saved it just in case an injury suddenly occurred, but felt now was the time for fresh legs. He sent Brad Warrener in place of a highly fatigued Mark Merrioneth.

Brad's first touch of the ball came quickly. He raced on to a Stu Wainwright pass and busted through two tackles into open space. The line appeared at his mercy apart from the Ensideleigh full back in front of him. He pinned back his ears and galloped for glory. The Hopton crowd roared once more, this surely was to be their day. A try here, followed by a conversion, and the miracle had happened. They would be safe.

From out of nowhere, Mickey King appeared. Diving at Warrener, he flailed and with the final flailing flicked Brad's right boot, which clicked against his left and he was going down. Brad was trying desperately to keep his footing, but knew he was going to hit the deck. Young Paul Davy steamed on to his last second release before Brad's arm touched the ground and now, with a torrent of Ensideleigh players chasing him down, made it to the corner.

The crowd went ballistic! Dugarry, Quinigan, Jardine, Caill and now Brodie all either held their heads in their hands, ran their hands through their hair or beat their fists in exasperation. Greg, Kenny, Stu, Brad and a delirious Davy, were in a mass heap on the pitch with the rest of the team and the whole bench and Trippett running wildly across to join them. Terry Derbyshire was ever more in dreamland. He hijacked a line from a famed commentary of years ago.

"Maggie Thatcher! Winston Churchill! Bobby Charlton! Gary Lineker! Theresa May! And now Billy Brodie! Your boys have taken one hell of a beating!" He laughed aloud at his line. *"Boy Oh Boy!*

You had to be here, folks, you had to be here." And then not wanting to alienate his listeners. *"But I'm pleased you're listening and I'm honoured to be bringing you commentary on this truly historic game, where Hopton Town have turned it around completely! But they still need to get one more point from somewhere and the conversion will be from way out. Hold on to your hats, everybody!"*

It wasn't all over by a long shot.

"My knee, shit, my knee!" Tony Estorino was clutching it in agony. Blood was pouring out of his left leg. The crack of the gunshot had not registered everywhere at first, with the crowd in such voice. He'd been pumping both fists towards the crowd in salute. Now he was down and those who had seen what had happened turned immediately silent. It rippled around the ground.

Veejay hurried to him in double-quick time. Players from both sides began gathering around, wondering what had happened. Veejay screamed for help quickly. *"Ambulance! Quickly!"* as he tried to stem the flow.

Bob Irvine hadn't been able to control his emotion. This had been an amazing rollercoaster and they were so close now. He had come straight from the stand as the try had been scored, ready to celebrate with the rest. He'd just made it to the pitch to go across when he'd heard the gunshot, seen Tony go down and had started running towards when the second gunshot went straight into him! He fell. Didn't move.

The crew in the mobile studio had screens popping from one to another as they desperately scoured the ground. Cameramen masquerading as video journalists were scanning everywhere. The crowd, initially hushed after the first shot, was now screaming and everyone was escaping as quickly as possible.

Greg looked towards the goalposts where the sound had come from, or at least the direction from which Bob had been hit.

The long redundant scoreboard behind the goalposts was a small old timber-framed building that stood fifteen feet high and had steps to get up to the box where tin numbers had been used to update the score line through the game in the same way some village cricket teams were still using on little floor stands. Its height had been such that fans could see the score rather than have to remember.

It was from here the barrel of a gun now appeared as Greg started running towards it. The third shot rasped in a quite different direction to the first two. No more on-pitch activity! This was straight at the main stand! Shrieks and screams everywhere now. Bodies trying to get away.

Greg carried on his course, breaking into full gallop as he passed the posts and saw the gun protruding from the scoreboard. He could almost see whoever it was in there. The barrel moved back inside.

Three of the video journalists had followed the action, heard the sounds and had seen Greg and now Kenny hurtling for the scoreboard. The mobile studio was now in full swing. Everything trained on it. The side door of the scoreboard burst open and the gunman leaped to the floor, gun in hand. The scoreboard had shielded him so far, but now he wanted better sighting for this.

Greg had only one game plan in mind – he kept running – and so did Kenny. Now only fifteen yards away, he realised who it was. No bloody way! He flew at him as the gunman took aim and fired.

Kenny knew instantly Greg had been hit. For all his Aussie bravado, he was transfixed by what had just happened and his first concern was for his team-mate, not the gunman. He stopped with Greg.

Fifteen cameras were now trained on the one man who had wrought all of this damage. And he wasn't finished. He'd run, gun in hand, towards the main stand, shouting with all his might.

"Where the fuck's Jardine!"

It was a shout of complete and utter desperation. He knew he had little chance of coming out of this with any degree of freedom, he just wanted what he saw as justice!

"George! … Why, why all this?" It was Greg, blood streaming from his shoulder, totally amazed by who it was wielding the gun. George Ramsbottom looked around to Greg, checking he wasn't about to make a move to disarm him. He looked back at the main stand. There was no sign of Jardine, nor Quinigan.

"Where's Jardine! … Where's fuckin' Jardine!!!"

Fred emerged from the throng. He calmly but carefully walked toward Hopton's previous coach.

"Still givin' 'im some stick, 'eh, George? Good on yer!" He paused, both in movement and speech, ten metres from him. His calming manner quelling George Ramsbottom's urge to find his next victim.

"He's gone … You know what people like him are like … any sign of trouble and they're off … how do you think the Mr Jardines of this world manage to keep themselves out of the way…" Fred shrugged his shoulders lightly.

"Now put the gun down, George, and let everybody get off home, eh?" It was delivered in Fred's typically off-hand style.

George Ramsbottom's shoulders slumped and his head went down for a second. There were movements all around him. He had nothing left. He raised his head, his eyes red with tears, angry and despairing, he held the gun close by his side ready to unload another bullet if needed, but intent on addressing everyone still around including, he now saw, Josie, who was nursing an arm after having been the unintended victim of the third bullet.

Nobody he'd hit had been the ones he'd wanted.

"I used to love this game! Still do! But the people who run it have ruined my life! And they're ruining this club – and yours!" he gestured to both teams now littered around the ground. *"Julian Jardine! Billy Brodie! They're money grabbing bastards, just out for what they can get, at all costs to our great game…"* He paused, gathering himself.

"Town were meant to lose today. They were meant to lose last week. They were meant to finish bottom! That's been the plan all season, so that this bastard," he pointed directly at Caill who had

stayed after all, *"this arsehole on the face of humanity, can pay off his debts and Jardine and his fucking cronies can earn millions from the deal they've done with Caill over buying the ground!"* He paused again.

"And you think Mr fuckin' Irvine will stick around once he's got wind of the fact there's no assets left?"

He dropped his gun to the floor.

AUTHOR'S NOTE

Tough Season started out some years ago as an exercise in moving from feature writing, short stories, sketches and songs to novels. In the meantime, I've written several non-fiction books that have offered me even greater understanding of the phrase 'you couldn't make it up' and that fact is sometimes crazier than fiction, but creation of characters and situations is a fantastic world and allows so much more imagination.

I used rugby league as my canvas for this crime thriller book in a similar way to Dick Francis used horse racing. Amazingly this started as a story I was able to read to my then young sons, but as you will have read by now that certainly wouldn't be the case today.

I'm extremely grateful to Emma Chapman, Tina Jackson and Phil Caplan for their help; my daughter Caroline Berry for cover design; regular sustenance from my wife Pauline; Ross Jamieson and David Burrill from Great Northern Books who have taken considerable care in looking after this first book in the Greg Duggan trilogy.

Enjoyed Tough Season?

Read on for an exclusive extract
from the sequel crime thriller
by Chris Berry

TOUGH SEASON 2
in the Sun!

TOUGH SEASON 2 in the Sun!

Chris Berry

CHAPTER 1

She'd stayed away. It hurt. Didn't matter how she tried to dress it up. She never believed in going back or at least that's what she'd always thought. New chapter, move on, forget, she'd done it all before – but this had been different, hard, she hadn't realised just how much she would feel, even now.

Stupid. She tried again to shake it off. Smiled as she thought of him, laid on her bed, blonde hair caressing the soft pillows, pictures of him coming as she closed her eyes. He'd taken photographs of her and selfies of them together on his mobile phone, but she'd never taken any herself and had never asked him to send any, preferring not to have anything about her that others could see. She saw him clearly now, she smiled again.

Those days when they had enjoyed each other, sensually, sexually and even more importantly it seemed now as two people very much in love, happy to be together, laughing and talking about anything and everything with nothing really mattering. She'd called him Mr Cool, he'd held her hand and had told her she was beautiful.

She wished she'd shown as much love back to him as he'd shown her, but she hadn't thought it possible given his circumstances. He hadn't been truly available, as she'd said, so she couldn't give herself totally. And even when he'd tried to show that he could and would be there, she'd rejected him – not out of the way she felt, but the way life had been. She'd moved on. But not enough it now seemed.

Another time. Another place. Another person.

'Juan? I need your help. Can you meet me?' she was close to tears, so near they'd already been quelled once, but were hurrying back to her moist eyes as she walked, checking behind her as she made her way.

'Just come, quickly,' as she began to pick up her pace despite her heels.

Another place. Another person. Another country. Another phone.

'So, what's stopping you, mate? ... You can't be serious? ... Listen, Greg, just get on a plane and get over. Put it all behind you for a few weeks. It's great out here. Sun, sea, sand and ...' He left the rest hanging with a laugh very nearly under-his-breath. If only he'd known how close his next word was to touch so close to home. He lost connection.

The other place. The phone had been flung after hitting the red button. Other buttons of a different kind were now being pressed, but little to do with mobile phone conversations. The breathing said it all.

'Oh ... Oh... Oh, baby ...' It was all she could muster but it was enough, even though she had stayed away so long. This was heaven – a heaven she hadn't anticipated returning to given all that had happened, all that had passed. 'That's so ... oh ... nice and slow ... oh ... yes ... just .. there ... oh ... now harder, deeper ... oh, yeah ... don't stop ... mmm ... yeah ...'

Clear blue skies, blazing sun and a beautiful sandy beach greeted the young couple as they made their way down from the lone bar where they'd enjoyed a carafe or three of sangria. They were holidaying and taking in the island's delights in an area that had once been known as El Rubicon just a mile and a half from their beach resort in Playa Blanca.

The beach was deserted. The bar now out of sight. They stripped naked, he with blond hair, a swimmer's physique and endowed in the most established of ways, she also blonde, slender, perky boobs and shaven to the south. They held hands and made for the ocean. Warmed by the summer temperature, Lanzarote's waters were welcoming. They embraced, kissed passionately. Luke lifted Lucy who held him around his shoulders as she wrapped her legs around his body.

They collapsed into the water and kissed again. Then they no longer kissed.

TOUGH SEASON 2 – in the Sun!
Second Book of The Greg Duggan trilogy.